W9-AOM-724

Books & Baubles
103 N. Market
Benton, AR 72015

RAINSONG

RAINSONG

Phyllis A. Whitney

DOUBLEDAY & COMPANY, INC.
GARDEN CITY, NEW YORK

The charm of Cold Spring Harbor has attracted me ever since I came to live on Long Island. I have tried to catch something of its special flavor in this story.

My thanks to Laura Farwell of the Cold Spring Harbor Public Library for furnishing background material; and to Robert Farwell, director of the fascinating Whaling Museum.

My gratitude as well to Barbara and Keith Hoffman, who are professional musicians and helped me generously with the popular-music scene in *Rainsong*.

RAINSONG

1

I lay in my bed listening to Ricky Sands's voice on the air. That beautiful, haunting voice, singing the melody and words *I* had written.

> Let the rain fall sweetly
> On the children of the earth;
> May rivers run clean
> And forests stand tall.
> Let the sweet rain fall,
> Let the sweet rain fall.

Just the chorus. I couldn't bear to hear any more. Grief was like a physical aching inside me, and I touched the switch so that Ricky's voice fell silent and the melody died . . . as Ricky too had died.

I remembered how sweetly the rain had fallen during those long walks in San Francisco, when we'd hidden laughing under an umbrella so no one would recognize him. Now for me, rain would always seem bitter.

Here in our penthouse apartment high above New York, I hid from the clamor of the press and the endless ringing of telephones. Norris and Bea Wahl were with me, helping me to shut out the world, acting as a barrier to protect me. Norris had been Ricky's manager. He knew how to talk to the media people and stave off their questions, while Bea's comfortable presence asked nothing as she tried to console me with nourishing broth she made herself.

If anyone turned on a radio for news, I fled. All too often in those terrible first days the airwaves were filled with talk of Ricky Sands. His music was analyzed endlessly, every detail of his life raked over, with a great deal of wallowing in the circumstances of his death. The songs were played over and over—especially "Sweet Rain"—and my own name, Hollis Temple, began to sound like meaningless syllables pounding at me from those disembodied voices. After all, I was Ricky's wife and I had written most of his recent songs.

The word "suicide" echoed on radio and television, and was printed in newspapers and magazines, with the inevitable relishing of the juiciest scandal. It was a word that cut through me, frightened me. It rang of despair and desperation, and it pointed an accusing finger at the living as well. How much of the fault was mine? How far back had it all gone wrong? I'd tried so hard not to fail him, and in the very effort had failed him all the more.

Had I ever really understood what drove and haunted Ricky Sands? There had seemed to be no way in which I could meet whatever it was that he wanted and needed from me, except through my music. And lately even this bond between us had begun to fade. Now I must face my own failure and deal with my own lonely pain.

Drugs, the coroner had said. A word the news media pounced on at once and constantly repeated. He had died of acute toxicity from both cocaine and heroin. A volatile combination that Ricky certainly had known was deadly.

In my bedroom high above Manhattan, even with the windows closed, I could subdue the city's roar only to some extent. The month was November, and usually autumn was the best season of all in New York. Now it meant nothing but an ending, with desolation sure to follow. At twenty-three I was a widow.

Ricky hadn't died here, but in a miserable hotel room on the East Side, and he'd left a call for Norris that had seemed a cry for help that had come too late. There had been no word for me, no reassurance that what he was about to do was not my fault. The last words he'd spoken when he left me that day had been strange, enigmatic. I still didn't understand what they'd meant. Lost in his own solitary despair, he probably hadn't thought of me at all at the end.

Right now I was supposed to be resting, but my clamoring emotions matched the city's clamor, and there was no stillness for me anywhere.

Perhaps I could risk the radio again and hear some anonymous voice that would distract me. I reached for the switch once more.

Immediately Ricky was on the air with that voice that compelled his audiences, and held such an illusion of sweetness. Never cloying. Always bittersweet. No hard rock for Ricky. He'd made his own special place; young and old audiences followed him obsessively because he reached out in some universal, loving way through his music. His music —and _mine_.

I let my hand drop from the switch without turning it off. The tune had changed and he was singing the first Hollis Temple song he'd ever recorded, "I Love You, Laura Lee." His bittersweetness came alive in that song, because without knowing him, I'd written it just for him. Though the singer still loved Laura Lee, there _were_ other girls to love, and he was looking ahead. A laughing, weeping, tongue-in-cheek sort of song that I hadn't tried to repeat. And didn't want to. Not after I began to realize how much like Ricky it really was.

Listening to his voice, memory carried me back to San Francisco again. Nearly five years ago . . .

I grew up in Berkeley, right across the bay from the Golden Gate city. My mother had died when I was three, and my father's sister had raised me. Dan Temple, my father, used to stay with us whenever he could, and I'd looked forward eagerly to his visits.

Dan played piano, sometimes on his own in nightclubs, sometimes with a small band. "Big Band" or Cole Porter music of what he called the "classy kind" was his life. So he'd been out of work a good deal until America went nostalgic. He had never wanted me to go into any phase of the music business, but he couldn't entirely resist it when I began to pick out tunes on the piano in Aunt Margaret's house and make up my own little songs before I could read. When he accepted the inevitable, he saw to it that I had a good piano teacher. The guitar I picked up later by myself. When I was older, he even let me sit in on a few jam sessions with his band, and I was ecstatically happy. Eventually Dan ceased all warnings except the one about never marrying a musician.

My mother had married a musician, and I think she was happy. Even though I couldn't remember her, I grew up loving her image, because Dan talked about her so often and made her real for me.

I went to college in Berkeley and made a lot of friends. I was always falling in and out of love. What I thought was love. Though even then my real—and secret—passion was Ricky Sands. I wrote two or three songs just for him, and once I sent a song off to him—notes and words painstakingly written down on a music sheet. Not a recording. Of course nothing came of it because I was going about it in the wrong way to get a hearing. I could have asked Dan about placing a song, but I knew he'd have a fit. He hated the sort of singer he called by the old term of "crooner." Even soft rock was out of his ken, and he only grudgingly acknowledged the existence of the Beatles.

I can remember the Hollis Temple of those days almost as though she were someone else. Perhaps I was popular because I was so eager for new experience, so venturesome, and always ready to take a dare. There had been a lot of exuberance in me then—very different from the woman I'd become. I've often wondered what turns my life might have taken if Ricky Sands had never come to San Francisco.

Of course I sent for a ticket the moment I learned that he would appear on the Berkeley campus. Just one ticket. I didn't want anyone else to share my experience of hearing him in person. I was no groupie. I even wondered if there were some way I could manage to meet him, speak to him. Though I really knew better. Ricky Sands was always surrounded, protected, by bodyguards and business associates. His personal retinue. Otherwise he'd have been swarmed over by screaming females trying to get close to him. I wanted no part of that mob scene.

This was when fate—or something—stepped in. Ricky's motorcycle escapades were notorious. He'd had more than one accident, though nothing terribly damaging. This time, on the Marin County hills, before the concert could take place, he banged himself up seriously. I cried when I heard how badly he was hurt, and how he might be in a San Francisco hospital for a long time. It was a miracle that he hadn't killed himself or anyone else.

I watched the papers, so I knew when he was out of danger, and I followed his convalescence. When he was well enough to have visitors, I began to plot. This time nobody but me gave *me* a dare, and I decided just what I would do. Looking back, I can only marvel at how foolishly young and naïve I was, even at eighteen.

At least I knew by now that one didn't submit words and music alone. Producers wanted to *hear* what you had to offer. I had learned about "demos," the demonstration tapes or discs singers and song writers use to get their work heard. While I was far from being a professional singer, and had no ambition along that line, I had a small voice with a lilt to it, and I could manage all right on a tape.

The university had good recording equipment, and I found another student to help me and made a tape of my own "Laura Lee," accompanying myself on my acoustic guitar. No back-up, of course—I couldn't afford that. I did it over several times, never completely satisfied. The student who helped me was flattering—but I knew better, though I had to accept my own limitations and settle for what I could manage. It was Ricky Sands I wanted to have sing my song.

The next step was to get in to see him.

First I did a few dry runs at the hospital during visiting hours until I knew the layout of rooms on his floor and the routine. It wasn't hard to lose myself in those antiseptic corridors one afternoon when the last visitor had left. There was always someone on duty outside Ricky Sands's door during visiting hours, but afterward, now that he was so much better and could walk around on crutches, there seemed less need to guard him. His accident was old news now.

I'd gotten myself a hospital gown, and I hid in a washroom until banging trays told me dinner was being served. Then I flopped out in bedroom slippers and an old bathrobe I'd brought in a shopping bag. Not very flattering. But I'd looked at myself long and hard in the washroom mirror. The top of me would do all right. Red hair cut just above my shoulders, straight and thick before it curled in. Green eyes and black lashes, a pretty good nose, and a mouth that liked to smile. Not bad, really—sort of arresting. At least the kids in college seemed to think so. I was still filled with a sense of daring—a reckless emotion that kept me from recognizing the outrageousness of what I was about to do.

No one paid any attention, and luck was with me. When I passed Ricky's door, the chair outside was empty, and I heard no voices from his room. Only the sound of a knife and fork. Ricky would be eating an elegant meal sent in from an expensive restaurant—no hospital fare for him. I had my tape recorder in the shopping bag, with my demo in place, and I knew what my opening remarks would be. I had to get his attention at once, or out I would go on my ear. Before anyone else, I'd done a good job of convincing myself. Ricky's ratings had been slipping lately, and I thought I knew why. I was no novice when it came to music, and I could only agree with the critics that his songs were beginning to get boring. My little song had a bite, and that was what he needed. He needed *me*.

I had the overconfidence, nerve, and inner terror of someone young who hasn't yet been slapped around by life. Dan had brought me up to the principle of *Never surrender*. Especially not to my own fears, and I felt I was doing just what he'd taught me.

I slip-slapped into Ricky's room and stood at the foot of his bed. My heart was pounding so loud I was afraid he could hear it.

"Hello," I said. "I've brought you something. Something you really need."

He looked up from his tray, startled, immediately wary, and set down his fork with its bite of fillet mignon. Perhaps my robe and hospital gown reassured him a little, but in a minute he was going to ask who the hell I was and how I got there.

I didn't give him time. "You do need me," I said, "and I think I can help you."

His hand was already reaching toward the bell on his pillow, and I gave him my best, most brilliant smile.

"I'm not a patient," I said. "I'm pulling a great big bluff. But if you put me out right away, you'll never know what I've got for you here." I took out the recorder and held it up.

"Oh, God," he said, "you've written a song."

"Right. Your ratings are falling and the critics are calling you stale. You're turning out bubble gum when, with what *you* have, you ought always to top the charts."

Ricky Sands was used to sycophants and "yes" people. He was thirty-nine years old, which was getting on for a pop singer, even a star. I don't think he really knew what was going wrong, for all his years at the top. Besides, he must have been terribly bored lying in that bed, and I was at least a novelty.

When he made up his mind and smiled at me, I knew I'd won myself a hearing. I'll never forget that first smile I had from him. I'll never forget how he looked sitting up against his pillows. He wore a silk robe of ivy green, with a yellow scarf at the neck, and his pale hair was curly and mussed, his blue eyes filled with laughter. When he chose, he could look almost angelic—and very sweet. That was the way all his fans saw him.

"So you've written a song," he said. "And now you're going to sing it for me. Well, go ahead."

While I plugged in the cord I talked to him over my shoulder. "I'm a songwriter, not a singer. This isn't a very good tape, but it's the best I could manage."

These weren't things I'd planned to say, and I was glad when he cut me off. "Never apologize, and don't try to explain. If it can't speak for itself, it's no good. So just turn the damn thing on."

I touched the switch and held my breath. I knew the melody was catchy. Not honey-sickening, and perhaps with an unexpected turn or two. The words were pretty good, I thought. They carried a story—like Carly Simon.

He listened to "I Love You, Laura Lee" all the way through, and then he said, "Play it again."

My heart hadn't entirely quieted, and this time my hand shook as I ran the tape back. After he'd heard it the second time, he nodded soberly. No more enchanting smiles. This was business.

He gestured to a chair beside his bed. "Sit down and tell me about *you.*"

I did my best to put on a good front, though there wasn't much to tell, and I was getting more and more scared by the minute. Success one doesn't know how to handle can be more frightening than the finality of defeat. I hadn't thought ahead to what I would do once Ricky Sands had heard my tape. It didn't help that Norris Wahl chose that moment to walk into Ricky's room, and he and I began the uneasy relationship of suspicion on my part, and jealousy on his, that had lasted to the present.

Norris was in his mid-fifties, a shrewd, homely, powerful little man who had managed Ricky for the last ten years and done a great deal for him—until the recent slipping began. This perhaps was more Ricky's fault than Norris's, since Ricky was getting as tired as he sounded. From the first, Norris regarded me as a threat to his influence with his singer, yet even he quickly recognized something that might halt an ominous slide down the charts. Especially if Ricky himself responded with genuine interest.

Norris listened to "Laura Lee," and then said, "What else?"

This I wasn't ready for—not in my wildest imaginings. But Ricky Sands's own guitar leaned in a corner, and I gestured toward it boldly.

"Sure—go ahead," Ricky said, and he was smiling again.

So I tuned up and sang three other songs I'd written with Ricky in mind. The best one was something I'd never have dared to show him if it hadn't been for the heady atmosphere of excitement that was growing in Ricky's hospital room. I'd composed it a little sadly after I'd read an interview with him where he'd talked about growing older—he hated nearing forty. I'd called the song "Let the Young Years Go," and I'd put both heartache and hope into it because I could project myself into Ricky's faltering talent and what I thought he might be feeling.

"I'm going to do that song," Ricky said, and when I saw tears in his eyes, I began, idiotically, to cry myself. Out of nervousness, out of fear of too much good fortune happening to me so fast, and from sheer relief that my bluff had worked so astonishingly.

"First, 'Laura Lee,' " Norris said. "They'll go for that one."

As suddenly as this I was launched as a songwriter. Ricky's excitement matched mine, and that endeared him to me all the more. He recorded with O.T.M. Records in New York, and he insisted on calling his producer then and there. I was introduced to Chuck Oliver by telephone and sang two songs for him over the wire. Chuck wanted Ricky back at work under any circumstances, and saw me as the nearest route to get him recording again. Chuck was a creative, imaginative man, and I came to like him better than I ever did Norris Wahl.

Though I had two years to go before graduating from college, I never went back. Utter stupidity, of course. Dan was appalled. From the first he disliked Ricky Sands. Of course all my friends were madly envious and admiring. I was already out of their world, and the orbit they imagined for me was thrilling—filled of course with famous and successful people *I* would get to know. Only one or two thought me a little crazy, but I paid no attention to them. Nothing anyone said really mattered anyhow. Ricky *liked* my songs. He liked *me*.

"Laura Lee" was the first recording he made after he got out of the hospital, and it went to the top of the singles lists in two weeks. That this should happen with a first song by an unknown writer was a ten million-to-one shot. Maybe even more. Yet it was happening to me. "Let the Young Years Go" followed, and that was gold. Before I knew it, there was to be an album, with my name on it, as well as Ricky's. We were heading for platinum. *Rolling Stone* did a piece about this new collaboration—wildly heady stuff.

Of course Ricky's first interest in me was because I might be a gold mine for him. I was also a new experience in his life, and any novelty that might stimulate him, refresh and relieve his jaded boredom, was welcome. Yet, even in my darkest moments later on, I know there was more than that. He cared about me—he really cared as much as he could. At least for a little while.

We were both alone. Ricky had no one. Despite all the hangers-on, he really had no one. I had only Dan and my aunt, and even this lack of family drew us together. Someday, I'd told him, I'd write a "lonely people" song unlike any that had been written by anyone else. I never got around to it because the time came when I had to pretend with all my heart that I wasn't lonely, and then I didn't want to sing about it.

I hadn't run with a drug crowd at college, and I had no knowledge for a long time of Ricky's drugs-for-kicks, much less the hard drugs. He'd been cleaned out at the hospital and not until after we were married did I discover that there was a side of his life he meant to keep away from me. If I'd had visions of going to studio recording sessions and really learning the business from the inside, I had to forget about that dream. I had to forget my notions of becoming an intimate part of what I thought was an exotic and glamorous life. Though he knew a lot of those "famous and successful"—and even notorious—people, he kept me away from them. Except when he threw some grand party, at which I always seemed to be a visitor, I saw few of the celebrities he sometimes talked about.

Ricky did his recording in New York, and he had a penthouse there. So that was where he installed me as soon as we were married. What else did I need but a grand apartment, a grand piano, and all the grand money I wanted to spend? To say nothing of a loving husband who flew home sometimes when he could get away, and demanded to see the new songs I was always writing.

For a little while my sweet excitement burned high, and Ricky couldn't have been more thrilling and satisfying as a partner in love. When this began to fall off, I didn't know what to do, and when Ricky blamed me, I was too inexperienced not to blame myself. He still wanted my songs, but only occasionally did he want *me*, and even then there was an emptiness between us that left me always hungry. That I might have needs of my own never seemed to occur to him.

More and more, I found myself trapped in the circumscribed life he'd designed for me. Then my one refuge—my songs—began to fail me as well. Songs were my fantasy world, and I couldn't live there anymore.

It was never easy to explain anything to Ricky. I couldn't talk about our lovemaking, because that made him angry and vituperative, but at least I tried to make him understand about my song writing.

"Look—to write songs I have to get new vibes, new ideas all the time. I need something fresh and stimulating to light the right spark. Ideas, feelings, come out of *life,* out of people, out of the world, and—I just haven't seen enough. I'm living in a beautiful, sealed box where nothing ever happens. I'm being smothered, buried alive. The tunes that run through my head are all beginning to sound like someone else's. Or like old ones of mine!"

"*I* happen to you," Ricky said. And he really thought that was enough. "But I'll tell you what," he conceded, "I'm doing a concert out on Long Island next week. How would you like to come?"

I jumped at the chance to be part of his backstage life for once, though that wasn't the way it happened. He got me a seat in the fifth row of the auditorium, and I found myself for the first time a member of his audience. It was a disturbing event.

I'd read about the electricity Ricky could generate in person, but I'd never felt it along with thousands of other people before. There was almost a blue lightning between star and audience. Love and adulation flowed out toward him palpably. Suddenly I knew that this was the love affair of his life. I knew grimly that it would always be that way. No woman could ever love Ricky the way he wanted to be loved. No single woman could rival *this.* Nor could he ever love a woman with the same intensity with which he poured out his passion to an audience. Star and audience. Each was seduced by the other.

That night—early morning, really—when he made love to me I couldn't give him my usual warm response, still remembering, and perhaps accepting, that I could never compete with that monstrous emotional binge he went on whenever he stepped out on a stage. There was nothing left of him for me except what was, for him, a mechanical act of sex. He couldn't even love himself without the mirror an audience held up for him.

Yet I couldn't stop my own caring, loving, and the realization that I could do nothing to fulfill it tore me up. He would never change, but I had to do something—something real, to save myself.

I began to strike out in a new direction with my songs and went off on an ecology kick. I became obsessed with the awful things that were threatening the world. Pollution and toxic waste, dying lakes and rivers, acid rain, the extermination of birds, animals, and fish . . . it was pretty stirring stuff, and it helped my song writing for a while. I could feel emotional about all this and really care.

Norris was doubtful at first. Causes didn't make for high ratings anymore, and Ricky was no Pete Seeger. Ricky, however, liked the new songs and felt this fresh approach would sustain the image he wanted to project to his adoring public. I marveled at the feeling he seemed to put into "Sweet Rain," when I knew he didn't really care, except when he was singing.

I began to realize with a terrible certainty that Ricky Sands couldn't care deeply about anything. While he was singing he became what he really wanted to be. Certainly, whoever heard him believed. Out on a stage he possessed a strange power that compelled an audience. But it happened only onstage or when he was recording. I worked in a different way, because the idea had to matter to me—I had to believe in what I wrote. And I was afraid that I might stop.

Two years ago I'd written "Sweet Rain," and it had already been recorded by other singers, though Ricky's gold record was still the best. A few critics had said it would be a standard for a long time, and even gave me credit. For me, this wasn't enough.

As the months passed, I grew more rebellious. I determined to face him again, persuade him to let me take more of a part in my own life and in his. A meek, self-effacing background was never for me. When I told him that, he laughed and I noticed how excited and strange his laughter had become. Only Norris Wahl began to pay some attention to me.

After "Sweet Rain" I hit a real snag and my creative forces seemed to dry up altogether. One day Norris came to see me.

"Look, kid," he said, "you don't know what a tough, rough world it is out there. *Sick.* The whole damn music business is a zoo! Ricky doesn't want you exposed to it, and maybe he's got a point. How can you write sunny, hopeful songs that *build* if you find out what it's really like? Just the same, we both know you're getting stale—you're imitating yourself now. Maybe it's time you found out what's going on. A few good shocks might help you to recharge. Time to grow up, Hollis."

"Recharge" was an apt term, since Norris clearly thought of me more as a song machine than a human being.

He began to tell me things I hadn't known until then—perhaps hadn't wanted to know—about the drugs Ricky was taking, and about a soap-opera actress named Coral Caine. He was right. I was shocked—and angry and hurt, and knew I'd been determinedly blind. Norris was right. It was time for me to wake up. Perhaps by truly understanding I could reach Ricky again. I'd never faced the fact that what I saw some of the time was the effect of the drugs he took. Norris stressed that only I could help Ricky, and that he needed me. This argument slowly began to penetrate my growing fog of pain and alarm. I had closed my eyes because I hadn't wanted to recognize a new violence rising in Ricky, or to hear his slurred and sometimes crazy speech. I'd told myself that he was tired, that he needed a rest. Performing took an enormous lot out of him. Now Norris was forcing me to face the truths I'd closed my eyes to.

As it happened, his intervention came too late, and his timing couldn't have been worse.

2

On the day when Norris opened everything up, we were sitting alone in the penthouse living room. Ricky had left town rather suddenly a few weeks before. He wasn't working, and he'd been mysterious about where he was going. Norris had driven him off in his own Rolls and told me not to worry. His words didn't help, but I was accustomed to Ricky's sudden trips, and often he didn't tell me where he was going until later. So I hadn't been any more concerned than usual.

This was not my favorite room in the apartment. A famous decorator had done it over for Ricky at a time when beige and brown were very big in New York apartments. The furniture was chunky and without much grace; it was also piled with huge cushions that decorators doted on, and into which one sank as if into a swamp. Of course there was indirect lighting, which made everything bland. Only Ricky's piano offered a black, exclamatory statement. Glass doors opened on a terrace, with tremendous views of New York on every side.

When I'd moved in, the first thing I'd done was to *un*decorate my own room and put in a few things to remind me of California—of air and freedom and sunlight. And even of San Francisco fog. I'd come upon a lovely misty photograph in a shop on Madison Avenue, and I'd hung it on my bedroom wall to remind me of fog creeping in over the bay.

On that day, with Norris in the living room, I sat with my feet tucked under me on a sofa that turned at right angles to embrace the room, and I listened to him with the sick realization that for the whole time I'd been married to Ricky Sands I'd been skating on ice that was wafer thin. I felt frightened enough by the revelations of the moment, though Norris had only just begun.

It was early afternoon, and he had glanced at his watch and nodded. "Maybe we can catch her right now." He pushed a button to slide back the panel that hid the television screen, and found the channel he wanted. Close-up, wailing heads told me it was soap opera, and the woman was obviously playing a drunk, to the distress of the male actor with her.

"That's Coral Caine," Norris said. "She's the woman I've been telling you about."

I sat up and put my feet on the floor. The temperature of the apartment was exactly right, as always, but I felt suddenly cold.

The woman on the screen was almost beautiful, though with features that had grown a little sharp, and which were sharpened still more because she was playing an angry lush. Blond hair and brown eyes, a voluptuous figure—when the camera moved back carefully to reveal it. Her voice was good, though her words blurred together at times.

"They'll get rid of her in the next two sequences," Norris said. "These scenes were shot weeks ago. She's already been dropped from the show because she's not acting a drunk—she *is* one. Her looks are going—you'd think she was forty, but she's much younger."

"And Ricky is—in love with *her?*" I asked in a voice I didn't recognize.

"Love? That's for songs. They had a thing going for a while, before he ever met you. Look, kid, Ricky needs someone to build him up. He's scared of his own age, and he's picked this affair up again with Coral once or twice—mostly to keep her still. She didn't like him getting married. Now she's kicking up a real stink—with threats. That's why I want you to know about her."

I was staring at the screen, and my expression must have stopped him.

"Hey," he said, "you didn't think Ricky was celibate before he married you? Not with all those dizzy chicks around!"

"Of course not!" I said indignantly. "I'm not a fool!" But I was. I'd put from my mind any concern about the women who'd come before me, and he'd never talked about them. Nor did I want to think about how Ricky spent those long weeks away from me on the road. He'd always seemed scornful of the girls who fawned over him, and since *I* never looked at another man, I wanted him to feel the same about me. As though wanting something terribly ever made it so!

"You're coming with me now to see Coral Caine," Norris said.

My indignation had died, but I felt appalled at such a thought. "How could I do that? I don't want to see her, and if what you're telling me is true, I'm the last person *she'll* want to see."

"It's true, all right."

"I won't see her!"

"You're Ricky's last hope," Norris told me. "You had the guts to walk into a hospital room and face a spoiled, bad-tempered pop star. You tamed him and married him. Now maybe you're the one who can save that marriage. Save *him*. If his career caves in, he's finished. If you can't stop Coral, she's going public. If that happens, Ricky will give up. He's been a zombie lately anyway—or haven't you noticed?"

I'd noticed, but I'd turned into an expert at not seeing what I didn't dare to see. Now Norris Wahl was shaking me up, shocking me as thoroughly as though he'd slapped me across the face.

"I want her to see *you*," Norris said. "That's all. It doesn't matter what you say to her, or if you say anything."

I jumped up and walked around on rugs that were soft and furry under my feet.

"You can help Ricky if you go," Norris urged.

I swallowed my sick feeling. Because there wasn't anyone else at hand to turn to, I had to trust Norris.

The woman on the TV set started screeching in a temper tantrum, and when Norris turned her off I said I'd do as he asked, and hurried away to change my clothes.

Something in my bones told me that now was the time for another bluff, and I began to psych myself into a state of numb courage. This would be nothing like going to Ricky's hospital room. That escapade had been filled with fun and hope and daring. Now I had to meet something that had nothing to do with fantasy—something more real and destructive than I'd ever faced before in my life. And I had no hope at all to buoy me along. Just my life crumbling around me and a desperate need for action. My life had been crumbling for some time, only I just hadn't looked.

We drove down to the Village in Norris's big car. Coral Caine's apartment was undoubtedly expensive, but it looked at first glance like a junk heap, and it smelled even worse for lack of airing. Mostly of stale liquor.

She came to the door dressed in a long yellow gown that must have been expensive too, but was now only bedraggled. On the television screen she'd worn a wig. Her real hair was uncurled, and a fading blond she hadn't bothered to tint. She must have been beautiful once, but not anymore, and as Norris said, she looked older than she really was.

Since I was behind Norris, she didn't see me right away, and her expression of surprise indicated that she had certainly expected someone else.

"Oh, all right—come in," she said ungraciously to Norris.

He grasped my wrist and took me with him into her living room, so there was no time for her to shut the door in my face, as she might have done once she'd seen me.

"Hello, Coral," he said. "I want you to meet Ricky's wife."

Clearly she didn't need to be told who I was. For a moment she stood staring at me, taking me in—not entirely drunk. Or perhaps sobered by our sudden appearance.

"What do *you* want?" she demanded directly of me.

"Mind if we sit down?" Norris pushed me toward a chair. "I thought it was time for you two girls to meet—maybe talk things over."

I hated him for saying that, for bringing me here—to no good purpose. I hadn't yet seen how cruel his purpose was, and by the time I knew, it was too late.

"Okay, sit down," Coral told us, picking up a glass from a table and swallowing a large gulp of brown liquid. Her manner seemed overly agitated, though I had the feeling that it was not only our presence that had strung her out to such a degree. She shoved a pair of shoes off a chair and sat opposite me, talking to Norris now, yet not taking her eyes from my face.

"It's no use bringing *her* here," she told him. "Nobody's going to change my mind. Ricky knows what I mean to do, and if he sent you here to stop me, he's crazy."

I couldn't bear to watch her and I let my gaze wander about the room. Obviously she'd been a woman of taste. Mixed in with the present clutter were several fine, though shabby, pieces of furniture, and some objects of real value. A millefiori paperweight on the Queen Anne desk, a temple dog from some ancient Chinese dynasty on the mantel, as well as a few good original paintings on the walls; all hinted of a happier past. One rather strange pencil sketch of a woman's face caught my eye. It was oddly linear and flat, without modeling or shading, yet the old-fashioned artist had caught a certain impertinence of character in his model that was arresting. So arresting that an impression of that sketch stayed with me, though it didn't surface for a long time.

"Nobody's going to change my mind!" Coral ran on, sounding even shriller than before. "I mean to give *Rolling Stone* the scoop. They'll love this! Then everybody else'll pick it up. You know how it will go— your beautiful, divine, pure-hearted Ricky Sands is an all-out bastard. Look what he's done to me—and to you, too, Miss Songwriter. Even if you did manage to marry him."

Norris sighed as though he'd heard most of this before. "I brought Hollis so you'd know it wasn't any use, Coral. Just look in your own mirror and then look at her. This is the girl Ricky's in love with."

"In *love* with!" She spat out the words. "You're both stupid if you think it's possible for Ricky to love anyone but himself. At least *I* understand that. I never asked for more than he could give, and he was never afraid with me. Though he will be now!"

"Look, Coral," Norris spoke sharply, "your dragging everything through a dirty scandal won't get him back. And it'll wreck you. Nobody'll ever give you a job again. What will you gain except the feeling of paying him off?"

"Maybe revenge has its own rewards. At least I'll gain support for Ricky's child. Millions. This baby of his I'm carrying right now. And that isn't going to help his bloody sainted image either. Maybe it's okay for some pop stars to play around and crawl in the gutter—but not Ricky Sands. His fans will never stand for it."

If Norris was startled by her announcement, he didn't show it. Perhaps he'd already known this too. I felt as though a fist had been driven into my stomach.

"It won't work, Coral," Norris went on more quietly. "Of course he'll look into this matter of a child—if there is one. But that doesn't mean it's his."

"So what do you think, Miss high-and-mighty Songwriter? Did you even consider me when you stepped in and took him away?"

"Oh, come off it." Norris was impatient again. "You and Ricky broke up years ago. Nobody took anything away from you."

"That's what you think. Don't you know he's been seeing me again?"

By this time, however, she was wearing down under Norris's unyielding attack, and her very defiance sounded sad and hollow. Harsh daylight from a window made her look a pitiful shadow of the woman in full makeup whom I'd watched on television, and for the first time I sensed what Norris was doing so brutally.

Nevertheless, she stormed on, still defiant, though her voice began to crack. "How could Ricky Sands possibly care about this insipid kid he married? All he wanted was her songs. She must know that by now!"

The probable truth of her words cut sickeningly deep. I tried to brace myself, understanding the pain out of which she struck to wound me. I was no novice when it came to the pain Ricky could inflict. Now I could see fully what Norris was doing, and I felt sick and ashamed. By setting me down in this woman's presence, confronting her with me, Norris meant to prove to her that she'd lost. I suppose I looked young and healthy and able to cope—all the things that Coral Caine would never be again—and I couldn't bear what was happening to both of us. How we were being used. Even in this moment of confrontation, even hearing her disastrous news, I knew where the blame lay—and it lay with Ricky.

"Norris should never have brought me here," I told Coral, and heard the break in my own voice. "I—I'll talk to Ricky. I know he'll help you."

She stared at me. "You're crazy if you think that! Nobody can get Ricky to listen to anything. And never mind being sorry for me! I've taken all I can. Now there's going to be a showdown and a big blowup. So just get out—both of you! And don't ever come back here again!"

Moving unsteadily, she crossed the room without another look for either of us, and slammed the bedroom door.

When we stepped into the hall a florist's messenger stood before the door, holding a sheaf of roses half covered by tissue.

"Miss Caine's apartment?" he asked.

"I'll give them to her," Norris said.

He took the roses and I glimpsed the deep pink of petals and a card tucked into them. Norris carried the sheaf into Coral's living room and called to her. When he rejoined me, I followed him down narrow stairs. I found myself hoping sadly that the flowers, whoever had sent them, would bring Coral Caine a little solace. Everything inside me felt raw and wounded and exposed.

"Bringing me here was an awful thing to do," I told Norris when we reached the street. "It was cruel to both of us."

That didn't bother him. "Sure, but it may work. Now that she's seen you, she won't have the guts to keep on. She's too sick. And she'll know better than to think she can get him back from you. That's what she really wants. All this revenge stuff is hot air, and I don't think she's pregnant."

I had nothing to say. I couldn't make him see what a dreadful thing he'd done. All I could do was hurry away down the sidewalk. When he came after me and took my arm, I pulled back.

"I want to be by myself. Please leave me alone."

"Look," he said, "I know you're upset right now. But I had to do this to save Ricky. In the long run you'll be glad I did. Now let me take you home, Hollis."

I stood still and looked him straight in the eyes. When he turned red I walked away, and he let me go. I never looked back but moved blindly, too sick over what had happened to know where to turn, where to go.

When I stood at a curb waiting for a light to change, a man stopped beside me. "Mrs. Sands," he said, "my name is Barron. I play bass guitar with Ricky's band."

When the green came on I crossed the street. Norris had sent him, of course, and I didn't want to talk to this man or anyone else.

"You look a bit rocky," he said, coming along beside me. "Will you let me take you home?"

I glanced at him then and saw a tall, mild-mannered man with angular features. Clean-shaven, since Ricky never wanted beards in his band. Old stuff, he always said. Though I'd heard the name Barron, I didn't know him. Ricky had never allowed me to meet, much less mix with, his musicians.

"Thank you, no," I told him, stiffly polite.

He still showed no sign of leaving me, so I spoke again more firmly as we walked along. "I suppose Norris sent you after me. But I don't need anyone to take me home. When I'm ready I'll get a cab myself. I just want to walk around the Village for a while. By myself."

"Wahl shouldn't have taken you to see her. Let's stop for a cup of coffee—here's a place. Then I'll put you into a cab."

He seemed to know where I'd been and something of what had happened, and I lacked the strength to go on opposing him. I didn't ask how he happened to be around at this particular time. I didn't care. At least coffee appealed to me.

We went into a cafe and sat in a dim side booth. When the mug came,

I warmed my hands around it and sipped slowly. Black and strong was what I needed.

The man named Barron seemed to have no small talk and neither did I. He appeared to be observing me, as though he waited for something, though I had no idea what. Making an effort to start home seemed too great at the moment, and it was simpler to sit here and try not to think or feel. I was afraid of what would happen if I indulged myself by giving my emotions free rein. I had to grow up and never again allow myself to be so vulnerable.

"How is your father?" the man across the table asked.

That startled me out of my vacuum. "You know my father?"

"No, but I've heard Ricky talk about him. Dan Temple sounds like a great guy."

This was even more startling, since Dan disliked Ricky so intensely, and I'd thought Ricky felt the same way about him.

"Ricky admires your father a great deal," Barron went on. "But of course you know that."

I didn't know it, and if it was true, the fact saddened me. Why hadn't Ricky told *me* if he admired my father?

"Were you in San Francisco when Ricky was there five years ago?" I asked, coming to life a little.

"Sure. The whole band was there, though we never got to play that concert. When Ricky smashed himself up, we scattered for a while. He kept us on full pay, but gave us a vacation. So I hiked around the Northwest for a few weeks."

"What did Ricky say about my father?"

"He respected him as a musician. He said he could learn something by listening to Dan Temple."

"Are you making all this up?"

"Do you think I am?"

I didn't know. Barron's presence was somehow unsettling, and suddenly I was ready to go back to the apartment.

He took me outside, hailed a cab, and helped me into it.

"You'll be all right now," he said.

I wondered how anybody could ever say that to anyone—and with such senseless confidence!

I thanked him, feeling bemused by this total stranger who had stepped so suddenly into my life. As the cab pulled away, I was aware that he stood looking after it. I didn't think about him again for a long time.

During the endless, traffic-blocked ride uptown, I sat watching the streams of people on every sidewalk, not really seeing them. Mostly I felt numb. Events that rock one's whole life can't be assimilated quickly. Even the cab driver gave up trying to talk to me.

When I walked into the apartment, the phone was ringing. Someone wanted to speak to Ricky, and I said he wasn't home.

"Mrs. Sands?" Its was a reporter. "We'd like to have a comment from your husband or you about Coral Caine's death."

I set the phone down and left it disconnected. When a peremptory buzzing began, warning me to hang up, I ignored it and went back to my own room to stand at a window, as I'd done so often since coming here. Sometimes the spectacular view had raised my spirits. It did nothing for me now.

I stood for a long while watching the sun go down across the river, its reflection blood-red in a million windows on this side. Great flat apartment buildings, looking too thin to stand, layered away from me in row behind row, with others cutting in at right angles. In a narrow slot between two giants stood the wedge end of another building, with strips of sky on either side.

For the first time all this seemed real—immensely frightening, threatening. All those windows that faced me with their lights burning all day, and most of the night, represented thousands and thousands of human beings living and working close together, none of whom I knew. The buildings seemed oppressive in all their steel and concrete, and I had a crazy vision of them all tumbling in upon one another, felled by some bolt from the sky—to end our millions of futile lives behind the windows.

Thoughts like this weren't like me. I didn't feel like myself. Somehow I managed to hold everything away and waited for news time. Then I went into the living room and turned on the television set where I'd watched Coral earlier today. The announcer said that the popular soap-opera actress Coral Caine had been found dead by a woman friend in her Greenwich Village apartment. The death appeared to be from drugs. She also noted that Miss Caine had been involved at one time with the pop singer Ricky Sands. Someone had seen a man and woman leaving the apartment shortly before Miss Caine's death, and the police hoped these two would come forward with any information they might have.

I switched off the set and sat in silence. Eventually, Ricky would come home. He would walk through the door, and I would say . . . I hadn't the faintest idea what I would say. In any case, I had the feeling it wouldn't do any good, because he'd turned into that zombie Norris had talked about. I didn't even know where he was so I could call him. So what was left? What was left for any of us?

Nothing at all for Coral Caine. Or the child she carried. And probably Norris and I were responsible.

Norris came to the apartment as soon as he heard. He told me he'd taken Ricky away two weeks ago to a place upstate where the rich and famous could disappear in order to cool down, and bring their drug habits within the bounds of survival. It was a good thing he wasn't in town right now, so there'd be no possible connection with Coral's death. However, since the police were looking for us, we'd better go over to the precinct station and clear ourselves. There'd be no real problem.

There was none, though we were questioned rather thoroughly before they let us go. Norris wove a plausible enough tale about our visit, inventing an invitation from Coral Caine. Since she was drunk when we got there, we still had no notion why she'd wanted to see us, and we hadn't stayed long. I could do nothing but back him up. By that time everything was beginning to hurt a great deal. I hated all the lies and subterfuge. Dan had never taught me how to cover up.

The police asked us one odd question. Had we noticed a spray of roses still in their tissue at the apartment when we were there? Norris told them about meeting the messenger at the door. Apparently the police were curious about those roses. While they hadn't been taken out of their tissue, no card had been found to identify either florist or sender.

Later a reporter was to pick up on the roses, mentioning their unusual "coral" color, as well as the lack of a card. But at the time, roses were the least of my concern.

On the way home from our visit to the police, Norris emphasized that *we* had nothing to do with Coral's death. She was already teetering on some brink, and, God knows, we weren't to blame, whatever had happened. I listened and couldn't believe. He was being hypocritical. If we hadn't gone to see her, if Norris hadn't been so cruel, she might still be alive. For me it was as simple as that, and had to be faced. Just as I must face her existence in Ricky's life.

When we returned, Norris used my key to let us into the apartment, and we walked into the living room to find Ricky sitting there waiting for us. He had heard the news and he looked awful—gray and stricken and sick. Norris took charge, wasting no time.

"Did you go to see Coral Caine today?" he demanded.

Ricky didn't look at me. "Whatever happened, she had it coming to her, but I haven't been near her in months." His voice sounded flat, mechanical—not like the voice of a singer.

A new fear gripped me. In the time I'd been married to Ricky, I'd learned all too well how easily he could lie. What if he *had* seen her? What if he were connected in some way with her death?

Norris must have been thinking the same thing, for he sat down beside Ricky abruptly. "Just tell me why you came back to New York."

When Ricky didn't answer, Norris shook him by the shoulder. "My God! Why did you have to come back *now?* Were you in her place today? Or did you call her on the phone?"

Ricky put his head in his hands, and I noticed absently that his beautiful pale gold hair was turning silvery at the temples.

"What's a phone call got to do with anything?" Ricky murmured.

"What did you say to her? If I'm to help you, I have to know."

Ricky looked up, his eyes on me for the first time since we'd walked into the room. "When did you learn about Coral, Hollis?"

I hadn't moved from the doorway since I'd seen Ricky sitting there, and now I came slowly into the room. "Norris took me to see her today."

Tears welled up in Ricky's eyes, but he didn't speak. Pity, I'd discovered, could be almost as powerful an emotion as love and certainly as abused—even though I knew his tears were for himself and not for Coral.

"What are you on now?" Norris asked roughly. "Is it ludes this time —or what?"

Ricky shook his head. "I'm just sick. Sick of everything."

"Well, it doesn't matter one way or the other. What's important is to get you out of the city right away. As soon as it's dark, I'll drive you back upstate."

"I won't go," Ricky said, sounding weak but obstinate.

Norris was growing angrily impatient, and I stepped in.

"That's enough! Let him alone. You can see he can't go anywhere now. I'll help you get to bed, Ricky. Tomorrow you can decide what to do. If there's anything to be done."

Ricky came with me, leaning heavily with an arm about my shoulders. We left Norris staring after us, still furious. When I returned to the living room later, he was gone.

The next few days were terrible to get through. Ricky was genuinely ill, and I could see that it was better to let Norris take him away than allow him to stay here to answer all the endless questions. In the long run, no one ever knew that he'd returned to New York. Norris took care of that. In me, however, the one unanswered question went on and on: *What had Ricky done that might connect him with Coral's death?*

The verdict when it came was suicide. Mixed drugs on top of alcohol. Coral's fading career was motive enough. There was never any mention of a baby, so her claim of pregnancy had been a lie, as Norris suspected. If Ricky had seen or called her, that never came out in the investigation. No one mentioned the coral roses again.

I telephoned my father several times during the weeks that followed Coral's death. Dan wanted me to come home to Berkeley for a while, but Ricky might return at any time, and I couldn't leave. Besides, how could I ever admit to my father that I'd been living a fantasy life ever since I'd married, and that it was all falling to pieces around me? What had happened, what *was* happening, was ugly and real, and I didn't know how to deal with any of it. Nor would I dump it into Dan's life.

With Ricky gone again, the apartment seemed quiet and empty. I missed the bustle and excitement that had always surrounded his times at home. There had been telephones ringing, arguments about album covers, interviews, bookings—and Ricky exploded through it all with enormous energy, almost convincing everyone that he was still that young singer who had burst upon the world twenty years ago. Now it seemed frighteningly quiet.

Music had always been my life and we had a fine stereo and collection of records, many of which were my choice. I played singers I'd enjoyed—Carly Simon, Anne Murray, Olivia Newton-John. Terri Gibbs singing "Ashes to Ashes" brought me to tears and I turned off the stereo. Right now music only made me feel empty, since I lacked any desire to create my own songs. It was a reproach, rather than a comfort, and no new tunes sang through my head.

Norris grew anxious about me. One day when we were in the beige and brown penthouse living room again, he started prowling like the bear he sometimes reminded me of. A small bear, but powerful, and much too clever. I remember that he turned abruptly and banged on the piano.

"Okay, Hollis—use it!"

I stared at him.

"You write songs, don't you? Then use it! You don't use emotion for anything else—so put it into some songs. What are you afraid of?"

His words made me furious, as though that were all there was to my life—song writing. Yet at the same time I knew he was right. Songs had always been my way of trying to understand what I thought and felt, even when I'd been afraid to face my own feelings. I swallowed my anger.

"I'll try," I told him meekly.

During the weeks before Ricky came home, I really did try to take his advice. I wrote "Other Woman," though I never showed it to anyone. Strangely, it was a cry, not from me but from the heart of a woman I'd met only one time. A tune with a sob in it. As though by trying to *be* Coral Caine I could find out who I was and what I meant to Ricky Sands.

I also wrote a sad little song, "Wanting Doesn't Make It Happen"— which I disliked later, though when Ricky made it, it gained a sort of cult following. He'd come home by that time and he was recording again, though not accepting any out-of-town gigs. I wrote "For Just a Little While," and he made that one too, but the special quality that he could put into a song was missing. He was off the hard drugs—at least that's what I hoped—but he was like a blank page on which nothing was being written. Perhaps he'd always been that way, unless he had a false stimulant. Now there was nothing more he seemed to want from me emotionally, or in any other way, though I still ached with love for him.

Sometimes I grew so angry that I wanted to hit him, shake him up, make him feel what I was feeling. But nothing I said or did got through to him. Except once, when I tried to talk to him about Coral. Then he cut me off with a fury that alarmed me.

"Let it alone, Hollis! She's gone now—so let it alone or you'll be sorry."

That chapter wasn't closed, but there was no way I could make him open it in order to clear the air. In the end I grew afraid to find out what might really have happened when he'd come home to New York, and Coral had died. He would never admit whether or not he'd seen her, or talked to her on the telephone. The only thing that ever surfaced was a bone-deep rage he still felt against her. He was angry over what she'd meant to do to *him,* and that anger was more important to him than her death. It appeared to be the only thing he could feel anything about, and that alarmed me even more.

In the year that followed Coral's death, I kept trying to work. I couldn't live with emptiness forever. A songwriter *has* to make up songs, or she dies a little. A good song can come easily on a wave of inspiration, but often it has to be tried over and over again—both lyrics and melody—in order to get it right. A great many more songs are written than are ever sung, and you can't know which ones will make it and which won't. A few get recorded, and only a few climb to the top and become big hits.

Because it had been at the top of the charts, "Sweet Rain" came up for a Grammy Award, and that pleased me, though Ricky couldn't have cared less. Someone else sang it at the award ceremony because he was in no condition to appear, and I didn't attend at all. Though the song didn't win, it went on growing in popularity, being sung in colleges, at church affairs—anywhere at all where people had a will for change. It was a cult song, I guess, the sort of rallying song they'd done in the sixties, but it was different because it belonged to *now.*

Ricky hardly seemed present anymore. Something was gnawing at him, and I couldn't tell what it was, or get him to talk about it, hard as I tried to encourage him. There were drugs again. He sank into the deep depression that always results. The highs he craved became harder and harder to reach, the depths more frightening and lasting. Strange people came and went in our apartment now at all hours of the day and night. They looked dangerous sometimes, yet mocking, as they virtually ignored me. Even though I was more knowledgeable, I didn't know how to help my own husband.

Nearly a year to the day of Coral's death, Ricky walked out of the apartment for the last time. He came to where I sat at the piano, trying to get something started.

"It's no use, Hollis," he said. "I've known it wasn't for a long time. I've got to run. There's nothing else for me to do."

"Run where? *Why?*" I cried.

He stared at me with vacant eyes. "If you need it, the answer's in the song," he said, and closed the door in my face. I never saw him alive again.

3

It was all over and I had to begin picking up the pieces. I felt as though something inside me had shattered and there were too many broken bits that I didn't know how to reassemble.

Sometimes at night I cried, but mostly I held everything back. The worst thing of all was having no one I could talk to openly and freely. I might have done this with Dan, but he was far away, and telephones and letters weren't the same. Besides, he'd never liked Ricky Sands or understood what he was all about. Not that I understood either. It was a strange grief I felt. Perhaps more for something lost long before the real man had died. There was self-blame as well—a feeling that I should have done something—should have understood more and helped. I should have *known*.

The uproar that followed Ricky's death shouldn't have surprised me, yet the fury of it did. And the sickening exploitation in all the media. I couldn't step out of the building without facing TV cameras and mikes, and attracting a crowd that followed me everywhere. Mostly I stayed inside, trapped. Until I'd met Ricky I'd been like them, a heedless watcher and reader who craved all the tragic details in the news instantly. I hadn't thought much about the victims of an aggressive medium whose job it was to deliver the news, at whatever cost.

Now I found out what it was like to be recognized at the door of the building, to be reached for, whispered about, gossiped over in print—often with no connection to the truth—to have microphones thrust in my face and questions hurled at me. This would have happened at Ricky's memorial service too, if I hadn't been protected.

The pop music world turned out in force, and I listened numbly to a famous singer whom I'd never met give Ricky's eulogy. I could only pray that the whole truth would never be known about a man who had been a public idol.

Those people who stood before our apartment building in an endless vigil, and had nothing to do with the press, gathered outside the church as well, wanting me to respond, to carry on the legend that was Ricky's. Because I'd written some of his songs, I was part of that legend, but this wasn't what I wanted for *me*.

At the service I was glad to have Norris Wahl on one side of me and Chuck Oliver on the other. Chuck had been Ricky's producer and I admired his special talents, though I'd met him only three or four times. He seemed a kind man, with a genuine grief over Ricky's death that was not merely connected with the loss of a valuable "property."

When Ricky's own band played "Sweet Rain," I dissolved in tears that brought no release. What had driven my husband to this black state of desperation? And how was I to live without him? As long as he was there, I could pretend that everything would change and that he would be again the Ricky I'd first thought I knew.

After the service, Ricky's musicians crowded about me, offering their help if I needed it. For the first time in a year I remembered the bass guitar player who had rescued me in the Village at the time of Coral's death. He was not among those who came to speak to me.

Norris and Chuck got me away as quickly as they could. Since Chuck had to return to the recording studio, only Norris and Bea came back to the apartment with me.

"This business can dish out some pretty rotten deals," Norris said, pouring himself a drink. "There's too much pressure all the time. It's pressure that caused Ricky's death, just as it did with Janis Joplin, and Jimi Hendrix, and all those others. Everything's so hyped up that you get to feeling you can never meet all the expectations that are piled on top of you. That's what it was, Hollis, so don't go blaming yourself."

I knew this was part of the truth, but there was so much more. More than I was ready to face.

"There's something you better know," Norris said. "Something the police have kept out of the papers. Which is just as well, as they'd have sensationalized it."

"What are you talking about?"

"Remember the roses that were delivered just as we were leaving Coral's apartment? Exactly the same sort of roses were found beside Ricky's bed in the hotel room where he died."

A chill crept through me to my very fingertips. "Why—*why?*"

"Nobody knows," Norris said. "Are you sure you don't?"

"Of course I don't!"

"The detective I talked to said there might be some connection with Coral Caine's death, but with Ricky gone, it probably didn't matter."

It mattered to me, and I would think about those coral roses over and over again in the coming weeks. Think fearfully because of what I'd feared about Ricky since Coral had died. Had he sent them to her as some sort of signal—and then brought the same type with him to the hotel room? None of this made sense.

By now I wanted only to get away from New York and everything that reminded me of Ricky Sands. But where was I to turn? Where could I hide?

Ricky's following in this country was fantastic, and now there were some who began to wonder about me. If I wasn't going to step out in public and become part of the legend, then perhaps I was to blame. Some of the letters turned especially vituperative.

Hundreds of letters poured in every day—whole boxes of them that we stacked in Ricky's office in the apartment—what he'd called his Trophy Room. Here he'd kept his gold records and two that were platinum. They were mounted on black velvet and covered with glass, and they hung on the walls keeping company with other awards and special citations he'd once been proud of. Then a few months ago he'd suddenly taken everything down and packed it all away in cartons.

When I asked him why, he had said, "It's over," and the words had shocked me. They weren't true, didn't need to be true—unless he believed them. He hadn't needed to kill himself.

During those days after his death I sampled a few of the letters. There was a strange ambivalence in me. On one hand I wanted to push everything away that reminded me of Ricky. If only I could forget, the pain would stop. But there was an equally strong need to hold any reminder of him close to me, to press my cheek against a jacket he had worn, to speak his name out loud and talk about him. So I dipped into the fan letters.

The outpouring of grief disturbed me because much of it seemed unwholesome, unreal. These fans weren't mourning a real man and his music, but someone they'd built up in their own minds—to answer their own pathetic needs. Already there had been suicides around the country because of Ricky's death—as always happens when some public idol died—and these terrified me still more. How could I stop this avalanche of emotion when I couldn't even handle or understand my own?

Once when I was sleepless I found myself standing at the terrace parapet in the middle of the night, looking down from the penthouse to a nearly empty street below. The attractiveness of death could be an insidious poison, almost contagious, promising surcease from pain, and a false peace. Was that what Ricky had sought? And Coral Caine? But it *wasn't* what *I* wanted. I wanted to live again and somehow work through the empty pain.

During this time a man named Alan Gordon telephoned and talked to Norris. I knew nothing about him, though the name of Geneva Ames, at whose request he was calling, sounded vaguely familiar.

"I think you'd better see him," Norris advised. "Mr. Gordon has some sort of plan for rescuing you."

"Who is Mr. Gordon?" I asked. "And why should he rescue me?"

"Who he is doesn't matter. It's the woman who's sent him that's important. You must have heard of Geneva Ames. She's rich-rich. Gives enormous gifts to worthy causes. She seems to've decided that you're someone she wants to invest in."

"Invest in? What are you talking about?"

Norris shrugged. "Maybe you'd better see him and find out."

Norris and Bea were being kind by staying with me for a while, yet by this time I wanted to get away from Norris as much as I wanted anything else. He'd begun to crowd me too much, trying to salvage something from the collapse of his own investment in Ricky. Not that record sales hadn't picked up since all the splurge in the media, but Norris felt I was the future, and he was pushing me.

I gave in abruptly. "All right. You can tell Mr. Gordon to come and see me."

Norris grinned. "I already have. He's coming this afternoon—about two hours from now. He wants to take you to see Mrs. Ames, so you'd better be ready to face those mikes and cameras again. Every move you make is still news."

"I'll see him here," I said. "But I won't promise to go anywhere with him. First, I have to know what this is all about."

At least something had caught my attention, and I was mildly curious. I put on the heather-toned tweed I'd bought in Scotland on one of those rare trips when Ricky had taken me along, without the band.

I didn't leave my room, however, until Bea came to fetch me. She was more excited about this development than I was.

"Wait till you see this one!" she whispered. "Be nice to him, Hollis. Norris seems to think he's got a good idea for you."

In the mirror I looked too pale, so I added a touch of flame lipstick and tied a green scarf at my throat. Ricky always said green complemented my red hair.

In the living room Norris Wahl sat against beige cushions, while Alan Gordon stood at the piano looking over old efforts of mine on the music rack—things I would never finish because of lost interest but hadn't bothered to put away. I thought it impertinent of him to be looking through my music sheets, but I didn't know then how little Alan Gordon cared about doing what was acceptable to others.

When I came through the doorway he stayed where he was beside the piano, so that Norris had to bring me to him for the introduction. He was also arrogant, I thought, suspecting that this scheme was not of his devising, and that he didn't approve of me, or of whatever Geneva Ames planned to do.

First impressions are important, and as I moved toward him I looked at him as intently as he stared at me, trying to add him up. Very tall. More than six feet. Hair slightly wavy and almost black. I was to learn about a Spanish grandmother later. Eyes a rather wintry gray, and narrowed as he watched me come toward him. A small scar raised his left eyebrow in a permanently quizzical expression, and his long nose was strong and slightly crooked. The imperfection seemed a relief, since otherwise he'd have been much too good-looking, and I distrusted handsome men. They had popped up rather often in Ricky's theatrical world, and he'd sometimes brought such friends to the apartment. I'd always been the outsider when it came to their jargon, and had never felt comfortable with any of them.

Alan Gordon took my hand firmly, but briefly, and I noted that his own was brown and sinewy.

"Thank you for seeing me, Mrs. Sands."

I gestured him toward the sofa, and chose the one chair that wouldn't sink me into cushions up to my chin. Norris asked if he'd like a drink, but he shook his head.

"I'll get right to the point, Mrs. Sands," he said. I liked his voice better than I did the rest of him. I always noticed voices, and his was deep and resonant. "Mrs. Ames has asked me to bring you to see her. She's had serious heart surgery and is recuperating in a hospital not far from here. Her car is waiting downstairs."

I was already shaking my head. "You must know what else is waiting for me down there. I'm not going to face that just to go with you when I haven't the faintest idea why."

He fixed his gray eyes at some distant spot far over my head, and I decided that this was the key thing about him—he was a very distant man.

"As I understand from Mr. Wahl," he said, "you would like to get out of New York. Mrs. Ames wants to offer you her home in Cold Spring Harbor for as long as you care to stay there."

Cold Spring Harbor, as I knew vaguely, was somewhere on the north shore of Long Island. But why I should go there, rather than to any other place, I couldn't think. Nevertheless, he had made me even more curious.

"Why is Mrs. Ames suggesting this?"

"She would like to tell you that herself. She understands what you've been through recently, and feels she can offer you a safe haven until the uproar dies down. No one needs to know you're there and you'll have the time and solitude to decide what you want to do later. When she comes out of the hospital, she means to visit friends in California for a while. So her house will be empty all winter."

"I already know what I want to do," I said. "I'm a songwriter and I want to write songs."

"Hey," Norris put in, "you've lost your singer. It won't be that easy now."

"It wasn't ever easy," I told him curtly. And that was true. In spite of quick success, I had worked very hard on my songs for Ricky.

Alan Gordon stopped looking at the spot over my head and seemed to discover me. "There's a grand piano at Windtop," he said. "A very fine one. What else would you like to know?"

"Let's begin with you," I challenged. "If you can't tell me about Mrs. Ames, tell me about you. Why are you doing this for her?"

He settled more deeply into the sofa, crossing his long legs, perhaps making an effort to lose some of his stiffness.

"The story of my life? I grew up in Cold Spring Harbor, and I still live there. My mother was Geneva Ames's closest friend, and after my parents died, when I was still in my teens, I lived for a time at Windtop, her home. Geneva—Mrs. Ames—has no children left, so in a sense I've been her son. I would do anything for her."

Though he said all this calmly, without emotion, I sensed his sincerity. He was a man very sure of himself.

While Norris scowled as he tried to think up new arguments to convince me, I made up my mind. After all, what could I lose by looking into this? Suddenly I wanted to know more about the mysterious Mrs. Ames, and what *she* wanted of me. I had a feeling there was a catch in this curious plan and that it wouldn't surface until I saw Geneva Ames herself.

"All right, Mr. Gordon. I don't really know why I should, but I'll go with you to see her."

Norris nodded, pleased, and stood up. "I'll come along, Hollis. As Ricky's manager—"

"Thanks, but I'd rather go alone," I told him. Norris wasn't *my* manager, and he had to understand that sometime. I'd felt for quite a while that Ricky had been too much in Norris Wahl's hands, and I didn't want that for myself. I still had no idea where I would go now with my music, though producers and agents—all sorts of people—had been trying to get in touch with me since Ricky's death. The only one I'd talked to was Ricky's producer, Chuck Oliver, who'd called me several times after the memorial service. I could only say that I had nothing for him, and I let Norris handle the other calls.

I put on a short jacket of expensive fake fur that I rather liked. Ricky had wanted me to have the real thing, but I didn't want to wear skins for which animals had been killed.

I'm not sure how Alan Gordon did it, but when we reached the vestibule he took my arm and propelled me straight through the mikes and gabbling reporters to Mrs. Ames's Lincoln Continental, waiting with its chauffeur at the curb. I saw him push one reporter aside when he tried to shove a mike in the car.

Apparently we'd taken them by surprise, and when we pulled away they didn't have time to follow us.

Clearly Alan Gordon didn't believe in idle conversation, so there was little talk on the way to the hospital as he became remote again. I didn't mind. It was Mrs. Ames who interested me.

His only remark on the short drive to the hospital took the form of a warning.

"She can be rather excitable at times, so speak to her quietly, if you will, and don't argue with anything she says."

This didn't sound reassuring. I might very well want to argue.

Alan Gordon had called ahead from the apartment to let Mrs. Ames know we were coming, so she was ready for us when we walked in.

Once she must have been a beautiful woman. The indications were there in the fine bone structure of her face, the large gray eyes, and well-formed chin. She was still a handsome, commanding presence, even propped up in a hospital bed. Probably in her sixties, she didn't seem especially frail, in spite of her medical ordeal. Her gray hair had been drawn back and tied with a black velvet ribbon that didn't look in the least coy. Her complexion was good, and enhanced with a touch of blush on the cheekbones, and a hint of light lipstick. When a nurse ushered us into her room she charmed me at once with her warm smile. Only the hand she held out looked fragile, and the pressure of her fingers lacked strength.

"Thank you for coming," she said. "I've been following the newspapers and I can imagine what all this must be doing to you."

She waved a ringed hand to a chair beside her bed, and nodded imperiously at the nurse, who left at once. Alan Gordon withdrew to a window, where he stood looking out.

I sat down stiffly, waiting for her to continue. The ball was in this woman's court and I needn't do a thing until I found out what the next play would be.

"Alan's told you of my offer?" she asked. "Invitation, really."

"He's told me, but I don't know why you've made it."

"Perhaps it would be nice to have someone in my house besides the housekeeper and caretaker."

"But why me?"

She didn't seem to mind my abruptness and her smile remained friendly. "I'm not entirely removed from your music world. When I was young I was a rather successful concert pianist. I even composed a few little pieces that are still played here and there."

Not good enough, I thought. There was still no reason to pick me out of the blue and make this offer.

"Do you like my songs?" I asked.

"I'm sorry, but I'm not sure if I've heard them. Though I know Alan has made it his business to listen. I'm not familiar with the popular field, I'm afraid. That is—" She seemed to hesitate and broke off, looking toward the man at the window.

He turned, still unsmiling, and I suspected that he hated my songs. All I wanted was to know what was going on, and I needn't play games with these two.

"Did you know my husband, Ricky Sands?" I asked her.

Again she hesitated, and her smile turned wistful. Then she made up her mind. "I knew your father when I was Geneva Lake. I knew him rather well before I married John Ames and moved into Windtop—our house in Cold Spring Harbor. That was before Daniel Temple married your mother."

This was the last thing I'd expected, and my astonishment must have shown in my face.

"You might telephone him," she said gently. "I think he'll remember me. Let's just say I'm paying a sentimental debt in doing this. You could have been my daughter."

But then I'd have been someone totally different. *I* wouldn't be here at all. How strange the threads—a turn here, a twist there, and generations ahead were affected.

"We've lost you," Geneva Ames said, and her smile charmed me again. "You understand, don't you, that I couldn't explain something like this through another person, or on a telephone."

I shook myself back into reality. "I think I'm just stunned." Suddenly I found myself returning her smile—really smiling for the first time in weeks. "Daniel," she'd said. No one I knew had ever called him that in my hearing. It seemed enchanting to know that when they were young this woman and my father had loved each other. I would call Dan, of course—not to check on Mrs. Ames's words, but because I wanted to know more about the past. About what this woman had been like when she was young, and what Dan had been like.

Alan Gordon moved from the window. "We mustn't tire you, Geneva. If Mrs. Sands decides to accept your suggestion, I can take care of everything."

"A moment longer," she said as I started to rise. "I know what it's like to need a total change. I lost my husband too—though that was years ago. It was my fault that Daniel and I parted, and it happened only because I put my career first. Which was right for me at the time. Now, my dear, you must put *your* work first and return to your piano.

There's a beautiful Bechstein at Windtop, and the house has been empty of music for too long."

"I don't know how to thank you," I said. She was opening up my life, giving me a place and time in which I could find myself.

"It will be enough to have you staying there," she assured me. "Birdy and Luther are getting old. Some years ago we had a serious fire at Windtop." Her voice broke for just a second, and Alan Gordon came toward the bed at once. She waved him back and went on. "It was arson —we know that—and I lost some valuable things. I've had to let most of my staff go because I wasn't sure whether I'd ever get back to Windtop. It will help to know that Daniel Temple's daughter is staying in a house I love very much."

"I've never heard him called Daniel before."

"That's what I always called him, and he used to call me Jenny. He was a brave, kind young man. A proper Daniel. I could never see him as Dan. It's too bad that he lacked a driving ambition, since he had his own talent."

I couldn't allow anyone to put Dan down. "People can be successful in other ways," I told her quickly.

"Of course. And he always was. Now I've seen his daughter, I know that it's right for you to stay in my house. I wasn't sure at first, but sometimes—don't laugh at me, my dear—sometimes I catch glimpses of what can be. Perhaps *you* will find yourself at Windtop."

Her deep-set eyes had brightened, and her cheeks had warmed beneath the hint of blush. At once Alan Gordon moved toward her, and she sighed.

"Everyone tries to keep me calm and quiet these days, and I hate it! Good-bye, my dear."

She held out her hand again, and this time I took it more warmly. There were questions I'd have liked to ask, but this wasn't the time, and she lacked the strength.

Alan Gordon bent to kiss her cheek, and then went to open the door for me. We stepped into an echoing hospital corridor that again plunged me back in memory to the first time I'd seen Ricky Sands. But I had to hold such memories away. It would be good for me to move into a place where he had never been. There would be fewer reminders.

We didn't speak until we were once more in the sleek black car. Then I asked Alan Gordon how I could keep the press from finding me out in Long Island. Cold Spring Harbor wasn't all that far away.

"I'll manage the details. It won't be hard. We'll get away at a time when no one's watching. How soon can you be ready to leave?"

Now that I'd decided, I was eager. "Tonight? Tomorrow? Anytime!"

He almost smiled. "When you turn yourself around, you really turn around! Let's say day after tomorrow. That will give you a little time, and give Windtop time to get ready for you. Will you let your apartment go?"

"No, I don't think so. Not just yet." I might still need a home base, since I wasn't in the least sure of this plan as yet.

"What about your help?"

I laughed. "I'm the help. Oh, I have a woman who comes in regularly, but mostly there's only me. I never wanted an entourage around me, the way Ricky did when he was working. I like to cook, and since he was away so much, there was only me to cook for. Besides, I need to be alone in order to write and think." That was true, though being alone had become more of a pattern in my life than I'd ever expected.

He went on almost absently. "There's one song of yours they've been playing a lot lately. I rather liked the idea behind it. I believe it's called 'Sweet Rain.' "

He hadn't said he'd liked the words or the melody, but this was something, at least.

"What do *you* do?" I asked him directly. He'd be in stocks and bonds, probably. He had that air about him of assurance and success.

"I work mainly in research at a laboratory called Sea Spray. Mrs. Ames was generous enough to fund the project, just outside Cold Spring Harbor. We have our own experimental greenhouse, where we study methods of growing plants for food, and for other useful functions. You've probably heard about the famous genetic lab at Cold Spring Harbor. We're an offshoot."

I revised my appraisal of him abruptly. I wasn't much of a judge, after all.

When we reached my apartment building we found only a single television van, but still a crowd of fans. Sometimes I'd wished that I could say something comforting to these people who were so loyal to Ricky, and so deeply wounded by his death. Norris had warned me, however, that I might get mobbed trying.

Once more Alan Gordon moved with an authoritative presence that cleared a path for us. When he chose, he seemed to exude a quiet strength that was reassuring. He would be a good man to depend on in a crisis.

When we were in the downstairs foyer, he didn't come to the elevator with me. "I'll see you tomorrow some time, to make last-minute plans. Better not tell anyone but Mr. Wahl and his wife where you're going."

"I won't," I promised. "Thank you, Mr. Gordon." I felt considerably meeker with him than I'd been in the beginning, and even grateful.

"Good," he said. "I'm glad you've dropped those boxing gloves." As the elevator door started to close, he added in parting, "Bring country clothes."

I would bring what I had, I thought, as the elevator car rose. Mostly staying-at-home clothes. Of those I had plenty.

Norris had gone out, but Bea was waiting for me, and in spite of the concern she'd shown for me, I had a feeling she was relieved that I would now stop being the Wahls' responsibility. As always, she was good-natured, and began at once to help with my preparations. I let her pick out whatever clothes she thought I ought to take, while I went to clear the piano of my music, and select a few books to take with me. And of course my guitar and tape recorder.

I couldn't touch any of Ricky's things yet. Not the awards or the gold records that he'd thrown hurriedly into cartons this last year—as though he meant to bury his career. There were boxes of photographs as well, albums of press clippings that I'd been putting in order for him, and of course reams of business and personal letters that I couldn't yet face. I especially couldn't touch his letters to me.

If Ricky had died in any other way, I'd probably have been reading those letters over and over, trying to bring him close to me. Now I wanted only to push him away. I couldn't forgive him yet for what he had done, and going through his papers, his possessions, would only upset me further. I wasn't able to understand the agony that must have driven him, nor was I ready to give in to my own grief. It seemed safer to be angry—now that I was no longer numb. The Ricky Sands I'd fallen in love with had died for me many months ago. The newer Ricky had frightened and alarmed me, and I couldn't bear to face what he'd become.

Around five o'clock, which would be early afternoon in California, I phoned Aunt Margaret, and found that Dan was home.

"Do you remember someone named Geneva Lake?" I asked my father.

There was a little silence, and then he answered me cheerfully, "Nobody ever forgets his first love."

I told him what had happened, and he sounded pleased. "Imagine Jenny's remembering all this time and wanting to help you! When I knew her, she was pretty single-minded about what she wanted to do—much too strong a character for me."

"She's still a strong character, but I have a feeling that she thinks sometimes about what she *didn't* do."

His chuckle was warm, amused. If he'd been badly hurt a long time ago, it didn't matter anymore. There had been my mother since, and he had never really gotten over her death.

I hung up, feeling reassured that my decision to go to Windtop was sensible, and would rescue me for a time at least from a life of siege. I was foolish enough to believe that I could really put myself out of reach. Of course at that time I had no cause to think that anyone except the media would be interested in me.

The second time I saw him Alan said it would be simpler if we were on a first-name basis, since we'd be seeing more of each other from now on. Seeing more of me, I suspected, was due to Mrs. Ames's orders, and not his own choice, but I accepted readily enough. I mustn't make judgments against him when I'd been so wrong before.

He planned to smuggle me out of the building around midnight of the following day. The press was interested in other things by this time, and all-night vigils were thinning out. Besides, the forecast was for heavy rain tomorrow, and that would clear out the few emotional fans who had been gathering to light candles, sing Ricky's songs, and create a disturbing atmosphere at all hours.

On my last night in the apartment I got up after Bea had gone to bed and sat at the piano for a long while, with my hands on the keys forming silent chords. I'd written my best songs here, and now the silence in my head seemed devastating. If I couldn't create something for others to enjoy, if I couldn't hear my own songs stirring in me anymore, what was I?

Surely my move to this house called Windtop would make melodies and words start flowing again. The change would mend and restore me, so that life—not death—would begin to matter once more.

4

The predicted storm obliged, and it was raining hard when we left Manhattan's still-lighted towers and went through the Midtown Tunnel. There was no chauffeured limousine this time. Alan Gordon drove his own Buick.

Traffic flowed in and out of New York night and day, but at this hour it had thinned, and our headlights cut through rainy darkness on the Long Island Expressway. My suitcases and guitar had been stowed in the trunk, and I had a duffel bag at my feet.

It was a relief that money, at least, was no problem for me, even though Ricky's expenditures had been enormous. He had left everything to me, including royalty income on records, permissions, and all the rest. My own earnings had been kept separate to some extent, and I had them to draw on before the legal details of Ricky's will were settled.

Norris had pointed out that I had a lot going for me as the writer of some of Ricky Sands's best songs, but he added that a songwriter was only as good as what she continued to turn out. That was a reminder I didn't need, even if his notion wasn't entirely true. Excellence has nothing to do with quantity or speed or the trend of the moment.

Alan Gordon had been efficient in his arrangements, as I would have expected. There was no one around when we left my building, and we'd escaped without being noticed. He drove in silence for some time and I was left to my own thoughts. There was a tug I hadn't expected about leaving New York and the places where I had been with Ricky, the streets where I'd walked at his side. As I was discovering, there were times when I wanted to hold every reminder close to me. Even pain was a tie with Ricky, and I found it hard to let go.

But I didn't want this now. I'd had enough for a while of pressing my wounds, and to break the silence, I asked an innocuous question.

"How is Mrs. Ames?"

"She's not doing as well as she likes to pretend," Alan said. "She put on a pretty good performance for you the other day, but it will take time for her to recover her strength."

"I telephoned my father," I went on. "He was pleased that she remembers him and has been kind enough to do this for me."

Alan made no comment, lost again in his morose silence. Taciturn was another word for this man, I decided, and gave myself to watching a car coming toward us, the beam of its yellow headlights streaked with slanting rain.

"My father used to call her Jenny," I mused, following the direction of my own thoughts.

He gave me a quick glance, and I saw in passing lights a look in his eyes that was strangely like pain.

Another interval of quiet went by, and I tried to stir the silence again. "Tell me about Cold Spring Harbor," I said.

This started him off. "It's rather small. It was a whaling town in the nineteenth century, and a seaport, thanks to the deep harbor, where fairly large ships could come in. Lots of history there, with buildings of real character that are still standing on Main Street. Mrs. Ames's grandfather was mate on a whaling ship. Cold Spring Harbor raised its own captains and seamen, though, oddly enough, whaling captains all came from somewhere else. A number of Victorian houses are still standing in the area—beautifully ugly."

I liked the phrase. What seemed ugly to one generation could often be transformed in the eyes of the next.

"Is Mrs. Ames's house like that?"

"No—not the house where she lives now. It's one of those Gold Coast palaces you've probably read about. John Ames's father built it on a hilltop, with thick woods all around that have been preserved. There used to be extensive gardens with statuary, fountains—the works. Those were the days when money didn't matter—if you were rich. Now, of course, much of the house is closed off. No one can afford to live in a museum these days and keep the whole thing going."

My imagination began to stir a little. "Mrs. Ames mentioned a house-keeper and caretaker."

"Yes. Geneva's kept them on because they've been with her so long—Miss Birdy Quinn, and Luther Sykes."

There seemed a smile in Alan's voice, and I glanced at his strong, slightly crooked profile as we drove through the lighted area of a small town. We were off the expressway now, following irregular roads north across the island. Roads I could make little sense of in the dark.

"What fascinating names," I said. "What is Birdy Quinn like?"

"A little dotty. But she keeps things in order and is ferociously loyal to Geneva. She bosses anyone who works there—the crews who come in to clean, and so on. She'll boss you, too! It's not like the old days, when there was a big live-in staff. Most of the people who stay in those big houses today contract with outsiders to come in and do the heavy work. Birdy has her own upstairs rooms in a corner of the house."

"And Luther Sykes?"

Alan hesitated for a moment. "Luther's still the gatekeeper, and he lives in a cottage near the gates. He's had some misfortunes and isn't the friendliest soul. But he, too, is devoted to Geneva. You'll have to get used to his ways. I hope you won't mind being isolated—because that's what Windtop is."

I'd been lonely and isolated in Manhattan, so it wouldn't be a new experience. Right now I felt it would be wonderful to hide away where no one would know me, and I could move about easily.

"What name have you decided to use?" Alan asked.

I hadn't thought about that at all, and said so. "In my song writing I've always been Hollis Temple."

"This is a small town. People are going to be interested in someone who moves into the Ames house. And you'll be shopping, appearing in the village from time to time. You'd better decide on an identity. That is, if you don't want it published all over the place that Ricky Sands's widow has come here. Newspaper pictures of you haven't been all that good, so you won't be easily recognized if you don't advertise."

This was sensible, and as we passed a lighted sign I picked out a word —BAKERY.

"All right," I said, "I'll be Mrs. Baker. Kate Baker, since my middle name is Katherine. But won't Miss Quinn have been told my real name and who I am?"

"I've said merely that a young friend of Mrs. Ames, who's been recently widowed, is coming to stay for a while. And that I'll be responsible—take care of any problems that arise. This should reassure Birdy and Luther about having a stranger brought in so suddenly."

"I'll have to think up a story to go with the name," I said. "Where I come from, who I was married to—all that."

"You'd better keep it as close to the truth as possible. Then you won't trip yourself up at every turn." He sounded almost stern now.

This too was wise, and I wandered away in my mind, setting down "facts." I was born across the bay from San Francisco. My father still lived out there. I was twenty-three years old. I like to play the piano and make up tunes. *And* my husband was dead. That was at the center of everything my thoughts kept returning to, and which I wanted only to push away.

"Are you all right?" Alan asked so suddenly that I blinked.

"Of course. My mind goes skittering off at times these days."

"Why did your husband kill himself?"

I suppressed my resentment over the callous directness of the question. How dare he ask me this?

"I don't think I want to talk about it," I told him coldly.

"It may be better if you do." His tone was calm, unemotional, and it quieted me, though I was still indignant.

"I don't think audiences—fans—ever dream what they can do to a popular singer, or how rough it is at the top," I said more quietly.

"Explain it to me." Again his clipped words seemed without feeling.

Suddenly I wanted to *make* him understand. Wanted to smash through a cold facade that seemed inhuman, and force this man to see how it had been.

"Ricky used to talk about it sometimes. He never liked me to come to his concerts or nightclub appearances, or even to the recording studio, where I might have helped. But I've been in an audience once or twice, so I've felt some of it myself. His kind of music breeds a special emotion. There's an enormous energy out there—a tremendous wave of excitement and adulation that comes pouring out to hurl itself at one man or woman who's in the spotlight. It must be the biggest high there is to feel all that coming at you. The applause and whistles and screams of approval . . . it gets pretty wild." He was silent. "Can you understand that?" I added tartly.

"I imagine the performer loves it. After all, he asks for it."

His tone disapproved of performers, and I felt angry again. While I didn't perform, all that had been my world, too, in a secondhand way.

"Of course they love it! It's their lifeblood. But they're just people, like anyone else, and sometimes it makes them feel inadequate. No one's all that great. No one can deserve what fans poured out to Elvis Presley, for instance, or lavished on the Beatles. Though they weathered it better than poor Presley did. Some performers take to alcohol or drugs to keep them going and to help with that big, terrifying bluff they must put on to make it all work. Or they can go the other way and start to believe they're really that great. Which is as bad, or worse. Sometimes it's a mixture—up one minute and down the next. Only the strong ones come through, and they have to make a fight."

I knew I sounded defiant and challenging, and I didn't care. Alan Gordon might know about greenhouses, but what could he possibly know about a man like Ricky Sands?

"Ricky was one of the weak ones, wasn't he?" Alan said.

"Ricky was one of *the* greatest!"

"I'll take your word for it. Obviously you've thought about it a great deal."

"Of course I have. I've had to, since I'm part of it. Some of the pressure's been on me too. I've felt it anyhow. To keep writing more and better songs. Hit songs. The charts become our thermometer of health —and that's hardly good for any artist."

"Well, you needn't ever touch a piano again if you don't want to."

That wasn't my idea of bliss either. By this time I was wound up, however, and I went on.

"Nobody ever lets a star alone. Once your face is known, you're public property. Ricky kept me out of it as much as possible, thank goodness. It's only lately that anyone's even taken an occasional picture of me. I hide behind dark glasses and comb my hair over my face when I go out. Ricky and I couldn't even enter a restaurant together without being mobbed for his autograph. So mostly I didn't go. But I know what it was like for him."

Had I really known? Because if I had, if I'd said and done the right things—I cut the thought off sharply. It led down a futile road. Whatever I'd done, or not done, it was all too late to help Ricky now. My explosion of words had left me feeling empty and dejected. It had been foolish to try to convince this man of anything. And what did I care what he thought?

He didn't speak again until I saw the shine of water on our left, with a few lights cast across it. Houses rimmed a curving shoreline, though I couldn't see much in the darkness.

"We're getting close now," Alan said. "This is the turnoff along the Shore Road. That lighted street right ahead is Main Street in Cold Spring Harbor. We're heading now for Windtop, on Snake Hill Road."

At this hour there was no traffic, and most of the houses were dark and asleep. The road we climbed wound away from the water, and lived up to its name in twisting curves. Near the top, ornate wrought-iron gates shone wet in the headlights as we came to a halt.

Luther Sykes had been alerted to our coming, and he darted out of his lighted cottage to swing the gates wide and greet Alan. He was a wiry, rather jumpy little man with a scarred face that I glimpsed in the car's headlights. His gray hair stood up as if in a constant state of alarm.

"I told Birdy to go to bed," he grumbled to Alan. "But she had to stay up and know all about everything. So she's waiting for you at the house." He acknowledged my introduction as "Mrs. Baker" with a curt nod, and stood aside to let us through.

"Thanks, Luther," Alan said. "Birdy likes to do the proper thing."

The gates closed behind us, and we followed a narrow, gravel-paved road that wound upward through deep woods. When we reached the circular driveway at the top, I could just make out the huge structure of the house as a vague black shape with tower and chimneys that blocked the sky.

"This was a sea captain's home?" I murmured.

"Hardly. John Ames's father was into oil and railroads and a few other enterprises. He built Windtop. It's an anachronism now, and I suppose it will be turned into a museum someday, if it's not torn down, or burned down, first. But it was a wonderful place for a boy to spend his growing years."

He sounded more natural in speaking of his fondness for this house than at any time since I'd met him.

The rain had lessened, and as I got out of the car I could see light shining in a number of windows. I was to learn later that the house was built in the shape of a "T," with the top bar forming the front. On the right of the central door mullioned windows glowed with light. The left wing extended away into darkness.

"That's where the fire was," Alan said. "Better stay away from that area. There're still burned timbers and debris that haven't been cleared out. Come along—Birdy's waiting for us."

The door had opened and a woman stood in the light. Inevitably, I'd imagined a woman who would look like her name—small and trim and chirpy. This "birdy" was more like a stork. Long-legged and narrow of face. Her white hair swept into a crest on top of her head, with a few wisps escaping to curl around thin cheeks. Her mouth seemed as narrow as the rest of her, even as she pressed it into a determined smile. She was probably in her late sixties, though she made few concessions to age. She observed me with eyes that scarcely opened, so I couldn't tell their color, but I was instantly aware of her lack of enthusiasm in greeting me. This, too, she shared with Luther Sykes.

"Hello, Birdy," Alan said. "It was good of you to stay up so late. I think Mrs. Baker will want to go straight to her rooms. I'll bring up her bags right away."

Birdy bent her long neck and murmured something I couldn't catch. When she stepped aside to usher me in, I saw a wide entrance hall paved in flagstones and paneled in dark wood. A massive staircase rose on one side to join a gallery at the second-floor level.

"I've prepared the Azalea Suite for you, madam," Birdy said, and started up the stairs, her back straight and thin and stiff.

I slung my duffel over one shoulder, picked up my guitar, and followed her.

At the upper level the leg of the "T" disappeared into darkness toward the rear. Birdy marched ahead of me past closed doors for most of the front corridor's length, stopping before one near the end. When she opened the door for me, I was greeted by the glow of lamps and a cheerful wood fire. The room's ceiling was high, and pale, pink-flowered draperies hid the windows.

"You have a fine view of the water from here, madam," Birdy said. "You'll see it tomorrow."

I'd been given a sitting room with a large bedroom adjoining, all glowing with touches of an azalea pink that was warm but not disturbing. In both rooms fires burned in the grates, welcoming me in from the rainy night.

Alan appeared with my bags and set them down in the bedroom.

"The rooms are lovely," I said. "Please thank Mrs. Ames, Alan. And thank you, Birdy, for choosing these rooms for me."

"I had my instructions, madam." Birdy sniffed as though the choice would not have been hers.

Alan went to the door. "I'll see you sometime tomorrow, though I'm not sure when," he told me.

"I'll be here. Thank you for driving me out tonight." I sounded almost as stiff as Alan himself, but I couldn't relax with this man. We seemed to exist on altogether different planes.

His quick departure suggested that he'd had enough of his role as unwilling messenger for Mrs. Ames, and I could only feel relieved to see him go.

"May I get you something from the kitchen, madam?" Birdy asked formally. "A pot of tea? Hot milk? A bite to eat?"

"No, thank you. I'll be fine. I don't want to be any trouble while I'm here, and of course I'll fix my own meals."

"As you wish, Mrs. Baker. We don't have a cook at this time."

"I understand. Good night, Birdy."

She nodded and took herself off, drawing the door shut on my azalea bower. I'd received the impression of a slightly malicious attitude on Birdy Quinn's part. The "madams" had seemed exaggerated, yet it was equally jarring when she'd suddenly called me "Mrs. Baker."

I knelt before the sitting-room fire and held my hands out to warmth. My very bones felt cold, and a wave of sadness that was all too familiar enveloped me. In this new place I could no longer look around and expect Ricky Sands to walk through a door, or appear beside my chair. He had never been here, and perhaps that very fact would be good for me. At this late hour of weariness, low spirits were natural, and I'd better get to bed. Sleep could always stop the hurting.

The bedroom was like a glowing jewel with its satin slipper chairs and pale pink rugs. A muted azalea print covered the quilt and the bed was turned down on pale pink sheets. None of this was my style, yet there was something soothing about it, as though I'd been tenderly enclosed in the pink interior of a shell. For a little while I could feel safely shut away from a world that had turned hostile and threatening.

My night things were at hand in my duffel bag, and I could leave my unpacking until tomorrow. In the adjoining bathroom—of pink marble, of course—I got ready for bed as quickly as I could. Before I slipped between the sheets, however, I went in my robe to part long draperies that had been pulled across the balcony door. I opened the door and felt night air cold on my skin, breathed deeply the scent of a wet forest world. It was no longer raining, but the woods dripped softly in a steady murmur. Snake Hill Road wound inland, and was not on the water, but this balcony was high enough for me to see out over dark banks of trees that crowded the hillside below. A few lights still shone across the water, and I knew that Birdy was right. By daylight I'd have a tremendous view.

The nearer grounds of the house interested me most right now, however. At the foot of wide brick steps that led down from the terrace to a stretch of lawn and garden, two lamp standards illuminated the scene. In the center of the lawn a circular pool with a marble bench on each side offered a place for quiet reflection, while beyond rose a white marble structure with columns shining through the darkness to offer entrance to a make-believe Greek temple.

As I watched, something stirred in the shadows, and a dark figure moved near the pool. For an instant it stood still, as though looking toward the house, where a patch of light must reveal my open door. Then the figure moved again and disappeared between white columns.

Was Luther Sykes still up at this hour? His cottage wasn't visible from the house, and it seemed unlikely that he would be about now. Alan's car had left long ago; I'd heard it descending the drive. Nor did I think Birdy, whose gaunt face had looked weary when she'd left, would be out there roaming wet grounds.

In any case, I was too tired to worry. I remembered that Alan had told me the house was wired with an excellent alarm system that Birdy turned on every night. So if it was someone who had no business on the grounds, he couldn't get into the house, and all I wanted now was to sink into bed.

I woke up late to a dim pink glow that was not the sunrise but my room responding to daylight that seeped around the draperies. I felt wonderfully rested, my depression gone, even though awareness of loss came first to my mind, as usual. But now I could cope.

Today would bring fresh scenes and activity. More than anything else I needed to keep busy, to be distracted. Sooner or later I must face what Ricky had done, confront and try to understand it—if that was possible. Even if the trail of his death led back somehow to Coral Caine—which was what I most feared—I must learn how to accept this and work through my own grief to calmer waters.

Right now, however, I would welcome whatever the new day offered.

Even before I showered and dressed, I flung back the draperies in the sitting room and gasped with pleasure. Beyond woods that rolled away down the steep hill, the harbor shone clear and blue, rimmed by land that looped in and then thrust outward toward the Sound in a peninsula. Close at hand, the grass was still green, though November had painted the leaves of a great beech tree a dark garnet that was different from the maples and oaks and dogwood. The reflecting pool was embroidered across its surface with red and yellow leaves, and beyond that the marble columns that I'd noted last night shone dazzling white under the sun. What a relief from concrete towers! And how clean and fresh the air smelled, tinged with the scent of salt water and nearby pine trees.

As I turned from the window, someone tapped at my door. When I called, Birdy entered, as tall and gaunt as I remembered her from last night, and with an expression no more welcoming than before. She carried a tray set with a silver coffee pot and china of an oriental design —brought over, perhaps, on some long-ago sailing ship. Birdy had folded hot toast into linen to keep it warm, and there were coddled eggs and imported marmalade. I was suddenly ravenously hungry, as I hadn't been in weeks.

"I *do* thank you," I said. "After I'd dressed, I was going downstairs to look for the kitchen."

She gave me her usual sniff as she set the tray down on a small table. "Don't expect that I'm going to do this every day. But I thought you might need a good start this first morning."

Apparently I had stopped being "madam," which was fine with me. I sat in the chair she pulled to the table and picked up a napkin embroidered in one corner with an elaborate "A."

"Last night before I went to bed," I told her, "I looked out the balcony door and saw someone moving about down near those marble columns. Who would be out there at that hour?"

She widened her eyes and for the first time I could see their watery blue. "Nobody'd be down there at that hour. The wind makes the shadows swing deceptively. That's probably what you saw."

What I'd seen hadn't been a shadow, but I didn't argue with her. "I'll bring the tray downstairs when I'm through. Will I need a guide to find the kitchen?"

"Just keep opening doors," she said curtly, and went away.

With a house like this to explore, perhaps I would start coming to life again. Eventually a phrase of melody, or the words of a lyric would start running through my mind. While I had no urge to sit down at a piano yet, I was nevertheless lonely for something that had been part of me for most of my life. I wrote music because I couldn't help it. Or that was what I'd always thought.

The coffee was hot and wonderfully rich, and I heaped butter and marmalade on my toast. Even the eggs tasted country fresh—a pleasant change from Manhattan.

When I'd finished, I showered and dressed in tan slacks and a blue chambray shirt—suitable, I hoped, as "country clothes." When I was ready, I carried the tray along a green-carpeted corridor outside my room, remembering the direction of the stairs. I found the gallery that overlooked the baronial hall, cold with its great flagstones. At the foot of the stairs I gazed up at the gallery rail, half expecting to see crossed axes and banners, and the flags of the castle. But only a red Moroccan rug had been thrown over the center of the railing.

This main foyer, though wide, was not very deep, and several closed doors, impressive in their carving, offered me a choice. I opened one on my right and found myself on the threshold of a splendid drawing room, its draperies drawn across long french windows, and its formal furniture covered with white sheets. Not what I was looking for.

I crossed to the opposite door and drew in my breath with pleasure. Here was a music room such as I'd never seen before except in pictures. The huge Bechstein piano stood near shrouded windows, its top down and keys covered, the dark satin of its wood shining in the dim light. Little gilt chairs had been set in a half circle nearby, and there were music racks before them, as though musicians had gathered here to play together only a little while ago. The room was large enough to hold an audience easily, and even dwarfed the great piano.

In one corner stood a harp, its shape unmistakable, though it was covered against dust. I'd never so much as touched a harp, and wondered if I might learn to play one. Later perhaps I'd bring my guitar downstairs and shock this august company with its uninhibited presence.

The piano drew me, even though I was a little afraid of it. I set my tray on a chair and went to raise the lid. Ivory keys looked old and faintly yellow, the black keys smooth and dull. I put a finger on middle C and struck the note tentatively. Even with the top down, the sound was strong, true, vibrant. This was a loved and well-cared-for instrument. If I sat down and tried some chords, would a melody come to life? But I'd attempted that more than once at the apartment since Ricky died, and the emptiness in me had been frightening. I could play other people's songs, but not my own, and I had the dreadful feeling that no tune would ever stir in me again. Certainly I wasn't ready to risk touching this magnificent instrument.

For the first time I looked around at the rest of the paneled room, discovering the black marble fireplace with a portrait hung above it. In the painting a young, handsome woman sat at this same Bechstein grand, half turned, so that she looked over one shoulder. Her arms were bare and white, and her steel-blue gown glittered. Blond hair, smoothly coiffed, gave her an air of distinction and dignity. Her long-fingered hands rested on the keys and I knew that when she played it wouldn't be Cole Porter. Geneva Lake when she was young! Perhaps at the time when my father had known her? Strange that those two had ever come together. Yet it was her memory of Dan Temple that had brought me here, and I felt a sudden closeness to the woman I'd met only in a hospital room. "Jenny," I said softly, and felt closer to her.

I lowered the piano lid with a faint riffle of sound, picked up my tray again, and walked through another door.

Adjoining the music room was another dark-paneled room—a library, with books on the shelves that looked worn, as though they'd really been read by those who'd lived in this house. High on top of one bookcase stood the lovely model of a sailing ship, and when I looked at it closely I saw the name *Geneva* on the prow. Named for the grandmother of the present Geneva, perhaps?

Still another door opened at the back of the library, and I continued my search for the kitchen area. This time I found myself in a smaller room—clearly a family sitting room. Here the furniture had been left unshrouded, and peach draperies were drawn back from long windows. A gold oriental rug on the floor felt comforting beneath my feet, and two small sofas and a chaise longue looked inviting. Near one sofa a round table draped with gold-patterned fleur-de-lis cloth held a Limoges tea set. The small desk and chair near a window must be where Mrs. Ames had written letters and done her household accounts in happier times. Always I felt her presence in this house—a dominant, living presence that had set its stamp everywhere.

On a coffee table an old issue of a popular magazine lay open, face down. I recognized the cover with a sense of misgiving and turned it over to the open pages. Ricky Sands's face looked out at me from a photograph that illustrated an interview he'd done a year or so ago. Recognition was like a blow. I hadn't liked the article, though Ricky had been indifferent to the misquoting, the sly put-downs, and misinterpretations. This was part of being a public figure—that though you were often at the mercy of interviewers, these "facts" would appear in print and then be picked up by future researchers, so that errors would be repeated forever as though they were true.

The sight of Ricky's face twisted my heart. It was a candid shot of him singing at a mike, with his guitar propped at his own individual angle. How beautiful and golden he'd looked—as though he would never age, though the picture had been taken only a year or two ago. These last months he hadn't looked like this at all. How terribly he'd feared getting old—and now he never would.

It was disturbing to find this magazine left open to Ricky's interview and picture. Who could have been reading about Ricky Sands? Mrs. Ames hadn't been home for some time, and surely Birdy Quinn wouldn't have been interested.

I shivered and set the magazine down, closing it. Then I took up my tray again and went on.

The maze of doors continued, and I turned back to the main hall. Big double doors stood closed on the far side, and when I went toward them I heard Birdy's voice behind me.

"You can't go through there. That's the burned-out wing. We're lucky the fire was contained before it got through. The other side of those doors is scorched black."

I was to learn that Birdy had a habit of wandering about the house, moving so silently that she was able to turn up at my side without warning. This first time it happened she'd startled me, as I hadn't heard a sound, and didn't even know what direction she'd come from. She looked a little smug when I jumped, and I tried to cover my surprise.

"What caused the fire?" I asked.

Pale blue eyes stared directly at me for a moment. Then she said, "Who knows?" and stalked away down the hall as silently as she'd appeared.

She knew all right, but she wasn't going to talk to me about it. There'd been no time to ask for directions, and I was still carrying the tray she hadn't offered to take from me. I wandered down the leg of the "T" past more doors that opened on rooms that were shrouded and unused—rooms so numerous that I wondered how anyone could ever have lived in them all. Perhaps the early Ames family had been large and able to overflow even this huge place. While there was central heating, a minimum of heat was used, and only a few rooms were comfortable.

Eventually I found what looked like a state dining room, obviously not in use now, but a room that could easily seat fifty at the long table.

A pantry opened off this room, and next came the big kitchen. Here there had been modernization—shining steel sinks, two huge refrigerators, one of which purred softly, a massive stove with electric burners, endless rows of copper pots, and cabinets filled with everything imaginable that might be used in a kitchen. An intimidating room where expert cooks must have worked, yet in its way a good bit more cozy than the rest of the house.

I set my tray on a sink, rinsed the few dishes I'd used, and found a cloth to dry them.

From the kitchen a door led outside, and I crossed a brick porch to what must once have been a thriving vegetable garden. Untended and weed-grown now, though still fenced in from marauders, it had a neglected look. More evidence of Geneva's absence, I supposed. I walked through a far gate and around to the front, where I came upon the hollow of burned-out desolation where the fire had struck.

This side of the house looked as though a rocket had been shot into it. Ceiling beams that had formed the second floor had fallen into a jumble of black timbers. Yet the flames hadn't reached the attic floor, and the roof was still intact. Even the back wall of this wing was still standing. The fire had been contained in one area, so that the charred ruins made a dark indentation—a cave that was still wet from yesterday's rain, giving off a stench of old, burned wood. I could see why the lower part of this entire wing had been cut off from the rest of the house, even though the attic floor continued to make a bridge across, high above.

Fallen timbers lay at angles, some on the ground, some propped against blackened walls. Deep gray ash covered the ground, except in a rear corner, where an effort to clear away some of the debris had been made. That task had apparently been abandoned, and I wondered why anyone had started to work in that remote corner. Perhaps to search for something that had been lost in the fire? It seemed strange that if this disaster had occurred several years ago no real attempt had ever been made to clean out the ruin and rebuild.

Recalling Alan's warning about falling timbers, I walked past at a good distance and followed the front driveway to the right wing. When I'd rounded the far end, I found myself near the terrace I'd looked down upon from my window last night. Here was the garden with the marble pool, and now I saw the graceful marble maiden in its center, pouring water from an urn. At least she'd have been pouring if the fountain had been running. The surrounding lawn, still summer-green though strewn with leaves, was set below terrace level, like the pool, and ran down a gentle slope of lawn and flower beds toward the white-columned whimsy of the Greek temple. Near the pool a man raked leaves, working in a leisurely fashion, and he didn't look around as I came near.

"Good morning," I said. "You're the gardener?"

He wore a shaggy brown beard, and his hair grew well over his collar at the back, so that it was difficult to tell whether he was young or old. He continued to rake toward his growing pile of leaves as he answered me.

"Good morning, miss. I suppose that's what I am—the gardener."

A strange reply, and I paused beside him. "Don't you know?"

He flashed me a quick, unsmiling look and went on with his slow raking. "I just started here yesterday. Luther needs all the help he can get with these leaves coming down."

"I've just arrived too," I said pleasantly. "I came in last night." A thought occurred to me. "Do you stay here at Windtop?"

He shook his shaggy head. "No, miss. I live with my sister for now—down the hill. I'm to come in every day for a while. My name's Pete Evans."

"And mine is Mrs. Baker. Were you here for any reason late last night?"

Again he shook his head, but this time he stared at me with a steady, searching gaze. The directness of his look seemed neither hostile nor friendly, but was merely an examining stare—and it disconcerted me.

"No, Mrs. Baker," he said. "I wasn't here last night."

As I nodded and walked on I sensed that he looked after me, perhaps curious at my questions. His presence made me vaguely uneasy. No one had mentioned a gardener in speaking about the small staff at Windtop.

I forgot him, however, as I returned to the front drive and stood looking up at the dramatic architecture of the house. Last night I'd seen only a dark silhouette with chimneys that stood against the sky. Now I could see the details.

The wing I'd just walked around seemed imitation Tudor in its half-timbered construction, its mullioned windows overlooking the drive. The central facade that housed the main door and Great Hall was more austere, with bare stone walls and plainer windows. Above the arched front door that looked more like the entrance to a monastery than a home, a few vines had been allowed to straggle. High above, tiled in gray-blue slate, the wide roof slanted steeply toward me. At either end rose squat towers, with windows all around, and between them were spaced the four chimneys that had once heated the house from all its many fireplaces. The architecture seemed far from controlled, but it made a bold statement of individuality that no one could argue with.

I turned and crossed the driveway to stand looking out toward thick woods that crowded in all around. Even in bright sunlight the trees looked dense and dark, though a good many bare branches were now emerging after last night's punishing storm. Well, I'd wanted isolation, and I would certainly find it here. It was strange to think that hardly anyone knew where I was—and not altogether reassuring. I must telephone Dan soon and let him know that I'd arrived.

As I continued to study the woods, a curious back-of-the-neck sensation crept over me. Someone was watching me. I whirled to face the house, but no one was in sight. One after another, I stared at the windows, but nothing stirred behind them and no one looked out at me.

Birdy's sudden appearance in the wide arch of the front door made me suppose that it was she who'd been watching me.

"Mr. Gordon is on the phone asking for you, Mrs. Baker," she announced.

I hurried into the house, unexpectedly glad to hear from Alan Gordon. We hadn't exactly hit it off last night, but at least he was someone I was acquainted with. The house and its grounds were beginning to give me a strange feeling that I hadn't stopped to examine. Perhaps a feeling of something inimical to my presence. The feeling seemed real, not whimsical, and I could only suppose that the source was Birdy herself.

She indicated a phone extension in the main hall and I picked up the instrument.

Alan sounded less stiff. "How are you, Hollis? Feeling more rested, I hope?"

"Yes, thank you. I had a good sleep and a wonderful breakfast, thanks to Birdy. So now I'm exploring."

"Good. Would you care to come into the village for lunch with me today?"

I accepted with more eagerness than I'd expected to feel, and he set a time to pick me up at Windtop.

When I set down the phone, I saw Birdy vanishing up the stairs and I called to her.

"Birdy—who is the new gardener? I didn't know there was anyone else here."

"Pete Evans? His sister used to visit Mrs. Ames. A fine woman. She lives down the road at The Shutters."

That didn't tell me much about her brother.

I went upstairs to unpack and to try to shake off my growing sense of uneasiness—as though something was wrong about the house. That was nonsense, of course. It was a fascinating, fabulous house, and I meant to explore it thoroughly. I would explore not only Windtop and its history, but my own changing self as well. I *had* to change, with Ricky gone, and I would naturally feel restless and lost until I found my own direction.

I wished that the notion that I was whistling in the dark hadn't occurred to me.

5

In my sitting room I once more felt safely enclosed by a pink and cream shell. The sensation was peaceful and relaxing. With these protecting folds around me I could hide like some sea creature from a roaring ocean outside. The faint echo of a seashell song stirred in my mind, but when I tried to grasp it, it slipped away. I wasn't ready yet. But if I waited, surely it would all come alive again. Keeping busy at almost anything was the only answer I knew right now.

I had risen late and time was running on, so I unpacked, shaking out my clothes and hanging them up. Bea had included two or three dresses, and one fall suit, along with an assortment of slacks, shirts, and sweaters. I put on the dark green suede skirt with its cocoa brown jacket—an outfit Ricky had liked—and tied my hair back with a green velvet ribbon. As a little girl I'd often wished for hair less brightly red, but I didn't mind anymore. Ricky had liked my hair, and once he'd written the words to a song I'd set to music—"The Girl with the Bright Red Mane." It hadn't caught on, but we'd enjoyed it as a joke between us.

There was still a little time left when I'd dressed, so I unpacked the rest of what I'd brought with me. I placed my tape recorder on the table beside my bed, and plugged it in. An empty tape waited in the machine —just in case. I'd always kept a recorder handy at night, because some-times I'd dream a tune, or a phrase, or sometimes lie awake and let whatever wanted to drift through my mind. If something seemed possi-ble, I'd hum it to the tape, or speak whatever words or ideas came to me. Otherwise, by morning, these would be lost. Often this way I could capture an idea that I could develop later. "Sweet Rain" had come to me in just that way, and now I didn't want to lose the slightest possibility that might draw me back to work.

When I'd taken everything else out of my suitcase and stored my bags in the room's ample closet—built at a later time, I was sure—I returned to the sitting room. A few books were piled on a table—all novels except for a volume about seashells. Perhaps I'd look at that later, play around with a sea song.

Right now I felt restless, and I went to the balcony door that I'd opened last night, and stepped out into wind that always seemed to blow across this hilltop. We were a long way from the sea, since Long Island Sound ran clear to Montauk Point to meet the Atlantic at the eastern tip of the island. This north shore was the hilly side of Long Island. Only the south shore was on the ocean. I thought of all those ships that had sailed the long way down the Sound to Cold Spring Harbor, and of the whalers coming into port.

The sound of a car winding up the road from the gates warned me that Alan was on his way, and I caught up my purse and hurried downstairs. It was a long journey in this house, so that by the time I reached the front door Birdy was opening it for Alan Gordon.

He looked more informal today in gray trousers, with a blue pullover under a subdued sport jacket, but he seemed grave and a little absent. I still had the feeling that I was a duty he must take on because of Geneva Ames.

I hated to become a chore for anyone, and I stopped him before we went out to his car.

"Look, Mr. Gordon, you don't have to do any of this. I'm here now and settling in just fine. I'm grateful to Mrs. Ames and to you, but I don't need to be looked after or taken around. I haven't asked yet, but perhaps there's a car I could use when I want to go shopping. Then I won't have to depend on anyone."

The scar that lifted one eyebrow seemed to give him a quizzical look. "You were going to call me Alan, remember? Of course there's a car you can use. And I wouldn't be doing this if I didn't want to."

As I went out to the Buick with him I offered no further protest, but I still didn't feel entirely satisfied.

Pete Evans was working on leaves that had drifted across the circle of lawn in front of the house, and he didn't look up as I got into Alan's car.

"Do you know the new gardener—Pete Evans?" I asked. "Apparently he started working here just yesterday."

Alan glanced out the car window and nodded. "Luther brings in extra help now and then when he needs it. I knew Pete when we were kids. I'm afraid he's something of a drifter. A few years ago he left a perfectly good teaching job at the high school and dropped out of sight. He's turned pretty aimless, I'm afraid. Though I expect his sister Elizabeth is glad to have him home, now that she's a widow. If he gives you any trouble, we'll get rid of him."

He had given me no trouble—just the feeling that he was observing me, even when he didn't look in my direction.

Alan sat for a moment longer with his hands on the wheel before he turned the key in the ignition. Something was troubling him this morning—I could feel it strongly. But when he started the car he seemed to shrug off his inner preoccupation.

We drove down the winding road to the gates, and now I could appreciate the density of woods all around. Except for a few stands of evergreens, the trees were mostly oak and dogwood and maple, with that magnificent beech tree up near the house. Shining through brown tree trunks, the gold and red of fallen leaves lay everywhere, forming a carpet that glowed with light, penetrating the gloom of the woods.

As we left the gates of Windtop and drove down Snake Hill Road toward the harbor, I found myself wondering about the man beside me. Last night my concerns and tensions had been different, and there'd been an antagonism between us that seemed to have vanished now, for all his preoccupation. I had no idea whether he had a wife and children, or whether he was a bachelor living alone. He'd been careful to tell me nothing about himself. I felt mildly curious, though I wouldn't ask questions.

At the Shore Road we turned toward the village. Last night when we'd driven through, the area was dark, but now I could see the low stretches of land bordering the harbor, and offering space for a town that was well sheltered by the hill rising behind. A few houses edged the road we followed, and more were dotted across the harbor but there was no density of building here.

Inland, on a tranquil pond, a graceful white church raised its steeple. "That's St. John's over there. Beautiful, isn't it? You must go and see it soon. It's been there since the early 1800s, and when the Tiffany estate burned down, some stained-glass windows that Tiffany himself had made were saved and put into the church."

Most of the newer homes were built on the hill above Main Street. The lower land was apt to be marshy because of the springs that gave the town its name. In fact, a stream had once run parallel to Main Street, and had been filled in in an effort to lessen flooding.

We drove past a red-brick building with a central tower that was the public library and another historic site, judging by the sign outside. Main Street itself was the old village.

"They used to call this Bedlam Street." Alan smiled. "Either because of roistering sailors who came ashore or perhaps because of the mix of languages spoken here in seafaring days. We're more decorous now, though maybe not as interesting."

Locust trees lined Main Street, and the long block of buildings glowed in the sun—peach and white, gray and pale green—housing small shops with imaginative names and assorted treasures for sale. Clearly, standards were held to, and nothing seemed junky. Alan told me that many of the buildings that had lasted were built back in the 1800s by the same carpenter, and thus were similar in architecture. Often there was a single high window in a distinctive central gable. And there were still white picket fences here and there, adding to a sense of Long Island's past. Once the picket fence had been a status symbol, and the carving of the pickets could be as fanciful as anyone chose to make them.

"We're not incorporated," Alan said. "The village is a sort of appendage to Huntington—our metropolis. We like our independent identity and hold onto it."

When he'd found a space along the street to park, we entered a small, charming restaurant, with glass tabletops rimmed in white metal, and white chairs of scrolled and gracefully turned wrought iron. One corner of the room housed a little tree growing in a pot, its branches forming a canopy over our table. White milk glass held purple asters, lending a bright splash of color. Since the tourist season was past, there was no crowding—a quiet time to visit Cold Spring Harbor. Everything seemed a world apart from New York. I needn't wear dark glasses anymore, since no one would pay much attention to me.

Of course everyone knew Alan Gordon, and spoke to him casually. He didn't introduce me, for which I was thankful, and as I studied the menu I thought how long it had been since I'd eaten quietly in a restaurant. To go out with Ricky had always meant a mob scene, and sometimes I'd been thoroughly annoyed by the way I could be pushed aside so some gushing female could get near him.

"I like this," I told Alan, relaxing for the first time in a long while.

Perhaps he'd forgotten me, because he looked startled when I spoke, as though his own thoughts had carried him far away.

"What would you like to order?" he asked.

"I'll have the fish chowder," I decided. "I'm really hungry, for a change."

He smiled his wintry smile that never lighted his eyes. "You're feeling better?"

"Right now—this minute—yes. It comes and goes. I'm glad for a change of scene."

"What do you think of Windtop?"

"It's marvelous. But I have a feeling that it's watching me. Maybe it hasn't accepted me yet, maybe it's waiting to see how I'll turn out. This morning I found the music room and a portrait of Mrs. Ames when she was young. I wonder if I dare carry my guitar down there and set it next to the harp?"

He seemed to discover me again, as though my words had caught his attention. Though I suspected his awareness was that of someone meeting a creature from another world. Perhaps even Geneva could understand better where I came from than this man ever would.

"Will you keep on writing your popular songs?" he asked.

The word "popular" seemed a put-down as he spoke it, but I didn't take offense. One shouldn't with another species. "I only hope I can. I haven't been able to coax out a tune in ages."

Our waitress brought our orders, warning me that the chowder was scalding hot. It was delicious, with crusty French bread and a mound of butter to accompany it. We found little to say as we ate, and the return of Alan's absent manner indicated that he didn't notice silences.

With the chowder relished and finished, I was eating broiled Long Island scallops when a man in the uniform of the Suffolk County highway police stopped beside our table.

"No luck, Mr. Gordon," he said. "But of course we'll stick with it. Something will turn up—don't worry. I just hope . . ." With a glance at me, he left the remark unfinished and went toward the back of the restaurant.

I didn't look at Alan. He would explain or not, as he pleased. Obviously, something serious had happened, since it had brought in the police.

"I'll tell you sometime, Hollis," he said quietly. "I'd rather not talk about it right now."

"That's all right. But you'd better not call me Hollis out in public. I'm supposed to be Kate Baker, remember?"

He came to life a little. "Right. I'm sorry. What will you do with yourself now? I mean, it isn't enough to run to ground and hide."

"I'm living from day to day. That's all I can manage. Getting acquainted with Windtop will keep me busy for a while. Though I'm afraid Birdy doesn't approve of my being there."

"I'm fond of Birdy, but I know how difficult she can be. Perhaps your interest in the house will win her over. She's as devoted to Windtop as she is to Geneva. When the west wing burned, it was as though she'd lost a piece of her own body."

"What was in that wing?"

"That's the unfortunate part. It wasn't only rooms and furniture. Geneva has been interested in Cold Spring Harbor whaling history for years, and she'd collected all sorts of things. Her scrimshaw was especially fine."

"It seems strange that the wreckage hasn't been cleared away before this."

Alan's mood seemed to darken. At times he could be a deeply somber man, and again a flicker of curiosity about him stirred in me.

"It was the fire that caused Geneva's first heart attack," he said. "She's been in and out of hospitals ever since. Without her orders, no one can touch the place, and she keeps saying that she must be here to supervise any rebuilding. Yet when she does come home for brief stays, she does nothing about it."

"What else was in her collection?"

"She had some pieces from her grandfather's ship, *Geneva.* He was the sea captain. On the maternal side her grandfather was mate on a whaling ship—so there're sailors on both sides. I remember a weather-beaten figurehead, which used to fascinate me when I was a kid, that burned. She'd planned to give everything to the Whaling Museum in the village eventually, and some of her scrimshaw did go there before the fire."

"What a shame so much was lost," I said, but I knew better than to question him about how the fire had started. I was aware by now that he didn't welcome questions that became too searching.

When we left the restaurant and returned to the car, he asked if I would like to stay in town for a while and explore. The little shops looked inviting, but I shook my head.

"Another time. I'd rather go back to Windtop now, please."

From the road that followed the shore we could see a sailboat tacking out on the water, even though the season was late. I watched the skimming white sail, remembering times when I'd gone sailing with Ricky. And with my father when I was little. Too many reminders! They could spring from anywhere.

When we reached Windtop's wrought-iron gates I said, "Don't drive me up—I'd really like to walk. Thank you for lunch. I'll be fine now, so don't bother about me."

"I'll keep in touch," he said gravely. "If you want anything, let me know. Birdy knows how to reach me."

I watched as he turned the car and drove away. Luther Sykes had seen me and he came nimbly out of his cottage. Standing before the gates, I could admire the great scrolls and curlicues.

"They're beautiful gates," I said as he swung one side open to let me through.

As with Birdy, Windtop was Luther's pride. "Brought over from France," he informed me. "That's the way it was done when old Mr. Ames was building the house. He brought a lot of things from Europe. Fireplaces and mantels and sculpture for the gardens. Even those flagstones in the main hall—they came from a Rhine castle. And the big front door's straight out of a Spanish monastery."

"Pillaging" was what it had been called, I thought, and men of great wealth had done a lot of it. But now it was Luther who interested me. His speech was that of an educated man, and seemed to contrast with his rough clothes and manner. He was clearly sensitive about the scarred side of his face, turning it from me. When he'd put his hands on the gate I'd seen that his right hand, too, was scarred, so that the fingers were permanently clawed.

"You walking up?" he asked testily over his shoulder as he closed the gate.

"I like to walk. Thanks for letting me in."

"That's my job. One of them." His tone was far from friendly, and I supposed that some of Birdy's hostility had rubbed off on the caretaker.

"Mr. Gordon said there might be a car I could use. Do you know about that?"

He considered for a moment, his eyes closed, as though he visualized a vast number of cars. Then he waved a hand in his quick, nervous way. "Sure—there's Mrs. Ames's own car. She keeps the Lincoln in New York, but there's another one here. I'll get it ready for you. Be careful on these roads. Snake Hill can be treacherous."

I thanked him again, and started on my way. The drive wound upward from the gates, cutting through thick woods. Once more I was aware of the golden autumn shimmer. Since the trees weren't wholly devoid of leaves yet, no glimpse of the house was visible for most of the walk. That didn't bother me. I liked the sense of being solitary but safe.

Most of the birds had gone south, but there were still jays and chickadees scolding and twittering at me from high branches. Stands of evergreens made the woods seem even more dense and mysterious, and the underbrush was a source of constant rustlings as I walked along. Now and then I glimpsed a squirrel, disturbed by my presence.

After yesterday's rain, blue sky above the treetops was a welcome sight, and as I climbed the winding road I found myself relaxing, letting everything flow away from me for this little while. Having lunch with Alan Gordon had helped, even though it hadn't been entirely comfortable. At least he'd seemed less formidable than before. Now I could live in this quiet moment, while my body was active, and my mind still.

Leaves along the roadside were still wet and soggy, so there was no crunching underfoot. The peace of hushed woods that harbored only bird and animal sounds was deep all around, so that it was startling to hear sudden voices. I was still well out of sight of the house, but I could hear a woman's tones nearby, answered by the slow, deeper voice of a man.

Rounding the next curve uneasily, I came upon the car—a green Pinto parked on the road, with a woman at the wheel. The new gardener, Pete Evans, leaned in the front window speaking to the driver. He looked around as I came into view.

"Here's Mrs. Baker now," he said, as though they might have been talking about me.

At once the woman got out of the car. "Hello, Mrs. Baker. I was up at the house just now, but Birdy said you were out. I'm Pete's sister, Liz Cameron."

Standing together, the two made a picture of contrasts. She was prob-

ably older than her brother—perhaps in her late thirties. I suspected
that he was the younger, in spite of the deceptive beard. There seemed a
cared-for prettiness about her. Her fair hair had been styled, not just
cut, with every lock held perfectly in place by invisible spray. Her jeans
undoubtedly carried a designer's name on a back pocket, her shirt was
expensive, and so were her buttery soft leather boots, worn to the shape
of her feet. Pete looked unshaven and careless in khaki pants and shirt,
and shaggy-cut hair. I never knew what he really looked like behind all
that foliage.

As she came toward me, holding out her hand, I noted the intense
deep violet of her eyes, the lashes darkened, with penciled lines beneath.
Eyes that appraised me coolly, for all the warm pressure of her fingers.

"Since I'm a neighbor, I wanted to look in on you," she said. Her
voice too was distinctive, low with good timbre.

"Won't you come up to the house?" I invited.

"I'd love to. Jump in and I'll drive you up. Do you want a lift, Pete?"

He shook his head, but I got in. As his sister turned the Pinto around
and drove up the hill, he stood looking after us.

"It's silly—Pete working at Windtop," Liz Cameron said. "I wish
he'd cut off all that hair and get a decent job. But he's not been one for
settling down for a long while. So don't be surprised if he takes off day
after tomorrow. He's turned into a gypsy." She sounded mildly exasperated, but loving, nevertheless.

"Mr. Gordon mentioned that your brother used to teach in a local
high school," I said.

Without answering, she parked her car before Windtop's massive
front door, and at once Birdy was there to welcome us. Clearly she still
disapproved of me, and her look offered little cheer as she glanced my
way. Pete's sister, however, seemed accustomed to her manner, and
asked her warmly how she was feeling.

Birdy sniffed and shrugged, indicating the worst.

I didn't want to sit in one of these great downstairs rooms for a visit,
so I invited Mrs. Cameron up to my suite.

"I'd love that," she said quickly. "And please call me Liz. Since I
mean to call you Kate. We must get acquainted. Geneva and I don't
always see eye to eye, but she sent word by Alan that I should look in
on you."

I wondered warily how much Liz Cameron had been told about me.
At least Alan had said my name was Kate.

Birdy watched us start up the stairs, but when I looked down she had done her vanishing act and disappeared without a sound.

"How do you like Windtop so far?" Liz asked as we reached the upper gallery. Apparently this was a favorite question—to be expected with such a house.

"It's fascinating—what I've seen of it. But I've never lived in a museum before, and it may take a little getting used to."

As we followed the long corridor that led toward my rooms, a distant shadow seemed to move. I put my hand on Liz's arm, startled.

"There's someone down there. It couldn't be Birdy. Even she couldn't fly fast enough to get ahead of us."

I ran along the hall, which ended at a narrow flight of stairs leading to the attic floor. Whatever I'd glimpsed was gone. Only rows of closed doors—like those of a hotel corridor—stood silent, as though nothing had moved past them in years. I went back to Liz, who shook her head at me, smiling.

"Windtop does that to people. I've stayed here overnight a few times, and I was always sure I saw things that really weren't there."

I remembered that Birdy had said it was only shadows in the wind when I'd asked her about the figure in the garden last night. Though still unconvinced, I let the matter go and opened the door to my sitting room.

At once I knew that someone had been in there. The subtle moving about of things whose position I remembered indicated an outside presence. Even my guitar, still in its case, had been picked up and shifted from where I'd left it.

"Someone has searched my room," I said.

Liz seemed unalarmed. "It's only Birdy, I'm sure. She's as curious as a magpie, and she's everywhere. Sometimes I think she rides on a broom, or maybe roller skates. Or, if this was the right day, it could just be someone from the cleaning crew that comes in regularly from the service Geneva uses. There's nothing missing, is there?"

As far as I could tell, what little I'd brought with me was here.

Liz looked about in delight. "What a lovely room. I haven't seen this suite before. You've a real view of the water up here. My house is lower down, so I can't see the harbor."

We sat in opposite pink chairs, and though there were no long silences, because Liz talked easily and constantly, I still had a feeling that she regarded me with a certain wariness, as I did her. There was something about her that I couldn't quite put my finger on. As I hadn't been able to in her brother's case either. I wondered if Geneva had asked her to watch me. And if so—why? Did Geneva worry that I was on the edge of a crack-up? I wished I could question my father about Geneva, but I wasn't ready to call him yet.

"Birdy said you were having lunch with Alan Gordon. How do you like him?"

"I don't really know him," I told her. "Of course he's been very kind and helpful these last few days."

She smiled ruefully. "He's the most eligible bachelor around here. But he's never gotten over his broken heart enough to marry."

While I was curious about Alan Gordon, I didn't want to learn through gossip.

"He's only helping me out because of Mrs. Ames," I said.

"Of course he would. He's been like a son to her, and she's done a great deal for him—practically building Sea Spray Lab just for his research. So he jumps whenever she whistles." Was there a dry note in her voice? "I suppose I do too—or used to when we were speaking. I never set foot in this house without hearing her voice and feeling her presence. I understand there was an old romance in the past with your father."

Liz's manner seemed so direct and open that I couldn't resent her remarks, however personal.

"So she told me. I never knew about it till recently. That was long before my mother, of course."

"But Geneva would remember. Old love dies hard, doesn't it? Was your husband your first love, Kate?" She spoke lightly, carelessly, so the question seemed almost impersonal, and before I could fend it off, she went on. "Mine wasn't, unfortunately. So marriage didn't always work out for me."

I could find nothing to say in response to such frankness.

Her manner seemed almost dreamy as she went on. "I understand you've lost your husband recently, so of course you need a change. We have a point of sympathy between us, since we've each lost a husband."

I wished that my life with Ricky hadn't given me a new tendency toward quick suspicion. When I'd first met him I'd been more trusting and sure of other people than anyone I knew. Now I found that Liz's candid remarks were not only in poor taste but made me uncomfortable. I wondered what was behind them. Perhaps they weren't quite as artless as they seemed.

"Tell me what you do with yourself around here," I asked.

Her smile was still rueful. "I read a lot, and I ride. I still keep a couple of horses. In the summertime there's sailing, boating. There are always committees that need volunteers, and I'm interested in helping to preserve Cold Spring Harbor history. For a time I worked for Alan, but I don't have a green thumb, and I got terribly bored setting out little seedlings and keeping notes on what this patch of wheat grass did against that. Besides, Alan's a stern taskmaster. Unfortunately I'm not like you—I don't have a talent. I understand you've had a few songs recorded. Is that what you like best—to write songs?"

At least whoever had informed her seemed to have been carefully general. She didn't seem to know about Ricky Sands, and I drew a breath of relief. "I play around at song writing a little. I don't know exactly what I'll do right now."

There was a tap on the door, and Birdy brought in a tray with a coffeepot and cups and set it down on a low table.

I thanked her, and when she started for the door, I spoke to her again. "Birdy, do you know if anyone came into my rooms this morning?"

She turned her tall, thin body toward me, staring, and the white crest of her hair seemed to bristle. "Who would come in? I haven't been upstairs at all today, till now. Why do you ask, madam?"

So we were back to the "madams" again.

"Nothing. I just thought I saw someone in the hall a few minutes ago." There seemed no point in telling her my room had been disturbed.

Birdy's sniff was eloquent and just short of insolence. When she'd gone I poured coffee, and as Liz took her cup she nodded toward my guitar.

"Do you sing your own songs?"

"I'm not much of a singer."

"There's a lovely music room downstairs."

"Yes, I found it this morning. I want to try the piano—when I can get up the courage."

"Courage?"

I couldn't explain what I meant by the word—that these days I risked myself whenever I sat down at a piano, or picked up my guitar. When nothing came, it was frightening and discouraging, and not to be chanced too often.

"Geneva used to invite some pretty famous people out for her private concerts," Liz said. "I've heard Itzhak Perlman play here, and a few other greats. Though Geneva's tastes can be catholic. She's even been known to invite popular performers. That singer who died recently in New York—Ricky Sands? He came out here a few years ago."

I tried not to look at her too quickly or sharply, but when I turned my head her manner seemed unconcerned. Yet I couldn't be sure whether her mention of Ricky had been casual or deliberate. I remembered the magazine I'd found open downstairs with Ricky's picture. Someone *knew*. And if Ricky had been in this house in the past, all sorts of ramifications opened up. Why hadn't Geneva told me she'd met Ricky, or that he'd actually been here? I recalled that when I'd asked her if she knew him, she'd sidestepped the question. And why hadn't Alan told me either? This new knowledge was unsettling.

Liz finished her coffee and set down her cup. "Thanks. I must run along now. My mare has a sore hoof, and the vet is coming out this afternoon. It's been lovely talking with you, Kate. I'll be in touch again soon. We mustn't leave you to brood in this mausoleum. Besides, I want you to see my own funny old house."

She insisted that I needn't accompany her all those miles downstairs, told me to work her brother *hard,* and went off with a cheerful wave of her hand. A little of her wariness seemed to have lessened, though mine hadn't, and I wasn't sure whether we might be friends or not. In fact, it had been so long since I'd had a real friend that I wondered if I'd lost the talent for friendship. Ricky had isolated me and it was only in the last year that I'd fully realized why he'd thought it necessary to keep me away from his other life. If I'd made new friends, they might have told me the truth about my husband.

Now I must absorb the unexpected news that Ricky had actually been here at Windtop, had probably sung his songs in the music room downstairs. I was no longer safely away from places where he'd been.

When Liz Cameron had gone, I went into the corridor and looked at the long line of closed doors. Then, one after another, I opened each one and looked into the room behind. I found nothing but empty suites and bedrooms. Nothing seemed to have been disturbed, and I had no feeling that I was being watched. I saw no more shadows that moved. The narrow flight of stairs that led to the floor above intrigued me, but it looked dark and uninviting, so I wouldn't explore right now. If there were rooms up under the eaves, they were surely closed off these days.

It was as Liz had said—Windtop could get to me. There was only one way for me to dismiss all spells and cobwebs, and even Ricky's shade. For me there had always been one solution to unhappiness—if only I could find it again. This was the moment to take my chances.

I picked up my guitar and went downstairs to the music room.

6

_____

My guitar was acoustic, since I'd never liked electronic sounds. I set it down deliberately near the harp and stood looking at the Bechstein.

A piano had always been *the* instrument for me. Guitar chords were different, and it was a piano I wanted now. Nevertheless, I had to force myself to prop open the great top, and then sit down to raise the lid. Idly I let my fingers wander across the keys, picking out whatever came to me. The notes were minor, melancholy. I changed the key and tried something more determinedly cheerful, but there was nothing I wanted to play. Not my own songs or anyone else's. The young Geneva watched me from the wall, and I wondered fleetingly if she had cried when she parted from my father. Had it been hard to stop being Jenny? What I must *not* think of was Ricky singing in this room

I tried to recall the wisp of sea melody, but it escaped me Sometimes just a sound led me to some unusual phrasing that could be repeated effectively as the hook that would lead the listener into the song. Sometimes words came alone and I would set a tune to them. Occasionally both worked together in a rare burst of inspiration. But I knew that a songwriter should write songs every day, or at least work at it, whether anything came or not.

When I was really working, when the ideas were flowing and the music singing through me, I could make the outside world literally disappear. It was as though time could be suspended while I existed in a universe more satisfying to me than any other. Once I'd heard a famous author say that a book he'd written years before, and which was still enormously popular, didn't mean a great deal to him. What mattered more was what he could create *today*.

That was true for me, yet I seemed able to create nothing in the present. Vainly I tried to visualize the blue water I'd seen this morning —the harbor with its sandy spits of land, and a few white sails. Nothing came. No seashells, no harbor, no sails. I banged the piano lid down, put my head on my arms and wept. It was as though all the grief I'd tried to suppress since Ricky's death came bursting through the dam to pour out in wrenching sobs.

Engrossed in my own misery, I didn't hear someone come into the room. When I finally raised my head and looked up with my face wet and streaked, I found Pete Evans beside the piano watching me. I resented his presence, resented his standing there silently while I cried.

When I saw him, he moved closer, and I caught a scent of leaves and pine needles, of the outdoors, about him.

"I'm sorry, miss. I was on the terrace just now and I heard you. Is there anything I can do?"

Because of my resentment, I snapped at him. "You can stop calling me 'miss' for one thing. If you're Liz Cameron's brother, you're not a proper gardener."

He grinned at me through the shaggy beard. "I guess I've never been a proper anything. But right now I'm working here, and I'd like to keep the job. Why are you crying?"

He was like his sister in being outspoken, but my anger had died, and I was far too submerged in my own pain to hold back.

"Because everything's lost, gone, wasted. Everything! And because I can't write songs anymore."

"Maybe if you'd stop looking at surfaces and go down inside whatever's bothering you, the songs would come."

With that astonishing remark he walked out through the french door and disappeared from sight. I could only look after him in surprise and outrage. At least my tears had stopped, and I had no further impulse to weep.

I told myself that I'd simply tried to face a piano too soon. I wasn't ready yet. Nor did I need any cryptic advice from Liz Cameron's offbeat brother.

I left my guitar defiantly near the elegant harp, and returned to the front hall. Alan Gordon stood on the flagstones talking to Birdy, and he gave me the first genuine smile I'd had from him.

"It's a beautiful day," he said. "Since I haven't put my boat away for the winter yet, I thought I'd go for a last sail. After all, it's Saturday. Want to come along?"

Saturday? I'd lost track of days and dates. I only knew that it was November—the sad month when one was forced to let go of all that was cheerful and hopeful. But that was self-pity, and I didn't want to drown in gloom. I tilted my chin and looked at him.

"I'd love to go sailing," I told him firmly.

"Good. Though you do sound a little grim. You'll find jackets in the cloak room off this hall, and maybe a scarf to tie up your hair."

There was a little powder room as well, and I stared at my tear-smudged face in the mirror, wishing Alan hadn't seen those traces of a grief I wanted to keep private. I wiped away the smudges and turned to the clothes rack. A navy pea jacket would do fine, and I pulled a blue scarf from its pocket and tied it over my hair. These things belonged to Geneva Ames, I supposed, and once more I had a sense of her presence.

When I rejoined Alan, Birdy, her long neck bent, looking more like a stork than ever, was talking to him earnestly.

"Don't worry," he said when she paused, "it will work out somehow."

This time he was driving a gunmetal foreign sports car, and I settled into the bucket seat, willing myself to relax, to take each moment as it came—and no more.

What a lovely, strange afternoon that turned out to be. Since I'd sailed with both my father and with Ricky, I wasn't a novice on Alan's graceful sloop. I noted its name, *Mary,* and remembered Liz Cameron's remark about Alan's broken heart. Had Mary been the girl he'd loved?

He must have noted my interest in the boat's name, for he spoke casually. "She was someone who died years ago. She used to sail with me when we were in our teens."

I couldn't help feeling that it was strange for a grown man to name a boat after a teen-age love, but I said nothing. Who was I to judge anyone? Look what I'd done at eighteen!

We used power until we were out on the waters of the Sound, where a breeze took the sails and we went skimming across the rippled surface. There is hardly any motion more soothing than to glide swiftly in a sailboat with the wind at your back. It seems almost like flight, except that there's no vibration, and the only sound is the soft rush of water parting at the prow and flowing by in white foam on either side.

We didn't need to talk and I was grateful for a silence that seemed for once to have no harsh undertones. If he had noticed my smudged face, he said nothing, asked nothing, and for this little space of time I could put everything that troubled me aside.

In the late afternoon we returned to the harbor, took down the sails, and woke ourselves up with the engine.

"Did you try Geneva's piano today?" Alan asked as we headed for the dock. His tone seemed mild enough, and without the ready condemnation he often seemed to show toward me.

"Yes. But it was a mistake."

"Why?"

"Because there aren't any tunes in me that want to be played. That crazy urge I've always had to make up songs seems to have vanished."

"It's like that sometimes in my work," Alan said. "There can be dry spells when nothing comes together. Then suddenly everything opens up, and solutions appear."

I hadn't thought of Alan Gordon in this light. "Tell me about what you do," I said, watching him maneuver the boat skillfully among other craft in the yacht club marina.

With a quiet intensity he told me about his work, speaking of new ways to grow plants that were useful to man. Nothing decorative like flowers. He was interested in what could be used as food, or in industry.

"The greenhouse we've built at Sea Spray is my special project. It's solar heated and we can raise what we like all winter without outside fuel. You must come and see it sometime."

I told him I'd like that, and meant it. But as we nosed into the dock, he seemed to change again, to revert to indifference as suddenly as he had come alive, and we were quickly back to our old, faintly antagonistic footing. I wondered why he'd ever asked me to go sailing with him, when the moment he returned to land he became distant again. Perhaps it was the spell of the water that had changed us both for a little while.

When we were in his car again, he asked casually about Liz Cameron's visit, and I suspected this must have been what Birdy was whispering to him about so earnestly when I'd come upon them earlier.

"I felt uncomfortable with her at first," I admitted. "She seems to know a lot about me—that I've lost my husband, and that I like to write songs. I suppose you've talked to her?"

"Only in a general way. But be a little careful. Elizabeth is a formidable and persistent woman when she chooses to be. She doesn't have enough to do with her time and energy these days."

"She told me she worked for you at one time."

"Yes. She didn't care to stay."

He didn't elaborate and I asked nothing more, noting that he'd called her Elizabeth rather formally.

Once more Luther Sykes let us through the gates, and as we wound our way up to the house, I looked for Liz's brother, but he'd either gone home or was working in another part of the grounds. It was a relief not to see him. The memory of my weeping with such abandon this afternoon was still sore, and I hated it that anyone had seen me.

At Windtop's door I thanked Alan for the afternoon and assured him again that he needn't feel obliged to look after me. "I do understand about your duty to Mrs. Ames, but I'm really all right, so don't bother about me."

"You understand very little," he told me curtly. "I never take on anything I don't want to do—not even for Geneva." He sounded almost angry as he spoke, and when he returned to his bullet-nosed car and drove off I stood looking after him for a moment. Alan Gordon mystified and aggravated and thoroughly baffled me. He was one person in his Buick, and another in that sports car. And he'd been still someone else on the *Mary*.

For once Birdy wasn't at the door, and I found my way to the kitchen without getting lost. It was disconcerting to discover Pete Evans at the long table, a bowl of hot stew before him, and Birdy hovering solicitously. As I was to learn, she loved to feed any man who drifted into her orbit. Not women—whom she sniffed aside as poor eaters—but any man with a hearty appetite.

"I'll come back later," I told her. Pete was the last person I wanted to see right now.

"If you want something to eat," she said, "you'd better stay and fix it now. You'll only have to take that walk upstairs and then come down again. The kitchen's big enough so you won't bother me. Madam."

Pete chuckled softly. "Better not call her that, Birdy. She doesn't like to be called 'miss' either. Mrs. Baker is a democratic lady."

If he was trying to rile me, he'd succeeded. I ignored them both and went to the refrigerator to consult its contents. A salad would do for tonight, and I set out what I needed on a butcher-block table. Pete finished his stew, thanked Birdy, and went quietly away. An aggravating man to have around. Perhaps because he fit no pattern I could find for him, and could be much too unexpected.

"Did you know Pete Evans before he started working here?" I asked Birdy.

"I know everyone around here," she said, sounding grumpy.

I let her alone after that, and she sat at one end of the table with a pot of tea and a plate of cinnamon toast. I pulled a chair to the other end and picked at my salad.

I'd expected to be hungry after our sail, but the appetite I'd had at lunch had deserted me, and I knew why. I was beginning to hate the lengthening of shadows, the moment when the sun went down—early, now that it was November. These things meant the coming of another restless, soul-searching night. Hope and life were born fresh every morning, only to expire at evening. It had been like that ever since Ricky had died.

Loneliness could grow too intense at night—sometimes to a degree that frightened me. I didn't like it that there were times when a dark, desperate personality seemed to take over in me. A stranger who occupied my own psyche and whispered of solutions I would never choose. Yet at the same time, solutions that held a certain fascination when they came in the dead of night.

The *dead* of night. Coral Caine and Ricky Sands were dead and I could only wish them peace. But I mustn't begin to envy them. I'd always cared about life. I wanted to care.

As I climbed the stairs to dimly lighted upper halls, the old whys began to stir in me again. Why had Ricky killed himself? Why—when he had everything in the way of success, money, recognition—why had he thrown it all away? To resort to the course of drugs, alone in a depressing hotel room, where no one could console or comfort him. Or say, *Wait! Don't do this terrible, irrevocable thing.* What was it I hadn't done, hadn't said—what words or actions of mine might have saved him? If only I had seen in his face that last time what he meant to do! I had never stopped puzzling over the words he'd spoken to me: "If you need it, the answer is in the song."

I had looked back through songs we had done together, and listened to recordings. I'd studied the words, looking for special meaning—and finding none. Those last months Ricky had been frightened, driven by something I didn't understand, coming nearer all the time to that last surrender. But to what? The possibility of his own guilt was what I feared the most, and because of this fear I couldn't report his last words to anyone. Not even to Norris. The truth couldn't matter to Ricky now, but it mattered to me, and I would go on puzzling over an answer.

Now, in my bedroom at Windtop, I sat at an azalea-skirted dressing table and stared into the mirror. My cheeks looked windburned, and my hair beneath the scarf was a mass of bright tangles. I sat brushing it long after the snarls were out, just because the motion seemed soothing and distracting. So I needn't think.

The evening ahead stretched endlessly long, but I knew better than to go to bed early and lie awake with my thoughts. For a time I stood on the dark balcony, with the wind cold on my face, and looked down toward white marble in the side garden. Tonight nothing moved within the aura of the light standards, and moonlight touched only the tops of trees that crouched black and formless down the hillside.

Had it been Pete Evans there last night, in spite of his denial? A strange man. Not what he seemed. Though I wasn't sure what he really seemed. He didn't fit into his sister's world either. Or into any world I understood. A drifter, Alan had said. A man who had run away from being a teacher.

Yet he had stood beside Geneva's piano in the music room this afternoon and spoken those strange words about going deep into whatever was troubling me, because that was where I would find my songs. He was wrong about that. For me, songs came out of joy, out of exhilaration. Or out of fervor because of some cause I could believe in. I had never written out of grief. Or at least only once or twice, and those songs hadn't been successful.

Had it also been Pete Evans who had come to my room, searched through my things, and then disappeared toward the far stairs when I'd glimpsed his shadow down the hall? Who else would it have been?

There were too many disquieting questions I couldn't answer.

The cold air made me shiver, and I went inside and picked up the seashell book I'd noticed earlier. I settled down in the cheerful sitting room to read. It was no use. My eyes followed words that made no sense, and I turned pages without any knowledge of their content.

I gave up and undressed. I put on a long gown of rose velour that Ricky had liked. Though now there was no one to dress up for, as I'd always done when he was home. Not that he'd troubled to notice for a long time. I didn't want to remember all those nights when I'd lain at

Ricky's side, achingly lonely, and hungry for his love, yet knowing that though he was awake he didn't want me. Only now, it was still worse, with an empty bed and no Ricky to lie beside ever again.

Before I turned out the lights I opened the bedroom door and looked down the long hallway. Neither my bedroom nor my sitting room had a door that locked, and this made me uneasy. Tonight I had a strong urge to bolt myself away from the rest of the house, as though it really was inimical to me.

As I held my breath, listening to silence, a sound drifted toward me —a faint strain of music. The back of my neck prickled as a distant voice began to sing.

> Let the rain fall sweetly
> On the children of the earth . . .

My impulse was to slam the door and rush to my bed, put a pillow over my head so I could shut out the sound. Instead, I stood frozen, with all my senses alert. That must be the recording Ricky had made. Someone in the house was playing that recording of my song. Of course that was it!

But as I quieted, still listening, the sound grew stronger, coming closer, and I knew it wasn't a recording at all. This voice was of a different timbre from Ricky's—huskier. And it lacked that hypnotic quality Ricky could put into his songs. What I heard was a real guitar— a *live* voice singing.

I had to know the source of this eerie music. Moving swiftly on slippered feet, I followed the corridor toward the front of the house, and as I moved the singer moved as well, slipping away ahead of me. Near the head of the stairs a lamp burned—but the hall below was dark except for a single slanting band of light, and I couldn't see the bottom steps clearly. The singer was down there now, strumming softly, coaxing me on. Like the Pied Piper, beckoning me to—what?

By this time nothing could make me turn back. I must know the singer's identity, his intention.

Clinging to the broad rail, I went down into a darkness that was cut by that single band of light. He had reached the chorus again—"Let the sweet rain fall." . . . Whoever it was knew every word.

From the lower steps I could see the shaft of light that thrust into the hall from an open door at the rear—the door to the music room. Suddenly the song ended, and the guitar was silent. My heart pounded in the silence, and I felt cold, frightened. Yet none of that mattered. I had to know. I ran across flagstones and stood at the door of the softly lighted music room.

There was no one there. The piano remained closed, as I had left it, and on its top, out of the case, lay a guitar. *My* guitar! I went quickly to put a hand on the instrument. There was no place to hide in this long, open room, and whoever had been here had simply disappeared by way of another door. In fact, one of the french doors stood open on the terrace, and wind stirred the heavy draperies.

I ran to the opening, but the moonlit bricks outside lay empty, and nothing moved in the shadow of the great beech tree near the house. I clutched my robe about my throat and came inside, shutting the door behind me. What of the alarm system? Why hadn't it gone off?

Reaction made me shiver again, and I went to the piano to pick up my guitar. Not again would I leave it downstairs for some ghostly presence to play.

When Birdy spoke suddenly behind me, I cried out and whirled around. She still wore her gray dress and a sweater, so she hadn't gone to bed.

"Are you looking for something, madam?" she asked, her tone correct, courteous—and a little sly.

"Indeed I am!" I told her. "Someone came upstairs just now playing a guitar and singing a song that . . ." I stopped myself in time, remembering that I wasn't supposed to be Hollis Temple Sands. "You heard it, didn't you?"

"A song? A guitar?" She sounded incredulous. "Perhaps you were dreaming, Mrs. Baker. I was down here locking up for the night, and I didn't hear anything."

"Well, I did! I followed the singing down to this room."

"As you can see, there's no one here," she said, her calm unruffled.

She would admit nothing, I thought angrily. Yet she knew very well who the singer was. She must have heard, she must know.

"Someone *was* playing a guitar—*my* guitar." I held it up for her to see, recognizing the futility of arguing with her.

"Of course, madam," she said politely. "I hope you sleep well for the rest of the night."

Meaning that I was batty and should be humored. I walked out of the room and upstairs to my own suite, carrying the guitar with me. The room's pink calm awaited me serenely. This was not a room that would hear ghostly singers in the night.

What had happened had shaken me badly, and it seemed impossible now to sleep. My watch told me it was only eleven o'clock, though it felt like the early morning hours. I sat on the straight desk chair in the sitting room and held my guitar to me tightly. As though it were my one friend. Surely it wouldn't lend itself to playing such tricks on me. Yet it wasn't I who had taken it out of its case and placed it on the piano. It wasn't my fingers that had warmed the strings. Was I going crazy?

I found the pick tucked in place, but not where I usually kept it, and I took it out and strummed a few soft chords. Perhaps now, in this haunted moment, when all my defenses against feeling were down— perhaps now something would come. It was the only thing I could think of that would relax me.

The sound that spoke to me was like water rushing, and a snatch of melody, a snatch of lyric skimmed through my mind.

Wind in the sails, and the sea running fast . . .

Perhaps a gull following the wake, as I'd seen this afternoon. I didn't want to go on with a song that would lead me only into more pain. Yet there might be something here. I could at least put the snatch of melody and words on tape, so I wouldn't have lost them by morning. A lifeline to reach for, perhaps. A talisman to hold against voices that tried to haunt me.

Sitting on the bed, I turned on the recorder and took up my guitar. The tape purred, but before I could touch the guitar strings, a voice spoke to me from the machine. "I know who you are. I know what you did. You're to blame for his death and you *owe* for that. Just wait and know that I'm watching you, Hollis Sands."

The guitar slid from my knees to the carpet while the tape spun on, empty of further sound. When I could move, I ran it back and played it through again, this time listening intently to the voice. A man's voice— just as the voice I'd heard singing had been. Soft, husky, hardly more than a whisper, unrecognizable.

I'd spoken to only three men since I'd come here yesterday—Alan Gordon, Luther Sykes, and Pete Evans. I couldn't imagine Alan or

Luther doing anything like this. With Pete Evans, I could suspect anything.

The voice frightened me. This seemed no empty threat, and I'd never felt more alone and vulnerable. There was no one at Windtop to whom I could turn. No one I could talk to. In fact, there was no one anywhere, except my father, whom I could trust completely. But he was too far away. This was for *me* to face, and I was no longer a child.

It seemed especially threatening that someone had used my guitar, used my tape recorder, violated the privacy of my room—and my life. I'd become too accessible, with no means of protecting myself. Birdy's assurance that no one had entered my room had been false, and that made her suspect as well.

But who around here cared about Ricky's death enough to accuse me? Who had left that magazine open for me to find? I knew now that this must have been deliberate. Yet only Alan Gordon knew who I was, and tricks like this were surely out of character for so mature a man. Worst of all to think about was the question of my own blame. This was something I didn't know how to face.

Pete Evans's words ran through my mind again, all too clearly:

Maybe if you'd stop looking at surfaces and go down inside whatever's bothering you, the songs would come.

It wasn't merely songs I wanted—or at least not songs alone. It was answers. And I had to do something quickly to find those answers because I could feel myself nearing the edge of a dangerous, helpless despair. In some way I didn't understand, that sort of despair must have been what drove Ricky to his final desperate act. But I'd always thought I had courage enough to stand up to whatever happened, and if I had any of that trait left, it must support me now.

I knew the action I must take, the ordeal I must face. The answers I needed didn't lie inside me, but back in New York in whatever was left of Ricky Sands's life in those boxes of papers that I'd refused to look at till now. Threads had surfaced here, but their source was still in New York.

Once I'd decided on the step I must take, I was able to turn off the lights and go to bed.

No one sang a rain song during the night. My guitar lay silent on the carpet near my bed, and, after a time, release came and I slept.

7

In the morning I called the gatehouse and asked Luther Sykes to get out a car for me. Then I announced to Birdy—who seemed openly suspicious—that I was driving to the city and might be away for a day or two, so would she tell Mr. Gordon?

When I'd packed my duffel bag for overnight, I put it and my guitar in the trunk of the car and started for Manhattan. I didn't need the guitar, but when I thought of strange hands touchings its strings, I couldn't leave it behind.

Sunday traffic into New York was light at this hour, so I had time to drive peacefully and think. At least I'd chosen a direction, and I knew what I must do.

After Ricky's death, the thought of examining the files of letters and papers he'd collected over the years had made me feel ill. Now I needed to face whatever was in those cartons. I must learn more about Ricky than he'd ever been willing to tell me. Some connection with him had reached into Windtop to threaten me, and I must discover what it was.

I even wondered if there was anything I could gain by talking to Geneva Ames. Was it only because of my father that I'd been invited to Windtop? Ricky himself had been in the house, performing, and Geneva had never mentioned it to me. Nor had Alan Gordon. This seemed much too strange.

When I reached our apartment building, I found no one around. Television trucks and equipment were gone, and so were the reporters. The media had discovered that their bird had flown, and apparently the fans had too. I hated to think that a search for me might already have begun, and that for *one* person it had ended by finding me.

When I opened the door to the penthouse, I saw that lights, which shouldn't have been burning, were on, and I heard the sound of rustling papers in the living room.

Norris Wahl looked up from a nest of cartons as I walked in.

"Hollis!" He didn't sound pleased. "Why didn't you let me know you were coming?"

"Why should I? What are you doing, Norris?"

"Someone had to get started on Ricky's papers, and you weren't ready to tackle them yet. I meant to get the worst of it done, and pick out things you ought to see. Then you could decide what to keep and what to discard. There're Ricky's clothes too. Do you want me to take care of them?"

I was suddenly furious—angrier than I'd been in a long time. "What right have you to touch anything here without my permission? How could you *dare?*"

Norris was accustomed to the exploding emotions of the "talent," and he only smiled at me blandly.

"I'm trying to help, you know."

I didn't know. "What are you looking for?" If there were answers to be found, I might as well start with Norris Wahl.

"Looking for?" His tone was carefully blank.

"You might as well tell me." I set down my guitar and bag, but stayed on my feet, trying to contain my indignation. Flying at him in a rage wouldn't help, though I was still angry. "Was Ricky in some sort of trouble he couldn't get out of? Is that why he killed himself?" The thought of Coral was always there at the back of my mind, though I didn't speak her name.

Norris dropped a batch of letters and bent to pick them up. When he straightened he looked at me guardedly.

"Maybe it's better if you go back to Windtop and leave all this to me. Why upset yourself any more than you need to?"

I didn't want to tell him that Ricky's past had already reached into Geneva Ames's grand house.

"You'd better explain," I said grimly.

"There's nothing to tell you, Hollis. I just know Ricky was running scared. He wouldn't talk to me, but something had him so frightened he couldn't take it anymore. I thought an answer might be found in whatever he left behind."

That was what I had begun to think. Though Norris had no right to search Ricky's papers on his own, I needed to learn the source of his suspicions, and I held back my indignation.

"Why do you think this is important *now?*"

"Who knows? Maybe I'm curious. Or maybe—you might as well know—though I hate to see you upset about something you can't help. Bea has had a couple of peculiar phone calls in the last few days that seem to connect with Ricky. It was a woman's voice, but she would never give her name."

"What did she say?"

Clearly he didn't want to tell me.

"Look—I've had enough mystery!" I snapped. "Stop trying to protect me, if that's what you're doing."

Again that familiar shrug. "If that's the way you want it. The woman told Bea that it wasn't over. And that she should tell *you.* Of course I said she wasn't to do anything of the kind."

As long as I was on my feet, I had a slight physical edge over the power I always sensed in Norris Wahl. But I couldn't stand up any longer and I dropped onto the sofa beside him and punched one of the beige cushions weakly. The fury that had driven me ever since I'd found him here had faded, leaving only a frightening emptiness to take its place.

"Perhaps I'd better go home to California after all."

"Take it easy," he said. "You aren't alone, and I mean to get to the bottom of this. Just forget about the calls. It's probably some crackpot female who had a crush on Ricky. There were plenty of those. Anyway, now that you're here, you might as well help. It's important to get this job done for another reason as well. I've been approached by a very good writer who wants to do a biography of Ricky—while all this interest in him is high. His fans are already clamoring, and this man has an agent with two possible publishers bidding. Ricky's papers need to be made available and—"

"No biography," I told him flatly.

Norris stopped sorting and stared at me. "What did you say?"

"No biography. Not yet."

"But this would be *authorized.* We'd have some control over what went into it. If we help the writer and give him all the assistance we can, we'll be able to keep a rein on what's written."

"Not yet," I said.

He looked still more exasperated with me. "Look, kid, you owe it to Ricky."

Norris, of course, would profit. He would see to that. Not that I cared, except for an instinct to hold off on anyone writing about Ricky. All those fans out there still loved and idolized him. Once I had been one of them, and I didn't want the truth about what he'd become to be revealed. Or lies to be told. Like all those John Belushi horrors. Even at the end, the image Ricky cared about had been protected, and I meant to go on protecting it, however futile that might be. I wanted his real talent to stand on its own. I did owe him that. But he had owed me something too. What was left of my last control crumbled.

"Ricky owed it to *me* not to kill himself!" I cried. "I don't know why he did it, but he about finished me at the same time, and I don't know how to go on."

Norris watched me warily, and I knew I could never really open up to him. Basically, he was afraid of emotion. Men usually are.

"Take it easy," he said again. "You need to collect yourself and really think about this. Sensibly and calmly. There are probably books about Ricky Sands being crashed through right now for the soft-cover market. Trash that can be on the stands in a few weeks. You can't keep that from happening. They'll probably do a docu-drama for television too. So isn't it smart if a more careful account of Ricky's life is published to counteract whatever garbage they rush out with?"

I hadn't thought about any of this. I supposed that Norris was right, but I hated to think of the exploitation that might begin, just as had happened after Elvis Presley's death. It had already started with the commotion downstairs. And with reporters whose job it was to forget all sense of human decency.

Norris changed the subject abruptly. "How do you like it at Mrs. Ames's house? Bea thought you might call her and report."

"There hasn't been time. I'm not ready to sort it out yet. I—I think there's something wrong at Windtop, and I don't know yet what it is."

"Wrong? What do you mean?"

I wasn't ready to give Norris the details. "Did you know that Ricky once played a gig at Windtop?"

He looked convincingly surprised. "When was that?"

"I have no idea. But he was there."

"I suppose I knew at the time, but I don't keep track of those special invitation things. It must have been a while back. Maybe before he met you."

"But then why wouldn't Mrs. Ames, or Mr. Gordon, mention it to me?"

"Maybe they forgot too."

"No one would forget something like that. Well, never mind. Hand me some of those papers and I'll start reading."

Instead, Norris picked up an envelope he had laid aside on the sofa. "First you'd better read this. It's addressed to you in Ricky's hand, and it's sealed. I was going to send it to you. I don't know why he didn't leave it out where it would be found sooner. Why bury it in stuff like this? Anyway, it may give us some answers."

For a moment I couldn't touch what he held out to me. When I hesitated, Norris picked up my hand and put the envelope into it.

"You'd better have a look at this now, don't you think?"

A curious mixture of eagerness and fear was stirring in me. Eagerness because of a faint hope that Ricky might, after all, have written something comforting for me to read. Perhaps words of reassurance that would absolve me from blame, even words of love that he might have written to me in the last days—or hours—of his life. Yet at the same time I had a sense of dread. What he'd written might tell me why he had died, and I didn't know if that was something I could face right now.

"I need to be alone to read this," I said, and Norris nodded.

"Sure, go ahead. I've got plenty here to keep me busy."

I picked up the guitar that was like a part of me, and went into the room that had been mine for the years of my marriage. Draperies were pulled across glass that looked out toward the Hudson, and I opened another set to let in late morning sun. The usual pigeon strutted on the terrace outside the window, bubbling importantly.

I sat staring at Ricky's handwriting on the envelope. He had always written in a strong but unformed hand, and he liked to use a black felt-tipped pen.

Feeling as though the very paper burned my fingers, I slit the envelope and took out a single sheet. The message was short—only a paragraph or two—and the moment I saw the date I knew desolation. This note—it was only that—had been written more than a year ago. There would be nothing here to comfort me.

> Dear Hollis,
>   How can I sing your beautiful songs when I live in constant fear of my life? From day to day I hear footsteps following me, as though the threat is coming closer. I'm ready to go out of my mind.
>   There is a woman named Coral Caine. I've never told you about her, but Norris knows. If anything happens to me, look for her. But be very careful, Hollis. She is dangerous.
>
> > In my way I love you,
> > Ricky

I sat with the single sheet in my hands, reading the lines over and over until they blurred before my eyes. The words were clearly a warning, in case anything happened to Ricky, but they had been written while he was in one of his near-zombie phases and before he'd gone to that place upstate where they'd treated him. In fact, this had been written months before Coral Caine died. In the end, *she* had been the one to die a year before Ricky, and none of the words in this note had any meaning for me now. Not even the closing line: *In my way I love you.*

In what way? He had killed himself in almost the same manner in which Coral Caine had died, and he had left nothing at all of comfort or explanation for me. I supposed I could understand that. Those about to take their own lives aren't concerned with what the living may feel. Their own agony is stronger. It is *their* hurting they want to stop, and how they hurt others doesn't matter. As sometimes I wanted to stop my hurting—even to the point of thinking about that dark, irrevocable road.

Hardly realizing what I was doing, I took my guitar from its case and smiled ruefully as I found myself tuning the strings. Music had been a comfort to me for so long that I instinctively sought its help. As I played a few chords absently, a hint of melody came to life. Notes that were sad and haunting, with a refrain that seemed different from anything I'd ever written—notes that could be readily repeated. No distinct words yet, but a *feeling* that came with the music. Something about memory . . .

Perhaps I'd have captured it if Norris hadn't tapped on my door just then. At once the tune vanished. I told him to come in and returned the guitar to its case. There was no need for concealment now. I gave him the note, and when he'd read the few lines he handed it back to me, shaking his head.

"This is too old to matter. We both know he was afraid of Coral. But why did he kill himself a year later when she was no longer a threat to him? Anyway, Hollis, you'd better destroy this. It's not the sort of thing some reporter—or biographer—should pick up."

He led the way back to the living room and went to work again, sorting more of the papers I hadn't wanted to touch.

"How would your biographer treat Coral Caine?" I asked.

He answered calmly enough, "Oh, he'd just change things around a bit in Ricky's favor. After all, you've been sheltered, Hollis. I don't think you have any idea of the women who were after Ricky Sands. Coral can just get lost in the crowd, and nobody needs to be any the wiser."

"The garbage rakers may not think so."

"That's why we have to furnish Ricky's fans with something better as soon as we can."

I moved about the room, looking with a stranger's eyes at plump beige cushions and golden brown furniture. The room seemed no more real to me than the Azalea Suite at Windtop. Had I lived in these rooms as Ricky Sands's wife? Had I sat at that piano to write "Sweet Rain" and all those other songs?

I went to a glass door and stared out at the terrace garden on which I'd worked so lovingly for the last few springs. Now it had shriveled with the coming of November, and it drooped in neglect.

"Norris," I asked, "haven't you ever felt guilty about Coral Caine? Haven't you ever felt that she might still be alive if you hadn't taken me to see her?"

He looked up from a letter he was scanning. "Why should I think that? I told you she was already over the edge. It wouldn't have made any difference whether we'd seen her or not. Or maybe a day or so, more or less."

"I wonder. Anyway, I have felt guilty ever since it happened."

"Did you and Ricky ever talk about her—have it out between you?"

"We didn't talk," I told him, "because Ricky wouldn't discuss her. He must have thought about suicide a lot. I suppose there were hints, if only I'd noticed. I don't think I understand suicide. I hope I'll always want to stay around to find out what happens next."

Even as I spoke, I wondered how true my words were. How did one resist the terrible despair a suicide must feel?

Nuances didn't interest Norris, however. "Sure, kid—you and me both. I always want to last another day."

Before I could return to the piles of paper, the telephone rang.

"That's probably Bea," Norris said. "She'll want to talk to you."

I picked up the phone but it wasn't Bea. It was Alan Gordon, and I found myself welcoming the sound of his quiet, assured voice with a pleasure that surprised me.

"I thought you might be there," he said. "Are you all right?"

"Why wouldn't I be?" I fenced.

"Birdy is full of dire warnings. It seems you upset her badly last night."

"Did she tell you what upset *me?*"

"She told me what you thought upset you."

"She claims she didn't hear or see anything, Alan, and I don't believe her. I can prove someone was there. I have something I want to show you when I get back to Windtop."

"When will that be?"

"There are a few things I need to do here. I'll drive back this afternoon," I said, deciding after all not to spend the night at the apartment.

"Good. Suppose I come to the house around five?"

"I'll see you then. I have a lot to talk to you about."

Norris had been listening openly, and when I hung up and sat down beside him, he gave me a long, searching look. "Don't you think you'd better tell Uncle Norris too?"

"No! And don't try to play uncle!"

His sigh was exaggerated. "No uncle—no agent! What am I, Hollis?"

"I don't really know," I said, and he seemed to accept that without resentment. He was remarkably impervious to verbal darts, but I could never tell whether this meant he was insensitive or merely patient and wily.

In any case, since Alan had called I felt restless and unable to concentrate on the task at hand. None of this had to be done here, and there was no reason why I shouldn't return to Windtop now.

"Norris," I said, "will you help me take these cartons down to Mrs. Ames's car? I've parked it in the building garage."

This time he was thoroughly annoyed and for once showed it. "Now, look here, Hollis—this job needs to be done right away, and I'm not sure you know enough about Ricky to do it properly. I knew him a hell of a lot longer than you did, and I understand all sorts of details about his career that you know nothing about. I doubt if you have the faintest notion . . ."

"I'll learn," I said, picking up my duffel bag and guitar. "Bring what you can, please, and then we'll come back for the rest."

He knew when he was beaten, and between us we made several trips and carried all the boxes downstairs. Norris put them into the car, and by the time I was ready to drive off he had recovered his nonchalance. He reached in the car window to pat my arm.

"Maybe I'll come out to Windtop to visit you one of these days, Hollis."

"I don't think that's a good idea," I told him. "But I'll be in touch with you as soon as I've gone through all this stuff."

"And you'll think about a biography?"

"I'll think about it."

I drove into Manhattan traffic that was still thin. I knew I was right. It was far better to get Ricky's papers out to Windtop and go through them slowly than to stay in the depressing atmosphere of the apartment, and I would seal each box so there could be no tampering with the contents. It felt good at last to be doing *something*. Windtop was where I lived for now. Whatever happened must be dealt with there. The answers I sought, if they existed in Ricky's papers, could now be found. I might need help, but not from Norris Wahl.

It was early afternoon when I reached Snake Hill Road and wound my way to Windtop's gates. Luther Sykes was nowhere in sight, but the gates were unlocked, and I could let myself in.

When I reached the upper driveway I found Pete Evans still raking leaves that the trees dropped almost as fast as he could take them up. He was just the man I needed.

I got out of the car and went around to open the trunk. "Pete, will you help me, please?"

He came over and saw the load of cartons. "Where do you want these?"

"Perhaps there's an empty room near mine where we could pile them. They're papers from New York I'll need to work on."

Norris had folded the tops together, flap under flap, so that nothing was exposed, and I would use the tape soon.

"No problem," Pete said. "There's probably a service elevator. I'll ask Birdy."

Since I'd had no lunch, I went with him to the kitchen to make myself a sandwich. We found her there examining the contents of the big refrigerator.

"Good afternoon, Mrs. Baker," she said. "Mr. Gordon has phoned and he is dining here tonight. You want something, Pete?"

"A service elevator, if there is one. Mrs. Baker has brought back some boxes she wants carried upstairs. Can I put them in a room near hers?"

"I'll show you," Birdy said, and they went off together.

I found bread and some sliced ham, and made myself a sandwich. When Birdy returned, I was pouring a glass of milk, and I placed everything on a tray to carry up to my room.

"It's a lot of trouble for you to make dinner," I said. "May I help?"

"No, madam. I enjoy cooking an occasional meal. And there's a girl from nearby who comes in to help when I need her."

She looked slightly offended, though since she often looked that way I couldn't tell whether it was because she considered my offer improper as a guest in the house.

I carried the tray upstairs and down the long hallway, to find a door open opposite my rooms. When I'd set the tray down, I went to look in, and found Pete Evans standing beside two cartons he'd placed on the bare springs of a bed. One hand rested on cardboard folds, and nothing appeared to be disturbed. Nevertheless, I had a sense of quick movement just as I'd reached the door. As if those flaps might not have been so innocently intact a moment before. I should have used the sealing tape in New York, I thought uneasily.

"The service elevator's near the stairs," Pete said. "I'll bring up the rest of the boxes right away."

"I'll help," I said firmly, not wanting to leave him alone again with Ricky's papers. I was becoming too suspicious of everyone, but I couldn't help it after the things that had happened.

He accepted my assistance without comment, and we loaded the rest of the cartons into the small elevator, then walked upstairs where I helped him carry them to the room Birdy had assigned. All this was managed in silence until the task was done. Then he stood beside the piled-up bed regarding me quizzically.

"Anything else, Mrs. Baker?"

"No, thank you." As he started away I asked an abrupt question. "Pete, do you play the guitar?"

He stopped instantly and his turn was slow. I wished he didn't have all that concealing hair on his face. Even his eyes seemed shadowed by unruly locks of brown hair.

"I suppose I could play one if I tried," he said. "Any particular reason?"

That was a strange answer, and I couldn't tell him that my reason was that someone had played a guitar in this house last night. Someone who *knew how.*

I asked a rude question instead. "Have you ever thought of shaving?"

A grin appeared in his mass of beard. "Not very often. Have you any objection, Mrs. Baker?"

"Perhaps it's not usual these days, but I like to see the faces of people I talk to," I told him.

It was the first time I'd heard him really laugh and the sound was full —a laugh that rang unconstrained through the halls of Windtop.

"You're jealous," he said, and walked off in his own unhurried way. I supposed that I deserved rude laughter, since I'd been equally rude.

When he reached the bend in the corridor, he turned back for a moment. "Since you can't grow a beard, you ought to figure out a good way to conceal all that openness you wear on *your* face, Mrs. Baker. A mask, or something?"

He was gone then, and once more I felt baffled and uncertain about Pete Evans.

I went into my room and looked around, but nothing seemed to have been disturbed this time. I took the roll of glued tape into the empty room and carefully sealed each carton shut. This was no real guarantee of privacy, but it was all I could manage. At least the door to this room had a lock, and perhaps I could get a key from Birdy.

While I was finishing my lunch the phone in my room rang. It was Alan on the line.

"I just wondered if you were home," he said. "Did Birdy tell you— I've invited myself to dinner. Elizabeth Cameron would like to come too. Is this all right with you?"

"Of course," I said. "It's your house more than it is mine, and I'll be happy to see you both. But Alan, will you come early? There's something I want to talk to you about."

"I'll come around five, as we planned," he said, and hung up.

Unexpectedly, I found myself looking forward to the evening.

8

Alan would be here in an hour, and then I could ease myself of some of my worries. Just telling someone would help. I was already aware of Alan's strength and his ability to deal with problems in a practical way. In the meantime, I had no wish to do much of anything.

Certainly I wouldn't take out Ricky's note to read his words again. I knew them by heart; they'd repeated themselves over and over in my mind until they became meaningless. My guitar held no comfort for me now, and even if Geneva's piano might have helped, the music room was too far away. Nor would I replay that voice on the tape. This was what Alan must hear, and I wouldn't torment myself with it until he came.

I went outside on the small balcony and stood for a little while staring at the panorama of view. This had a quieting effect that helped me to blank out my thoughts and deaden feeling. Close to the house nothing moved. Pete was probably still working around at the front, and the side lawn with its pool and marble maiden was empty of all but a few birds. White columns on the far side of the lawn shone among spreading shadows of late afternoon, and the marble bench was empty. Only bands of sunlight slanting through the trees were stirred by the shadow of branches moving in the wind. Everything else was still.

It was time to overcome my apathy and change for dinner.

When I'd showered, I dressed in a smoky India silk with touches of amber. How often I'd dressed up for Ricky when he was in town, and put on my best smile—only to wait endlessly while meals grew cold and he didn't come, even though he'd promised to be there.

Stop it, I told myself. All that was over. I would never have to wait for him again, and perhaps it was better to be angry than to grieve. The sooner I recognized that and accepted the fact that my life could be better from now on, the sooner I would recover.

But not yet. I wasn't strong enough yet to sustain the anger. I still missed him too much, and I'd always forgiven him.

Amber drop earrings I'd bought for myself were the final touch. There was still a little time before Alan would come, and I returned to the soothing view of the harbor and its arms of land. From up here I could see the whole panorama, including the white steeple of St. John's church. But now something had changed in my closer view of the garden.

The marble bench beyond the pool and sloping lawn was no longer empty. A man sat smoking a cigarette in the shadow of the columns. It wasn't Pete—this man was clean-shaven. He was too far away for me to make out his features, but I knew he was someone I hadn't seen before.

I ran inside and hurried along the corridor and down the stairs, apathy forgotten. There was no need to hunt for Birdy. She appeared at the foot of the stairs as I clattered down in high heels.

"Come with me!" I cried. "Come with me right now!"

I took her by the arm without ceremony and led her through the music room to the side garden. Out here where the sun had nearly vanished, it was cooler than on my sunny balcony. Still holding a reluctant Birdy by the arm, I marched her out to the terrace.

The marble bench on the far side of the lawn was empty. No one moved among the columns. No man sat there smoking a cigarette.

"There *was* someone there!" I told her. "Whether you believe it or not, someone is using this house. I saw a man sitting on that bench, just as I saw him out in the moonlight the night I came. He was sitting there only a moment ago!"

Birdy released her arm from my hand. "Madam, you are very excited. There is no one using the house. Don't you think I would know if a stranger were about? Mr. Gordon has told me of your sad loss, and I'm sure it must be very unsettling to be in a place like this where everything is unfamiliar. You can so easily be fooled by shadows."

"Stop telling me it's shadows!" I cried. "Shadows don't come into my room and leave messages on my tape recorder. They don't play tunes in the halls at night and sing songs I know very well."

She stepped back as though she thought me dangerous. "You must talk to Mr. Gordon about these fantasies, Mrs. Baker. You mustn't go on like this."

I was so angry I was shaking. My own helplessness to convince her made me more furious than ever. Yet there was nothing more I could say or do, and when Alan, following the sound of our voices, came out on the terrace, he saw my state at once.

"It's all right, Birdy," he said. "Mrs. Baker is upset. You go along and I'll take care of everything."

"Let's sit down inside." Alan spoke gently. "Then you can tell me what's troubling you."

I cast a last look at the empty garden, and went with him. A fire had been lighted in the sitting room downstairs and he led me in and seated me on the small sofa close to the blaze. The coffee table where I'd found the magazine with Ricky's picture was empty, and I wouldn't mention that. I didn't want still another denial of what I had seen and heard.

"Birdy will bring us her special drink," Alan said. "Do you want to sit quietly and wait till it comes, or would you like to tell me what's worrying you?"

I held my hands to the fire and managed to stop shivering. When I began, I spoke slowly, quietly, holding back the edge of frenzy that wanted to creep into my voice. I told him all of it from the beginning. About the figure I'd glimpsed the night I arrived—up to the moment just now when I'd seen a man smoking in the garden. I told him about the guitar and the voice that had sung "Sweet Rain," and of the frightening message that had appeared on the tape in my recorder.

He listened intently, and his manner remained gentle and sympathetic—something he'd never shown me before. Yet I had no idea whether he believed anything I told him, and I knew that Birdy had already denied it all.

"I'm not crazy," I insisted, suspecting that was what the unbalanced always said. "These things happened. Come upstairs with me and I'll show you the proof."

He came, his hand on my arm, steadying me on the way up—when I didn't want steadying, didn't want sympathy, or pitying gentleness. All I wanted was to be believed!

The pink shell of the Azalea Suite glowed serenely as I went directly into the bedroom, where my tape recorder waited.

"Listen," I said, and touched the play button.

Of course I might have expected what happened. The tape turned softly and there was no other sound. No warning voice whispered its ugly threat. Whoever had placed the message there in the first place had easily erased it while I'd been in New York. Why hadn't I thought to take the tape with me? But I'd been intent on other matters, and this hadn't occurred to me.

"There *was* a message!" I wailed. "The voice told me he knew who I was and that I was to blame for Ricky's death. He said he'd be watching me. Alan, there really was a message!"

He took my hands and held them, warming them with his own strength and vitality. "Hush now, Hollis. It's all right. I do believe you. Of course you're not crazy. Perhaps I even have a suspicion about what's happening."

"What do you mean? Who could it be?"

"Let me track it down first," he said.

"Does Birdy know who I am?"

"I'm afraid she does." He looked uncomfortable. "Geneva felt we shouldn't try to conceal anything from her, and I agreed reluctantly. But Birdy is discreet, and she isn't gossiping around, so I'm sure she hasn't told anyone. If any further messages appear, put the tape away safely so I can hear the voice. I may have some ideas about this, but I've got to track it down myself. Now let's go downstairs and have that drink. Elizabeth will be here any minute."

We returned to the cheerful sitting room and drank the spiced mulled wine that Birdy served us. While she remained stiffly formal, her eyes questioned, and Alan smiled at her.

"It's all right, Birdy. I've told Mrs.—Baker—that you know who she is. Mrs. Ames and I trust you to say nothing. The pretense must be continued to protect her from intrusion. In the meantime, Birdy, please keep your eyes open for any possible trespassers, either inside the house or out."

Birdy bowed her head in response to Alan's words, but she didn't give an inch. "There is no one around, or I would know about it."

"I certainly hope you would, Birdy," Alan said.

She gave him a dark look and fled from the room.

"She's in on it!" I cried. "I'm sure she knows something."

"It's quite possible. Sometimes she has mistaken notions of loyalty."
Loyalty to whom? I wondered. But he didn't elaborate.

"Perhaps I shouldn't stay any longer," I told him. "If someone knows about me, then this isn't going to work."

"Where can you run to that you won't be followed?" Alan asked. "Dashing off somewhere else won't solve the problem. Let's just put our wits together and catch this fellow, whoever he is. I really don't believe he means you any bodily harm. Probably he just wants you upset enough so that, when he shows himself openly, you'll be ready to talk."

This sounded even more alarming. "Talk about *what?*"

"You're the only one who can answer that."

"Well, I can't answer it! If you mean do I know something about Ricky's death that hasn't been discovered—I certainly don't."

"What if someone thinks you do?"

I must have looked even more horrified, because he came to sit on the sofa beside me and put a quieting arm about my shoulders.

"I'm only supposing out loud. There has to be a reason behind this mysterious presence, and it's better to figure it out and deal with it without panicking. I'm just trying out possibilities."

"Are there keys to my doors upstairs?" I asked. "I'll feel better if I can lock myself in at night, and lock the doors on my belongings whenever I go out."

"Birdy will know about keys. Or better yet, I'll get a man in tomorrow to put in good locks on your doors. Would you like me to stay here tonight? I can sleep in one of the rooms nearby."

"No, I'll be all right." I didn't want to be dependent on Alan. I'd never been helpless before, and I needed and intended to face this on my own.

"What about your husband's manager in New York?" Alan asked. "He knows you're here—how trustworthy is he?"

That was something I couldn't answer. Yet neither could I imagine that Norris Wahl would dream up ways to frighten and torment me. Or that he or Bea would tell anyone where I was. We might disagree, but it still served him to play the game my way because there were things he wanted from me. And besides, there were the peculiar phone calls Bea had received, so the Wahls were victims too.

Voices sounded from the front of the house, and Alan went to look out a window. "Elizabeth's arrived," he said, and a few moments later Birdy showed her into the sitting room.

Liz Cameron looked chic in amethyst crepe, with a handsome cameo on a silver chain about her neck. Silver combs shone in her high-piled blond hair, and as usual every lock was sleekly in place. She looked big and beautiful—like one of those goddesses of mythology.

When she'd kissed Alan on the cheek, she held out her hand to me. "This is a lovely surprise—coming to dinner at Windtop again. It reminds me of old times. And it's a good idea for you, too, Kate. We must try to keep you busy and cheerful while you're here." She stood back at arm's length and examined me frankly. "You look terrific—I like that dress!" Then, noticing Birdy hovering at the door: "I do hope you're putting us in the grand dining room tonight, Birdy."

"Of course, Mrs. Cameron," Birdy said, and went away.

Liz sat in the chair Alan drew toward the fire, still chattering, so that I wondered if she was uneasy about something. "This *is* cozy. I just stopped for a minute outside to talk to Pete. I can usually walk through the woods the short way up from The Shutters. But not in the dark and with high heels. So Pete will drive my car home and come back for me later."

This seemed a curious arrangement, and I looked at Alan. "Since you all grew up together, why didn't you invite Liz's brother to dinner tonight?"

Alan raised his shoulders quizzically and nodded at Liz. "You explain."

"Because he wouldn't come," she said readily. "Pete has a few problems he needs to work out, and he's not ready for social occasions yet."

"Did he ever tell you what he's been doing for the last few years?" Alan asked.

"Not a word. And I know better than to ask."

I was more and more curious about Pete Evans. "What made him leave Cold Spring Harbor in the first place? Or is that something I shouldn't ask?"

His sister made a face. "Everyone knows. He ran away because something happened that he couldn't take. He won't talk to me about it, and never has. So I only know a few bare facts."

She accepted a cup of mulled wine from Alan and sipped it gratefully. "It *is* getting cold tonight. I hope we don't have an early winter."

She didn't say what the "bare facts" were, and the talk wandered off to horses and riding, and then to Alan's research work at Sea Spray. Both tried to include me in their talk, but they seemed more at ease with each other, and I recognized the difficulty of drawing me into conversation except on a superficial basis. Liz knew nothing about me, and Alan knew too much. My world had been the popular music scene, and it had been sometimes full and sometimes empty. But I could touch on none of that. Nor did I want to talk to this woman about the disturbing happenings that had occurred since I'd moved into Windtop. Mostly I listened and tried to make appropriate responses at the right times. When Liz invited me to go riding with her, I told her I'd love to, and I said again that I'd visit Alan's greenhouse whenever he wanted to show me around.

Birdy came to announce dinner and we went into the splendid, rather overpowering dining room.

"Geneva had this room done over herself years ago," Liz said. "It used to be dark and depressing. Though of course the floor is just as it was originally."

Large squares of parquet made a foil for ivory walls and woodwork and the light draperies that covered windows that reached nearly to the ceiling. A Flemish tapestry on one wall picked up the dark gold tones of the floor, and antique English chairs were upholstered in delicate needlepoint. Above the long table hung a Waterford chandelier, electrically lighted, and again there was a fire burning beneath a white marble mantel.

The young woman who served us had once worked for Geneva, and she moved skillfully under Birdy's watchful eye. Birdy had outdone herself with the tenderest of roast beefs, a potato soufflé, and broccoli hollandaise.

When we began to talk about music I found that Alan and Liz Cameron shared the same tastes in the classical. My classics were the music of my father's time—Gershwin and Porter, Berlin, Rodgers and Hart, Lerner and Loewe, and all the others. Liz had a fondness for this music too, but Alan didn't commit himself and I couldn't tell what he thought.

As the meal progressed, I became increasingly aware of the rapport between Alan and Liz. Of course they had been friends since childhood, but this seemed more—something more intimate and accepting. Though if there had been a love affair, it was probably long past. At least I sensed that it was past for Alan. About Liz I wasn't sure. There was a look at times in those violet eyes that seemed enigmatic—as though she held back something, or perhaps suppressed her true feelings. Alan didn't seem to notice one way or another—or didn't want to notice.

At one point Liz spoke to him solemnly, not chattering now. "Have you had any word?"

"None at all," he told her flatly. "Though I may have a lead to follow up. But let's not be gloomy with Mrs. Baker."

Again the subject of what troubled him was to be taboo with me.

Birdy had pulled the brocaded draperies across the windows, and I was just as glad that no one could watch us from outside in the November dark.

I'd begun to feel more relaxed and almost peaceful when Birdy came to tell me I was wanted on the phone. It could only be Norris, and my heart jumped. Norris meant trouble. I excused myself and went out to the main hall to pick up the phone, and found that I was right.

"Bad news, Hollis," he said at once. "After I left today, about the same time you did—someone broke into the penthouse and searched it thoroughly. Drawers were turned out, your desk ransacked, the closets disturbed. As far as I can tell, nothing of value has been taken . . . You okay, Hollis?"

I'd gasped at the news, and dropped into a chair beside the telephone table. "How did you find out?"

"The building super was doing the rounds, and he found your door jimmied. So he phoned me and I called the police. I've been going over things ever since. Maybe it's a good thing you took those cartons of Ricky's papers out there with you."

"Do you think that's what they were after?"

"Who knows? It's possible, isn't it? Maybe Ricky had something on someone. Is that likely?"

"I suppose it could have been. I wouldn't know."

"You needn't come to town unless you want to," Norris went on. "I'm taking care of things. I doubt if the police will find any leads. They think it might be the work of some fan who broke in for whatever he could collect."

I doubted that, but I thanked Norris for calling me and we hung up. For a few moments I sat thinking about what he'd just told me. At any other time, my first reaction would have been to rush home and see for myself whether anything had been taken. But right now too much else was happening here.

When I returned to the dining room I told them in general what had occurred. "Someone broke into my New York apartment. Nothing seems to be missing, and I don't believe I'll go back to New York immediately. My husband's manager is in charge there. I brought some boxes of papers back here with me this afternoon, and that might be what someone was searching for."

"What was your husband's work?" Liz asked casually.

I was silent for too long and Alan answered for me. "He was a musician."

True enough, and it gave nothing away, but I felt thoroughly tired of a masquerade that had already been penetrated by someone.

"You might as well tell her," I said to Alan.

He agreed. "Elizabeth is practically family," he said, and went on to give her a few details about my identity. She sat quite still as she listened, and for the first time since I'd met her she seemed a little guarded, so that I wondered if these were facts she already knew.

"Well!" she said when he'd finished. "This *is* a story!"

"We can count on your discretion, of course," Alan said.

They seemed to exchange a look that carried a special meaning not meant for me.

"Of course," she promised readily. "My lips are sealed!"

I returned to the subject of Ricky's papers. "Birdy said I could put the cartons in a room across the hall from mine," I told Alan. "That's where they are now. Do you suppose a lock could be put on that door too?"

"I'll have it done tomorrow," Alan said.

We finished dinner with fruit and nuts and piping hot coffee. After the meal we sat in the sitting room for a little while and sipped brandy. Liz didn't stay very long, and I thought she looked restless and uneasy, as though something about my story had upset her.

"Kate," she said, and then corrected herself. "I'm sorry—Hollis—you look tired, and we shouldn't keep you from resting. I'll call Pete to come for me now."

"Don't bother," Alan said. "It'll only take a minute to drive you home." He looked at me. "I'll come back here. Under the circumstances, I'd better stay for the night. Birdy can fix a bed for me in a room near yours. I'll feel better until we can get those new locks installed."

I was grateful—not only because he would stay, but because he'd begun to believe me.

When they'd gone, I asked Birdy about temporary keys for my two doors, and for the room across the hall. She searched a drawer and found some that were tagged for the rooms in question.

"A lot of these doors have interchangeable keys," she warned. "So locking them tonight won't mean much."

"Anyway, let's see if they work," I said.

She came upstairs with me and we found that one of the keys worked perfectly for both doors of the Azalea Suite, and another slipped noisily into the lock of the room across the hall. Under Birdy's eyes I checked my cartons and found the sealing tape undisturbed.

Before I went into my room I asked her to wait a moment while I looked around. For once she refrained from sniffing, and she waited while I looked through both rooms and went out on the balcony.

"Is everything all right, madam?" she asked when I'd finished my quick search.

"Just one more thing." I turned on the tape recorder. It ran softly, and no husky voice spoke to me from the machine. My guitar was still in its case, and nothing in either room appeared to have been touched.

"Thank you for a wonderful dinner, Birdy," I said.

She nodded stiffly and went away.

I began to get ready for bed, and when Alan returned he tapped on my door. "Everything okay, Hollis?"

"Everything's fine. And, Alan—I really enjoyed the dinner. I'm glad you invited Elizabeth Cameron."

"I enjoyed it too," he said. "If you need me, I'll be right down the hall. After a while I may go out for a walk, but I won't be gone long, and I'll stay on this side of the house."

Tonight I would be able to sleep without anxiety, and that was what I wanted more than anything else at the moment. I was weary enough to go to bed right away. Oblivion meant not thinking of Ricky. Not feeling pain. Not trying to cope with all that was disturbing me at present. I didn't want to remember anything.

A wisp of tune ran through my mind. The same notes I'd thought of back at the apartment this afternoon, and as I hummed them softly to myself, a possible title and theme came to life in my mind: "I Don't Want to Remember." Ricky'd always told me to look for the common denominator in my songs. Something that would speak to people out there. There had been "remembering" songs before, but this would be different.

I hummed the snatch of melody to the tape in order to preserve it, and played it back. It wasn't right yet, but perhaps something was surfacing in me and this was a beginning.

9

I woke to the gentle sound of rain against the windows, and when I got up to look out I found the day gray and misty again, with woods hemming in the horizon, and no harbor visible.

Strangely, I felt almost cheerful—or at least hopeful. A song coming to life could do that for me. This morning I would stay inside and start working through Ricky's papers. Rain that would keep me indoors might also keep intruders out, and that was a reassuring thought.

The phone calls to Bea Wahl and the way my apartment had been searched nagged me still, but answers to both the invasions in New York and here might lie in Ricky's papers, and I must find them.

Early morning courage always helped and I had a feeling that today I would be able to cope.

When I'd put on slacks and a pullover, I unlocked one of my doors, closing it behind me and pocketing the key. On the hall carpet lay an envelope with my name on it—a note from Alan.

> Hollis, I'm leaving early—behind in my work. Here's my phone number at the greenhouse. If you need anything, call me.
>
> Alan

The words reassured me. Alan might seem remote at times, and preoccupied with his own problems, whatever they were, but he possessed a quiet strength that could be leaned upon. He was *there*. Unlike Ricky, who had so seldom been around when I needed him. But I mustn't think about that. Like the wisp of song that kept running through my head—I mustn't remember.

When I went downstairs I found Birdy washing dishes at the sink. I fixed my breakfast, and ate it at the kitchen table while I planned my morning. First, I'd face the unhappy task of working on Ricky's papers. Yet all the while I knew that, whatever I did, the comforting knowledge of a tune stirring in me would be there—getting ready to become a song.

Often it was like that, with music and words fluttering under the surface, starting to grow like a green plant. When I had done the dutiful thing with those papers, I would go down to the music room and discover if something was ready to come to life on Geneva's beautiful piano.

For a time my morning went as I'd planned. The first carton seemed to be mainly bills and receipts—records that had been kept for old tax purposes. More recent records were probably stored in a safe. Sometimes Norris had sent over a girl from his own office to run through papers for Ricky and sort and label, since he never wanted to bother with a full-time secretary. Now I needed only to take the packets out, read the labels, and put them back. All they gave me was a glimpse of Ricky's tremendous expenses and overhead.

The next carton was mostly old business letters. Some of the dates went back to long before Ricky and I were married, and could probably be thrown away. Norris had been right about knowing much more than I did about such matters, and I needn't have been so edgy with him. My real indignation had grown from his taking over without consulting me, and even that was natural for him, since no one had ever consulted me about anything before. I was supposed to turn out hit songs, and otherwise keep out of Ricky's affairs. Now, late as it was, I had to discover what was still happening to Ricky's songs. A lot of them were my songs too.

I went on reading, carefully here, skimming there, resealing each carton as I finished it and marking the tape with a black "O.K."

Another carton held fan letters, though I hadn't brought all of those from New York. They came in by the bushel, and I'd read them eagerly when we were first married. Mostly they were thrown away, though I'd answered some of them for Ricky myself when he wouldn't bother.

Since this box of letters had been placed with his papers, it must contain special ones.

I ran through a few quickly, not reading every word. Some of them asked for autographed pictures, while others wanted only to praise. A few—and these were the ones that mattered most—told of how much Ricky's songs had helped someone to get through bad times, or perhaps think seriously about the world we all lived in. There were a great many letters from young girls. *I am fifteen and I love your songs. I love you.* Often sad, lonely, ill-expressed letters. One that I picked up was signed merely "Tim."

> I will always remember the time when I met you, Ricky Sands. Nothing mattered much in my life until that day. When you wrote to me afterwards and said you'd help me, everything changed. I want to be a singer like you someday. I want to make up songs that will touch people and make them think.

Well, good for Ricky, I thought. Though this letter was pitiful, too, since the chances against the writer's succeeding were so enormous. Just the same, everyone ought to try for that gold ring on the carrousel. Or the gold record. The chances had been enormous against me too. Perhaps, without Ricky, they still were. I left "Tim's" letter on top of the pile I was running through, and picked up the next one.

I had closed the hall door when I came in, and had opened windows in this unoccupied room. Soft, steady rain sounds were soothing, and made an accompaniment while I worked. When someone rapped on the door I was startled out of my concentration.

"Who is it?" I called.

"It's Pete Evans, Mrs. Baker."

I opened the door and he grinned at me, holding up a brown paper bag. "Good morning. Alan sent me to a hardware store for new locks, and I've brought them back. If you'll open your doors I'll get to work installing these."

I did as he asked, and returned to the cartons, leaving the door open so I could keep him in view. As I'd noticed before, he moved in a leisurely, unhurried way, as though time meant little to him, and nothing in his life was urgent.

After a while I asked him a question. "Pete, since you've been working here, have you seen anyone on the grounds who doesn't belong?"

He was on his knees before my sitting-room door, and he looked around. "I don't think so, Mrs. Baker. But then—I don't know much about who belongs and who doesn't."

There was always something about Pete Evans that made me wary. He seemed to watch me, to study everything I did, and my very uneasiness about this made me want to bait him.

"We had a lovely dinner last night," I said. "You should have been there."

"Mr. Gordon doesn't invite the hired help to dinner."

"You grew up with him, didn't you? You called him Alan a little while ago. And he probably would have invited you, except that your sister said you wouldn't come."

"She's right." He went on with his task, the sound of the drill cutting off further talk.

Some of the business letters I examined—a lot of them written *for* Ricky, not *by* him—brought more of his past life to light. All those concerts he'd played here and abroad. Events that had happened while I was still in high school. I'd tried to steel myself against emotion, tried to hold on to the cheerful mood with which I'd awakened, but these letters brought Ricky vividly to life in a time when he'd been only a distant idol to me. How strange and unreal it seemed now—that for a little while I had been an intimate part of Ricky Sands's life. I'd wanted to share that life, wanted to be a real wife and bear his children. It hadn't worked out that way, and now our children would never be born.

Norris was right again. Going through these papers was more painful than I'd expected.

The next box I turned to was smaller, and when I pulled off the paper tape I found the flaps already glued down. Someone had sealed it earlier. I crossed the hall and borrowed a tool from Pete, so I could pry the cardboard open. The box contained a pile of loose clippings, and all the dates were old. Ricky's young face looked out of newspaper print and stabbed at my heart. I wished I could have known him then.

When Pete came to retrieve his screwdriver he found me dissolved in tears again. He always seemed to find me weeping.

"Go ahead and cry," he said, glancing at the news photo in my hands. "I wish I could cry."

I pulled a tissue from my pocket and dabbed at my eyes. "Who would you cry for?"

He regarded me thoughtfully for a moment before he answered. "I suppose you might as well know. Someone's likely to tell you anyway. I'd cry for a young girl. A girl in this town who died a few years ago. She killed herself and I feel that a lot of the blame was mine. She was a kid in one of my English classes—a promising young writer. But I didn't have the wisdom to see what was happening to her, or I might have helped. Maybe I could have turned her around. I just wasn't a good enough teacher."

Pete's words were stark, without emotion or self-pity. They asked for no sympathy.

"So that's why you felt you had to run away?" I said.

"You could call it that. Anyway, I quit before I could do any more damage."

I wanted to ask how he'd occupied himself in the years since, and why he'd come back now. But I remembered Liz saying that she didn't dare ask him questions. I didn't dare either. He was a strange man, and for all his easygoing manner he could sometimes be forbidding. I could sense the self-blame he put on himself. I, too, knew about self-blame and about regretting actions that might have been taken and weren't.

Pete went back to his work on the locks, and I found myself wondering how he'd dealt with *his* despair. I went to stand in the doorway and watch him.

"Do you ever feel angry with the girl who died?"

He still didn't look at me. "Sure. I used to, more than I do now. Angry with her for what she did—all that foolish waste. And with me for what I didn't do. I guess that's a normal reaction when death tears up our lives."

I supposed that was true. I only knew there were times when it helped me to be angry.

I still held the news clipping in my hands, and Pete looked at it. "Your husband was Ricky Sands, wasn't he?"

I should have hidden the clipping, but it was too late. "Yes. I've had to run away too—from the siege in New York. That's why I came here when Mrs. Ames invited me. I'm Hollis Sands."

He nodded gravely.

It would have been better if he hadn't found out, but I couldn't help that now. I returned to my search, reminding myself that I wasn't

merely checking these papers Ricky had left behind but was also looking for some dark motivation that lay at the core of his life and his
death.

Now I began to read every clipping carefully, though nothing seemed
to illumine the darkness. Someone had ransacked our New York apartment looking for who knew what. So I must look too, and try to recognize answers when I found them.

Pete finished installing the shiny new locks on all three doors, and
came to give me the keys.

"Try them, please, Mrs.—Sands," he said. "Just to make sure they
work for you."

Each key turned easily, and when I thanked him, he stood for a
moment regarding me in that strange, rather provoking way. I couldn't
read his expression, but his look seemed wary again, as though, somehow, he might not trust me.

I spoke impulsively. "Why do you always look at me like that?"

"Maybe I just wonder about people. Wonder what makes them tick."

"Did you know who I was before you saw that clipping just now?"

He merely grinned and went away, carrying his tools. A disturbing
man. I was glad to be alone again. Glad to work behind a locked door
that no one but me could open.

At the bottom of this smaller carton that had been so carefully sealed,
I found a manila envelope with a few letters and one more clipping.
These were items dated more recently, and they'd been tucked beneath
everything else, as though to hide them from casual view.

The clipping was the *Times* obituary of Coral Caine's death. The
letters were from her. Words sprang out at me from the one on top:
Thank you for my special roses, darling.

I felt physically ill—sick with grief as I fumbled the letters back into
their envelopes. I couldn't stand any more. Emotion had been piling up
inside me since I'd opened the first carton, and reading Coral's words
had brought me to my breaking point.

To stop the rising wave of nausea, I stood up, breathing deeply. Overhead something thudded heavily. For a moment I stood listening to a
soft, shuffling sound, as though something was being dragged across the
floor above me. Probably Birdy was up there on one of her housekeep-
ing tours. But what if it wasn't Birdy? What if my tormenting intruder
was up there, shut into the house with me on this rainy day? At least
this was something to pull me away from pain I could no longer handle.

I locked the door of the carton room with a new key, and then ran down the hall to the back stairs I'd discovered earlier—stairs that led to the floor under the eaves. If I stopped to find Birdy, whoever it was would be gone by the time we got there. At this instant my intruder—if that's who it was—might be trapped. I would move carefully, but I would investigate. I would *not* think about roses. I wouldn't think about pain I could no longer handle.

I could move fast if I needed to, and I also had the advantage of surprise. He wouldn't be ready for me. I crept up the stairs softly, stepping lightly, so the old wood hardly creaked.

At the head of the narrow flight, an uncarpeted hall ran toward the top of the "T" that formed the house, with closed doors lining either side of the stretch of corridor. No one was in view. The sound I'd heard had seemed to be moving along the front of the house. Only a little dusky light from a window at the end of the hall guided my way as I moved softly past closed doors.

At the place where the crossbar of the "T" met this hallway I could turn in either direction. Most of this enormous front area had been left open for a cluttered storage space, and the roof slanted steeply down overhead, interrupted by places where the chimneys cut through. At the far end of either wing were two closed doors. These, I supposed, were rooms in the end towers I'd glimpsed from the ground.

As I hesitated, not sure what to do next, a whispery sound made the hairs rise on the back of my neck. Someone beyond the far door on my left had struck chords on a guitar. I knew that if he started to play "Sweet Rain" I would run. I would fly downstairs and lock myself in my room. To hear that song now, in these distant reaches of the house, would be too ghostly, and I couldn't bear it.

Then the rather hoarse singing I'd heard before began softly—so softly that I couldn't make out the words, but the tune was one I didn't know. In this remote attic area, with windows closed against the rain, the singer probably thought himself safe from being heard below. But I had heard him dragging something in the hall above me.

Surprise was still on my side. Someone playing a guitar alone was probably sitting down, and would be hampered by his instrument. He couldn't move as fast as I could.

Feeling my way past obstacles of furniture and trunks in the dim light, I crept toward the sound. When I could touch the closed door to the tower, I stopped, and so did the music. There were soft sounds beyond the door, but I couldn't identify them. I must move fast now. I would fling the door open, look quickly inside, so I would have a clear view of the room's occupant. Daylight showed at the strip of sill, so it wouldn't be dark in there. But *I* would be in the dark, and I'd have that extra advantage. Once I had seen, I would run for the stairs. I'd go down them shouting for help, and I didn't think I'd be followed. So far, the intruder had chosen to be elusive, hiding himself. This was my chance to see who was in the room.

I drew a deep breath. The cracked china doorknob felt slippery in my fingers and I knew I was sweating. I turned it softly and pushed. Narrow steps wound upward into the tower room, so I could still see nothing from here, though there was a flooding of light from windows above, and I no longer had the advantage of darkness. Clinging to the rail, I circled upward until I could peer into the room at eye level.

There was no one there.

Gray daylight pressed against the windows all around the tower, showing me a big room with a peaked roof. There were no corners in which to hide. A narrow cot, set at an angle from a window that overlooked the roof, had been made up as a bed, and a guitar lay upon the blanket. The indentation of a head marked the pillow, and someone had been sitting on the side, for the covers were wrinkled.

Before one window stood an easel with a faded watercolor upon it, and on a nearby table a dusty paint box stood open, its colors crumbling and dry. Unused brushes stood in a glass from which water had long evaporated, and cobwebs trailed across everything. None of these things had been touched for years, it seemed. The room's present occupant played a guitar and didn't bother to dust!

A familiar smell seemed to permeate the air, as though something had been burned in here, though it was being dispelled by a breeze from an open window where spatters of rain slanted in. A sound like wind bells reached me, and when I crossed the room I found a rack with empty hangers tinkling together, sounding the chimes I'd heard.

From this window I could look out across the steep pitch of roof where rain cascaded down to the gutters at the edge. Four wet chimneys cut into the sky between this tower and the one at the far end of the roof. There, too, a window stood open, and I had my answer.

I must not have moved as silently as I'd thought, and whoever had been here had escaped across slippery slates to the opposite tower. I shivered to think of anyone crossing that rainslick roof, but he must have done so safely and escaped through the opposite window. It would do no good now to rush downstairs and call for Birdy. She would either not believe me, or pretend not to. In any case, my quarry was gone. More and more I was sure that Birdy knew very well who was hiding in this house. When I closed the window it moved without a sound on tracks recently waxed.

As I started to leave the tower, my attention was caught by a portrait hung on the wall space between two windows. It was an oil painting of a little girl with a laughing face. Though not expertly done, the artist had caught the child's spirit, her joy, so that the picture became arresting. I wondered why it had been left up here—hidden away.

It was cold in this tower, with no heat and the gray rain outside. Even Windtop's halls were warmer, and I hurried to the door, noting a big plastic bag that had been dumped there. It was filled with foodstuff in cans and packages, and was probably what I'd heard being dragged over my head earlier.

I pulled the door shut behind me and went down the circling stairs to the main part of the attic. When I reached the leg of the "T" I began to look into one room after another on this attic floor. The rooms were small and crudely furnished. This must have been where the servants lived at Windtop in the old days, when big houses were run with large staffs. Such plain little rooms they were. A single small bathroom served them all, and was probably considered a luxury. Each room had been supplied with a washstand, and most of the old-fashioned basins and pitchers were still here, dusty now, and often cracked. The bare beds were narrow and made of iron, and none of the chairs looked comfortable—probably cast-offs from the house below. I was sure that anyone Geneva Ames had employed would have been given better quarters than these, but this was the way servants had been housed early in the century.

To me, it seemed a place of ghosts. Young girls who'd worked here as house or scullery maids had lived in these rooms with their private dreams and sorrows. All gone a long time ago. These were gentle ghosts. Not like the man who played a guitar and threatened me with a whispered voice on tape. Sooner or later I must come face-to-face with him, and the thought of what might happen was hardly pleasant. If a confrontation occurred when I was unprepared and had no plan, nowhere to flee—what then?

I'd had entirely enough of this haunted attic floor, and I hurried down the back stairs and found my way to the kitchen. Birdy sat eating hot soup and crackers at one end of the table, and she looked up at me as I came in. If she was expecting more complaints about a mysterious presence, I said nothing immediately. I wanted no more of her pretense of disbelief. She knew, and I knew. What I wondered was how much Alan Gordon knew, and whether some conspiracy was in progress against me.

She offered me soup from a pot on the stove, and I thanked her and sat down at the far end of the table.

"I did some exploring this morning," I volunteered. "I expect it will take me weeks to cover the whole house. It's all right, isn't it? You don't mind?"

"Why should I mind?"

"This time I went up the back stairs and I found what must have been the former servants' quarters under the eaves."

She seemed to stiffen, but she said nothing.

"There's a tower room at the front of the house that looks as though it was used as a studio at one time—there's an easel and old watercolor paints. Who was the painter who lived in this house?"

Birdy took another spoonful of soup, not looking at me. "Mrs. Ames's small daughter fixed that room up for herself. She liked being up above the treetops. After she died, Mrs. Ames left the room as it was. She used to go up there sometimes just to remember her little daughter. But not anymore."

"I'm sorry," I said. "I'd wondered whether she had any children."

"She had only one daughter—Mary. That's her picture on the wall up there."

"It's a charming portrait. It almost bubbles with laughter. Do you know who painted it?"

"Of course I know. It was Luther Sykes."

I could only stare. *"Luther?"*

"Why not? As a young man he was a very good artist. Not quite professional, maybe, but good enough. Of course he doesn't paint anymore. Not since his right hand was damaged."

I revised my mental picture of a surly little man who seemed more suited to work with a spade than with delicate brushes. However, it was the child he'd painted who interested me more right now.

"You knew Mary Ames, of course?" I asked.

"I was here when she was born. I knew her all of her life. It was

Luther who taught her to paint a little. Things were different with him then. There's a better portrait of her in the downstairs sitting room." Birdy hesitated and seemed to swallow old pain. When she spoke again it was almost defiantly. "Mary died many years ago, and her death changed all our lives."

Until this moment I'd seen Birdy as an adversary—a woman who guarded Windtop and resented the intrusion of an outsider with unreasonable prejudice. Now I could glimpse her, as well as Luther, in another light. Windtop had taken her whole life, and she had given it gladly. The house and its occupants had been her life. I felt touched by this and moved by her dedication. Nevertheless, she was involved in something more now—something that affected me so strongly that I couldn't let it go.

I spoke to her quietly. "I'll have to meet him sometime, you know— whoever it is you've allowed to stay in the house."

Dark blood rushed into her cheeks, and the white crest of her hair seemed to stiffen. "I don't know what you're talking about."

"Does Mrs. Ames know?" I asked. "Does Mr. Gordon know?"

This time she gave way to agitation. She jumped up to carry her dishes to the sink, where she began to wash them furiously.

In the face of her open distress I had to push my advantage. "In a way, we're stalking each other, aren't we—your guest and I? Each time we just manage not to meet. But it must happen soon. Do I need to be afraid, Birdy? Or perhaps he's the one who's afraid of me? He must have taken a nasty scramble across the roof this morning to get away from me."

She left the dishes and stalked from the room with her head held high, and there was anger in every inch of her carriage. Anger and perhaps anxiety too.

I walked out of the kitchen and found my way again to the butter-yellow sitting room, where Alan and Liz Cameron and I had talked together last night. The portrait of a girl about twelve hung on the wall behind the place where I'd sat—which was why I hadn't noticed it. This was the same young face I'd seen upstairs, though she was a few years older in this picture. A lovely child in a yellow dress, with a yellow bow in her clouds of dark hair—as though the artist had painted her to match this room.

I remembered that Alan's boat had borne the name *Mary* on its prow.

Perhaps he had grown up with Mary Ames and remembered his old playmate.

This more professional portrait had been done with greater skill than the one upstairs, yet there had been more indication of an entrancing and mischievous character in the cruder painting in the attic. Luther's portrait had been painted with greater sensitivity to character.

So much death, so much sorrow! This long-ago loss brought my own closer. If I could just remember the happy times with Ricky and let the rest go! Old letters from Coral Caine had nothing to do with me. But those deep pink roses *had* been from Ricky.

In the music room the piano still waited for me, shadowy and dark on this rainy afternoon. I didn't go to it at once, however, when I entered the room. A french door stood open on the terrace and when I went to close it I stayed for a moment looking out at the wet garden. There was no one there, and I wondered if Pete Evans had gone home, or if he worked at other odd jobs around the house. Had he come across the intruder? And if he had, would he tell me?

Rain splashed softly on the bricks outside. This was no pounding storm but a steady autumn rain that could soak golden leaves in the gutters and seep moisture into the ground against the coming of winter. Wherever a crease in the earth offered a channel, water ran away in rivulets, turning any bare space into mud.

Remember one of the happy times, I told myself, and closed my eyes deliberately. A scene from the past began to drift through me, hazily at first, like smoke. A strange memory to come out of the past, and not altogether happy. I gave myself to it and went back to when it had happened.

One night late I'd gone to a Manhattan nightclub to hear Ricky sing —something he'd never wanted me to do. I went because everything had seemed to be going wrong for him lately. The record business was in a bad way and money was tight. To have a hit, a singer really had to be at the top. Ricky's bookings had been slipping too, so this place wasn't one of his better gigs. I wanted to see for myself what was happening. Then perhaps I'd know how I could help him.

I went alone in a cab, and told them at the door who I was. I said I didn't want Ricky to know I was there, but would just wait somewhere backstage where I could watch his performance and not be noticed. I was humored and taken into cramped quarters at one side of a small stage. A stool was found for me and I sat in a dark corner out of the way, where I could see the stage.

As it happened, I was safe enough, since he wouldn't have recognized me even if he'd looked my way. He brushed past so close that I could sense his tension, almost smell his terror. He'd told me that it was always like this before he went on, and he could shake with fright before a performance. His stomach would turn over and if he hadn't taken something to lessen the terror and quiet his nerves, he might never be able to perform. An assistant was with him, mopping at his wet forehead with a handkerchief, whispering encouragement.

When the band began to play the vamp of a song I had written, I began to sweat too, and I clasped my hands together, not only in fear for Ricky, but for me as well. What if they hated him because of my song? What did I know about writing songs for those indifferent people at the crowded tables out there? Ricky wasn't even the headliner, and this was a far cry from the huge auditorium where I'd watched him once in the past.

Nevertheless, seeing him now, I caught the very moment when the adrenaline began to work, and saw his shoulders straighten, his head come up in that gallant way that used to set an audience screaming. These people didn't scream. Those I could see near the front hardly looked up when he came on, and there'd been only a smattering of applause. How quickly idols could die.

Then Ricky began to sing, and a sudden hush came over the room—a listening quiet, as the strange magic he could project took over. I left my stool and crept to where I could watch him better, and glimpse the audience beyond him. The nearer faces looked rapt, hypnotized. His band was backing him up softly, supporting, but never overpowering. Even the drums could whisper when he sang "Sweet Rain." Ricky had something that only a few greats possessed in any field. And what he had he was throwing away.

Before it ended, I returned to my stool and I saw him when he came off, saw how high he was, how gloriously excited. He had conquered the odds once more and won the room. He was up there on the mountaintops, and he wouldn't be able to come down for hours. No drug could ever give him such elation as he felt after a successful performance. They could only destroy it, if only he would realize that fact. Now he'd probably go out on the town with members of his usual entourage, have something to eat, and unwind for a while. If he came straight back to the apartment he wouldn't be able to sleep, and I could understand why. I could understand everything a little better. I stole away and asked the doorman to get me a cab. On the way home I thought about what I'd seen.

This experience, this love affair with any audience, was what Ricky Sands lived for. All his energy was given to *this,* and he had nothing left for anyone else in his life. Everything that touched him, everything that he touched, must be bent to this single driving force. No wonder he was so afraid of growing old, when audiences might not want him anymore. Yet even when he was slipping, he was better than anyone else!

At home I went straight to bed and lay awake for a long time, desperately needing a man whom I'd probably never had and never would. An imaginary man who existed only on a stage.

Of course I never let Ricky know what I had done.

Raindrops danced on Windtop's red-brick terrace, and rippled the surface on the pool where the marble maiden now poured real water from her tilted urn.

The scene I'd just lived through again had seemed so real, so vivid in its detail, that it was hard to return to a present where there was no Ricky Sands. Yet now, looking out at the rain, something strange began to happen. In spite of what memory had brought me out of the past, suddenly I couldn't recall exactly how he'd looked. I couldn't see his face. This was frightening—and yet, wasn't it better to forget and wipe everything out of my mind, never try to bring it back, but just let it all flow away from me like the rivulets of water out there running toward the harbor?

Words began to whisper in my mind, and the piano drew me. That snatch of tune that had come to me earlier was clearer now, and growing. A feeling of excitement that I hadn't experienced in a long while began to rise. In my head I could hear the notes, listen to the words. I could forget everything but the song that must be born. Sometimes this was a high moment for me—while it was all still in my mind and I'd committed nothing to the piano or to paper. The sounds and the vision always had a shining quality that I would never find again. Reality couldn't equal the lovely vision that sang in my head. Yet always I had to try to capture it.

I raised the piano lid and sat down on the bench, put my hands on the keys, and let the feeling of a song flow out through my fingers. Softly at first, hesitantly, then gathering strength as the tune affirmed itself and became real.

10

My fingers seemed to find the notes of their own accord. It was always best to let the music lead the way, and for me to follow wherever it took me. The melody was emerging quickly now, and words came alive in my mind, fitting lyric to music.

Whatever came through as strongly as this would stay with me, and as soon as I'd carried this as far as it wanted to go, I'd get my tape recorder and set it down. This was a *piano* song, so I would record it here. Writing notes and words on paper could come later.

Softly I sang the words as I played:

> "I've forgotten your face
> In the rains of November.
> I've forgotten your voice—
> I don't want to remember . . .
>   I must not remember."

Yes, this would ring true. The emotion was right. It was what I wanted to convey. Others would respond to a song of longing denied.

I played the tune over and it grew under my fingers. There would be more, of course. As Ricky always said, "Half a song is no good!" There must be a bridge to connect verse and chorus—something to offer a rest, a change. Then the verse itself—sometimes harder to do than a catchy chorus. Perhaps more about memories denied. At least the main hook that every song should have to pull listeners back and send them away humming was here: *I don't want to remember—I must not remember.* A song that touched on life with real feeling could help for a little while. Words were potent healers, and when they were combined with music, they became powerful, memorable.

I'd found that the very sound of the words was important. Many a good tune had failed until new words gave it a second life. With me, the voice of the singer was paramount. Whether I liked it or not, I was still writing for Ricky. I had no one else. A song must be sung before it really existed.

Suddenly I was drained, exhausted. Using my creative faculties to the hilt could do that, so that I felt used up both mentally and physically. But this was a good tiredness, with accomplishment behind it, and it was something I hadn't experienced in months. Not since long before Ricky had died.

I closed the Bechstein and went upstairs. Now I must give this time to grow. I was still rusty, but at least I would bring down my recorder and catch what I had, so I wouldn't lose a note of it.

It was a relief to know that this time no one would have come into my room while I was out, and I slipped the new key into its lock with confidence. A confidence that evaporated the moment I stepped into the sitting room and smelled the odor of burned wood.

The door to the balcony stood open, and I knew my intruder had come over the roof again. For a moment I was too frightened to move—yet I had to see who it was. I crept to the bedroom door and peered around the edge. He was there, sitting on my bed, though all I could see were outstretched legs in jeans, and my tape recorder on his knees. He must have sensed my presence, for he leaned into my view.

I saw his eyes and froze. We stared at each other for a tense moment. He moved first, jumping toward me, and for an instant I thought he would strike me. Instead he pushed me heavily, so that I fell back into a chair. Then he bolted through the open door to the hall and went pounding along the corridor, thudding down the back stairs. I'd had a swift impression of height and strength, and I'd caught the acrid odor of dead woodsmoke from his jacket.

I realized I was breathing as hard as though I'd been running. There was no need to hurry now. I knew where he would be, and, though I was frightened, I must find the courage to confront him. But not alone. When I reached the stairs I called for Birdy, only to find her waiting for me in the lower hall, looking as shaken as I felt.

"Did you see him?" I cried. "How dangerous is he?"

She didn't answer, and I went past her to double doors that had once led into the other wing of the house. When I pulled them open upon the drop-off into ruin, the stench of wet, scorched wood rose sickeningly in my face. It was a smell that could last forever. In the corner that had been partially cleared, and which offered a little shelter, a foam-rubber mattress and sleeping bag had been placed. He lay curled on top of these, with his knees drawn to his chin. It was as though by his very position he could protect himself from the world. He seemed much younger than I'd thought—probably no more than sixteen.

Birdy came to stand beside me looking down. "He's insisted on sleeping out there ever since you came. Punishing us all, I suppose. Until a few days ago, he was using that studio room of Mary's upstairs. Today he packed everything up and was going to bring it down here, when you nearly caught him. You might have killed him, chasing him off across the roof!"

That was hardly my fault, but I could see how upset she was.

"Who is he?" I asked.

She raised her hands in helpless surrender. "He's Timothy Gordon. He's Mr. Gordon's younger brother. The police are looking for him now."

"What's he done?"

"Nothing—so far—except run away."

That wasn't entirely true, considering the way he'd been tormenting me.

She sensed my resistance to her defense. "Why shouldn't he come here when he had nowhere else to go? He's lived here since he was practically a baby."

This was the problem Alan had been facing—a runaway younger brother.

I was feeling less alarmed, but still wary. "You might as well come out of there," I told him. "We need to talk things over. You owe me that, at least, don't you think?"

His answer was to burrow his head more deeply into his arms.

"Mrs. Baker is right." Birdy was on my side for once. "You needn't hide anymore, Timmy. It's damp and cold out there, so come in and get yourself a hot bath. I've washed some jeans and a shirt for you, and you can stop hiding now."

This time he sat up. "Don't call me Timmy!"

"I'm sorry, Tim," she said. She knelt at the blackened edge of the floor and held out a hand, speaking more gently. "Come now, it's going to be all right."

I could hear the affection in her voice. If Alan had been like a son to Geneva Ames, this younger boy was someone Birdy must have taken to her own heart long ago.

He got up, reluctantly, and clambered to our level—tall and thin, with tousled brown hair, not as dark as his brother's, but with a far darker expression in his eyes.

"Are you going to tell Alan?" The direct question was hurled at me, and I sensed how quickly violence could rise in him again.

"I don't know," I said. "It's probably necessary. But I'd like to hear your side first."

He was much taller than I was, and though thin, I realized in him a strength that could be threatening. I backed away from his glowering look.

"You're not Mrs. Baker," he accused. "I know who you are."

"It seems that practically everyone knows who I am." I glanced at Birdy, who paid no attention, fussing over Tim, pulling off his wet jacket.

At her urging the boy went upstairs and she bustled after him, carrying clean clothes and a bar of soap. When he'd been shut into a bathroom she came down and joined me at the kitchen table, where I'd poured myself a cup of coffee. Reaction and shock had left me chilled too.

"Perhaps it will help if you'd tell me what this is all about," I said.

"It's simple enough. There was a big blowup with his brother, and Timmy came running here. He always knew he could count on me. He says he won't go back to school and he never wants to see his brother again."

"How does he know who I am? And why should he care?"

"He recognized you right away. I guess he's seen pictures—and he feels connected. He's crazy about that awful music." Her voice broke. "Ricky Sands was his big idol, and Tim thinks *he* wants to be a singer."

Tim? I remembered the note to Ricky that I'd read only this morning, which had been signed "Tim."

Birdy was running on:

"Mr. Gordon and I did all we could to stop the foolish turn he was taking, but we couldn't change anything. When Tim came to me a week ago, I had to take him in. Maybe Mr. Gordon knows what's best, but I'm not sure he can be fair to his brother. In fact, I don't know anymore what fair is for Timmy. Do you know, Mrs. Baker? You belong to that world out there that he wants to be part of. Of course he's too young, but he won't accept that."

I'd had a longing and a determination as strong as Tim's myself, and I couldn't say even now whether it had been a good or a bad road to take. How could one ever know, since there was no telling whether other roads would have been better or worse.

"I don't know how to answer that," I said. "Why does he dislike *me* so much? Why has he been trying to frighten and torment me?"

Birdy shook her head, unhappy. "I don't know that, Mrs. Baker."

"You might as well stop calling me Mrs. Baker," I said. "Everyone seems to know I'm Hollis Sands."

We sat at the kitchen table and waited, listening to the rain. When Tim came downstairs he was fresh and clean in jeans and a blue shirt, and his thick brown hair stood on end, curly and wet from the shower. The look he gave me was still defiant. The line of his chin was younger and softer than his brother's, but his will seemed as strong, and the sense of darkness that lay upon him might have been copied from Alan Gordon, and was troubling to see in so young a boy.

"What are you going to do about Alan?" he demanded of us both.

Birdy got up to pour a glass of milk that she set before him with a plate of cookies. "Drink that, and eat something. You've been starving yourself."

"I asked a question," he repeated stubbornly. But he sat down and drank half the glass of milk without stopping for breath.

"First I need to know a lot of other things," I said quietly. "For instance—what do you have against *me?*"

His look was too old for his young face, and filled with a wildness that was unsettling. "I really scared you, didn't I?"

"I don't know why you should want to."

He finished the milk as any thirsty youngster would, and stared at me again. "Because of Ricky. I wanted to pay you off for Ricky."

Birdy snorted impatiently. "Why you should fasten on someone like *that* for your idol, I can't imagine! He couldn't have been much, from what I've heard."

"You don't know *anything!*" he told her, but the underlying threat was still for me.

"Did you know Ricky Sands?" I asked.

"Of course I knew him! I coaxed Aunt Geneva to get him out here with his band one time when I was just a kid. I told her she ought to give other kinds of music a chance. She thought pop music was fun sometimes, but too loud. Anyway, she invited him, and he came. I *talked* to him, and he was super. He thought I was kind of young to be a singer, but he said when my voice settled down I could come to see him in New York, if I wanted. I could even come to the studio before that and watch him record. So I did when I was a little older."

His tone softened as he remembered, and suddenly there were angry tears in his eyes. "He said maybe I really could be a singer. And he liked one of the songs I took him—one I wrote myself. Of course I never told Alan when I went in. Ricky said when I was ready maybe he could help me. And he would have. He really would! If it hadn't been for *you.*"

I listened sadly, helplessly, seeing myself in Tim. He was as innocent as I had been, and he would need to be a lot stronger than he probably was to withstand what could happen to him in the pop music field. Either there'd be a lot of hurt for him—perhaps a broken heart because of failure, so that he'd turn into a permanent hanger-on, or else there could be the seduction of success. That was much more unlikely, but sometimes more fatal. I already knew that I could sway him from neither course. His last words, however, had carried a startling ring of hatred.

"Why should you blame *me?*" I asked him again.

"Because of what Ricky said that one time I saw him in New York. He took me out for dinner after the recording session, and we talked. He said I ought to finish high school anyway. And then if I really meant it, I had to be willing to work up from the bottom and not let anything stand in the way. Even if I only got odd jobs in a recording studio somewhere, to start with—until I made some friends and got someone to listen to me. Of course, if he was around, he would listen right away, and he'd tell me the truth. If I had something, maybe he could help me to learn. Only he's not around to listen now. He told me another thing too. He said, 'Never get too close to any woman because they're sure to do you in. They can take too much, take you off the main road of your life. There's a woman who's doing that to me right now.' It sounded like he was talking to himself. Like he was high on speed or something. But what he said made sense."

"I think I know about the woman he meant," I said gently. "I don't think it was me." I hoped it hadn't been me.

"Of course you'd say that. If you'd been any kind of wife, you'd have known what was bothering him. You wouldn't have let him kill himself. Why should *you* be here—and Ricky Sands gone?"

"Sometimes I've asked myself that," I said. "In a lot of ways, Tim, we probably felt the same about him." There could be more truth in the words he'd spoken than I could bear.

"Or," he said, "maybe Ricky was right—the choice he made. Maybe nothing's worth it. Maybe it's better to jump off a roof or something."

"Don't talk like that!" Birdy cried.

I tried to speak quietly. "I suppose we all feel like that sometimes. When I do, I tell myself to wait—just to wait a little while. Because things change."

"Then why didn't Ricky wait?"

"That's one of the things I'd like to find out," I said. "Maybe you can help me."

He began on the sandwich Birdy had brought him, and he chewed silently, not answering me.

"We'll have to tell your brother," I went on. "He's awfully worried about you."

Birdy moved nervously between table and sink. "Yes, that has to be done. Mr. Gordon is working at the greenhouse today. I can give you his telephone number, Mrs.—uh—Sands. I don't want to talk to him first myself. He's going to be furious with me, but I *had* to help Timmy."

The boy reached out and patted her hand, forgiving her the diminutive of his name. "It's okay, Birdy. It wasn't your fault. It's hers." The black look was there again, and he'd forgiven me nothing.

"I don't want to talk to him on the phone either," I said. "This is too important. If you'll tell me how to find the greenhouse, I'll go there now and tell him myself. Tim, promise us just one thing—you won't run away again until I've seen your brother? Maybe I can ease things for you a bit. I'm sure he'll want to come right over here to see you."

"I got no place to go," he said glumly, not trusting me.

When Birdy had provided me with directions, I pulled on a trench coat from the collection near the front door and ran through the rain to the garage. Pete Evans was inside doing a clean-up job. His hands were grimy, and he smelled of gasoline and grease.

"So you found out," he said, reading my face too easily.

I went to the Mercedes and opened the door. "Did you know about Tim all the time?"

"I began to catch on. I've talked to him once or twice."

"Why didn't you say something?"

"I thought about doing that," he said mildly. "Only I could never make up my mind whether I should."

"That boy might have hurt me. He still has an unreasonable grudge against me. I'm going to find Alan Gordon now and let him know where his brother is."

"I hope he'll take it easy. That kid's running on a pretty ragged edge. He scares me to pieces."

"Being scared isn't any way to help him, is it?" I said tartly, and turned the ignition key.

Pete answered before I touched the gas. "Maybe not. But it's a good way to make you think twice about anything you do that touches the boy. It pays to be scared."

I drove out of the garage without answering, more upset by his words than I wanted him to see. I was uncertain enough about my own decisions these days, so how could I know what was right for anyone else?

Back in town I followed the wet highway in the direction Birdy had given me until I came to a side road that led to a fenced-in area. A sign read SEA SPRAY INSTITUTE. I drove through the gate, parked beside other cars, and got out in the rain. The place had a country look about it, with autumn foliage lining a road that led past several modest buildings, among them a greenhouse.

Instead of the usual glass, wide strips of a heavy, transparent synthetic material ran from the center ridge to the ground, encasing the entire building. A door at the rear opened upon a small office, and I stepped through to find a gray-haired woman working at a typewriter. Beyond her desk were bookcases that overflowed with plant and gardening titles, and on the walls hung photographs that were mostly of strange-looking plants.

"Is Mr. Gordon here?" I asked.

The woman smiled at me pleasantly. "Right through there. You can go in, if you like."

I thanked her and went through a second door into a long stretch of building where plastic strips peaked overhead and ran down the sides, enclosing everything, yet letting in light that on a clear day would allow the full rays of the sun to enter. Wooden planks, damp in patches, marked a center aisle that extended the length of the building between board shelves that held racks of seedlings and small potted plants. At either end plants that were like small trees grew in their own soil. Down the center, a trough carried warm water, and numerous plastic water jugs, filled with darkened liquid to hold the heat, were lined up beneath the shelves. Solar-heated water would apparently help to keep the greenhouse warm all winter. Toward the far end several larger plants grew in pots, and Alan stood near them talking to two young people—a girl and a boy—with an enthusiasm and animation that I'd never seen in him before. Both were listening with rapt attention.

I spoke my "Hello" hesitantly, and he turned around. In corduroy pants and jacket, with a billed cap pulled over his eyes, he looked different. Even his manner toward me seemed changed. Perhaps he was too preoccupied to be surprised by my sudden appearance, for he greeted me casually, still intent on what he'd been discussing.

"Hello, Hollis. Have you ever seen Nicotiana growing?" He indicated a tall tobacco plant. "We're developing an improved variety to use in a safe organic spray for garden insects."

Until now I'd never really visualized Alan Gordon in his own work. Here in this greenhouse he was not the man I'd known during the last few days. He wasn't brooding and remote, nor was he silent and re- laxed, as he'd been when we'd gone sailing. Here he seemed to surge with vitality—alive and excited and clearly absorbed in what he was doing. When he reached down to touch the leaves of a tiny plant there was a tenderness in the gesture that told me how much he loved green and growing things.

I hated to call him back to a more somber present, yet when he looked at me I thought of Tim, and knew I must break my news to him quickly.

"May I talk with you, Alan?" I said. "Can you come outside for a moment?"

"Go on with what you're doing," he told the young people, and came with me to the outer office, explaining as we walked. "Agricultural students come to work with us from time to time. We run a training program with classes in the other buildings, you know, as well as in our main experiments here."

On another day I'd have wanted to hear it all, but now my news must come first.

We went outside, where the rain had stopped and there was a hint of sun breaking through.

"What's happened?" he asked. "Where's your car?"

"Near the gate."

"Okay, let's go over there and talk."

He hadn't left his work behind, however, and he waved toward a wet field of what looked like overgrown weeds. "Amaranth," he said. "We're trying to get a project going where people will grow it in their own backyards, and farmers will raise it for food. It makes a good flour, and it's a pretty plant with its purplish blooms. But the big thing is its protein value. Give it a chance, and amaranth can help feed the world. Over there we're developing Jerusalem artichokes for alcohol that could supplant gasoline in some cases."

For the first time he'd dropped the guard I'd always seen him wear, as his real interests came through. Now, however, there was the matter of Tim, and I must deal with it whether I liked it or not.

I gave Alan the place behind the wheel, and when I was beside him in the passenger seat, I made the plunge. "Your brother is at Windtop."

The familiar dark look came over his face like a curtain, and the easy friendliness he'd shown the two young people was gone. I could still sense his enormous vitality—something he hid most of the time.

"I'd begun to suspect that's where Tim was hiding out," he said coolly. "You'd better tell me about it."

The change in him promised little mercy for his brother, and I felt an increasing sympathy toward Tim.

"Don't be too hard on him," I said. "The quarrel you had upset him badly. I think he needed to get away for a while so he could figure things out."

"Birdy should have told me."

"Don't blame her," I said quickly. "Tim coaxed her into letting him stay for a few days."

"Give me the car key," he said, and held out his hand. "We're going to Windtop."

I put the key into it and watched his controlled motions as he drove through the gate and back to the highway. The very control he exerted over an anger that would explode around Tim in only a few minutes alarmed me. I couldn't forget what Pete Evans had said about the boy.

"Please listen to me," I said. "Please stop somewhere and just listen. We need to talk before you rush in and make everything worse."

He paid no attention, driving fast. I made my pleading stronger.

"While you're probably very good with all those plants, I don't think you're good at all with people!"

He gave me a black look and stepped harder on the gas.

"Do you want your brother to kill himself—the way Ricky Sands did?" I threw at him.

This time he slowed a little, and I knew I'd punctured his anger.

"Isn't there some quiet place where we can talk?" I urged. "I'm on your side, if you'll just give me a chance. I know something about that music world Tim thinks he wants for himself."

"All right," he said. "We'll talk before we go to Windtop. But I know what that kid needs better than you do."

We followed the narrow highway through Cold Spring Harbor, where water running down the hillside flowed across the road. Several ducks waddled about near the library—a familiar sight, I'd been told. At the far end, harbor water lapped into marshy land, where sea grasses grew tall, and around a curve we turned off to follow the road to St. John's Church. When Alan had parked, we walked beneath dripping trees and between wet shrubs, climbing to the level of the church. The white building had the graceful simplicity of New England, its steeple cutting into a clearing sky, St. John's location beside a calm, tree-surrounded pond seemed restful and inviting—surely a place to lessen anger and offer quiet contemplation.

A walk ran along the water on one side of the church, and we stood for a moment watching swans near the bank. On the far side willow trees dripped toward the water, hiding busy traffic from view. As we followed the walk, I looked up at the great stained-glass windows that had been rescued from Tiffany's home when it had burned.

"All right," Alan said, "tell me."

There was no compromise in him, I thought uncomfortably as I tried to find words that would bend him a little, make him more sympathetic toward Tim's problems.

"You don't want your brother to quit school," I said. "And perhaps he won't want to, if you handle this gently."

"And *you* know how I should handle it?"

"I'm not that smart. Maybe you're not either right now. At least I know what it feels like to be in Tim's position—determined to go in one direction, however foolish. I was there myself, not all that long ago."

I could sense that he looked at me more attentively, but I couldn't meet his eyes, for fear I might falter. Speaking hesitantly at first, I began to tell him how much I'd wanted to write songs, how much I'd wanted Ricky Sands's world. I even told him about the crazy thing I'd done to get Ricky's attention and trick him into listening to my music. Alan heard me without interruption until I paused. Then he asked a question.

"What did your father do about this?"

"He cared enough to tell me all the things he thought were wrong about my marrying Ricky. But he never threatened me or took away his love and support."

"So you went off and did all those wrong things anyway?"

"How can I know if they were wrong—even now? Dan understood that I had to find out for myself, and there was only one way to do that. If he'd opposed me, I'd have gone ahead in spite of anything he might have said. As Tim certainly will. But perhaps you can slow him down a little. You don't want him to run away and disappear."

We turned at the rear of the church and walked back to a bench that had begun to dry in the sun.

"What about now?" he asked as we sat down. "What do you feel about your own life now?"

"A lot of the time I think about how I might have helped Ricky. Perhaps I wasn't as generous toward him as my father was toward me."

"And as you think I ought to be toward Tim?"

"As perhaps you'd *better* be. It's possible that he can at least finish high school. But if you're too hard on him, he'll run off and you may lose him for good. I don't know if there's a right way, and I'm sure there's no easy way. I just think you shouldn't rage at him right now."

Alan was still raging inside, however. "High school! I want him to go to college. I want him to do something useful with his life."

"And you don't think troubadours are useful? Perhaps you're wrong there."

He snorted. "Have you heard him sing? He croaks like a frog!"

I smiled halfheartedly. "Maybe frogs are the coming thing—they've tried everything else. Yes, I've heard him sing. It was your brother who was doing those creepy things to torment me. Though when I heard him in the house singing Ricky's song—my song—he mostly whispered the words, so I couldn't tell much about his voice."

"Yet you're ready to forgive him for the things he's done to frighten you?"

"Forgiving doesn't come into it. There was a lot of malice in what he did, and that still upsets me. The way he blames me for Ricky's death upsets me. But he's young, and I'd like to understand how he feels and why."

Alan seemed ominously quiet, and I knew I was probably talking to a blank wall with this dark, unfeeling man. Besides, I had enough problems of my own. The moment of high excitement, of coming to life again at Geneva's piano, seemed far behind me. I wasn't sure that I could even recall the tune and words that had come to me. What use was there in writing songs anyway? Who was to sing what I wrote, now that Ricky was gone?

Hopelessness could be like a sudden smothering blanket. If only I'd listened to what Ricky *wasn't* saying—if only I'd seen . . . Futile thoughts that would haunt me for the rest of my life.

Alan took me by surprise. "Thank you for stopping me when I'd have rushed in." He sounded grudging, unused to concession. When he went on it was as though he sorted out his own thoughts, trying for a new direction. "One of the reasons I didn't want you to come to Windtop is because you were Ricky Sands's wife. I knew how Tim felt about him. That's why I didn't tell you that Ricky had been here that time, or that my brother had run away. I suggested to Geneva that she say nothing to you about this. Because of who you are—"

He broke off as though turning something over in his mind, and then came to a decision.

"Let me tell you about Tim," he went on. "We aren't blood brothers. When my mother died, my father married again, and Tim was the son of the woman Dad married. He took Dad's name later. That's why there's such a difference in age between us. When my father and Tim's mother were killed in an accident in Spain, Tim was hardly more than a baby. Geneva took us both in. Since I was older, I felt a special responsibility toward him."

Alan paused and sat for a while staring at the swans. I kept very still, waiting, and after a moment he went on.

"Geneva Ames was a close friend to both our parents. I'd always been in and out of Windtop as a small boy, and it was good to have the house as a base to return to. Tim grew up there. When I was older I became his guardian, and when I had my own place he came to live with me. As he does now. Until he met Ricky Sands, everything seemed fine, and I didn't worry about his imitating a few pop singers and making up his silly songs. I thought he'd grow up and forget about that. But once Sands came out here, everything changed. Now Tim's making a lot out of the fact that I'm not his real brother, and he's been saying that the minute he's eighteen he'll go off on his own. I suppose I'll be lucky if he waits that long."

I felt sorry for both Alan and Tim, but I'd said all I could for the moment. Alan would have to take it from here, and if I'd influenced him at all, perhaps he'd hold back a little.

When I'd have risen to return to the car, Alan took my arm and drew me down. "Wait," he said. "Hollis, I really am grateful . . ."

We were very close and his arm was around me. He held me with a strange intensity, and whatever else he'd meant to say fell into silence. When he kissed me I was taken by surprise, shaken more than I wanted to be. No man had kissed me since Ricky, and I wasn't ready. Yet there was a rising urge in me—a need to be held and comforted. It had been so long since a man had held me lovingly, and I knew I could turn easily into Alan's embrace. I could rest my head on his shoulder and give up some of my burdens. And if he kissed me again, all that was sleeping in me might come to life. And this was too soon. This was the wrong man—a man who sometimes frightened me—and I'd be turning to him for the wrong reasons. Whatever my burdens were, they were still mine, and until I'd dealt with them I couldn't be free. Or impose them on anyone else.

Perhaps the kiss had surprised Alan, too, for he drew back at the same moment I did, brusque with me now, as though he already regretted what he'd done.

"I'd better get over to Windtop and talk to Tim," he said. "I'll try to go easy with him, but I still have the same convictions about what he wants to do."

Not convictions—prejudices, I thought, and said nothing.

As we drove back to Windtop it was as if he hadn't kissed me at all. As if that sudden touch of his mouth on mine had been a mere thank you for whatever I had done to calm his anger. Which was fine with me. I would ignore what had happened, just as he was doing. It was better so, but I still waited for my heart to stop thumping.

By the time we reached the gates the sun was out fully, shining on wet gold and red leaves, glistening on dark branches where raindrops still clung.

Luther, small and wiry and strong, came to open the gates. I looked at him with new eyes, remembering the painting he'd done of little

Mary Ames. The scar patches on his right hand that drew it into a claw had new significance now. It must no longer be possible for him to hold a paintbrush. And that scar along one cheek that gave his mouth a sinister droop was something I must discount. Luther was an artist with a lost talent, and I hoped that I might talk with him one of these days.

The gates were open and we went through.

"Birdy tells me Luther used to be an artist," I said to Alan. "I saw that portrait he did of Mary Ames upstairs in the attic. Doesn't he ever paint anymore?"

Alan was driving fast again, impatiently, and he braked on a curve in the road and shot me one of his dark looks. "Stay out of the attic. Mrs. Ames won't like your going up there."

"I was chasing Tim," I said mildly.

That seemed to exasperate him. "Don't you have any sense at all?" he snapped at me. "He might have hurt you. He can be dangerous at times —that kid."

"If I had any sense I'd get away from Windtop right now," I told him.

We'd reached the drive in front of the house, and when he stopped the car he turned and touched my hand lightly. "I'm sorry, Hollis. I shouldn't take my foul temper out on you. Come on in."

Birdy was in a state of high excitement as we came up the steps. If she'd had feathers she'd have fluttered. "Whatever took you so long? I called the greenhouse and they said you'd left ages ago."

"Where's Tim?" Alan asked.

"He's gone! That's why I called—to let you know, so you wouldn't need to come home right away."

"Just tell me what's happened," Alan said.

She sniffed a few times, but continued more slowly. "Tim didn't want to wait for you. He said you'd be wild and he needn't take that. He started tearing around and yelling when I tried to persuade him, so Pete Evans heard him and came inside. Pete got him quieted down and then telephoned Mrs. Cameron. She told Pete to bring Tim over to her house, and said he could stay there as long as he liked. Maybe that's best for now, Mr. Gordon. But that's not all I'm upset about."

She still seemed breathless, and Alan put an arm around her and led the way to the kitchen.

"Tea's your treatment for everything, isn't it?" I'd followed them and he glanced at me. "Fix us all some tea, will you, Hollis?"

"I'm all right," Birdy told him grumpily. "Never mind tea! I've got more to tell you. I phoned Mrs. Ames at the hospital and explained about Tim. And do you know what she did?"

"I'm waiting to find out," Alan said.

"She postponed her California plans. She was leaving the hospital tomorrow anyway for her New York apartment, but now she's coming straight out here to Windtop. She'll arrive tomorrow afternoon. *Tomorrow afternoon!* And nothing's ready! I can't do it all myself."

Alan spoke soothingly. "You'll be fine. You'll manage everything, just as you always do, Birdy. Get in any help you need, and I'll stay for the rest of the day and do what I can."

She managed to steady herself, planning aloud. "We'll have to fix up a bedroom for her downstairs—perhaps in the yellow sitting room. Stairs might be too much for her now. And I'll have to find a proper cook." She reached for a pad and began to make notes.

"We'll manage," Alan said and looked at me. "You look done in, Hollis. Why not go upstairs and rest? I'll postpone talking to Tim for now. That will give us both a chance to cool down."

I was glad enough to escape, and I climbed slowly to the room I'd left such ages ago—when I'd discovered Tim sitting on the bed with my tape recorder on his knees. The door stood open, as I'd left it in my hurry, and I felt like a different woman as I walked in—more alive. Some things had been cleared up, while others were more doubtful than ever.

At least I knew the identity of the intruder who had tormented me, but that alone hadn't brought me to life. Was I different because a man other than Ricky had kissed me and made me feel like a woman again? A man who had meant nothing by what he'd done? Or was it because I had started work on a song that made me feel like a different woman?

Of course it was because of the song. Of course that was what had renewed me. I wouldn't allow it to be any other way.

11

My tape recorder lay on the carpet where Tim had dropped it, and I picked it up with a twinge of uneasiness. Had he been in the room long enough to leave another message for me? Of course it wouldn't matter if he had, now that I knew who he was.

A little of the cassette had been run. So there *had* been time. I ran the tape back quickly, and touched the play button. The hoarse, whispering voice spoke to me as it had before, and again I was struck by the eeriness he could put into the sound. It compelled me to listen.

> What foolish songs you wrote for him, Hollis Sands. They didn't succeed because they were good. It was his voice that made them wonderful. He spoke to everyone who listened. He put his own spell into what he sang. And in the end you destroyed him. Think about that. Think about it in the night. Are you going slowly crazy, Hollis? Are your thoughts going round and round and making no sense . . . because of what you did to Ricky? Why should you live and Ricky die?

I clicked off the switch and went out on the balcony, where I could look over treetops to shining water and a single skimming sail. In the summer the harbor would be alive with white boats.

All my elation was gone. Suddenly neither a kiss nor a song mattered.

I must not think of Tim's voice or his words. I would order my thoughts. They needn't go "round and round," leaving me feeling lost so much of the time. These were the words of someone who wanted to frighten me because of his own confusion. No, that was false. This boy could be dangerous, as Alan had said.

Then there was the matter of the roses. Special roses of a particular coral color that Ricky had sent to Coral Caine the day she died. What had they meant to her, when by her own earlier words she'd treasured such roses? Even more terrible to think about—why had Ricky taken similar roses with him to the hotel room where he'd died?

If only the hurting would stop, and the aching of self-questioning and self-blame. I mustn't go on with this, when I knew how futile it was.

I looked down upon the flagstone below my balcony, and it was as though the very stones promised an end to pain—a way to sleep, to peace and nothingness. That was what Ricky had achieved—by his own choice.

In an instant I stepped back from this treacherous fascination, angry with myself. How could I allow Tim's malice to get under my skin? But of course it wasn't just Tim. It was my sense of hopelessness that had been piling up lately, but that must never be listened to. Sometime soon I must talk to Norris Wahl. I needn't handle everything alone.

I wasn't fearful and timid. Even though I'd had enough of pain, I must use it now, turn it to some sort of purpose. Norris had told me that once, and it still held true.

With new determination I returned to the bedroom and erased Tim's words. Then I carried the recorder downstairs. I wasn't ready to rest yet. Too much resting only encouraged depressing thoughts.

A great bustle was going on throughout the lower floor. Alan, under Birdy's direction, was carrying parts of a bed to be set up in the sitting room. They paid little attention to me as we passed in the hall, and I went straight to the piano in the music room.

I hadn't forgotten a note or a word, and I sang softly to the tape, accompanying myself. It was all there solidly, and I felt the familiar elation rising in me. Energy always flowed from my own creative forces. When that was high, I could do anything, face anything, and now the juices were stirring in me again. I must work on the verse and finish the song. Ward off the darkness in the best way I knew.

A misty day in Frisco town . . .

No, that sounded like "A Foggy Day." I had to be on guard against the easily familiar, and sing my own music, my own words. I tried again with a bit of melody.

> Mists roll in through the Golden Gate
> As we walk the hills together.
> Now I walk alone and remember.

It was flowing through me. The verse would remember, while the chorus would deny, and what I was singing would touch a chord of response in those who listened. Even a melancholy song could comfort and console. It could lessen the loneliness because it said, *I've been there too. I know what it's like.*

Tim claimed that my songs were no good, but he was wrong. He could hear me only through his own pain, his own fantasy about Ricky —which hadn't been any more real than mine.

I ran through the music again, repeating the words, as the song began to grow.

"I like that," Pete Evans said behind me. "It's pretty good."

I crashed discord on the keys and swung around. "Don't do that! You're always creeping up on me. I hate it!"

"Sorry," he said. "I've brought you a message, and I couldn't help hearing."

"What makes *you* a judge?" I demanded, still annoyed, as I so often seemed to be with Pete Evans.

"I'm a listener. I've heard Ricky Sands's songs."

"Now they have to be *my* songs. And I don't like anyone around when I'm working."

"Do you want to hear the message? It's from my sister, Liz."

"All right. What is it?"

"She's been very good with Tim, and he's feeling better. Liz thinks you should see her this afternoon, if you can. As Ricky's wife, perhaps you can talk to the kid, and to Alan too. Keep him from jumping on Tim too soon. I'll walk you down there when I'm through here."

"I haven't any influence with Alan, and I don't think I can take any more of Tim right now. He left a few more unpleasant words on my recorder before I caught him."

"I'm afraid he needs a lot of help."

"Not from me. He detests me."

"So you won't come?"

"I don't know," I said. "I don't seem able to help myself, so how can I help anyone else?"

"You were doing all right just now. You were doing the best possible thing to bring you out of that funk you've got yourself into."

"Just go away and leave me alone!"

His grin was maddening in all that beard. I had no idea what he really looked like. I only knew that he could irritate me more than anyone I'd ever known. Alan might disturb me deeply, but this man was like a fly—buzzing at me, stinging, darting away, and darting back to sting again.

"You'll be okay," he said cheerfully. "I'll meet you on the front terrace around four."

He went off, not waiting for a reply, and I closed the piano with a bang. The interruption had dispelled my mood and I couldn't concentrate now. Never mind. Whatever I'd done was safely on tape. In fact, I realized that the machine was still running and the tape had probably caught my exchange with Pete Evans. I turned it off and left the recorder on the piano when I went to look for Birdy and Alan.

In spite of Pete's interruption, I felt better. Getting something down for a new song helped, even though that wonderful, high elation couldn't last. It never did.

Now I must find out what Alan planned, and deliver the message from Liz Cameron.

In the sitting room Birdy was making up a bed, while Alan moved other furniture around. The room was big enough to take this new arrangement comfortably and still not look crowded. If either of them had heard me playing the piano, nothing was said. Birdy, tall and thin, was busy at her nestmaking. Lost in her own plans, she shook her head at my offer to help.

"Mrs. Ames will like this," Birdy said. "She always loved this room. She had that very wallpaper put in herself, you know. That shade of primrose yellow is her favorite color, and it makes the room bright, even in midwinter. I'll bring a few things down from her rooms to welcome her. It's the right choice, don't you think, Mr. Gordon? Though perhaps we'd better move that picture."

"You're right," Alan said. "I'll take it down."

They were speaking of the portrait of Mary Ames in the yellow dress that matched the sitting room. Its company too painful for Mrs. Ames?

"I wonder if she's on any special diet?" Birdy ran on. "I must call Hazel and see if she can help out with the cooking for a while." She was talking to herself, and required no response.

Alan said, "If you don't need me anymore, Birdy, I'll go down to Elizabeth's and talk to Tim."

I spoke quickly. "Mrs. Cameron thinks you shouldn't see Tim for a little while."

Pete appeared in the doorway. "Anything I can do around here?"

"You can tell Mr. Gordon how your sister feels," I said.

"Sure. Liz thinks it's best not to come right away. She's got Tim calmed down, and if you wait, Liz thinks he'll be more receptive. Then maybe he'll listen to you."

Alan stared at Pete for a moment. "I'm not sure she's right, but I'll wait awhile. Pete, will you drive me to the greenhouse after lunch? My car's still out there. Birdy, how about some quick sandwiches?"

Since I wasn't hungry, and wasn't needed, I returned to the second floor and let myself into the room where I'd stored the cartons of Ricky's papers. Working here would keep me busy until four o'clock, when Pete would take me to Liz Cameron's house. I didn't look forward to seeing Tim again after the additional words he'd placed so spitefully on my tape, but I'd have to talk with him eventually.

I pulled out one of the smaller cartons to open, and as I tore off the paper tape, it occurred to me again that such a sealing was hardly tamperproof. Anyone could open one of these boxes and then replace the tape. At least I had a key to the room now, and that should keep out anyone who was merely curious.

The cardboard flaps sprang open, and at the sight of what was packed in this box I remembered sadly the day when Ricky, in one of his depressed moods, had taken his framed gold and platinum records from the wall of his office at the apartment, and had packed them away in this same box.

"They don't mean anything," he'd said. "When I'm not making new records, these don't count."

"But you'll record again," I'd protested. "You just need a rest, Ricky. You drive yourself too hard."

That wasn't all he needed, however—and in the end he'd chosen the longest rest of all.

I lifted one frame after another from the box and looked at each in turn. He'd had several golds, and two platinums. Most were before my time. Even with the two golds that were mine, I'd had little part in their actual making. Not once had he allowed me in the studio where I could watch the production of a record. I'd never been able to see Chuck Oliver at the mixing console, though Ricky had told me how good he was.

Of course I knew about what happened. First Ricky, with headphones on, did the pilot—a rough vocal. Later, the overdubbing of the band was done, and the final vocal track was laid down. Then came the mixing of sound that brought something up here, emphasized something else there. The producer who worked this final magic had to be an artist too, though he got no public credit.

The gold record for "Sweet Rain" was in my hands. It shone against the black velvet on which it was mounted, and it had been framed in narrow, gold-toned metal. Somehow the glass had been broken. Slivers and shards were strewn across the top, with some of the larger pieces missing. I looked into the box, took out the other records, but none of the glass in them had been broken. The mounting on the velvet background seemed a little askew, though when I tried to pry up the record with my finger, it was firmly attached.

I felt puzzled. If this breakage had occurred on the way out here, why weren't the other records damaged too? Of course anyone could have opened this unsealed box back at the apartment. Norris, perhaps? Or even Ricky himself? I hadn't touched the collection since he'd packed it away. Suddenly memory was sharp in my mind of Ricky the last time I'd seen him alive. He'd stood at the door of the apartment and spoken those cryptic words that I'd never been able to understand: *If you need it, you'll find the answer in the song.*

What answer in what song? Goodness knows, I'd thought about that and I had no idea what he meant. Neither had Norris when I'd finally told him. Certainly Ricky hadn't been himself at the time and I'd been fearful about his going off alone. How right I'd been to be afraid!

I picked up the frame and carried it carefully downstairs to the kitchen, where Alan and Pete sat at a table eating lunch.

"I have some broken glass here," I told Birdy. "I don't want to leave it in a wastebasket."

She gestured toward the rubbish bin and I tipped the broken bits out of the frame, and wiped the gold disc with a piece of tissue. Then I picked up a small kitchen knife and sat down at the far end of the table to work the shining gold disc gently up from its backing. It came easily enough, not firmly attached, as I'd already suspected. There was nothing underneath. No hidden message that Ricky might have left for me here in some desperate moment.

The kitchen was silent, and I realized that all three were watching me intently. I gave them a vague smile.

"This is one of Ricky's gold records. The glass seems to have been broken, and I wanted to make sure the disc hadn't been damaged."

"Give it to Pete," Alan directed. "Next time he's in a hardware store, he can get new glass."

I pushed the frame down the table.

"Sure," Pete said. "I'll take care of it."

Birdy had been watching me, and now she brought me a glass of milk and a chicken sandwich. I found I was hungry after all, and I ate in silence at my own end of the table. The time was after two o'clock. It had been a long day.

The hours till four seemed to drag. I went back upstairs and worked for a while longer on Ricky's papers without unearthing anything important, and trying not to be upset by them. Then I wandered idly about the house, keeping out of Birdy's way, and I even sat outside in the welcome sun for a while. I did everything but go near the music room again. Let my new song rest for now. Something would be going on under the surface of my mind, and tomorrow I would return to it fresh, to find that it had grown mysteriously.

I wondered what the coming of Geneva Ames was going to mean, and whether I would now have the chance to know her better. I thought about Tim, too, and what I might say to him that could help. I didn't want to think about Alan at all.

Eventually, I went out to the front terrace and found Pete waiting for me.

"We'll walk," he said curtly. "There's a shortcut between Windtop and The Shutters. There'll be some mud after the rain, but your shoes look okay."

We crossed the drive that looped before the house and I saw there was an opening in the trees where a path ran downhill. Even though rain had beaten more leaves from their branches, the woods were still sparsely aflame, and bright-colored piles heaped the earth around every trunk, and were thick and spongy on the path we followed. We walked with care over slippery gold and crimson, with Pete leading the way.

Windtop was quickly out of sight behind us, as the path pitched downward through deep woods.

A few minutes later we came into the open at a level stretch of meadow that ran to the stone wall surrounding Windtop.

"There's the back gate," Pete said. "Mrs. Ames put it in years ago, when our mother was her good friend. It hasn't been used much lately. Not since Liz had a falling-out with Mrs. Ames. She may not be happy to hear that Geneva's returning."

Pete had brought a key to open the gate. "This belongs to Liz," he told me. "There should be another key at Windtop, if you ever need to use it." He pulled the gate open and we walked through.

A wide slope of grass that was still green spread beyond the wall, and now the house came into full view. I'd always loved old houses, and I stopped, entranced by my first sight of The Shutters.

"It's beautiful," I said to Pete. "Windtop is grand and European and awesome, but this house is New England America. I love it!"

"Our grandfather built it." Pete sounded pleased.

The house was both tall and wide—cedar-shingled, silvered by the weather, with a good deal of white trim. It rose three stories and was crowned by a domed white cupola topping the mansard roof. A wide, inviting porch ran across the front and along the near side, with pairs of slim white columns, spaced at intervals, supporting the porch roof. I could see at once where the house got its name, for dozens of dark green shutters were evident at the long doors downstairs, and at the many windows above.

We cut across the leaf-strewn lawn that sloped to a loop of Snake Hill Road, and followed the drive to the front steps. Liz heard us and came onto the porch.

"Thanks for coming," she said, holding out her hand to me. "Tim is worn out, and he's sleeping right now. I've put him in the upstairs bedroom where he used to stay when he visited us as a small boy. Come in and we'll talk awhile before you wake him, Pete."

The hall that cut through from front to back wasted no space, but was narrow, with a flight of stairs running up at the left. On either side, the rooms were large and high-ceilinged and gracious. Liz led us into a drawing room that occupied the entire depth of the house along the side porch. At the front of the room the furniture seemed old and a little shabby, but the far end had been turned into a comfortable sitting space with a few pieces that were less traditional. There were two fireplaces, and the one at this end of the room flamed with burning logs.

More than anything else, however, it was the radiance of the room at that particular moment that struck me. The sun went down early in November, and its rays slanted through golden trees outside, filling the entire room with reflected autumn radiance. Even without lamps, the room glowed and shimmered with light.

A tea service before the fire awaited us, and we sat down in a friendly grouping while Liz poured. As always, her hair was groomed and lacquered, with not a lock out of place, and the pale lemon of her silk dress suited the room.

For the first time today I could push everything that troubled me away and allow the lovely room with its serene golden light to work its soothing magic. Even the spiced mandarin tea was fragrant and quieting. For a little while it was as though Windtop and a man named Alan Gordon ceased to exist. And as though the pain of Ricky's loss had slipped for a moment into the past and become less urgent.

"I love the autumn dusk in this room," Liz said. "When I was a girl, it always seemed a magic time to me."

"Yes, it's like that," I said contentedly. A hint of music drifted through me—something to do with this shimmering light. Not Ricky Sands's sort of song. A song as old-fashioned as this house, and one that I might set down just for my own satisfaction.

Pete spoiled everything. "What did you expect to find underneath that record?" he asked.

I drank hot tea and tried to collect myself. "Find? What do you mean —find?"

"You were looking for something—that was clear enough. How did the glass get broken? Was it cracked in any of the other frames?" He seemed to take it for granted there were others.

"I don't think so," I said, feeling resentful under his steady, not entirely sympathetic, look.

He turned to his sister. "I'm not sure Hollis should be staying at Windtop. Something's going on up there, and I don't know what it is."

"That's because you've never liked Alan," Liz said. "You two were never on the same wavelength. What could be going on?"

"Don't you feel it sometimes?" Pete asked, looking at me again.

"I've been too busy coping with the tricks Tim's been playing on me," I said. "It's better with him out of the house."

"It's not healthy the way Geneva has gone on mourning Mary, and at the same time shutting her out," Pete said.

Liz smiled. "My brother's given to sensing things no one else can." Her wide violet eyes regarded her brother with mocking affection.

"I just keep my eyes open more than most," he told her. "Did you know that Geneva is coming home tomorrow?"

Liz seemed disconcerted. "I'm glad she's recovering, of course, but I'd hoped she'd go straight to California. It's much more peaceful when she isn't here."

"Birdy told her about Tim," Pete said, "and she's concerned enough to come home."

"She'll never let Tim stay here." Liz shook her head in exasperation. "Yet up at Windtop he'll be under both their thumbs. At least Alan can be reasoned with—sometimes. But Geneva is a born autocrat."

I had no idea what this was all about, and in any case old feuds had nothing to do with me.

Liz studied me thoughtfully. "If you could make your peace with Tim and correct his notions about *you*, it might help to have you up there at Windtop. As Ricky's wife, you may even be able to help him."

"It's because I'm Ricky's wife that he's angry with me. He has a notion that I'm responsible for what Ricky did. And for all I know he might be right."

Pete snorted derisively. "Don't talk nonsense!"

"How do you know it's nonsense? I should think you would understand." I was thinking of his own load of self-guilt.

He looked away from me, and I realized that I'd snapped at him again.

"I'm sorry," I said lamely. "I guess we both live in glass houses and shouldn't pick up stones to throw."

The golden shimmer in the room had darkened, and Pete began to turn on lamps. Now there were shadows in the corners, and I missed the reflected glow.

"Will you get Tim up, please, Pete?" Liz asked. "It's time to bring him down. There's a lot to be done before he can take a visit from Alan."

Her brother went out of the room, and at once Liz edged her chair closer to mine. "Good! I've wanted us to talk alone. Tell me how things are really going at Windtop. Not all that spooky stuff that Pete worries about, but how Birdy and Alan are doing."

"Why, they're all right, I suppose. Alan's in and out. I don't think he wanted me there in the beginning, and Birdy still doesn't. I won't need to stay long. I just needed time to figure out what to do with my life."

"And what will you do with it?"

"I hope I can write songs again. But first I had to get away from all that morbid publicity surrounding anything that touches Ricky Sands."

"That could be rough, I imagine. I saw him just the one time when Tim persuaded Geneva to invite him out here. He stayed only a couple of days, but in that little while he managed to upset all our lives. I don't think he meant to. Maybe he just had a talent for destruction."

I'd never heard it put more clearly, though I hadn't thought of Ricky in that light before. It was true that he had damaged almost anyone he'd touched closely, though I didn't want to discuss Ricky with Liz Cameron, and I could be equally blunt.

"What was your falling-out with Mrs. Ames?"

For a moment I thought she wouldn't answer me. Then she shrugged and went on with a wry smile. "She didn't want Alan to marry me. She did everything she could to see that he wouldn't."

There seemed a challenge in her manner, though I wasn't sure what she was challenging, or why she'd told me this so openly.

"It doesn't matter anymore," she continued. "I expect it would never have worked out between Alan and me. He leads a deep, dark emotional life that he suppresses most of the time. I hate that side of him, so we get along better as friends."

I wasn't sure she spoke the truth about its not mattering to her, and I had the odd feeling that she was still challenging me.

"What makes him like that?" I asked.

"Who knows what makes any of us the way we are?" She reached for a cigarette and picked up a silver lighter. "Anyway, who cares?"

She must have sensed my discomfort with this turn in our conversation, for she changed the subject abruptly.

"You visited Sea Spray today? What did you think of the greenhouse?"

"I wasn't there long, since I'd just come to tell Alan about his brother. What I saw was fascinating."

"He's a different man out there. His work is what he cares about most. Perhaps it's all he cares about these days. I saw that clearly enough while my job there lasted. Admirable, I suppose—but limited."

So the subject hadn't really been changed. She still wanted to talk about Alan.

"Tell me about Tim," I countered. "How can we change his mind about me?"

"I don't know. That's up to you. He's on the verge of running off on his own to New York, even though he's underage. He has some crazy idea about getting work at a recording studio. Now if Alan starts storming at him, and—"

"Perhaps he won't," I said. "I can understand how Tim feels, because I've been there with Ricky Sands. And I've talked to Alan a little. At least he's postponed seeing his brother, and that's something."

"Did he tell you about the relationship?"

"That he's not Tim's natural brother? Yes. But I think he feels as much responsibility as if he were."

"Responsibility's not good enough," Liz said.

"At least it's a start. It's something to build on."

The look she turned on me was critical, knowing. I sensed her antagonism and found myself flushing. But before I could respond, we heard Pete and Tim coming down the stairs.

When they paused in the wide doorway, I saw that Tim looked much less wild and distraught than when I'd last seen him. Cleaned up, he was a good-looking boy, though too thin, and too solemn and humorless.

"We've been talking a bit." Pete spoke casually. "Just trying to figure out a few things."

Tim stared glumly at his own feet.

"Come in and sit down, both of you," Liz invited. "We can't talk with you two out in the hall."

Tim ambled in his disjointed way to a sofa, and sat down with his legs outstretched. Pete came to sit beside him.

"I think Tim has been mixed up about you, Hollis," Pete said. "We've been trying to straighten things out. He didn't really understand about the drugs and what they must have been doing to Ricky. None of that was your fault."

I glanced at Pete in surprise. "How did you know about that?"

He answered calmly. "There was plenty in the papers. And a lot of those hyped-up singers and musicians are on drugs. It's a logical deduction. And it is true about Ricky, isn't it? That's the way he died—shooting up."

I closed my eyes against the familiar tide of pain.

"Tim would like to sing for you," Pete said quickly.

I managed to push the hurting away once more and stared at the boy. "Do you want to?"

He gave me a defiant look. "Why not? Pete thinks I should."

"All right," I said. "But if I listen to you, I'll have to tell you the truth about how I feel. Suppose I don't like your singing—what then?"

"That won't change anything," Tim said, glowering.

"That's probably the right answer," I told him. "Of course I *have* heard you before, remember, but it wasn't exactly a good way to judge."

The familiar hint of malice came into his look, and I suspected that Pete hadn't changed his feeling toward me very much.

"We brought down Tim's guitar," Pete said, and went to fetch it from the hallway.

The boy took the instrument and sat down in a chair without arms, slinging the strap over his shoulder. For a few moments he tuned the strings, and Liz went to the piano and struck a few notes for him.

When he began to sing I listened intently. Alan would be pleased if I was forced to condemn Tim's voice, but first of all I was a songwriter and I had to be fair.

The first sound of his singing was startling. Froggy indeed. Harsh, but not unmelodic. It didn't fit in with anything that was being done now, but that didn't necessarily condemn it. Pretty voices weren't as much in demand in this rock age. It was the song, however, that caught my attention. It was a song about running away, about escaping—a song filled with the yearning of the very young. Though the words were crude and unpolished, the tune and the meaning touched me. There were times when I had felt like that—not so long ago.

Tim repeated the chorus—or started to. Then he struck a discordant note and silenced the strings with the flat of his hand. "That's enough!" His head came up and he stared at me across the room, young and defiant, and ready to be hurt.

I could offer him nothing but the truth as I saw it. "Your voice has an unusual sound, Tim."

That was equivocating, and he knew it. "Ugly," he said defensively.

"Ugly-beautiful. It's a special sound that listeners would have to get used to. If someone really got sold on it, you might find that people would pay attention. I think you'll need to work on it. I don't mean take lessons, because a teacher might try to change the sound and make it more conventional. It's yours and you need to stick with it and try to convince someone to listen. That won't be easy. Maybe even impossible. It's too soon to tell."

"I'll make them listen," he said grimly.

"Not by beating anybody over the head, Tim," Pete said. "I think Hollis has something, if you'll hear her out."

"Where did you get the song, Tim?" I asked.

"It's mine." Again he was defensive.

"It's interesting. Touching. If you've written others I'd like to hear them. I'm not sure the words are right yet, but what you're saying has a lot of feeling in it. It rings true. And the tune is good."

"Then I'll take it to New York," Tim said. "Or maybe Nashville. Alan will try to stop me, but I'll make it on my own. I don't care what he says!"

"Don't take it in until it's ready," I told him. "Then maybe I can help you."

"How?" He glowered at me, unconvinced.

"Introductions can be useful. They won't necessarily sell a song, but there are people in the business I know. I want to get back to song writing myself, and perhaps we could see some of these people together. Just so someone—the right person—might hear you and really listen and start thinking about you. But you're not ready yet, Tim. Stay home and work on what you have. Make some tapings and listen to yourself. If you've done other songs, get them ready."

"If I stay here I'll have to go back to school," Tim said, and I could hear the brittle edge in his voice. Too much emotion surged too close to the surface in this boy.

I spoke quietly. "There's nothing wrong with finishing school. You can use the time to get ready for what you want to do. Some maturing will help, and you need to put a few more years of life behind you. I know you don't want to wait. I remember how impatient I was. Alan's right about school—you need that first."

I knew by his face that I'd lost. I had brought in his brother's name, and as suddenly as a firecracker Tim exploded into profanity. Holding his guitar across his chest, he tore out of the room and out of the house.

"Stop him, Pete!" Liz cried.

Pete was already running after the boy.

When Liz sat back in her chair, I realized how tense she'd been. Her voice quivered when she spoke.

"I'd hate to be that age again. All that sensitivity and anger, all that rebellion so close to the surface! I remember."

I could remember too. "I know I upset him, but I had to speak the truth."

"Ah, the truth . . ." For just an instant I caught something unsettling in Liz's eyes. As though she were on the verge of saying something too revealing, and had held it back.

The room's lovely golden light had turned gray at the long windows, and early dark was coming down.

"I'd better get back to Windtop," I said. "I shouldn't be here when Pete brings Tim in. I might upset him all over again."

She agreed a little too quickly. "You're probably right. I'll walk up with you."

I was already at a porch door. "You needn't bother—I can find my way. Lend me a flashlight and I'll manage fine."

She rummaged in a drawer and handed me a sturdy outdoor light. "This will do, and it probably is best if I wait for Tim. I'll walk you to where the path begins."

She came with me up the sloping lawn and pulled open the gate that Pete had left ajar. I went through and turned to face her.

"Why did you want me to come down this afternoon? Was it really because of Tim?"

"There was something I wanted to know—and now I think I do."

She hurried away toward the lighted house, and I stood for a moment looking after her. *What* did she think she knew? I had an uneasy feeling that it concerned Alan Gordon, but there was nothing I could say to change any mistaken conclusions she'd come to.

I turned the beam of the flashlight upon the path that curved away into thick darkness, and started up the hill.

12

Though pale light still showed in the sky above the trees, the moment I was out of sight of The Shutters woods crowded in around me, thick and black. I was grateful for the light beam that kept me on the right course and prevented me from stumbling over stray roots. Always there were thick leaves underfoot, slippery at times, or crunching loudly where they'd dried out.

As I climbed, I thought about what I'd learned during the time I had spent with Liz Cameron. I was beginning to put bits and pieces together. She'd been a widow for a long while. She was close to Alan's age, and had grown up with him and wanted to marry him. A wish that Geneva had frustrated. I wondered how Alan felt. If he had wanted to marry her, I didn't think Mrs. Ames could have stopped him. But what did Geneva have against her old friend's daughter? Of one thing I was growing sure. In spite of Liz's words to the contrary, she was still in love with Alan Gordon.

None of this concerned me, I told myself firmly. I was merely curious. No matter what Liz chose to suspect, *I* wasn't going to fall in love again for a long time. I didn't like it that a memory of the moments I'd spent with Alan beside the pond at St. John's Church was still sharp in my mind. All I wanted was to reject the momentary longing I'd felt to be in his arms. I wasn't ready for that.

The path seemed to take longer on this uphill course, and parts of it were steeper than they'd seemed coming down. I disliked the dark shape of trees whose branches reached to snag my hair at every turn. I suppose no one can walk in strange woods after dark without a feeling of uneasiness that supplants reason.

The quiet all around seemed at first too intense. At least until I began to hear the underlying rustlings. Small night animals abroad, I supposed. The sounds were eerie when I could see nothing beyond the path of my light. At first I'd thought it a strong, far-reaching beam, but it seemed to have grown weaker, and I wondered anxiously if the batteries were failing. Perhaps it was just that any light would be quickly dispelled against that vast company of trees that closed me in.

A sudden louder crashing in the brush a little way off startled me. That must be some larger animal. A deer, perhaps? There were still deer on Long Island, though I didn't know if any were left around here. I began to hurry on the steep path, feeling breathless now as I climbed. Of course a deer wouldn't hurt me—it would only run away. But I still didn't want to encounter one alone out here in the woods.

Surely I should have reached Windtop by now. There'd been no other way to go. Was that a light out there among the trees? But I didn't think the house was in that direction. Perhaps it wasn't a deer, after all.

The thought of Tim escaping Pete's pursuit, and perhaps stalking me out here among the trees, was disturbing. What was it he had said? *Why should you live and Ricky die?*

But it wasn't Tim. The crashing sound came closer and so did the light, and suddenly a man's voice hailed me.

"Hey! What're you doing here? You don't belong in these woods!"

The shout carried a threat, and I wanted no argument with someone who might not know I was visiting at Windtop—perhaps wouldn't care. I started to run.

"Stop there—you!"

I could hear him crashing after me, and knew he would catch me in a moment. I swung about, turning the light beam full on the figure that came rushing through the underbrush. It was Luther Sykes, carrying a lantern. I lowered the beam and stood still in relief, waiting for him.

"I'm Mrs. Baker," I called. "It's all right, Luther. I ran because you scared me. I've been down the hill visiting Mrs. Cameron."

He covered the last few feet in a rush, and I saw with alarm that he'd picked up a heavy tree branch in his free hand. My name seemed to mean nothing to him, and he looked wild and strange.

I turned and ran again. I must be close to Windtop, and this man didn't look sane.

Luther, however, knew every inch of these woods, and he could run with a loping gait that overtook my shorter steps. In a moment his hand was on my shoulder.

He swung me around and I knew that I was facing no mere anger over a trespasser. There was something far more violent in this wiry little man.

"You came back!" he shouted, shaking me by the shoulder. "You shouldn't have come back. I know what you're up to and I won't let it happen—not again!"

Somehow I twisted from his grasp, but he'd knocked the flashlight from my hand and I ran blindly into a tree. Somehow I righted myself and found the twist in the path that led me onto the open, grassy space before Windtop. Alan's car was in the driveway, and lower windows were lighted. I ran toward the house shouting.

I'd given Luther only a temporary slip and he was after me at once, swinging the tree branch. It struck me across the side of my head and I fell dizzily to the grass. At once he was over me, pinning me down.

"You think you're going to set another fire! Oh, no you don't! Not ever again! Your mother almost died over what you did that time, and you're not going to hurt her anymore. Not ever again!"

The breath had been knocked out of me, and I felt his hands around my neck so that I couldn't cry out again. I squirmed and kicked, and knew I was fighting for my life.

Then the door burst open and Alan came running out. He plucked the old man away from me, and I could only lie gasping helplessly for breath.

"Stop it, Luther!" I heard the sharp command in Alan's voice as the old man still struggled to get at me. "What's the matter with you?"

I could breathe now, and in the light that streamed from the house I saw Luther falter and put his hands over his face. "I—I didn't know. I thought it was *her.*"

Alan picked me up and carried me through the open door, where Birdy stood waiting anxiously. I let my head rest against his shoulder and remembered the tenderness this man had shown when he'd touched the young plants in his greenhouse. Suddenly I wanted that tenderness for myself. Perhaps it was there, a little, as he laid me down gently on a sofa and smoothed the hair back from my face.

"Did he hurt you, Hollis? Can you talk?"

I put my hand to my throat and felt it carefully. "You came just in time. Is Luther crazy? What happened to him?"

"A confusion in his mind, I'm afraid. Were you walking through the woods alone? You shouldn't risk that at night."

Birdy had followed us in. "You need to talk to Luther, Mr. Gordon," she told him. "He's out in front now, waiting for you. I wouldn't let him come in, though I think he's recovered himself and—"

I broke in on her words. "Who did he take me for? Why was he connecting me with the fire?"

"He must have thought you were Mary Ames," Alan said sadly. "It was she who set the fire and burned out a good part of that wing."

"He took me for the little girl in that picture he painted so long ago?"

"She wasn't so little when she tried to burn the house down," Birdy said grimly. She exchanged a long look with Alan, and seemed to make a decision. "Mary died in that fire she set years ago. So she can't come back. But Luther still thinks he sees her sometimes."

"Let's not bother Mrs. Sands with old history," Alan said. "Will you help her upstairs, please, Birdy? I'll go talk to Luther."

She bowed her head. "Come along and I'll help you upstairs, madam. I can bring your supper up in a little while."

The "madam" told me that Birdy held me partly to blame for what had happened, and I supposed she was right. But no one had suggested possible danger in the woods at night between The Shutters and Windtop. No one had ever warned me about Luther. Had Liz Cameron known and kept silent?

Alan was still there, watching with concern in his eyes as Birdy helped me up. I must collect myself and tell him about Tim.

"I've seen your brother," I said.

Both Birdy and Alan looked at me, and I went on. "I'm not sure, but I think he'll stay with Mrs. Cameron for a while. Maybe he'll even go back to school when he cools down. I've heard him sing, and I told him he needed to do a lot more work on his voice and his songs before he'd be ready for New York."

"More work?" Alan was indignant. "Didn't you tell him it was hopeless when he croaks like a frog?"

"I don't know that it's hopeless." I felt exhausted, yet I still had to speak up for Tim. "*You* don't know that it's hopeless, Alan."

At once he was angry again, the concern I'd sensed in him already gone. "I must ask you not to see my brother again," he said, and turned to Birdy. "I'll come early in the morning, and I'll be here when Mrs. Ames arrives. Right now I'd better talk to Luther. Please stay with Mrs. Sands until she feels better."

He sounded authoritative again. I would certainly make no promise not to see Tim—*if* I stayed much longer at Windtop.

He must have seen my chin come up, and recognized his own arrogance. "I'm sorry, Hollis. I wouldn't have had this happen for anything. We'll talk about Tim another time. I wish—" He broke off with an odd gesture, as though he cast something away—his anger perhaps?—and went out of the room.

He was too many men rolled into one for me. There were more sides to his nature than I could ever understand.

Birdy helped me upstairs. My knees were still shaky and my throat felt sore, but Alan had come in time, and I only hoped I wouldn't dream about Luther Sykes tonight.

Upstairs my azalea rooms glowed with a rosy welcome. I would be glad to have a locked door between me and the world tonight. No one but Tim could come climbing in by way of the balcony, and there would be no more scares from him—I hoped.

"Shall I turn down your bed, madam?" Birdy asked, still stiff and displeased with me. "Would you like me to stay? You don't look at all well, madam."

"I'm fine," I assured her. "But I would like to know more about the night when the fire was set, and why this has happened to me. Did Mrs. Ames's daughter really set the fire?"

Birdy considered me for a moment, standing very stiff and straight, her eyes narrowed and her mouth pursed. "I suppose it's all right to talk about it, now that you know. After she grew up Mary could be unbalanced some of the time. Everybody spoiled her when she was little, and she thought she could have anything she wanted. She'd had a terrible quarrel with her mother and she wanted to pay her back. So she got up in the night and set that wing on fire. Luther tried to stop her and put it out, but she was in a crazy rage and she pushed him right into the flames. Those scars on his face and his right hand came from the terrible burns he got that night. Mrs. Ames wanted to have skin grafts done, but he wouldn't stay in the hospital for proper care. Maybe it was a good thing Mary died." Birdy's tone was bleak and grim.

"That's awful," I said. "And especially tragic for Mrs. Ames. That picture of Mary upstairs makes her look like a laughing angel. Luther must have been fond of her when she was younger, since he painted her like that."

"Everybody loved her then," Birdy said. "The fire changed everything. When Luther came here as a young man he worked at Windtop only because it was an easy outdoor job that left him free to paint."

"How long ago did the fire happen?"

Birdy considered. "It must be six years or more."

"It's strange that Mrs. Ames never had the wing repaired."

"She kept putting it off. She didn't want to talk about the fire, or face what happened that night. She had those doors inside the house closed, and the lower wing shut off. I think she began to pretend there was nothing beyond those doors. When she went outside she never walked around that end. Mr. Gordon told me that while she was away in California, he intended to have the whole thing cleaned out and perhaps rebuilt. If it was done when Mrs. Ames couldn't watch, it would probably be all right."

"Thank you for telling me," I said. "Since Mrs. Ames is coming home tomorrow, it's better if I know."

Birdy bowed her long neck primly. "I'll bring your tray after a while, madam. There's something I need to do first."

"Don't hurry," I said, and locked the door after her. Then I stepped out on the balcony and breathed deeply of the cold, bracing air. A wind had risen, sounding like the rushing of water through the trees. But these woods would never seem friendly to me again.

At least I felt a little stronger, and there was one thing I could do right now. It was a question that had been troubling me for some time, and seeking an answer would be the sort of distraction I needed. Besides, I needed to talk to Norris.

I sat down at the telephone in the sitting room and dialed New York. When Bea Wahl answered, I spoke with her for a few minutes, assuring her that everything was fine at Windtop. She volunteered that there had been none of those odd phone calls for at least twenty-four hours, and she hoped they had stopped. I asked for Norris, and when he came to the phone, I chose a direct attack.

"What did you find underneath that gold record of 'Sweet Rain' when you broke the glass?"

He was silent for a few seconds. Then he said, "I don't know what you're talking about."

"Do you remember, Norris—I told you Ricky said I'd find the answer in the song? Isn't that what you were looking for—an answer?"

"Sure, I remember. Hollis, you sound upset. What's the matter?"

I had more reasons to feel upset than I could count, but I wasn't going to discuss them all on the phone. "Just tell me—was it you who broke the glass?"

There was silence again. Then he said, "Hollis, I need to see you. When are you coming to New York?"

"Perhaps never, the way I feel right now. Answer my question!"

"So you found Ricky's note?"

I stared at the ivory mouthpiece as though it had a life of its own. "What are you talking about?"

"I don't know if we should discuss this—the way you sound. It was just that I got to thinking about what Ricky had said, and I kept wondering. He said, '. . . *the* song.' That had to mean 'Sweet Rain.' So I decided to look at that framed gold record and see if it told me anything. I didn't mean to break the glass. I was trying to get the backing off and it cracked. Anyway, I did find his note underneath."

"And you kept it without telling me?"

"It didn't make any sense. He was off in that crazy world of his when he wrote it. You didn't need any new mysteries, so I just put it back, with the broken pieces of glass on top. I supposed you'd find it eventually. Maybe at a calmer time."

"I didn't find it at all," I said. "There was nothing under the record. Norris, what did Ricky say?"

"Look—I can't quote offhand. It was too crazy. He must have been high on something when he wrote those words."

"What did it *say,* Norris?"

"I told you—I can't remember. Just let it go, honey. It doesn't matter now. It wouldn't help you. But if you want to come to New York—"

"Good-bye, Norris," I said, and hung up the phone.

I shouldn't have called him. I had an answer, but it told me nothing, and it opened all sorts of new questions. Who had Ricky's note now? Talking with Norris hadn't helped, and it had been the wrong time to mention roses.

I stretched out on the chaise longue and closed my eyes. How to be calm? How to thrust everything disturbing away from me? Once, ages ago, I'd meant to go downstairs and play Geneva's piano. That was when I'd heard Tim on the attic floor, and I'd been dashing from one thing to another ever since.

I wished that I'd brought my tape recorder upstairs so I could listen to my new song. That might quiet me, give me something happier to think about. I lacked the energy to make the trip to the music room. Yet if I didn't go—if I left the recorder there on the piano, with the tape still in it, something might happen to it, and I knew that, in spite of everything else, I didn't want to lose that song. It was already fading a little because of all that had happened to blank it out.

With an effort, I roused myself and unlocked the door. One side of my head felt sore, and a lump was rising near my temple, where the tree branch had struck. My throat was still tender, but at least my knees had stopped trembling, and I felt stronger. I could certainly walk downstairs and get the recorder.

When I stepped into the hall, however, I hesitated, drawn once more toward the back stairs. The horror of what had happened on the night of the fire was still vivid in my mind, haunting me, and not to be shaken off. I felt achingly sorry for Geneva Ames, who had lost her daughter so terribly. And even for Luther Sykes, who had tried to hurt—not *me*, but the shade of a girl who had died six years ago.

Compulsion drew me to the attic, to her picture. I climbed the narrow stairs, flicking light switches as I went, and found my way through crowded storage space to the tower. The door stood open, as I'd left it, and I went up into the room.

The portrait of a little girl in a blue dress drew me and I stood before it, studying every detail. Luther Sykes had caught her laughing spirit— what a pretty, open-faced little thing she had been. Only to grow up into a young woman so emotionally unbalanced that she'd tried to burn down her mother's house.

I left the portrait and went to look out the window through which Tim had escaped from me across the roof of the house. Steep gray slates were invisible in the darkness, and I could just make out sentinel chimneys against the sky. Beyond rose the opposite tower, and the equivalent of this room. Tonight light glowed behind the glass. Who could be up there now—and why?

As I watched, a shadow moved against the light, a tall, narrow silhouette. Birdy. Probably she was getting something from the attic to help in welcoming Geneva tomorrow. The light went out, and I wondered if she had looked across the roof to the lighted window in this tower where I stood.

It didn't matter. The picture had told me nothing, and all that mattered right now was to retrieve my tape recorder from its vulnerable place in the music room.

I went downstairs, moving slowly and a little painfully, meeting no one in the empty hall below. The music room was dark when I opened the door, but the light from the hall was enough to guide me to the piano. My recorder was there, apparently just as I'd left it. I picked it up and climbed the stairs, feeling shaky again.

In my room I stretched out on the chaise longue, with the recorder on my lap, and reversed the tape to the beginning. When I pressed the play button I heard my own piano chords, and then my undistinguished voice singing words about not remembering.

It was good. I knew it was good. The tune had an unexpected turn to it, and there was an appealing repetition to catch the listener. It was a singable melody. And the words would grow and improve as I worked on them.

When the music ended, other sounds came on. That was Pete Evans approaching the piano before I knew he was in the room, startling me out of my concentration with his comment about my song. I heard my own retort, and his further words. But now it wasn't the words I listened to. It was Pete's voice that struck me in sudden recognition. Disembodied like this, with no concealing beard, no prickly personality to confuse me, I remembered very well the first time I'd heard that voice.

He'd been clean-shaven then, like all the members of Ricky's band, and he'd sat across from me in a Greenwich Village cafe. I'd thought at the time that Norris Wahl had sent him, but now I wondered. He had been there on the street where I was walking—near Coral Caine's apartment. He had taken over as though he knew everything about me and why I was there. What had he said his name was. With an effort, it came back to me—Barron. It would have been Peter Barron, of course. While I'd never been allowed to meet Ricky's musicians, I knew their names, and he had told me that Peter was his bass guitarist and a very good one.

Now he was more or less hiding out behind a beard, calling himself Pete Evans, and doing odd jobs at Windtop!

I switched off the tape and sat for a long while trying to understand still another thread of the tapestry that Windtop was weaving about me.

13

The next morning I breakfasted in the kitchen again. We would be dining more formally when Mrs. Ames came home, Birdy assured me. Hazel would come in today to do the cooking, and if Mrs. Ames decided to stay awhile, other help might be hired.

She asked how I felt—which surprised me—and told me that I needn't worry about Luther. He'd been really ashamed of himself when she talked to him last night.

Though I felt a lot better, I had plenty to worry about besides Luther. Especially because of the new questions in my mind concerning Pete Evans.

I'd just finished my eggs and toast when Alan arrived to join us for coffee. He seemed more subdued than usual this morning.

"Have you heard anything about Tim?" I asked as soon as he sat down.

"I've talked to Elizabeth on the phone." I'd noticed before that he always called her Elizabeth rather formally. "Pete brought him back to the house, and he seems to have quieted down. She thinks if I will bend a little, he'll go back to school."

"And will you?" I asked.

For just a moment the familiar brooding look was there in his eyes. Then he smiled at me wryly. "I haven't changed any of my basic opposition to what Tim wants to do, but I suppose I'll have to let him try. Maybe the whole thing will take care of itself, once he finds out how hard it is, and how little he's likely to succeed. The important thing right now is to get him back to school, and not have him run away."

For a man like Alan Gordon, such words were a major concession.

"I'm glad you'll give him a chance," I said. "Your relationship with him is pretty important—maybe more than you think. What about Luther?"

"That's still up in the air. He wasn't there when I came outside last evening, and he seems to have disappeared. He didn't sleep in his room at the gatehouse and I haven't been able to locate him. I'm not really concerned—Luther can take care of himself. He's probably upset over what he nearly did to you, but he'll turn up eventually. He's got no place else to go. Geneva wants him taken care of, and so do I."

The idea of Luther lurking about in the woods wasn't reassuring, but the circumstances that had thrown him off last night weren't likely to occur again.

"Pete's working down by the gate this morning," Alan went on. "So he'll be there when Geneva arrives. She'll come in time for lunch, Birdy, though I'm not sure exactly when. Is everything under control?"

Birdy said it was and turned to me. "Was there something you wanted upstairs last night, Mrs. Sands?"

So she had seen me across the roof, as I'd seen her. "Not really. After what happened, I wanted to look at that portrait of Mary Ames again. The one Luther did. I kept thinking about the injury that keeps him from painting."

"Nothing keeps him from painting except his own mind," Alan said. "He can use that hand on some pretty delicate stuff when he wants to. With Mary gone, there was no one he could punish, and he took so long healing that by the time he was well he'd convinced himself that he could never paint again. But he's never tried anything threatening until last night. How are you now, Hollis?"

"I'm all right." I'd tied a scarf at my throat to hide the bruise.

"I hope you won't say anything to Geneva about what happened with Luther," Alan went on. "At least not right away. There are enough unhappy memories for her connected with Windtop, so what he's done can wait a little."

While I agreed, I felt increasingly uneasy about Luther's disappearance, and the narrow edge of sanity on which he balanced, so that I wondered if it wouldn't be better to tell Mrs. Ames the truth right away.

After breakfast Alan phoned Liz and said he would come down to see Tim. He wanted that matter settled before Geneva Ames arrived. I'd noticed a tension in both Alan and Birdy concerning her coming, and it was clear who would be in charge once she arrived. Birdy's anxiety I could understand, but Alan Gordon didn't seem like a man who would be easily dominated by anyone. By now I was more curious than ever concerning this woman whom my father had once loved, and I wanted to see her again and know more about her. I'd already felt her presence, which had left its stamp throughout the house.

When Alan left, I walked with him into the hall. He surprised me at the door by putting his fingers gently at my throat and pressing aside the scarf so he could see the bruise.

"I'm sorry this happened, Hollis. Are you really all right?"

It seemed best to assure him that I was. He bent his head and kissed me lightly on the cheek, and I stood looking after him as he went to his car. I didn't want to admit to myself how much that light kiss pleased me. Where was I going with Alan Gordon? In a way, it was a good feeling to know that he asked nothing of me now. I was being left alone until I was ready, and I was willing to wait.

When he'd driven off, I put on a jacket and started down the road to the gatehouse, where Alan had said Pete was working. I had pressing business with Pete Evans, and the sooner I brought it into the open the better.

This morning the woods seemed less menacing, even though Luther might still be out there. Slanting bands of sunlight cut through branches that were nearly bare, so that I could see well into the trees. As I followed the road, there was nothing along the way to disturb me. I walked briskly and put all thought of Luther Sykes out of my mind. It was pleasanter to think of Alan in the gentler mood he'd begun to show me. I could be persuaded when there was no pressure.

Pete was polishing the ironwork on the big gates when I neared the entrance, and I stood still for a moment watching him, considering my approach. When I'd made up my mind, I walked up behind him.

"Good morning, Mr. Barron," I said.

He wasn't a man to startle easily, and he turned without hurry, his look guarded and searching, as though he would see into my thoughts but reveal nothing of his own.

"So you know?" he said. "How did you find out?"

"You gave yourself away when you came into the music room yesterday. I was recording my new song and your voice got onto the tape while it was still running. When I played it back later, I remembered where I'd heard it before."

He gestured toward the gatehouse. "Luther's not back yet. Come inside for a moment and we'll talk."

I went ahead up slab steps into a rustic room with a big fieldstone fireplace. Heavy beams extended overhead, giving the space an echoing quality. Some of the furniture looked hand-hewn, and I suspected that Luther had made these pieces himself, perhaps even to weaving the rush seats. There were two fine pottery jars on the mantel, one a rose glaze, and one cerulean blue. A vase of autumn flowers stood on a rough trestle table. For all its austerity, the room held a quiet beauty.

As I glanced around at whitewashed walls, I saw that Luther had hung no pictures anywhere—not his own or anyone else's.

Kindling and logs were ready on the hearth, and Pete knelt to light a fire. I knew he was waiting for me to ask questions, to challenge him, and that he meant to offer nothing himself. I moved indirectly.

"Have you heard what happened to me last night on the way home from your sister's house?"

He nodded without turning from the fire. "I saw Alan when he arrived this morning and he told me. Liz shouldn't have let you come home alone. It's the night hours that can get to Luther, though he's never done anything like this before. It was at night that the house was set on fire, and sometimes he remembers."

"Did you know Mary Ames?"

Flames on the hearth had begun to throw off a welcome warmth, and Pete rose and looked directly at me. "I knew her well enough when we were kids."

"Those portraits of her at the house make her look almost angelic. Why would she do such an awful thing?"

"Who knows why anybody does anything?" Pete said bleakly.

It wasn't Mary I really wanted to know about now. "Please tell me," I said. "I want to hear all of it. About *you.*"

He said nothing, and his reluctance to begin was clear.

"At least you can tell me how you made the jump from being a teacher to playing in Ricky's band."

Again he stared at the fire. "It happened accidentally. I suppose you know that Tim persuaded Mrs. Ames to bring Ricky Sands to Windtop for one of her concerts? Almost everything that happened afterward started right then. Ricky's bass guitar player got sick and couldn't come along. I volunteered. The guitar has always been my hobby and Ricky's music was my kind. Sometimes I'd amused myself by accompanying his records." He turned to look at me coolly. "It wasn't your music then. Ricky said I was good and asked if I wanted a job. That was about seven years ago and I was teaching at the time. It wasn't until a few months later, when things fell apart for me and I needed to get away, that I thought of his offer. I went to New York, and he took me on. We decided on the name Peter Barron for me to use, and I let Pete Evans disappear for a while, though Evans is my real name. I suppose I'd still be Peter Barron if Ricky hadn't died." His account was as stark as his tone—the bare bones of events that must have been filled with emotion.

"How long were you with Ricky?" I asked.

"Until about a year ago, when he put us on hold because of his own troubles. No one around here knew what I was doing. Not even Liz, though I kept in touch with her. I just dropped out for a while and made a clean break until I could put myself together again."

I waited for him to go on, and when he continued he sounded almost indifferent—as though he spoke of something far removed from his own life.

"After Ricky died, I didn't want to look for another job as a guitar player. So I came back to Cold Spring Harbor to work things out."

"Did you know I was coming here?"

He merely stared at me, and I knew he wouldn't answer. That in itself made me uneasy.

"Were you in San Francisco when I married Ricky?" I asked.

"I was there. He took us all by surprise. None of us thought Ricky would ever marry."

Silence could be heavy with the unspoken. Pete and the others had undoubtedly believed that Ricky had married me for my songs. Not even I knew whether that was true or not.

"Did you like Ricky?" I asked directly.

"Of course. Everyone liked him. We hated what he was doing to himself. And to the band."

"To me, too," I said softly. "But that's over now. He can't hurt anyone anymore." Even as I spoke I knew it wasn't over. It couldn't ever be over until the nagging questions had been answered—one of them a question I feared. How deeply had Ricky been involved in Coral Caine's death?

"Why didn't you tell me right away that you'd played with Ricky's band and that we'd met?" I asked. "Why the masquerade?"

Pete had seemed evasive from the first, even while he answered my questions. Nor would he tell me anything readily now.

"Maybe I didn't want you to make any connections," he said.

"I don't know what connections to make. From the minute you showed up outside Coral Caine's building that day, I wondered how you happened to be there. Will you tell me now?"

He went to throw open the door, as though the room had become overheated. The movement seemed to release some tension that had risen in him.

"All right!" He gave in abruptly, and sat down opposite me by the fire. "I was there because Ricky asked me to go with him that day to see Coral Caine. Sometimes Ricky talked to me more than he did to the others in his band. I knew he was wildly angry with her, so I thought it might be better if I went along. We were there when you and Norris rang her apartment bell. Coral let us out the back door before she let you in."

This was what I'd been afraid to face ever since Coral had died—the fact that Ricky might have seen her that day. Now I could understand her agitation when she'd let us in. This was the connection Pete hadn't wanted me to make—and that I'd been pushing away from myself all along.

I forced myself to ask another question. "Where did Ricky go when you left?"

"I'm not sure. We separated outside. I didn't want to leave him because of the state he was in, but he insisted that he wanted to be alone. There was nothing else I could do. I walked around the block, and when I reached the door of Coral's building again, Ricky was nowhere in sight. I hung around for a while until you and Norris came out. When I saw you go stumbling off by yourself I thought you ought to have someone with you."

I remembered the way he had rescued me that day and given me a little breathing space before I went home. I hadn't understood his motives then, and I didn't fully understand them now, but at least I could be grateful.

"I never thanked you properly," I said.

He seemed suddenly angry—the first hint of emotion he'd shown since we'd started to talk. "You're asking for more than you may want, you know. There's still time to back off."

"I have to hear it all," I said doggedly.

"You didn't learn about Coral's existence until that day, did you?"

I shook my head. "Norris came to see me. He turned on the television set and showed her to me." The words had a dull ring, but I couldn't feel strongly anymore about that part of what had happened.

"Norris would!" Pete was still angry.

"Go on," I said. "What happened after you put me into a cab?"

Whatever he was angry about faded, and with it went the control he'd been exerting over himself. His voice shook as he went on, and I knew his pretense of being calm and unemotional was only that.

"I looked around again for Ricky, but he'd cleared out by that time. So—I went back to see Coral."

"*You* went back?"

He fiddled with the open collar of his shirt, and his hand was trembling. "You sure you want to hear all this?"

"I must hear it," I said.

"All right. I hope you can take it. She hadn't locked the rear door after us, and I went in that way. I found her on the floor in the living room. She was already dead. After that I got out of there fast, and out of the neighborhood. Then I phoned a woman whose name was on the mailbox in the lobby—a friend of Coral's. I told her I thought she needed help, and I didn't say who I was."

I had a feeling that everything was going to pieces inside me. Ever since Coral's death I'd been holding off this deep, terrible fear. Now Pete's words had brought it into the open, and I had to hear the rest.

"You think Ricky went back to see her, don't you? You think he had something to do with her death?"

Again he gave me that wary, evasive look, and I knew that Pete Evans was still not telling me everything.

"There's no real evidence to make me believe that," he said.

"Except that afterward Ricky couldn't live with what he'd done?"

Pete stood up abruptly, his own moment of weakness past. "I've got work to do before Mrs. Ames arrives."

"There's one more thing," I said. "Ricky used to send Coral Caine roses. Do you know about that?"

"Sure. She told everybody. She bragged about the color that matched her name."

"Norris and I met a florist's delivery man bringing her deep pink roses just as we left her apartment that day."

Pete nodded. "I saw them there. They'd come to mean something special to her—that Ricky was coming back. She'd have been excited about receiving them, happy."

"Yet she killed herself without ever taking the roses out of their tissue." I stared at him blindly.

"Look," he said, "maybe Coral had to die. Maybe it was the only way out for her, and she took it. Maybe it was better for everyone."

He didn't sound convincing, and I knew he didn't believe what he was saying.

"Norris and I both saw a card wired to the roses," I told him. "Yet the police didn't find a card. Did you see one?"

"I took it," Pete said.

"*You* took it?"

"To give to Ricky. I didn't think the police should see it just then."

"What did it say?"

For a moment he didn't answer, and when he spoke there seemed a warning in his voice.

"Don't ask questions, Hollis."

"Why shouldn't I ask questions? I want to know!"

"Let it alone. For now. You may find out one of these days."

There was some sort of danger here, and I didn't know what it was. I got up and walked through the door into sunlight, feeling light-headed and queasy.

Pete came with me. "Holding your breath won't help."

I gulped in air and steadied myself. Questions would do no good, when he wouldn't tell me the truth anyway.

"You'd better start walking," he said. "Walk fast—it will make you feel better. Go straight back to Windtop and finish that song. That's what you need right now. Don't try to find out everything, Hollis. There are some things it doesn't do us much good to know. The police are satisfied, so let it go at that."

Why had *he* let it go? I almost wished I'd never recognized Pete's voice on my tape recorder.

"Does Alan know you played with Ricky's band?" I asked.

"No! So don't tell him. Because of Tim, he hasn't any love for Ricky Sands. He might start digging, and I'm in a vulnerable position. I've told you more this morning than anyone else knows. Nobody's ever asked me more than casual questions, or turned up the fact that I was with Ricky in the Village that day. I'd just as soon it stays that way."

He grasped my arm as if for emphasis, and his fingers hurt me. At once he stepped back. "Sorry—I didn't mean to grab you like that."

But he had meant it. His grip had been a warning to say nothing. I wanted to get away from him—away from everyone, so I could think.

"There's no need for me to say anything to Alan just now," I assured him, and started up the hill.

I walked as fast as I could. I had a crazy impulse to run, to hide, to avoid seeing anyone for a long time. All I felt—the whole muddle of my fears—would be clearly written on my face for anyone to read. And there was too much I mustn't give away. Ricky could have been there when Coral died. He could have been to blame . . . he might have given her the drugs, or administered them himself!

I was lost in my own turmoil and completely unprepared when Luther Sykes appeared suddenly on the road before me. His white hair had blown wild in the wind, he was unshaven, and his eyes under thick gray brows had a glassy look that was unfocused. There was no one within shouting distance on this private road—no help for me if he took me for Mary Ames again.

"I'm Mrs. Baker," I told him quickly. "You *do* know me, Luther."

His quick, wiry movements made him almost dance on the road. "Of course I know you! Last night I got mixed up in the dark and I thought you were someone else. I've been walking around in the woods all night, trying to forget what I nearly did. Maybe I *am* crazy, like some folks say."

"It's all right," I told him. "I wasn't hurt. Mr. Gordon explained about the mistake you made. He's been looking for you, and he'll be glad to see you again."

The old man relaxed a little, and some of the wildness went out of him. "He's not angry with me?"

"He understands, Luther. We know you didn't mean what you did."

It was difficult not to speak to him as if he were a child. He had undoubtedly had a good education, and once he'd been a young and talented artist. Somewhere inside him that younger man still lived.

"I've seen one of your paintings," I said, and realized at once that it might not help to mention the portrait of Mary Ames.

He waved off my words with his scar-twisted right hand, and I was afraid he might get excited again.

"Mrs. Ames is coming home today," I went on quickly. "I must get back to the house now and see if I can help Birdy."

He hadn't known she was coming, and he stared at me in surprise. "I thought she was gone for good. I thought she'd close up the house now —maybe get rid of it."

"Why did you think that?"

"Houses that stay around for a long time can get notions of their own. Especially when bad things have happened in them. You ought to get out of there before the house hurts you. It doesn't like us—not any of us!"

"I have to go now," I repeated.

"You don't believe me! Don't you know that people who go down into death and come back can see things other people can't? I can see what that house is all about. Come along with me and I'll show you."

Before I could escape, he'd grasped my arm with his powerful left hand and was marching me back to the gatehouse. Pete saw us coming and left his work on the gate, only to have Luther wave him off.

"I'm just going to show her something she needs to see," he told Pete and took me into the big room, where flames were still lively in the grate. Pete followed us to the door, and stood there watching.

Luther went to rummage in a cupboard, and in a moment returned with a rough canvas in his hands, propping it against another chair. I stared at the painting in dismay.

This time he had done a portrait of Windtop. It was crude and unfinished, and I realized that he must have painted it with his left hand— since the fire. Yet it was recognizably the house in much of its rough detail, viewed from the front and showing red embers still glowing in the burned-out section. The chimneys leaned a little, the corner towers wavered, as though under water, while the lower windows seemed to peer out through a gauzy veil. Some sort of metamorphosis seemed to be taking place that threw everything off from the normal and into some world that belonged only to the house. A world that was clearly evil. Or mad.

"Well?" Luther said.

Pete said, "You painted what you saw in your own mind, Luther. Maybe it helped a little to blame the house. Instead of Mary."

"She was part of it! *She* knew what the house was like. Now it doesn't want to go on without her."

"Then we'll have to watch out," Pete said quietly. "We'll have to see that it doesn't damage those who live there now. Maybe you can help on that, Luther. Just keep your eyes open."

It was the best thing he could have said. His quiet words seemed to turn something around in Luther's mind, and bring him into protective alignment with us against the house.

"That's right," he agreed. "We'll all watch it now. You watch it especially, Mrs. Baker. It almost got you last night."

Pete made a slight gesture of his head toward the door, and I hurried out to make my escape. This time I climbed the hill without seeing anyone, and when I reached the upper drive I stood for a moment staring at Windtop's imposing facade, half expecting the chimneys to lean and the towers to waver. Luther's macabre painting was something I wouldn't soon forget. Fortunately, the house shone serenely in the sunlight, its walls secure and foursquare except for the scar of the fire.

I went inside and offered my services to Birdy, who merely sniffed me away. Alan was still gone, and I could only hope that everything was developing well between him and Tim. There was still at least an hour before Geneva Ames was due to arrive, and I remembered Pete's advice. I needed a rest from horror, and I went determinedly into the music room to see if I could once more become absorbed in my song.

My years of learning to concentrate helped, and I was able to blank out everything but my music. Notes seemed to flow from my fingers, carrying out the melody I could hear in my head. I was too deep in my work to notice when the Lincoln drew up in front of the house. This room could hold itself apart in a shell of silence, away from everything else.

When Geneva Ames opened the door and walked in, I came back to reality with a start. At the hospital I'd thought her patrician and rather autocratic. Now, dressed in a well-tailored gray suit, with a gray fur hat pulled at a jaunty angle, she gave an impressive and slightly contradictory effect. A woman of importance, with just a dash of something less proper about her. But I didn't think anyone would call her Jenny now.

I slid off the bench and stood up, feeling young and respectful as she came toward me with her hand held out.

"I'm delighted to see you in my home, Hollis. And I'm glad you found the Bechstein. That was an intriguing tune you were playing just now. Is it yours?"

"It's something I'm working on," I said lamely. I found that she awed me more than a little—this lady who had stepped out of my father's past.

Until this moment her portrait had dominated the room. Now it gave way to the real woman. A comparison was not unflattering, since she'd aged with distinction and dignity. She was a handsome woman, and she possessed even more assurance than the woman in the picture. I had the feeling that everyone around her would always snap to attention and carry out her slightest wish.

"I'd hoped that Alan would be here," she said as she moved about, touching the cover on the harp, shifting a music stand an inch—as though she reacquainted herself with her own possessions. "Do you know where he is?"

"He went down to The Shutters to see Tim."

"Of course. Tim is why I've come home. I'm not certain that Alan handles the boy in the right way, and I thought I might be useful now."

I felt relieved. I hadn't known where Geneva might stand when it came to Tim, and the boy didn't need any more obstacles in his path.

"I'm sure you will be," I said.

She smiled. "You're already on Tim's side, I see. Suppose you tell me what this is all about."

There seemed no reason to hold back anything that concerned Tim, so I told her of the tricks he had played on me, and how I had caught him.

"I think it's mainly because of his brother's opposition that he ran away," I finished. "Alan hates the idea of Tim becoming a pop singer and a songwriter. But when a young person feels as strongly as Tim does, no opposition is going to stop him—and it may make everything worse. Perhaps you can persuade him to delay a little until he's older."

Geneva nodded. "Yes, I remember how it was for me. I had to have my career before I tried any other road."

She took off her hat and set it on the piano. Then she smoothed a lock of upswept gray hair and sat down in a chair near me, crossing elegant legs.

"Of course this is different with Tim," she went on. "A different field altogether. You must realize that your husband was to blame for what is happening to Tim. I should never have invited Ricky Sands to come here in the first place."

The tone of her voice had darkened, and I knew that I'd congratulated myself too soon about her making things easier for Tim.

"My husband tried to encourage talent whenever he found it in the young," I said mildly.

The look she turned on me was commanding. "I wanted you to come here where I might see you again because we needed to talk. It isn't only because of Tim that I've come home."

"When you invited me to Windtop, you didn't tell me you'd met Ricky."

"It wasn't necessary. And of course impossible really to talk under hospital conditions."

I wasn't sure where she was leading, and it was a relief when Alan came into the room. He went quickly to greet Geneva with a kiss on the cheek.

"I've never seen you look better," he said. "I'm glad you're home. Birdy is fretting for us to come to lunch, so let's go in now, if you're ready." He looked past Geneva at me, and his smile was unexpectedly warm. "You've helped Tim a lot, Hollis. We'll talk about it at lunch."

They went ahead, with Geneva on Alan's arm, and as I followed I had a strange feeling that I was walking inside Luther's painting of the house. If I turned my head quickly as we crossed the side square of hall, I might catch the staircase shimmering in its own light, or find that the floor had moved subtly out of balance under my feet.

But I mustn't be haunted by a picture. With Geneva Ames here, nothing would dare to move even slightly askew at Windtop.

14

Lunch was a rather grand affair, with the three of us sitting in state at the table in the formal dining room. The meal went smoothly enough for a while, though Geneva Ames could ask penetrating questions.

"Luther looked a little wild when he came to open the gates for us," she said to Alan. "Is anything more than usual wrong with him?"

Alan gave me a quick, questioning glance before he answered. "He wasn't feeling well yesterday. I'm glad he's up and around again."

"I met him in the woods a little while ago," I said. "I told him you wanted to see him, Alan. I think he's better today."

"And Peter Evans?" Geneva went on. "What is he doing here?"

Again Alan explained. "He's staying at The Shutters with his sister, and he came up here looking for temporary work. So we took him on."

She shook her head doubtfully. "He seems an unstable young man. Elizabeth must have her hands full. I don't like the idea of a *teacher* doing yard work."

"Why shouldn't he do yard work?" I asked impulsively. "Why shouldn't a concert pianist get married and turn domestic, for that matter?"

For a moment she looked startled at my temerity, but her smile was kind. "You're right, of course. I was speaking out of turn. I'm glad you're here, my dear. Do you know what we'll do later today? We'll call California and talk to your father. Alan tells me Daniel was pleased when you let him know you were coming here. I'll enjoy speaking with him again after all these years."

I wasn't sure about a joint call to Dan, when I'd been too disturbed ever since I'd arrived to talk to him myself. I had written him a quick note that said very little, and that was all.

Geneva, however, took it for granted that I would agree, and went right on. "There are a few other things I'd like to do today. Are you free to help me, Hollis?"

"Yes, of course. I'll be glad to." I liked the idea of keeping busy, even though I knew that no matter what I did a strong undercurrent was bearing me along at a different level, threatening to come to flood and submerge me in some way I couldn't anticipate. It was impossible to put out of my mind what Pete Evans had told me.

Alan had noticed my distraction, and while we were finishing coffee in the sitting room he spoke to me directly. "Something's worrying you, Hollis. Is there anything I can do?"

I wouldn't give Pete away, but I could tell him a little. "I've just learned some new details about Ricky's life that are upsetting. I can't talk about them yet."

"You needn't talk about anything you don't want to," Geneva said, and I suspected that my relationship to Dan offered the main reason for her interest in me. Unlike the theme of my new song, perhaps *she* wanted to remember.

After lunch, when Alan had accepted an invitation to dinner at Windtop tonight, and had driven off to his greenhouse, Geneva stood at a window and watched him go.

"A fine man," she said. "He's always been dependable and considerate. Not a bit like young Tim. I must call Elizabeth soon and ask her to send that young rascal up here to see me. There's so much that needs to be done. It's good to be home—good to be alive!"

She took a step into the middle of the room and surprised me by whirling about with her arms outstretched—the movement of a much younger woman. I remembered her tilted hat—when hats in New York were being worn straight across the forehead. Geneva Ames could still fly in the face of petty convention when she chose, and I liked her all the more for her unguarded gesture.

"Have you explored my beautiful house?" she asked, turning back to me.

"Only a little. I'll feel more comfortable with it now that Tim's not hiding out, and trying to frighten me. Mrs. Ames—did you ever see the oil painting Luther Sykes made of this house?"

"You mean before the fire—while he could still paint?"

"No. I think he did this afterward. He even put in the burned-out section."

She shook her head, puzzled. "No, I haven't seen any such painting. I didn't know he'd even tried to use a brush again. What was it like?"

"Crude," I said. "But it had an eerie sort of power. A disturbing picture."

"You've made me think of something, Hollis. Something I decided before I came home. I've put this off for too long a time. Come outside with me for a moment."

Birdy had been hovering, with a watchful eye on Geneva, as though she expected her to collapse at any moment. When she saw we were going out, she rushed for a cape to put around Geneva's shoulders.

Outside, I followed to where we could stand on the driveway before the blackened ruins left by the fire. When Geneva slipped a hand through the crook of my arm, I felt her tremble, felt her weight as she leaned on me. But she allowed no weakness to reach her voice.

"When I was in the hospital I made myself face this over and over again in my mind—as I never would for years after it happened. I've had enough of pretending. I don't want this ugly scar to remain for a moment longer. I'll consult with Alan and have this debris cleaned out. I won't rebuild, but perhaps we can turn this space into a garden, an arbor. I've even thought of planting espaliered fruit trees against those awful black walls. The sun gets in here every morning, and it will make things grow. We were lucky that night to stop the fire before it spread to the whole house."

Her words poured out in a release of old, long-suppressed emotion. When she spoke of her daughter, however, there was visible control as she reined herself in, though bitterness came through.

"Mary is buried a long way from here. I've never visited her grave, or wanted to. I lost her forever that night."

"I learned only yesterday about what had happened," I said.

She went on in the same cool tone. "I've forgiven myself at last—though it took time and a few stays in the hospital for me to accomplish it. For too many years I accepted a blame that wasn't mine. Mary came home angry that time—she wanted a quarrel. And she grew angrier every day during that last visit. But how could I condone what she was doing?"

Now emotion came through again, and Geneva's eyes blazed. Her hand tensed on my arm, and two spots of high color burned in her cheeks. I watched her in alarm.

"There's still a score to pay off," she said.

I didn't know what she was talking about, since Mary was dead, and I was glad to see Birdy come running out of the house. She must have been watching from a window.

"You must rest now," she told Geneva firmly, and then looked at me. "You shouldn't have let her come out here!"

I could hardly keep Geneva Ames from doing whatever she pleased, and I suspected that Birdy's loyalty would be more extreme than ever, now that Windtop's owner was home again.

Left to myself, I returned upstairs to my peaceful azaleas. I took music paper from a suitcase and began to set down the notes for my song. The words on the tape were insistent, running through my head: *I mustn't remember.*

By now I knew how hard it was not to remember constantly. I hadn't made *my* peace yet, as Geneva Ames had done. I hadn't forgiven myself. Besides, there was something else. What if my fears were wrong! What if Ricky had been blameless, and driven at the end in some way I didn't understand? If that was true, didn't I owe it to him to discover the truth? And to find out about the roses.

With key in hand, I crossed the hall to the room where I'd stored the cartons. However painful it might be, I must look at Coral's letters and learn whatever they might tell me. I unlocked the door and pushed it open—to be greeted at once by a draft of wind and a swirl of flying papers.

Tim sat on the floor in the midst of the cartons he had spread around him, and was in the process of opening. He wore an outdoor jacket, and the open balcony window gave evidence of another trip across the roof.

This morning there were shadows under his eyes, as though he hadn't slept, and his longish hair was uncombed and windblown. He sat cross-legged on the floor, and made no effort to stop the flying papers, his look defiant.

I closed the door to stop the draft. "Do you live out on the rooftop these days, Tim?"

His grin mocked me. "I like it out there."

"Why?" I asked. "I should think it would be pretty scary."

"Maybe that's why I like it. The first time I went across the roof, I was about eight. It gave me a good feeling—being on top of everything, with death all around and me in charge! Aunt Geneva had a fit, and Alan gave me a licking. But they never stopped me from going out there when I felt like it. I used to think I wanted to be a mountain climber when I grew up."

"It seems to be a useful talent for you these days." I sat down on the bed and waved a hand toward the cartons. "What are you looking for, Tim?"

The hint of cockiness vanished and he ducked his head to hide a misery I glimpsed for just an instant.

"It's all right to tell me," I said gently. "Maybe we're even on the same side. Maybe we're looking for the same answers."

"Okay!" Defiance was back, and he still didn't trust me, but he went on, groping for words. "I want to know *why* Ricky did it. Down at The Shutters, Pete was talking to Liz about all this stuff you brought from New York. And about putting a lock on the door. So I decided to have a look."

"No one knows you're here at Windtop?"

"I'm good at giving them the slip! I just came up through the woods to sneak inside and up the back stairs. Why did you bring all this stuff out here, Hollis? What *is* it?"

I decided on the truth. "For one thing I needed to sort through Ricky's papers. For another, I'm looking for the same thing you are, Tim. More than anything else, I want to know why he did it."

"What if you're the reason?"

"I really don't think I am. But I'd like to understand, no matter where the road leads. Maybe Ricky could have come out of drugs and gone back to work again. God knows, I wanted him to. The best I knew how, I wanted to help him."

Tim's eyes filled with tears, and he bent his head again. I felt pity for him, and a certain kinship. Ricky had given Tim a hero to love and admire. Which, in the beginning, was what he'd given me. That we'd loved a hollow man made it all the worse now. But of course Tim hadn't accepted that.

After a moment he sniffed and rubbed tears from his cheeks.

"Have you found anything interesting?" I asked. "Anything useful?"

After a moment of what seemed like inner wrestling, he dipped a hand into the nearest carton and brought out a packet of letters that he waved at me. "Maybe these have some answers—I don't know. I guess they're love letters from that actress—Coral Caine."

These were what I had come for and I stiffened. He went on quickly. "They're old letters, Hollis. From before he married you."

"In that case, I'm not sure either of us should read them. I'll put them in my room and just skim them later. To see if they might tell us something."

I half expected an argument from him, but he gave up the packet of letters, and I carried them to my room and locked them into a suitcase. When I returned, Tim was closing the window.

"Can I help with all this stuff?" he asked.

"Maybe you can. Let's go through the rest of the cartons I haven't opened yet, and see what we can find."

It was something to have him accept me at all, and I found a certain comfort in the company of this boy who had so admired Ricky and still suffered over his death. Perhaps Pete Evans ought to let him know that he had played in Ricky's band. That might be something for Tim to hold onto, since he seemed to like Pete.

We worked quietly on the remaining boxes, bringing nothing of special interest to light. Tim found a batch of fan letters that excited him, and he read through every one.

"Those used to come in by the thousands," I said. "We saved only a few of the best ones. There's even a letter from you that I found earlier."

"He kept one from me?" Tim sounded touchingly pleased. "Even before I went to New York to meet Ricky, I wrote to him. And sometimes he answered. I have every letter he sent me. Not that there were all that many, and they weren't very long. But they were in his own writing. He didn't use a typewriter, or have somebody else write to me."

"Yes." I remembered how Ricky had felt about his fans when he had been himself and feeling well. When I'd first known him, he'd have liked to answer them all. "He just picked out a few and wrote to those fans himself," I told Tim.

"I have all his albums. And most of the singles. Hollis—it wasn't true what I said to you on that tape. I mean that your songs weren't good for Ricky Sands. They're wonderful songs. I just wanted to hurt you."

"I know that, Tim. Maybe we can help each other now. We're about finished here, so let's reseal the cartons, and then I'd like you to hear something."

The contrasts in him could be startling. He could be angry and vindictive, even threatening, and then a moment later he would be amiable and considerate. In an "artist," as performers were referred to in the music business—this would be called temperament. Someday he might even command a few fans himself, strange voice and all. The important thing now was to get him to wait.

"Will Liz wonder where you've got to?" I asked.

"I told her I was going for a walk. She's not worried about me now. This morning I promised her and Alan that I'd go back to school next week. I guess it's okay. I guess that's what I have to do."

When the cartons were sealed with fresh tape, I helped Tim pile them on the bed again. Nothing of any special interest had turned up except for Coral's letters. I'd come here to read them, but not with Tim watching me.

He came with me across the hall when I returned to my room, and he looked around at the azaleas.

"This is where Ricky stayed that time he came here with his band," Tim said. "His musicians all had rooms close by. Ricky liked the view and the balcony, and I remember he said the bed was wonderful."

I dropped into the nearest chair. Ricky had been in these rooms? He'd slept in the bed where I slept every night at Windtop? I'd been glad to leave the physical sense of Ricky's presence behind in New York. Only I hadn't! He had sung in the music room downstairs, and he'd lived in these same rooms for two days, slept in the same bed I slept in now. He had stood on this balcony, looking out toward the harbor, seeing the same view I'd enjoyed.

"You okay?" Tim asked.

I nodded at him. "I'm being silly. I hadn't realized that Ricky'd stayed in these rooms."

"Birdy said that was why Aunt Geneva wanted you to have them. Alan didn't like it, but everybody does what she says. Mostly."

This seemed especially strange, when neither one had mentioned that Ricky had been in this house.

"You could ask Birdy to move you," Tim suggested.

"No, I won't do that. I'll get used to it. In New York there was too much to remind me." I was talking half to myself. "All the times we walked on Madison Avenue, looking at the shops, and sometimes hearing his voice come out of some music store singing 'Sweet Rain.' It was all so sharp for me in New York."

"I know," Tim said simply. "Just the same, I guess I can understand what he did. When I stop being mad about it and blaming other people.

Everything must have hurt too much, so all he wanted was to make the hurting stop."

He sounded wistful, and I knew that reasoning wasn't good enough. "If he'd just talked to someone! That's the best way to clear up confusions. Confusion is temporary—and his solution wasn't. There are better ways to get out of pain, Tim. Even making up songs helps."

This time he really seemed to be listening, and I pushed my advantage. "I've put some of my new song on tape. Will you listen and tell me what you think?"

"Sure. I'd like that."

He really meant it, and I reminded myself that I was now his one tie with Ricky Sands and a world he wanted to belong to. I must move very carefully.

I ran the tape back and played it through to the point where Pete had walked into the music room. Tim listened intently, and then said, "Play it again." I remembered the time in San Francisco, when Ricky had used those words.

When he'd heard it three times he nodded. "It's really like that. I mean what the song is saying. About not wanting to remember, but remembering anyway. There's one place, though, in the tune . . ."

He hummed a few notes, and I knew what he meant and that he was right. "That's good, Tim. Very good. Let me get it down before I lose it." I went to the desk and wrote in the slight changes. "I can even pick this up in the introduction—maybe vamp it a little. A vamp can be useful. You need to hear only a few introductory bars of the vamp to 'New York, New York'—and you know what's coming."

Tim looked pleased with my approval. "When you played the tape, just now, I could hear Ricky singing. I bet he'd have liked this song. I wish I had Ricky's kind of voice. But then, nobody else could have."

I smiled at him. "I think you may do all right, Tim—when the time comes. I did it too soon, even though I was older than you are. And that makes it harder for me now."

"You better send that one in. Somebody will want to sing it." He ran a hand through his windblown hair, mussing it still more. "Guess I'd better get back to Liz's now. I didn't think I'd be gone so long. Say— did Luther ever turn up? I heard about what happened last night."

"Yes, I saw him today. And I think he's sorry for what he did. He's a strange sort of man. This morning he showed me a horrible picture he'd painted of Windtop. Did you ever see it, Tim?"

"The one where everything is sort of off focus? It gives me the creeps. But after the fire, he was never the same as he was before."

"Were you here when it happened?"

"I was just a kid. Mary'd come home for a few days and she didn't do anything but fight with Aunt Geneva. I don't know what about. She did a lot of yelling. It used to be that everybody was crazy about her—until she changed. Alan and Pete both wanted to marry her. And old Luther was always painting her when she was little. Until she turned into somebody else. The last night she was here she got up in the middle of the night and set the house on fire. I think she picked that wing because she knew Aunt Geneva had so much there that she treasured."

"Then you saw the fire?"

"Sure. I went out on the roof where I could look right down and watch the firemen putting it out. I even saw what she did to Luther." Tim sounded excited, like someone remembering a play.

"It must have been awful," I murmured.

"It wasn't so bad—except for Luther—since the whole house didn't burn down. Though I guess Aunt Geneva lost all those family things she couldn't replace."

He was leaving out the main tragedy. "To say nothing of her daughter," I added.

"I know. We never saw her again."

"I feel terribly sorry for Mrs. Ames," I said. "I don't think she's ever recovered from Mary's death in the fire that night."

Tim stared at me as though I'd gone suddenly crazy. "Hey! What're you talking about? Mary didn't die in that fire. She just took her car and drove off like crazy, and we never saw her again. Anyway, I never did. I suppose she really did die that night for Aunt Geneva—and Birdy, too. Maybe that's how you came to be mixed up about her."

"Mary didn't die in the fire?" I repeated blankly. Birdy had certainly told me that deliberately. "But then what happened to her? Mrs. Ames told me she was buried a long way from here."

"I wouldn't know. Nobody talks about her. Aunt Geneva won't have her name mentioned, even though this was years ago. Sometimes I wonder if Mary is still alive, and I wonder what would happen if she showed up again. . . . Well, I better be going. Thanks, Hollis. I mean —*thanks.*"

"Wait a minute," I said. "Shouldn't you see Mrs. Ames while you're here? Or at least Birdy?"

"I don't want to see them now. I have to figure things out first."

Without realizing how badly he'd shaken me, he went off down the hall. I turned back to the rooms where Ricky had once stayed, and sat down, feeling more bewildered than ever.

A web of concealment and deceit had been woven around me ever since I'd come here. They were all part of it—Alan, Mrs. Ames, Birdy, Liz Cameron. Even Pete Evans. In various ways I'd been told—or at least allowed to believe—untruths. Seven years ago Ricky had come to Windtop with his band, and no one had told me that. Though I had been allowed to believe that Mary had died in the fire, no one had disillusioned me. In fact, Birdy had said this in front of Alan, and he hadn't contradicted her.

Perhaps there'd been no reason to tell me that both Alan and Pete had been in love with Mary Ames. Yet this might explain a good deal about both men. Was this why Alan sometimes seemed remote and lost in unhappy thoughts? And why he'd named his boat the *Mary?* I began to think of him in a new way—as someone with a wound that had never quite healed. Would Mary have married him if she'd stayed here? Was this what Geneva had wanted, and why she'd been against his marrying Liz Cameron?

Again I had the feeling of being inside Luther's painting—as though landscapes that had seemed to have clear, firm lines had wavered into shapes that were never what they appeared to be.

"Mrs. Sands? Mrs. Sands!" Birdy's voice broke into my thoughts as she came rapping on my door.

When I went to open it, she looked past me eagerly, as though she expected to find someone else there.

"Tim's gone," I said. "He was just here for a little while. I think he'll be all right now."

"I knew he was in the house! I always feel it when he's around. He should have waited to see me. Mrs. Ames wants you now. Right away, please."

That was fine with me. There were a few questions that I wanted to ask of Geneva Ames, and this was as good a time as any to confront her.

15

I could hear the piano as I went downstairs. When I walked into the music room Geneva smiled at me and went on playing Tchaikovsky's music for the little swans.

"My daughter used to dance to this here in this very room," she said. "Mary was a gifted child with a choice of talents, but most of all she loved to dance. She was *en pointe* in her early teens, and she had such grace. She was enchanting!"

I had come down primed with questions, but her words had disarmed me.

Geneva raised her hands from the keys and rubbed her knuckles. "I can't play as I used to. I haven't touched the Bechstein in months. I'm trying to make my peace and accept what can't be mended. But it's never easy."

How well I knew that.

She turned about on the bench. "Will you come upstairs with me, Hollis? There's a room on the attic floor I need to visit, and I don't want to do it alone."

"Of course," I said. "Can you manage the stairs?"

"With your help I can."

Birdy came into the room muttering and protesting, but Geneva shook her head. "Hush! It's perfectly all right for me to climb stairs if I move slowly. I'm a little weak, but I'm not an invalid. If you want to help me, stop scolding."

On the way up we paused frequently for Geneva to rest. When we reached the attic floor I expected her to turn toward the tower room that had once been Mary's studio, but instead she moved toward the opposite tower, where I'd seen Birdy the night before.

"We've always used the attic for general storage," she said, "but I've kept a few special things in this tower room."

Unlike the opposite tower, this space was crowded, and had little furniture. Birdy found a straight chair for Geneva, who waved an imperious hand as she sat down.

"First, that trunk over there, please," she directed Birdy.

While Birdy lifted the hinged top, I found an old camphorwood chest, where I could perch and watch silently. All my questions must still be postponed until the right moment arose.

The trunk appeared to be filled with old clothes, and when Birdy pulled out a wrinkled blue dress and shook it out, I recognized the dress of the little girl in Luther's portrait, painted in a happier day.

"You shouldn't do this," Birdy said as Geneva took the faded blue frock from her. She held the dress to her face for a moment, as though she wanted to recover the warmth and scent of the child who had once worn it.

"I don't like this," Birdy insisted. "It's time for you to face everything that happened. She's gone, and maybe it's a good thing."

"Birdy, Mary didn't die in the fire, as you told me, did she?" I asked softly.

"Of course she didn't!" Geneva laid the frock across her lap and smoothed the fabric. "Why would you tell her that, Birdy?"

"It was necessary." Birdy sniffed and tossed her head.

I had no idea what she meant. More questions were still there, waiting.

Birdy continued to bring other articles from the trunk, among them a small pair of pink ballet slippers with blocked toes, soiled from use.

Geneva held out her hand for the slippers, and Birdy gave them to her reluctantly. "All of Mary's young dreams were in these—and they all came to nothing."

"She wasn't that good a dancer," Birdy said.

"Where is the scrapbook?" Geneva asked. "It should be in this trunk with her other things. Why haven't we found it?"

Birdy shrugged, but the quick, silencing look she turned on me betrayed her. I had seen her in this room last night, and she didn't want Geneva to know.

"There are pictures of Mary in that book that I want to see again," Geneva went on.

"I'll look for it another time," Birdy said quickly. She seemed more flustered than I'd ever seen her, and when she cast another quick look at me she seemed almost frightened.

Geneva gave in. "All right, we'll let it go for now. I'm a little tired. May I visit your rooms on the way down, Hollis? I haven't seen that suite for a long time."

Whatever determination had brought her up here had evaporated with her fading energy.

"Please do come," I told her.

When Birdy had put everything away, we went down to the second floor to my rooms. At the door she turned to Birdy.

"Would you like to serve us tea?" she asked. "We'll come down for it in a little while. Don't bring it up here."

Birdy went off looking huffy over being dismissed, and Geneva smiled. "She's a dear. I couldn't get along without her. But she does like to be in the middle of whatever's happening, and perhaps it's time for you and me to talk alone."

She stood looking about the sitting room, nodding to herself. Anger and grief had retreated to their deep hiding place.

"I always feel calm and relaxed in these rooms. May I sit down for a few moments, Hollis?"

In the chaise longue she stretched out with her eyes closed, sighing gratefully. I sat opposite her and waited. Something would come out of this, when she was ready.

What came surprised me. "Tell me what you think of Alan?" She spoke without opening her eyes.

"Why—he's been very helpful ever since I came here."

"That's not what I mean. He has spoken of you quite warmly, my dear. He approves of you. I wondered what you thought of him—as a man."

"We hardly know each other," I said carefully.

She laughed and the sound had a rich, musical ring. "You mustn't mind an old woman's frankness. There's no time anymore for polite equivocation. Alan's been lonely for too long. He's like a son to me, and I want to see him happy."

And I was Dan Temple's daughter, I thought, not trusting myself to speak. There had been moments when I'd warmed strongly to Alan

Gordon, and I didn't want to give Geneva Ames the slightest edge, lest she run over me, and over Alan too. I wasn't ready yet.

She sensed my reluctance to talk and changed the subject quickly. "Let's telephone your father. I have enough courage now. We can do it from your phone right here. Do you think he'll be home?"

Courage was something she'd never lack. "He could be. I'll call him, if you like."

I sat down and began to dial. Even though I wasn't ready to talk to Dan, this would break the silence, and with Geneva here I needn't try to tell him anything important.

Dan himself answered the call, and at the sound of his voice I tried to speak cheerfully, assuring him that everything was fine, and said there was someone here who wanted to talk with him. Then I handed the phone to Geneva and went out in the hall. As I closed the door, I heard her say, "Hello, Daniel," in a voice that pretended to be steady.

I wandered out of earshot toward the stairs, and when I returned after a few moments, the door was open again, and Geneva lay back in the chaise longue, a slight smile on her lips that told me the conversation had not been unhappy.

"He called me Jenny," she said. "I suppose the someone young and foolish we once were stays inside us all our lives. We pile on layers of experience, allegiance to new loves, new lives. But underneath it all we *do* remember, Hollis. I liked the song you were working on, but it needs to say something more."

"I'm glad you could talk with him."

"I am too. I suppose I'll always wonder what would have happened if I'd taken the other road. What if I'd been willing to give up my music and marry Daniel Temple? We couldn't have made it otherwise, with each of us traveling off in different directions."

"You wouldn't have been happy. You had to do what you did."

"I'm afraid that's true and I shouldn't have any regrets. Mine was the greater talent. Daniel knew that. I had to have my chance."

"Yet in the end you gave it up to marry another man and retired from your music."

"I don't know whether that was right either. I was getting tired of a hard, strenuous existence, and I'd achieved what I wanted to do. But it wasn't enough—for me. John Ames was an altogether stronger man than Daniel. And I suppose I needed someone stronger in those days. I wonder if there aren't some women—strong women—who still need to be dominated? Maybe the old idea of looking up to a man was more comfortable in some ways. It required less of us. Though a part of me gets furious at the very thought."

"Were you happy with John Ames?"

"I'm not sure I know what that means. I wanted a child, and we had a beautiful daughter. *That* is what I must try to remember. That it wasn't all horrible and tragic. There were happy times."

I wanted to ask how Mary had died, if not in the fire, but I didn't dare. Though I could still ask something else.

"Why didn't you tell me that Ricky's band had come to Windtop? When I asked that earlier, you said it was irrelevant and that you couldn't talk about it in the hospital. Can you talk about it now? Why did you put me into the very rooms where he'd stayed?"

She answered me calmly. "These are lovely rooms, and you needed a haven. If I'd told you, would you have come?"

"I don't know," I said. "Perhaps not. But why these rooms? Wouldn't it occur to you that my memories of Ricky might make me unhappy, staying here?"

"If I thought about it at all, perhaps I thought it would never come up."

"Tim told me—just a little while ago. He came up to Windtop on a mission of his own, and we talked for a while. He said he wasn't ready to meet you yet."

"That was foolish of Tim. But I'll see him later. Would you like to be moved out of these rooms, Hollis?"

It doesn't matter now. I just don't understand not being told that Ricky had come to Windtop."

The telephone rang and I picked it up.

"Hello—Hollis? This is Liz Cameron. I'm going down to the village on a couple of errands. There's just time before everything closes. Would you like to come along?"

"I'd love to," I said. I was ready enough to escape from Windtop for a while. And escape Geneva, who made me uneasy with the imposition of her will on others. Liz said she'd pick me up in twenty minutes, and I told Geneva.

"That's a good idea. Will you help me downstairs now, please? I'd like to go to my room and rest before dinner. I'll see you then."

When I'd left Geneva in her room and called Birdy, I changed to beige slacks, a green pullover, and a light jacket. Then I went downstairs to wait for Liz Cameron.

Wind had whipped the trees nearly bare of their last leaves, though piles still collected on the ground. Pete was out in front raking them up and stuffing them into bags. The afternoon light was fading, and he was getting ready to stop.

I walked across to speak to him, remembering what Tim had dropped so casually—that Pete Evans had once been in love with Mary Ames. He was the boy next door, and they'd all grown up together, so it was natural enough. But how serious had it been for him?

"Have you finished your song?" he asked as I reached him.

"Almost. I played it on my tape this afternoon for Tim, and he liked it."

"Tim has a good ear, and he's in tune with the kids. Are you still trying to convince yourself that you mustn't remember?"

"I don't want to! I wonder why no one else told me that Ricky had come here? I even have the same rooms he stayed in."

"I know." He was watching me in that oddly intense way I remembered from the first time, when I'd sat across from him at a table in a Village cafe.

"I'm going into town with your sister," I said, moving away.

"Did Birdy tell you I put new glass over Ricky's gold record of 'Sweet Rain'? I left it on the hall table for you."

"Thank you." I could hear Liz's car coming up from the gate, and I started across the drive.

"I remember the party Ricky threw when that record hit the top of the charts," Pete said. "You weren't there."

I paused with my back to him. "Ricky liked to keep me under wraps. He never wanted me to come to those bashes. As though I might melt."

I still recalled how upset I'd been that Ricky hadn't wanted me to attend that particular party—when "Sweet Rain" had been my song too.

"Coral Caine came that night," Pete said. "Whether she was invited or not, I don't know."

I hadn't realized this, and I wondered why Pete should tell me now. To hurt me? To turn some screw that gave him satisfaction? I didn't understand Pete Evans, any more than I did Alan. There were times when Pete seemed almost a friend—and other times when he threw down challenges I didn't want to pick up. How much of a friend had he really been to Ricky?

Liz reached the house, and I ran toward the green Pinto and got in beside her. At first glance she looked as cheerful as usual, and I was glad to see her. Not until we were on our way down Snake Hill Road did I realize that the cheerfulness was a facade. Underneath lay something tense and jittery, even though she tried to sound as she usually did. Nor was she as well groomed as I'd always seen her. Unruly strands of blond hair escaped their combs; her jeans showed earth stains at the knees, and her blouse was wrinkled, with a spot of black grease on one sleeve. "Unkempt" was hardly a word I'd have used for Elizabeth Cameron in the past, and her careless appearance added to my sense of something seriously wrong.

"First we'll stop at the Whaling Museum," she said. "I'm a trustee, and I need to see the director. You can look around while I'm talking with him. This is one of the best little museums on Long Island, and perhaps you can pick up some of Geneva's family history."

The afternoon was darkening, and though there was still color in the sky, all the lights were on along Main Street, so the little shops glowed like miniature stage sets, inside and out. Old houses that were still homes climbed the hills above, and spread higher into the newer residential sections of town.

The museum was at the far end of the street, just before it became a highway again. We parked in front of a building that was in character with the rest of the street. Its wide, gray-shingled roof slanted over whitewashed walls. A white steeple rose in the center, topped by a weather vane whale flipping its tail in the breeze. On either side of a black central door, black-shuttered windows contrasted with white walls. Again there was the motif of a white whale on the entry panel. Next door, construction was going on to convert another building into an extension of the museum.

We went in innocently enough, though perhaps if Liz had guessed what I'd find, she might not have taken me there.

I liked the feeling of order without clutter, offering much to see, but with enough open space to make the two large rooms attractive. Leading the way past a long whaleboat that had once been used to row out from a ship, Liz stopped before a display of scrimshaw.

"Geneva gave the museum these pieces," she said. "She'd been collecting scrimshaw for years, and her grandfather, Joshua Dickey, carved some of these himself. When so much was lost in the fire, it was lucky that she'd placed her collection here. Joshua was mate on a whaling ship out of Cold Spring, as they used to call it. 'Harbor' was added later because there's another Cold Spring upstate. He might have been the town's first whaling captain, if he hadn't died young at sea. Amuse yourself, Hollis. I won't be long."

Only Japan and Russia still hunted the great sea beasts, and the need for oil and spermaceti and ivory was long past, so everything here belonged to a period of history.

Away from home for months and years, while their ships roamed the world's oceans, sailors had developed the art of etching scenes and decorations on the teeth and bones of whales, then inking in the designs. Some of the items in the case were utilitarian—sewing things, pie crimpers, and other household trinkets. Some were purely decorative and each sailor had carved whatever his imagination prompted. Some were scenes of the sea, or of a sailor's home, or represented historical events in the past. One broad whale tooth in the collection bore the exquisite face of a girl, and at once I focused on that out of all else in the case. A card beneath it stated that this was the work of Joshua Dickey, grandfather of Geneva Ames. The miniature face was haunting, the smile impudent, the dark eyes hinting at something tantalizingly withheld. Her ink-black hair was center-parted in the style of that day, and I saw by the legend underneath that Joshua had drawn the face of his young wife, Geneva.

I studied the carving thoughtfully, not only because she might have been the first Geneva, but because I had a strong feeling that I'd seen a depiction like this before. Somewhere I had seen a similar linear drawing. Perhaps of this very face. But where?

I wandered on through the rooms, looking at displays concerned with all aspects of whaling, stopping to enjoy a seaworn figurehead that had graced a sailing ship a hundred years and more ago. Yet all the while, the distinctively carved face of Geneva Dickey stayed with me, tantalizing, trying to tell me something.

When Liz rejoined me, I took her to the scrimshaw case and pointed out the carved tooth. "Do you know anything about this piece?"

"I don't think so. It seems to be Geneva's grandmother. Why?"

"I'm not sure. It seems familiar in a strange way."

Liz had nothing to suggest as we left the museum.

"Our next stop's the library," she said, when we were again in the car. "I've some books to return and pick up. We'll go downstreet now. That's the term people use for the busy end of the village. That's why you'll see the Downstreet Bookstore over there across Main Street. And notice the store Gilliwrinkles. That's what people used to call odds and ends."

Her words came breathlessly, as though some inner agitation still stirred beneath the surface, and I wished I knew what was troubling her.

Again as we drove along, I enjoyed the peach tones and greens and sparkling whites that had been used on old houses that were now shops and restaurants along the street, their colors still visible in the artificial lighting of late afternoon. The sky had clouded over and it was almost dark.

The library stood at an angle where the shopping area ended, and Elizabeth said it had been built early in the century. She parked at one side and we walked up to the red-brick building. Again there was a white steeple rising from the roof, and slim white columns on either side of the entrance. We entered a wide room with a beamed cathedral ceiling and bookstacks on both sides, the library desk straight ahead.

When Elizabeth had returned her books and checked out two that were being held for her, she nodded to me. "Here's a chance to talk without anyone from Windtop overhearing us."

I wondered at such secrecy, and at her agitation, which seemed to be increasing. Beyond the stacks on our right a bay window looked out upon the darkening sky, and a comfortable red-leather sofa offered a place to sit. The round reference table nearby was empty at the moment, and the bookstacks made a screen that gave us privacy.

"You're worried about something," I said as we sat down.

"Does it show that much? I worry about a lot of things. Tim, Pete, Alan—me. The way Tim is obsessed by Ricky's death scares me. Hollis, have you ever reached a place where everything seems so hopeless that it would be wonderful to do what Ricky did?"

Coming from Liz, the words shocked me. She, of all people, had always seemed cheerful and well-balanced.

"I suppose everyone thinks about this now and then," I said.

"I should think *you* might—with all you've been through. I don't know how you've endured all that's happened."

I didn't want commiseration, and I didn't believe she was really speaking about me.

"Would it help to talk about what's bothering you?" I asked.

She winced as though my words had stung. "There're some things I'm afraid to know more about. Pete's been behaving strangely. I didn't realize until now that he'd been with Ricky Sands's band for these last years. Oh, he wrote to me and phoned me after he went away, but he wouldn't tell me what he was doing, or where he was. As though there was some sort of expiation he had to perform before he could come back to us. We always used to talk—now we don't at all. After a while everything seems to pile up and becomes too much to take. Do you ever feel as though life is so pointless there's no reason to bother?"

Her words came too close to my own half-buried fears. "It's not that simple," I said.

"I know. Misery and desperation aren't anybody's private property. You're lucky to have your song writing. What else pulls you along?"

"I know one thing that pulls me," I told her. "I feel as though I can't rest or settle down to anything else until I know why Ricky died. Lately there are times when I feel as though I'm getting close to an answer. As though something is about to open up around me—if I just wait."

"What possible answer do you mean? You must know his motives by now."

"I don't think it was the right time for him to die. Sometimes I wonder . . . what if it wasn't suicide?"

This was the first time I'd put such a thought into words, and I wanted at once to take it back.

Liz looked startled. "How could it have been anything else?"

"I don't know. I don't know how it could have happened at all. There was a woman who died a year before he did—an actress he'd had an affair with. Sometimes I've wondered if there might be a connection. Pete has told me that Ricky went to see her just before she died."

"Do you mean he might have killed himself out of remorse because he felt responsible?"

"It's possible, though Ricky wasn't awfully good at remorse. You met him when he came to Windtop, didn't you?"

She sighed. "Yes, I attended that famous concert, just like everyone else. Except Alan, who had sense enough to stay away. I'm afraid I never found Ricky Sands as charming as others did. That sort of music isn't for me." She broke off apologetically. "Sorry! I forgot that it's your music too."

"I don't mind. It takes a good many years to become respectable and accepted."

She brushed at her knees abruptly. "Look at me! I'm a mess. I was working on my car this afternoon. I'm good at engines, you know. And then I raked leaves for a while before I realized how late it was."

It seemed revealing of her state of mind that for once she hadn't bothered about her appearance, hadn't cared.

"Hollis, why did you come here?"

The sudden question surprised me. "Why, I came because Mrs. Ames invited me. She used to know my father. You must have heard about that?"

"You could have refused. What made you accept?"

"It seemed a good idea to get away from New York. And I didn't know where else to go. Why does what made me come here seem important?"

She sidestepped the question. "What do you hear from New York about your husband's death? Pete was wondering if anything new had turned up."

"There's been nothing. As far as the police go, the case is closed. They don't think there's any mystery about his killing himself."

"That's good," Liz said. "Sometimes Pete comes up with strange ideas that I can't figure out."

"Such as?"

"I don't know . . . it's almost as though he feels guilty about something that happened around that time."

Pete himself had told me about going to Coral Caine's apartment near the time of her death, but where he'd been a year later when Ricky died, I didn't know. By that time the band was breaking up.

"I'm not in touch with anyone in New York but Norris Wahl," I told her. "Norris was my husband's manager, and I haven't let anyone but him and my father know where I am. Though of course if anything new came up someone would get in touch with me at once. Right now I'm happy to keep out of sight."

"That's probably wise. Well . . . we might as well get back. The library's ready to close."

As we returned to the car I wondered why she had wanted a quiet talk with me. Nothing of any consequence had come out that I could tell, and it was disturbing to find that Liz Cameron, who had seemed so capable, so confident and strong, was no more sure about her life than Tim was about his, or I about mine.

At dinner that night I noticed that a change had been made in the dining room. The portrait of Mary Ames—the professional portrait in the yellow dress—that had hung in the sitting room had been removed and placed on the dining-room wall, where Geneva sat with her back to it. I remembered that Alan and Birdy had spoken of moving the picture.

As Geneva and Alan and I sat down, I sensed quickly that something was wrong. Geneva's control was perfect, as always, but she wore a more haughty air than usual when she spoke to Alan, and at times she sounded tart.

He, at least, seemed unruffled by her displeasure, and even mentioned it to me. "We've had a small disagreement, Hollis. Partly because of you."

I looked blankly from one to the other.

"Not really because of you," Geneva assured me. "Alan exaggerates. This concerns Tim. You might as well explain, Alan, since you've opened this up."

"It's nothing for you to worry about, Hollis," he said calmly. "I happen to feel that it might be better for Tim to stay with me for the time being. He doesn't altogether trust me yet, and we need to break down a few barriers. We can't do that unless he's with me. Birdy mothers him, and he has a real affection for Geneva, but I still feel that he shouldn't move into Windtop now. Because of you, Hollis."

I started to protest. "But we've started to become friends. . . ."

Alan went on, "That's the point. You have helped him, but in this house the connection with Ricky Sands can only go on and on. You were Ricky's wife, and because of your music, Tim—"

"Is that so damaging?" I broke in. "Maybe I'm already getting him to see that he needs to wait."

"I want Tim where I can watch him and advise him myself." Geneva sounded unshakable. "But I'd rather you didn't encourage him about this music thing in any way."

"Then perhaps I'd better leave soon," I said. "I'd planned to accept your invitation for only a little while, Mrs. Ames—until I could get my bearings."

She was already shaking her head, dismissing my words. "I'd like you to stay, Hollis. And I want Tim here too. So let's not discuss this any more now. Why don't you tell us about your afternoon, Hollis?"

This settled nothing, but her will overrode both Alan's and mine. I could sympathize with him, since there was clearly no way to argue with Geneva Ames.

A bit self-consciously I tried to talk about my visit to the Whaling Museum, and as I spoke I found myself staring at the wall beyond Geneva's head, where the portrait of Mary Ames hung. It held my attention even more than it had before.

When I mentioned the scrimshaw collection, Geneva warmed a bit, and began to speak of her grandfather, relating stories that had been handed down in the family. Yet all the while, as she talked, my attention kept returning to the portrait behind her. This artist had certainly been more expert than Luther, though more conventional. Luther's cruder painting had caught something of what Mary's younger spirit must have been. There had seemed a sense of laughter about to surface —a hint of mischief, perhaps. Quite suddenly I saw the resemblance.

Of course—that was it! I felt relieved over solving a puzzle. Yet slightly disturbed as well.

Alan noticed the change in my expression. "What is it, Hollis?"

I explained about the likeness I'd seen that Joshua Dickey had been clever enough to catch in his tiny scrimshaw etching—the likeness of his young wife's face.

"I kept thinking I'd seen that face somewhere before," I said, "and I've just remembered where. It was in Luther's painting of Mary Ames that hangs upstairs in the attic. Did your daughter look like her great-grandmother, Mrs. Ames?"

Geneva and Alan exchanged a look with some meaning that escaped me.

"I believe a likeness has been noticed between her and old photographs of my grandmother. It's a resemblance that skipped my father and me."

Now I could relax, with the answer found, and stop thinking about the scrimshaw face. I wasn't in the least prepared for the lightning flash that seemed to strike just as we were finishing dessert.

The portrait upstairs brimmed with laughter, and the resemblance was there. But Luther hadn't caught the hint of impudence that Joshua had expressed in his primitive carving. The quirk of the mouth, the sly, sidelong look of the eyes must have revealed what Joshua recognized as a facet of his wife's character. Perhaps it had amused him and stirred his memory while he was away at sea. None of this showed in either the charming portrait that hung behind Geneva's chair or in Luther's laughter-filled painting upstairs. And I *had* seen it before, and suddenly, in this flash out of the blue, I knew exactly where.

Inwardly I began to shake, though I kept my hands steady and tried for once to give nothing away in my face. I could hardly wait to tell them I was tired, so I could escape upstairs to my rooms.

The place where I had seen that beautiful, saucy face was on the wall of a Greenwich Village apartment. A framed pencil sketch on Coral Caine's wall had been an exact copy of the scrimshaw face. It had seemed a strange drawing to me at the time because it was flat and linear, without shading—as I knew now, a copy of the scrimshaw face.

When I reached my room I locked the door on the inside and took out the letters from Coral Caine that I'd found among Ricky's papers. I put aside the one that referred to roses, and picked up the next one. When I sat down to read, the opening sentence sprang out at me, and I felt a growing sense of horror.

> Darling Ricky:
> Last night I tried to
> burn down my mother's house . . .

16

I sat very still, holding Coral's letter in my hand. They all knew—*all of them*—that Mary Ames had become Coral Caine. The conspiracy of silence around me was frightening. The very fact that I had been brought to this house was frightening.

The ruined face of the woman I'd seen that day in the Village in no way resembled the younger portrait, so I'd never made the connection. I wondered if Alan and Geneva had perhaps been waiting for me to discover the secret they'd kept.

Outdoors the wind had risen and I listened as it howled around the house. Before long it would be winter, and I could be trapped indoors at Windtop. Unless I got away soon. Why had they wanted me here?

When someone knocked at my door I sat in listening silence, my heart thudding.

"Are you all right, Hollis?" That was Alan's voice. I couldn't trust him now. Any more than I could trust anyone else at Windtop. "Hollis, open the door. I know something's wrong and I'd like to talk to you."

I couldn't sit here forever. I had to face them all eventually—and then get away as soon as I could. Answers didn't matter now, but only immediate flight from something that threatened me, and that I didn't understand. Was afraid to understand.

With an effort, I got up and opened the door. Alan came into the room, and he didn't look in the least threatening. If anything, he seemed concerned about me—but perhaps that was only because he thought I still didn't know.

I handed him Coral's letter.

He needed to read only the opening before he set it aside and came to take both my hands. "Sit down, Hollis. Don't look so terrified. There's nothing to be afraid of, though we owe you some explanations. Come on now—sit here. You're white as paper. Can I get you a drink? Coffee? Anything?"

I let him help me to the small sofa, and he sat beside me, close, but not touching me, and the eyes that I'd thought wintry were kind.

"I don't want anything," I said. "Nothing but the truth. Why did you bring me here?"

He shook his head unhappily. "I never wanted this to happen. I didn't want Geneva to invite you in the first place, or to use your father as an excuse for her invitation. But you know her a little by this time— you know we don't argue with her easily. She'd been very ill, and it seemed simpler to do as she wished."

"But *why* did she wish it?"

"She hasn't been entirely open with me, so I'm not sure I know exactly. Of course whatever it is has to do with Mary's death, and the part your husband may have played in it."

This was what I hated to face—what Ricky had done to them all.

"You loved her when she was Mary, didn't you?" I asked.

"I did at one time. We were engaged to be married. That was what Geneva wanted and planned for us, years ago. Mary didn't want it, and I'm not sure I did, really. In those days she was lovely—charming. Perhaps a little wicked, but in a playful sort of way. All that changed when Ricky Sands came here to sing. After she met Ricky she couldn't see anyone else, and she ran away to New York—followed him there. She'd wanted to be a dancer, but she wasn't good enough, and she lacked the discipline. So she got a job as a soap actress on television, and I guess she did all right. Until she started drinking and taking drugs. Geneva blames Ricky for that, and I'm afraid I do too."

I was still trying to understand, to absorb what I had learned so suddenly. "Ricky couldn't help the way he was. He drew people to him like bees to honey."

"He drew you in the same way, didn't he?"

"I suppose he did. But I had my songs and that made a difference."

"So he married you, where he'd never have married Mary."

I winced, feeling sore and bruised. The wreckage Ricky had left be-hind after his Windtop concert was hard to face. Nothing was coincidence. One thing happened—one portentous event, and everything led away from it in strands that wound out in a hundred directions like the web of a spider.

"It's bringing me here that I don't understand," I said miserably. "Why has everyone kept the truth from me? Even Liz and Pete knew the truth. And Birdy."

"Yes, that's so. Only Tim doesn't know. He has no idea what happened to Mary. She was like an older sister to him when he was small, and he was fond of her."

"Pete was in love with Mary, too, wasn't he?" I mused aloud. "So when that girl in his class died, and he blamed himself, he followed Ricky to New York. So he could be near Mary?"

"What are you talking about?" Alan said.

"You still don't know? You don't know where Pete went when he left Cold Spring Harbor? That he joined Ricky's band and had been with him all that time?"

Alan was staring at me. "I certainly didn't. Why wouldn't Elizabeth tell me?"

"She didn't know herself until a little while ago. Under the circumstances, I suppose Pete didn't want it spread around. He just stopped being Peter Barron when he returned and became Pete Evans again."

"Under *what* circumstances?" Alan demanded.

I thought again about Pete being with me right after Norris and I had seen Coral Caine. And of returning to her apartment after he left me— to find her dead. But all this was for Pete to tell Alan, if he chose.

"I mean under the circumstances of Ricky's death," I said. "Pete liked him. I think Pete just wanted to get away—as I did."

"You believe Pete *liked* Ricky?"

I had only Pete's word for that, and I didn't answer.

"I'm sorry about all this," Alan said more gently. "Of course it's upset you."

"I still don't understand why Mrs. Ames wanted me here."

"It's not hard to understand. No matter what Geneva says, or how she behaves, or how Mary behaved—she was Geneva's daughter. She never stopped loving Mary, even though she tried to cut her out of her life. She still wants to know how much Ricky Sands was to blame for all that happened to her daughter, including her death. Perhaps even how much *you* were to blame. But she couldn't come right out and ask you, could she? She thought if she got to know you—"

"How could I be to blame?"

"She read the papers. She heard the reports, though she deliberately kept her relationship to Coral Caine hidden. In her mind there's a real division between Mary and Coral. She loved Mary but wouldn't acknowledge Coral's existence."

"I should think the news people would have dug this out."

"Coral kept her own background secret. She wanted to disown everything she'd once been, and she must have destroyed whatever might have connected her with Geneva Ames and Cold Spring Harbor. None of her acquaintances knew—the police questioned them. And she had no real friends. So the truth of who she was never came out. Geneva arranged for her attorneys to take care of burying her as Coral Caine. As Coral, she wasn't important enough for the press to bother with for long. But Geneva knows that you were in Coral's apartment the day she died. Sure, the police cleared you and Ricky's manager. But have you ever cleared yourself?"

That was an honest question, but I didn't know how to answer it honestly. "Perhaps I never have." I told Alan what I'd said to Norris Wahl—that if we hadn't gone to see Coral when we did, she might not have died. "We could have been the last straw."

I was beginning to feel shivery and sick again. I still blamed myself, but I didn't want Alan to blame me.

He put an arm around me. "I'm sorry, Hollis. I don't want to be cruel. I just thought it might be easier for you to talk to me than to Geneva. I can smooth the way for you a little."

"I still don't know why I'm here."

"Let Geneva take her own time. Because of your father, she's ready to be sympathetic, but she still believes that you may have some knowledge that will help her. She hates quandaries."

I shook my head unhappily. "I don't know anything myself. I hate quandaries too."

I thought of Coral's letters and wondered what else they might contain. But I couldn't share this with anyone else right now.

"Anyway, what does it matter?" I asked. "None of us can change the past, no matter how much we'd like to."

"*I* don't think it matters," Alan said. "You wanted to know why you're here, and I've tried to explain how Geneva feels. Convincing her that it's all finished is something else."

"All I'm trying to do is get on with my life," I said, knowing in the same instant that my words weren't entirely true. I, no less than Geneva, was held by the past and its terrible questions.

"I'm not going to take on Ricky's guilt," I added.

Alan's arm tightened about me. "Good! You'll be all right. Just hold on to that thought no matter what Geneva says or does."

"Will you help me?"

The tenderness I'd seen before warmed his eyes. "I'll be right here. You aren't alone, Hollis."

I didn't want to be alone, and I knew that I was no longer fighting him, and that he knew it.

The shrilling of the telephone broke in on us, and Alan picked it up impatiently, handing it to me.

"If Mr. Gordon is there," Birdy said, "please ask him to come downstairs. Something has happened, and Mrs. Ames wants him here right away."

I told Alan and he touched my cheek with light fingers. "Unfinished business," he said. "I'll have to go downstairs."

"I'll go with you," I told him. "I don't want to stay alone just now."

We went downstairs together and found Geneva in the sitting room with Pete and Tim. Tim was insisting that he wanted to move into Windtop immediately, now that Geneva was home, so Pete had driven him up here.

Geneva sat erect against the pillows on her bed, gowned in a robe of gold crepe, looking like anything but an invalid. She challenged Alan the moment he walked in.

"I'd like Tim to stay here for now, and he's moving in directly. We would like your agreement, but if we don't have it he's coming anyway."

"I suppose that's up to Tim," Alan said.

Tim threw his brother a defiant look. "I want to stay with Aunt Geneva."

Pete had stayed in the background, but now he spoke in a mild tone, though the question he asked was hardly amiable.

"If Tim stays here, hadn't there better be some ground rules, Mrs. Ames?"

She frowned at him. "What are you talking about, Peter?"

"I think Tim would be better off with us at The Shutters than with either of you playing tug-of-war with him. If he comes up here, are you willing to let him do his thing?"

"Meaning what?" Geneva asked, knowing very well. I noted her flushed cheeks uneasily.

"Maybe it's smarter if we all try to look at things the way they are, instead of how we wish they were," Pete went on calmly. "Tim wants to be here at Windtop because Ricky Sands's wife is here, and he thinks she can help him. So maybe you'd better decide before you let him stay, Mrs. Ames, that this is something you and Alan can live with."

There was an uncomfortable silence, and then Alan shrugged. "Hollis has convinced me that we've got to go along with the way Tim feels. For now at least."

"You said it was the same with you when you were young, Mrs. Ames," I reminded her. "You did what you wanted to do against whatever odds there were."

"I was older and I'd finished college. Besides, no one opposed me. My music had some dignity to it."

Tim snorted, and Pete put a hand on his arm.

"You may stay here, Tim," Geneva told him firmly, "if you promise you will go back to school and do your best. For now I will tolerate this notion of yours, though I don't think it's appropriate or sensible. Perhaps in time you'll outgrow it. I feel that you will be better off under the circumstances with me than with your brother. For the present."

"Okay, Aunt Geneva. I promise." Tim threw his brother a look of triumph, and picked up his guitar. "Where do you want to put me, Birdy? I don't have to sleep outside any more, or even in the attic." His grin had lost none of its cockiness.

"I'll fix a room for you, Timmy," Birdy said. "Right next to Mrs. Sands, since that wing is heated." She looked more pleased than anyone else to have Tim in her charge again.

"Then it's settled," Pete said. "I'll get along now. Liz is waiting for me in the car."

"Elizabeth is outside?" Geneva asked. "Here? Why didn't you bring her in?"

"She wasn't sure you'd want to see her. The last time you met—"

"That's ancient history. Hollis, will you go and ask her to come in, please?"

I went outside into a high wind and crossed the driveway to the car. Evergreens thrashed and waved their branches, and the beech tree rattled bare bones. Liz rolled down a window.

"Mrs. Ames would like you to come in," I said. "She says your disagreement is ancient history."

Liz smiled as she got out of the car. "I'm glad. I've hated not seeing her. We used to be good friends."

Together we hurried across the drive. From outside, the big lighted house looked more like a museum than a home, and not especially welcoming. I paused at the door with my hand on Liz's arm.

"I've just learned what you've all been keeping from me," I said. "I mean about Mary being Coral Caine."

She pulled me inside out of the wind. "I'm relieved, Hollis. I never thought it a good idea to keep you in the dark, even though Alan told me it was what Geneva wanted for a while. Of course Mary was the cause of that quarrel I had with Geneva. Up till the time when Mary died, Geneva was convinced that she could bring her home and have everything as it was before. Even to having her marry Alan. She didn't want me to take that away from her."

"She felt that way even after the fire?"

"It was an obsession. As though marrying Alan would turn Coral back into the young Mary. Geneva never gives up an idea, once it's taken hold. So I was supposed to keep hands off with Alan. As though *he* could be manipulated. He pretends to go along with Geneva because he's fond of her and doesn't want her upset."

"Did *you* like Mary Ames?" I asked. "Did you know her after she took her stage name?"

"I saw her only once in New York while she was acting on television. Geneva asked me to visit her and find out how things were going. I suppose we were friends when we were children. But not after we grew up."

When we reached the sitting room, we found that Tim had gone upstairs with Birdy, and Pete was coming through the door.

"You can have the car," he told his sister. "I'll walk down through the woods. They're holding a council of war in there, and I don't want any part of it."

We went in to find Alan adding wood to the fire in the grate. He glanced up as we came in, and for just an instant when our eyes met I felt warm again, as though I were in his arms. I rather liked the thought of that unfinished business.

Mrs. Ames sat up in bed, her eyes bright and her cheeks pink. She held out both hands to Liz, who went to put her arms about the older woman. They held each other for a moment in loving reunion, and I might have felt touched if I hadn't caught Alan's gaze upon them, skeptical and a little mocking.

Geneva looked past Liz at me. "Hollis, my dear, you must be tired. Will you look in on Tim before you go to bed?"

The dismissal was clear. I caught Alan's warning glance and knew we must humor her, even when she was being autocratic.

I said good night and went out, closing the door softly behind me. Wind seemed to stir through the big hall, finding every chink to whistle through. Pete Evans sat on the bottom step of the stairs, waiting for me.

"What did you mean—a council of war?" I asked.

His grin could be maddening, because I never knew what hid behind it. "Come on," he said, grabbing me by the hand and pulling me toward the music room. "They keep it warm in here when Geneva's home, since it's her favorite spot."

He drew me along without ceremony, and led me to the piano bench.

"Were you always as rough as this with your students?" I asked.

"Only with those who made me impatient. Maybe I never was a patient enough teacher, though it was a job I'd like to have been good at. Let's hear you play 'Sweet Rain.' Let's hear you *sing* it—right now. Oh, I know you don't have much of a voice, but what's there isn't bad."

He leaned past me and struck an opening chord. Sometimes this Peter Barron, who had been Ricky's friend, had an almost hypnotic effect on me. Even while I resented him, and tried to think up arguments to oppose him, I did as he wished. Haltingly at first, I sang the words to my own accompaniment and he began to whistle—skillfully, sweetly. When I finished he added a few trills.

"Why?" I asked. "Why did you want me to sing this now?"

"Next the new song," he said. "The one about remembering."

"It's not finished. I'm still working on it."

"Never mind. Let's hear it."

It was all there in my head, and I sang what I had of the verse, and then the words of the chorus as far as I'd carried them.

> I've forgotten your face
> In the rains of November.
> I've forgotten your voice—
> I don't want to remember . . .
>   I must not remember.

"It's good," he said. "Very good. You already know how the final chorus needs to end. You're playing the contrast out in the verse, so now you carry it through in the last chorus. Go ahead."

"I can't," I said. "I have to be in the right mood to have a song come alive for me."

"You're a pro—you create the mood."

"With you standing there sneering at me?"

He looked astonished. "Hollis, I've never sneered at you! Play 'Sweet Rain' again, and this time don't sing the words. Just hear them in your head. Listen to Ricky's voice singing them."

I could find the keys with my eyes closed, and I could hear his voice clearly, poignantly. Sometimes his face escaped me, but I could hear him singing. Now I listened with my inner ear, clear through to the last lines.

> Let the children sing,
> Let the sweet rain fall.

"There's your mood," Pete said softly. "So go ahead."

I opened my eyes and watched my hands on the keys, found the notes that came to me, whispered the words as I went on. The last line of the final chorus came easily now: *I know I'll always remember.*

"That's it!" Pete cried, excitement in his voice. "That's what you need to say at the end. You've carried through all the pain and loss to a bittersweet ending that rings true. There's a sort of healing there that listeners will feel."

The excitement swept through me too. This was the "high" that came only when I'd done something right—brought something to life where there was nothing before, and I knew it was good.

Pete came around the piano and swept me up from the bench, waltzed me around the room, then gave me a huge hug and a smacking kiss on the cheek before he let me go.

"Now you can send it to Norris. Do something with it!"

"There's no one to sing it."

"Nuts! There are hundreds of voices out there, and one of them will snap it up. Maybe someone will sing it for you better than Ricky ever could. I'm not even sure this is his sort of song. There's a difference that's *yours.*"

I could almost believe him.

"Just hold on to the whole thing in your head and don't lose it. It says something that matters. None of us can forgive until we're willing to remember. Think about that. So long, Hollis. And don't let the council in there get you down."

He was gone, moving in the quick way he could manage when he wasn't pretending to be languid and slow. I wondered what it was that Pete needed to forgive himself for. Not only for the death of a girl he felt he might have helped, but something else. Something connected with Ricky?

When I reached my room the song was still running through my head, and I sat down to put the last notes of it, as well as the words, on paper. Perhaps Pete was right and I ought to send this to Norris Wahl. I must be a songwriter on my own now, and he would know what to do with it.

When it was all safely down, both on tape and on paper, I went outside to stand on the balcony again. A touch of winter chill laced the air, and I hoped we weren't going to have an early snowfall. Stars shone in a clear windswept sky and a moon trail glittered on the water. I remembered my first night here, and the figure I'd seen over near the marble columns. It had only been Tim hiding around the house, getting ready to torment me. I had a feeling that it wouldn't take much to put him back in that earlier state of resentment toward me.

When I'd come upstairs just now, the room next door was open, and Tim and Birdy were inside making up the bed. Tim seemed too keyed up and elated, as though he'd won the round of a private battle—as perhaps he had. I'd wished uneasily that his room wasn't next to mine.

"Hi, Hollis," he'd said when he saw me. "So everything's been decided for us, hasn't it? I start back to school tomorrow, and you'll stay and wind up marrying my big brother. *She* is figuring all that right now. Poor old Liz!"

Birdy sniffed. "He's talking nonsense, Mrs. Sands. Don't pay any attention."

I'd told them both good night and come into my room. Of course Tim was talking nonsense. If something had begun between Alan and me, it had nothing to do with anyone else. There was a fragility about it now, and I didn't want Geneva Ames or Tim or anyone to tarnish it.

Standing here on the balcony, movement down in the garden caught my eye. Once more someone sat on the marble bench between Greek columns. A dark shape that had risen to stand staring toward the house. At my lighted room—or at someone else's?

Not Luther, I thought. Alan or Pete? Which one might be watching my room—and why?

I went inside to light the fire in my grate. With doors and windows closed, I could feel safe enough here. There was nothing to fear anyway. No one meant me any harm. I was here, as Alan said, only for what I might know and whatever Geneva could pry out of me.

There'd been no chance to tell Pete Evans that I knew who Coral Caine was, or to ask why he had never told me. There'd be an opportunity tomorrow, perhaps. I still wished this knowledge hadn't been kept from me for so long.

In any case it was Alan I wanted to think about now. A gentler Alan who had sat beside me in this room and offered me the comfort of his arm about my shoulders. For this song that I was living, the lines still had to be written—and I wasn't at all sure what they would be.

17

I slept more soundly that night than ever before in this house, and I woke up early, feeling rested and more courageous. I needn't decide about anything right away.

When the telephone rang and I answered, Birdy said, "There's a man from New York here. Did you invite someone, Mrs. Sands?"

"Of course not," I said. "Who is it? What man?"

"He says his name is Mr. Wahl and that you'll want to see him. What shall I tell him, Mrs. Sands?"

I sighed. "I'll be right down, Birdy. Where will you put him?"

"It's warm in the music room," she said grudgingly. "Since Mrs. Ames is in the sitting room now, I'll take him there. The drawing room is still closed."

"Fine. Tell him I'll be down in a few moments."

I went as I was, in gray slacks and blue cardigan, and when I left my room I picked up my recorder with the new song tape in it. Perhaps I could make this visit worth Norris's while, and mine.

I found Norris standing before the portrait of Geneva Ames, and he turned as I came in.

"Hello, Hollis. You're looking a lot better. I take it you're not being hassled out here?"

Wasn't I? "At least nobody notices me away from the house," I said. "How are you, Norris? I didn't expect to see you at Windtop."

"If I called you, maybe you'd tell me not to come." He looked up at the portrait. "What's she like?"

"That's a long story. Why are you here?"

He walked to the piano and picked something up. When he turned I saw that he held the framed gold record of "Sweet Rain." The glass had been replaced and I'd forgotten to take it to my room.

"I came because of what Ricky put underneath this record," he said. "I saw this just now out in the hall. You've had new glass put in."

"What did you find? Why wouldn't you tell me before?"

"That's why I'm here now. I've been thinking about it ever since we talked on the phone, and I decided you ought to know. So I drove out to see you."

I went to the piano bench and sat down, waving Norris toward one of the room's straight chairs. "All right then—let's talk. When I took the record out of the box the glass was broken and there was nothing under the gold disc."

"That's what worries me. I mean—who has that scrap of paper now?"

"Just tell me what Ricky wrote—if you can remember."

"I can remember all right. I just didn't want to tell you on the phone. There was only a torn sheet with a line or two in Ricky's writing. I'll give it to you straight, Hollis. It said, 'Coral was murdered. Talk to Peter Barron.' How could I make anything out of that? I couldn't find Peter, and I didn't believe this anyway. The police know Coral killed herself. There isn't any doubt about that. So how could I take Ricky's words to the police? I put the paper back where I'd found it and waited to see if anybody else made sense out of it. Ricky's state of mind wasn't so hot those last weeks before he died. Maybe he didn't see pink elephants, but he saw other things that weren't there."

Talk to Peter Barron. The words kept running through my mind. What had Ricky meant? Perhaps only that Barron knew something? But what if he'd meant something worse? From the first, even when he'd helped me, I'd felt uncertain about Pete.

"Ricky was frightened about something," I said. "Terribly frightened. Do you think it was of Barron?"

"I doubt it. Peter always seemed a harmless sort. Mixed up but well-meaning. Ricky was scared of not being able to sing again. He was losing his main purpose in life, because if he couldn't sing, he couldn't go on. That's why he killed himself."

"But why would he want someone to talk to Peter Barron?"

"That's what I'd like to find out."

In a few minutes perhaps I would take Norris to Barron. But first there was something I wanted to tell him.

"Did you know that Coral Caine was Geneva Ames's daughter?" I asked.

Norris's surprise seemed real. He hadn't known. "Then why did she invite *you* here? She must have hated Ricky."

"That's another long story, and I'm not sure I know all of it yet. There's something else. The roses that were delivered that day when we were leaving Coral's apartment were from Ricky. They should have made her happy, and they didn't."

I ought to tell Norris that Pete and Ricky had been in Coral's apartment ahead of us, and that Pete had returned alone to find her dead, but I held back. The implications for Pete might be too serious, and I wasn't sure enough to take that step as yet. I would let Pete tell Norris this himself, if he chose to.

After a gloomy silence of several moments while I waited, Norris threw up his hands, dismissing all of it. "We're not getting anywhere right now. I need to think about this some more. Let's forget about it for a while. Hollis, are you doing anything about a new song?"

"As a matter of fact, I am. I have something to play for you, if you want to listen."

That caught his attention. I set the tape recorder on the piano and pushed the play button. When my recorded part ended, I reversed the tape and played it for him again, singing the words along with the recording. Pete had said it was good, and having been with Ricky's band, he should know. Norris, however, understood what would go commercially, and I had to face that realistically. Ricky had been able to put across whatever he wanted to, but I had no such influence.

Norris never went overboard with enthusiasm, but he nodded. "Maybe you've got something there, Hollis. I'll take it back to New York and see if anybody's interested."

"It's not as good as 'Sweet Rain.' I'm pretty rusty."

"We can't tell. It's the listeners who tell us. Anyway, don't compare everything you write with past hits. Nobody knew 'Sweet Rain' would make it either."

"This isn't exactly a demo," I said.

"Stop apologizing," he told me, and I heard an echo of Ricky's words back in that San Francisco hospital. "We can take care of that. Now get busy and write some more. You need to get up a whole catalog of just *your* songs. You can put in some of the old ones Ricky didn't get around to recording. I'll talk to some agents, and see if there's an artist in town who might be interested. Of course a lot of the talent are writing their own material these days. Still, we might sell some singles if you get to work."

"Thank you, Norris," I said meekly. He knew everyone in the business, and I'd be glad for any help he could give me. Sometimes in the past I'd judged him too harshly when he really was trying to help in his own way. "Would you like to talk to Peter Barron now?" I added.

Norris looked startled. "Sure I would. Do you know where I can find him?"

I went to a side door that opened on the terrace. "Come along and I'll show you."

The wind had died down since last night, and it didn't seem as cold. Though the sky was gray, and the woods presented the dead, bare look that comes between the fading of autumn colors and the coming of snow that would make the landscape beautiful again.

Pete was not in the side garden, and when we walked around to the front I saw him near the garage on the far side of the drive. He was washing Mrs. Ames's Mercedes. Norris's car had been parked nearby. I watched Pete as we approached, trying to consider him in the light of Ricky's words.

"There you are—Peter Barron," I told Norris.

He looked bemused. *"Peter!* With all that hair on his face! What's he doing here?"

Pete heard him and looked around. "Hello, Norris. I live here. I'm staying with my sister down the hill."

"I don't get this," Norris said.

"Pete is really a schoolteacher," I explained, raising an eyebrow mockingly at Pete, since he'd so often riled me. "Playing in Ricky's band was a—a sort of hobby."

"And now you wash cars?" Norris was still astonished.

Pete never seemed to mind what others said. "A respectable job. Gives me something to do. Hollis, have you played your new song for Norris?"

I nodded. "He'll take it to New York. But now he wants to talk to you, Pete. Where can we go?" I glanced around at the immense house with all its watching windows—and listening ears?

Pete went into the garage to clean his hands and then led the way around the intact wing of the house to the side garden.

We weren't out of sight, but at least no one could hear us. Norris and I sat down on the marble bench, and Pete leaned against a column, looking indolent. I could never tell what he was thinking or feeling, or whether Norris's coming disturbed him in any way.

"Tell Pete what you found under the gold record," I prompted.

I'd never seen Norris at a loss for words before, but now he sounded awkward, as though the discovery of Ricky's bass guitarist at Windtop had disconcerted him.

While he spoke haltingly I stared at the house, searching for the second-floor balcony outside my room, and finding the azalea draperies. Last night I'd stood up there looking down toward this bench, and had discovered someone here watching the house.

The draperies twitched slightly, parting a crack, and my heart jumped. The reversal was complete. Someone was in my room now, looking down at us in the garden. As I watched, the draperies parted farther, and the door to the balcony opened, allowing Birdy to step outside. Apparently I hadn't locked my door, and perhaps she'd gone in to make my bed—though she hadn't done this before. She stood at the balcony rail and stared at us openly. I could almost hear her sniff. At least it wasn't Tim up to his old tricks in my room.

Norris was talking to Pete when I turned my attention back to them. "There are a few things I need to discuss with you," he said.

"Sure," Pete told him. "Go ahead."

Again Norris seemed uneasy, uncertain, and suddenly I realized what was bothering him. He really didn't want to talk in front of me.

"I'm hungry," I said. "I'll go in and have breakfast. You're welcome to join me when you're through, Norris."

By the time I reached the kitchen, Birdy was there ahead of me, talking with Alan. He'd come over early to see how Geneva was before he drove over to Sea Spray. Birdy had already told him about Norris Wahl's appearance.

"What's he doing here?" Alan asked me.

"He wanted to talk to me. Business, mainly, I suppose. Right now he's having a reunion with Pete Evans."

Alan started to speak, and then stopped as a crashing of chords from the music room echoed through the halls, startling us. The music was full and dramatic, plunging into the middle of a phrase that sent the

Valkyries riding abroad at full tilt. Geneva had lost only a little of her skill at the piano.

"Oh, my God!" Birdy cried, and I saw that she'd turned pale and frightened. She stared at Alan for a moment, and then ran for the music room.

"What is it? What's the matter?" I asked.

If the outburst of music and Birdy's reaction had disturbed Alan, he didn't show it. "Superstition," he said calmly. "Legend of the house. We'd better go in there. She usually winds up feeling faint after an attack like this."

I followed him to the music room, where the rear door stood open. Geneva continued to send stirring strains soaring through the house. Birdy stood beside the piano, looking helpless in the face of this torrent of sound, while Geneva played on, her face set, and her long fingers moving powerfully on the keys.

"Why is she doing this?" I whispered to Birdy.

She ignored me, speaking to Alan. "Can't you stop her? This is bad for her."

Alan sat down on the bench beside Geneva and put an arm about her. "You know how much this music upsets you. You promised not to play it anymore."

She looked at him blankly for a moment, and then raised her hands from the keys, so that a tremendous contrast of silence fell upon the room. The sudden hush left my ears tingling in reaction. When she looked at Alan, it was as though she stirred from a trance, surfacing gradually to an awareness of the room around her.

At my elbow Birdy whispered, "Something awful's going to happen. I know it! It always does when she plays like that. The last time was when—"

Alan shook his head at her. "Don't add to the legend, Birdy. Geneva, this sort of music disturbs you, and it's better not to play it."

She turned her patrician head to look at Birdy and me across the great black piano, recovering herself. "You both look like startled fish," she told us tartly. "Do close your mouths."

I laughed, but Birdy was not reassured.

"Don't forget, Birdy," Geneva added, "that I still want to find that scrapbook with Mary's photograph."

Alan drew Geneva up from the bench. "I'll take you to your room, dear. Birdy will bring your breakfast and I'll stay awhile. Perhaps I'd better move into the house for a few days. Are you feeling better now?"

"I'm feeling fine," she said, and sailed through the door ahead of us, her manner plainly indicating that she thought us all idiots.

Birdy started after them, and then turned back to me. "You left your door open this morning, madam. I went into your room to see if everything was all right."

"Thank you, Birdy," I said, and returned to the kitchen.

I found Norris at the table and Pete dropping bread into a toaster, setting out butter and marmalade. I wondered what revelations they'd had for each other out in the garden. I meant to find out eventually.

Norris was shaking his head over the outburst of sound that must have come pouring into the garden where they sat. "Not my kind of music," he said. "Too noisy." Which might have been funny at another time, considering the rock stars he'd handled.

"What is the legend about Mrs. Ames playing Wagner?" I asked Pete.

"Mostly legends are built on coincidence," he said. "Two or three disasters have happened following those outbursts, so someone starts making a connection. When Geneva wants to let go emotionally, she rips out the Valkyries and lets them ride. So a legend gets started. You want to take over with Norris's breakfast, Hollis? Right now I've got a date with a razor. I'm tired of going around looking like a bush. As a disguise it's outlasted its time."

I had the feeling that his flippancy covered something else. He and Norris were both solemn enough under the surface.

"Why did you need a disguise in the first place?" I asked.

Pete rubbed a hand over his face. "Maybe it was a screen to hide behind. When I knew you were coming to Windtop I was glad I'd already grown a different look. I thought it might keep you from recognizing who I was. And it worked for a time."

"I still don't understand *why*."

"No need to understand," Pete said coolly.

None of this satisfied me, and I felt increasingly troubled. It was as though Geneva's dramatic music was still crashing through me to my very nerve ends. Warning me.

"I wonder if Geneva played like that the night Ricky died?" I mused aloud.

"Sure she did," Tim said from the doorway. *"I* remember."

I stared as he came into the room, yawning and stretching. "Aren't you late for school?"

"Right. I have to ease into this gently, don't I? Shock to my system and stuff like that. Pretty grody."

Pete said, "You'd better get going. Shall I drive you in?"

"I got up earlier than you think and tried out my motorcycle. Then I felt weak, so I went back to bed. I can get myself to school all right—thanks."

"Do you suppose I could talk to Mrs. Ames?" Norris asked of no one in particular.

Birdy had appeared in the doorway and she shook her head. "Mrs. Ames mustn't be bothered now."

"Then I'd like to hang around for a while. Is there a place in the village where I could stay for a day or two?"

"Do you think you could put Mr. Norris up here, Birdy?" I asked. "Will you check with Mrs. Ames?"

Birdy said grudgingly that it could probably be arranged.

"Thanks," Norris said. "Anybody mind if I look around outside for a while? This is a remarkable place." No one objected, and he wandered out the kitchen door.

Pete looked at me and seemed to see something he didn't like. "Let's go for a walk too, Hollis. You've been sitting around turning pale. It's a good bracing morning—so come along."

"I thought you had a job?"

"They're getting ready to fire me any day now. So I might as well help them along."

Since I wanted to talk to him, I picked up a jacket at the front door and we went out together.

Tim had gone roaring off on his motorcycle, and Norris's car was still parked near the garage. As we started off, I saw him standing in front of the burned section of the house, lost in his own thoughts.

Pete cut down through the woods in a different direction from The Shutters, and we descended steeply to a lower loop of Snake Hill Road. He walked briskly, as though he were alone, and he, too, seemed deep in his own thoughts. I had to stride to keep up with him, sliding now and then on slippery leaves. Once he put out a hand absently to steady me, and when we reached the road the walking was easier.

Near the foot of the hill we found a place with low cement benches forming a half-moon enclosure around a patch of cobblestones. It was a pleasant spot, an entrance to private grounds, where roads met and rayed away through bare woods. A lonely spot with little traffic going by. We sat down on cement to rest before we started the climb back to the house.

Since Pete obviously wasn't going to offer anything, I asked a direct question. "What did Norris tell you?"

Pete stirred leaves with one foot. "Sometimes, Hollis, it's better not to know too much."

I didn't like that. People were always protecting me—or pretending to.

"Did *you* take Ricky's note from under the gold record?" I demanded.

"Why not Alan or Tim? Or even Birdy? Why me?"

So he did know about it. From Norris?

"I was just asking a question," I said. "I'll ask them when I get a chance."

"Sometimes I wonder about you, Hollis. Why you're here at all."

I'd wondered myself. "You're not my keeper."

"I wonder about that too. It's not my choice to turn up in that role, but here I am playing it again. Look, I was fond enough of Ricky while I knew him, and I admired his talent a lot. Sometimes I was sorry for him. But I was even sorrier for Coral. I could see what Ricky had done to her—what he was like, aside from his music. Maybe she was better for him than you could ever be. Ricky had to be center stage all the time, and Coral understood that. She was strong enough—and weak enough—to let him be what he had to be for the sake of his music. Maybe some singers really love their audiences, and that love wave goes both ways. It wasn't like that with Ricky. He loved only the mirror image of himself that an audience could hold up to him. Coral held up that mirror, even after she knew what he was really like. You were beginning to see him too clearly, and your songs were falling off. Besides, he couldn't stand it when anyone looked at him with reproach. So he turned back to Coral for a little while. There was a time when she could do more for his ego than you could."

His words seemed cruel, yet I had the feeling that he was merely stating the truth as he saw it. As I needed to accept it? I remembered the time when he'd told me to go down into my pain and try to understand. Right now he seemed filled with a sadness that touched me.

"You loved her, didn't you? Coral-Mary?" I said softly.

He sat staring at a sparrow hopping along a twisted branch. "Don't sentimentalize about me, Hollis. Once I cared a great deal for Mary Ames. I could only pity Coral Caine. There was no way to help her, once she was obsessed by Ricky. You're luckier than she was, Hollis. She's done for. You have another chance. So think about that."

What I was to do with "another chance" I still didn't know.

Pete went on. "After alcohol and drugs set Coral off, she turned on Ricky and started to think of revenge. That was all that nourished her at the end. So she failed him too. And maybe she couldn't forgive herself for that."

The sparrow flew away, and we were silent for a little while before Pete continued. "Ricky brought a special sort of happiness to a lot of people. Even while he was taking, he gave, too, in spite of himself. That he wasn't as much a man as he was an artist isn't the whole point. He had only one big thing to give, and if it was narcissistic, what does it matter? Except that his own weaknesses destroyed him and destroyed his talent. Along the way he damaged a lot of people besides himself."

This time I found words. "I think he wanted to come back. I think he'd have changed if only he'd lived. Sometimes people do. I'm not even sure that he killed himself. I can't believe that!"

Pete was listening intently. "Do you know something you're not saying?"

"Only what Norris hinted at. That if Ricky knew Coral was murdered, perhaps he knew too much to stay alive."

"That's dangerous thinking, Hollis. Maybe you'd better not go telling people stuff like that." He stood up abruptly. "Let's go back to the house."

"Wait," I said, pulling him back to the bench. "Was it because of Coral-Mary that you went with Ricky's band?"

"Partly, I suppose. There were other reasons."

"Did you *really* care about Ricky? Or did you hate him?"

A drift of brown leaves had blown around our feet, and Pete stood up again, crunching them. "Let's go back," he repeated. There was a hint of suppressed anger in his voice—and some of it was directed at me.

I made one last try as we started up the road together. "I really would like to know what you and Norris talked about after I left you in the garden. I'm tired of being kept in the dark. You both wanted me away. Why?"

He strode along beside me, not answering, and I wished that for once

I could see his face behind the beard. I'd seen him clean-shaven in New York, but I couldn't remember now what he'd looked like. If Pete didn't trust me, I didn't trust him either.

He didn't answer my question and we walked in silence. The way back seemed longer as we climbed the hill. We might have gone the whole way on foot, if Liz Cameron hadn't driven by, coming home from the village.

"Want a lift?" she called, stopping beside us.

Pete waved me into the car. "Go ahead, Hollis—I'd rather walk. Thanks, Liz. I'll see you later."

She glanced at me curiously as I got in, and I thought how interlocked we all were, held together because of Ricky Sands.

Liz said nothing for a moment, and then made one of her sudden, direct attacks. "Are you falling in love with Alan Gordon, Hollis? Are you as foolish as all that?"

"I'm not falling in love with anyone!" I said sharply. "I'm still trying to recover from the loss of my husband."

"Who couldn't have been very real anyway, according to Pete," Liz said calmly.

I had no answer for that. It was just as hard to stop loving an imaginary man as it was a real one.

"Perhaps we all fall in love with what isn't really there," I said.

"*I* haven't done that." Liz was emphatic. "From the time I was very young, there's never been anyone but Alan for me. I knew he cared about Mary Ames, but that didn't make much difference either. Now we're back to the beginning of the game, and this time I mean to win. Just keep that in mind, Hollis."

At least she'd let me know where her battle lines were drawn. I wished I could decide about my own.

"I'll keep it in mind," I said dryly as we went through Windtop's gates.

18

We drove up to the house and I thanked Liz for the lift. When I got out of the car she would have driven away, but Birdy came rushing out the front door.

"Wait, Mrs. Cameron! Mrs. Ames wants to see you, please. You too, madam," she added.

We went inside together and found Geneva waiting for us in her sitting room. Out of bed, she looked regal and very much in command. Norris was with her, and he avoided my eyes. She had put on a black frock with a couturier look about it, and a double strand of pearls shone against the black.

"Good morning, Liz. Hollis. Sit down, both of you. Mr. Wahl has brought something he wanted me to hear. I'd like you to listen to it. All right, Birdy—I'll be fine now."

Reluctantly, Birdy went out of the room.

Norris had brought his own tape recorder, and a tape was in place. When he reached for the switch, Geneva stopped him.

"Wait. First tell them what you told me, Mr. Wahl."

"Hollis knows." He still didn't look at me. "Anyway, she knows part of it. About the phone calls that Bea was receiving at our apartment. Calls from a woman. They stopped for a time, and then yesterday we had another one. Only this time I was home, and I was ready. We taped the call. I brought it out here to play for you, Hollis—and then I decided to try it with Mrs. Ames. Just in case."

He touched the play button and I heard Norris's "Hello." A woman's voice followed, rather husky and soft, as though an effort was being made to disguise it.

"Get Ricky Sands's wife away from where she's staying," the voice said. "If you don't, something may happen to her."

"Who is this? What are you talking about?" That was Norris.

"Who I am doesn't matter. She's a valuable property, isn't she—your little songwriter? You don't want her mixed up in anything dangerous."

Norris started to ask another question, but the caller hung up, and we all stared at Liz. She'd made an effort at first to disguise her voice, but at the end, as she grew more tense, she'd spoken naturally. Her speech was distinctive, and there was no mistaking her identity.

"Why, Elizabeth?" Geneva demanded.

Liz stared at her hands, not answering.

"Give them the rest of the story, Mr. Wahl," Geneva commanded. "I mean the part that doesn't concern this tape."

Finally Norris looked at me. "I'm sorry, Hollis. I didn't want to tell any of this. Not even to you. Not at first. But then I got to thinking that you had to know, because maybe it connected with other things. After I left you that day in Greenwich Village, when we'd visited Coral, I went uptown to my office. There I tried several times to phone her and I kept getting a busy signal. Until the last time, when a man answered the phone. He wouldn't tell me who he was, and he said Coral couldn't be disturbed. Which, I'm afraid, was the exact truth." Norris hesitated, though he had sounded dry and emotionless. "I recognized the voice— it was Pete Barron."

"Pete can probably explain," I said. "His being in Coral's apartment isn't earth-shaking. He's already told me about it."

As I related Pete's story I watched Liz Cameron. Her guard was up and she was giving nothing away.

Geneva seemed satisfied with my account. "I'm afraid you're building molehills, Mr. Wahl. Why didn't you tell the police about this at the time, if you thought it was important?"

"That's all water over the dam," he said.

I could understand well enough why he hadn't. Norris would have been desperately afraid of Ricky's involvement in Coral's death, and he wouldn't have stirred up anything that might hurt his star. Liz's calls hadn't begun until Ricky's death a year later. All this must have been what he was talking to Pete about.

"The main reason Mr. Wahl came here," Geneva went on, "was to take you back to New York, Hollis. Would you like to go with him?"

"I've already told him that I want to stay for a little while longer, if you're willing to have me. I'm working again, and I'd like to hold on to that." I stared at Liz, and her eyes dropped. For the first time she spoke.

"Are you going to make anything of that tape, Mr. Wahl?"

He threw up his hands. "Just tell me why you did it!"

She shook her head vaguely. "It seemed a good idea at the time. Now I know how foolish it was."

She had, in fact, behaved so foolishly that it seemed unlike her, and I wondered whom she might be protecting. Or who it was that had put her up to the calls. Pete? Alan? In either case, I couldn't imagine for what purpose. She had her own reasons for wanting me gone now, but she wouldn't have had them when she started making the calls.

When Liz stood up as if to leave, clearly meaning to tell us nothing more, Geneva stopped her. "Please stay a moment, Elizabeth. Mr. Wahl is just leaving, and I want to talk with you."

If anyone could get the truth out of her, it was Geneva. Liz sat down heavily, giving up.

Norris looked at me. "Come out to the car, will you, Hollis? We need to talk about a few things. That biography of Ricky, for instance."

I didn't think that was what he wanted to talk about, but I followed him outside. Pete was working on Geneva's Mercedes again, and he didn't speak to either of us, lost in some world of his own.

"No point in my staying here any longer," Norris said glumly. "Just ride a little way with me."

I got into the car and we started toward the gate. When I looked back, Pete was staring after us.

"I guess I know now what you were talking to Pete about," I said.

"Yes. Neither of us thinks that Coral or Ricky wanted to die. I mean, we don't think they killed themselves. There's something more that hasn't surfaced yet. That's why I want you out of there."

This was the fear that had haunted me all along, yet it wasn't reasonable fear unless I knew more. "You'd better explain," I said.

"It's safer for you if I don't," he told me, and started down the driveway in too much of a hurry.

Luther heard us coming and the gates opened, so we could drive straight through. When he'd taken the first loop of Snake Hill Road at still greater speed, I knew what Norris was up to.

"Just stop the car," I said. "You're not taking me back to New York. I won't go. Let me out here and I'll walk back."

"Don't talk," Norris ordered. "This is trouble."

He took the next tight loop with increasing speed. As the big car skidded near a drop-off on the road, he tramped on the brake with no effect. I gripped the door handle as we went down, and I knew we'd never make the next curve. The lower hill dropped off steeply, and there was an outcropping of rock on the high side.

Norris swung the wheel wildly and we went off the road at top speed and a crazy angle. Leaves scattered like dust, and the wheels screeched for purchase as we flew straight for the pile of rock. The last thing I remembered was that rock mass coming right at the windshield. Afterward I could never recall the crash.

When I opened my eyes, I lay on my back looking up through bare branches to a smoky sky. For a few moments I couldn't figure out where I was, or how I came to be there. A yellow leaf clung to a twig above me, swaying gently, refusing to let go. I watched the slight movement, hypnotized.

After what seemed ages in which I had no will, I tried moving my hands and felt dry leaves beneath them. My head turned cautiously without pain, and at once leaves rustled over my face. Slowly I began to remember. The car. The hill. Failing brakes. Norris!

When I sat up I found that I'd been thrown clear into a huge pile of leaves. I raised myself to my knees and stood up shakily. I felt dazed, but I didn't seem to be seriously hurt. A bump on my head throbbed, but that was all.

The wrecked car was a little way off. It had smashed head on into the outcropping of rock at high speed. On the passenger side the door hung open, where it had released me to tumble out. The motor had died and there was no fire. I scrambled shakily up through leaves and went around the rear of the car to the driver's side. The steering wheel had smashed into Norris's chest. I tried desperately to open the door, but the metal was crushed and twisted, so that I couldn't make it budge. The glass had cracked into cobwebs, but hadn't fallen out, and I couldn't reach in to Norris. I screamed his name, but he didn't hear, and I gave up to look for help.

A house loomed on the hill above, and I stumbled up a steep slope and pounded on the door. When a woman came in alarm to open it, I waved toward the smashed car and asked for a telephone.

She saw the state I was in and took me inside. Then she made the call to the highway police. I asked her to phone Alan Gordon at Sea Spray as well, and he told her he'd be there right away.

After what seemed an endless wait, events began to jumble together in a confusion that was hard to sort out afterward. The police arrived and a wrecking crew got Norris out of the car. When Alan came he seemed shaken to find that I'd had so narrow an escape. He told me gently that Norris was dead, and drove me back to Windtop.

I was taken at once to Geneva's room, where everyone fussed over me, and I managed to tell her what had happened. Out of all the confusion, I remember a moment when Pete Evans came into the room and stood looking at me. But when our eyes met, he turned away and walked out of the room. There'd been no words of sympathy from him —nothing. He would do no fussing.

Everyone was enormously kind. When everything stopped whirling around me at too fast a rate, pain came again. There'd been too many senseless deaths. Norris had been trying to help me. He had known something about Coral's death, and Ricky's, and now he was gone too. But he had talked to Pete Evans. . . .

We were all questioned by the police, of course. No one seemed to be to blame. Even in a good car brakes could fail. Mechanics would look into this to find the cause.

I remember a few things about the next days. The police had told Bea Wahl, and I'd talked to her sadly on the phone. When arrangements had been made, Alan drove me to New York for the memorial service. The second one for me in so short a time. I stood beside Bea and kept expecting Norris to walk in and make some dry remark about the ceremony. Bea's sorrow and loss were mine all over again. She had family in Florida and would be going there now. A loving, generous lady, who placed no blame on me, even sensing my unhappiness enough to point out that it had been Norris's own choice to go to Windtop.

The only bright moments in the next week or two back at Windtop came when Tim and I met in the music room and experimented with a tune that might suit Tim's unusual voice. We worked on it together, and it was an exercise in distraction that cheered us both for a little while.

Tim had plenty of dogged determination, but he needed more than stubbornness to get him by. He had little real confidence in his own talent—just a driving desire to succeed. To prove himself. This alone wouldn't have been good enough, but I felt that he had the basic talent to back it up, and that he would sing and write songs because he couldn't help it. Which was the real drive behind any success.

At one point when we hit a block, he struck a discordant sound on his guitar and put it away from him. "It's no good. They're right about me—I *am* a frog!"

"So what? Then you'll make the whole country love frogs. In the meantime, start growing up. That's your main job now. You're like me when I started in—you haven't much to write about, or sing about. Time will take care of that. Right now you need to use what you have."

"Nobody wants kid stuff. Use what?"

"Fantasy. We can always sing about what we wish we had, what we wish we were. That's a whole world that anyone can draw from. And it's right there inside your head. You don't have any shortage of imagination, Tim."

He grinned at me sheepishly. "The trouble is, I'm stuck out here where nothing ever happens!"

"Maybe not to you," I said.

"I'm sorry, Hollis. I just meant that I could do better in a city, near a music center. Then I'd be around musicians and singers, and I could feel I was part of something."

"I know. And I suppose that helps. But you can be more creative off by yourself than when you're in the middle of things, and just copying —trying to produce what somebody wants. You've got a streak of originality, Tim. So start cultivating it. New York isn't all that far away and you can have the best of both worlds."

He brightened a little and picked up his guitar again, struck a few chords, and began to sing a snatch of something he'd been working on. It was about wanting terribly to be *somebody,* and I could see that fantasy was already working for him. What was more, his voice was beginning to get to me in its own strange way.

"That's pretty good," I said when he stopped. "Stay with it. You can make the listener feel something. Just an empty beat isn't ever good enough. One thing—you don't gobble your words the way some singers do. You don't swallow them or run them all together in a blur. I can understand everything you say. Ricky had that too, and it's one reason people sang his songs."

That afternoon with Tim was one of the good days, and I wished I didn't have a sense of marking time, of waiting for something to happen. My own music wasn't going well, and there was no one to give me advice. And no Norris to introduce my songs to someone who might help me. I missed him more than I'd ever thought I would. The whole house had a strange sense of anticipation about it that I didn't like. Sometimes the images in Luther's painting haunted me.

Once Liz took me riding, but that was scarcely a happy occasion. She was worried about her brother and kept questioning me—which was pointless, since I had nothing to tell her. Pete had chosen not to shave off his beard, after all, and he went around looking shaggier than ever—really wild. Nobody had fired him. He made me nervous by popping up around the house, where he'd been put to various jobs of repair. He hardly spoke to me, though I had the uncomfortable feeling that he was still watching me more closely than ever. Perhaps wondering how much Norris had told me. I avoided being alone with him.

Alan said he had planned to get rid of Pete, but Geneva had put her foot down. She'd been fond of him since he was a little boy, and now he obviously needed help until he could solve his own problems. She decreed that he could keep on working at Windtop. Then when he had a falling-out with his sister, she said he could move into the house for the time being. Liz had come in tears to Geneva, not knowing what to do about her brother.

Geneva was firm and confident. "We'll see him through. He's got good stuff in him, and he'll work things out."

I couldn't feel sure about this.

By his own choice Pete moved into the attic room where Tim had once hidden, and I found myself wondering how he got along with Luther's painting of the young Mary Ames.

Once or twice, on a weekend, Alan took me on a walk through the woods or out to dinner. Since the accident, he had been gentle with me, and I had the feeling that an unspoken and affectionate acceptance was growing between us. We had both been badly hurt, and while there were moments of strong attraction, we were both being cautious. So everything stayed safely impersonal between us, though with a feeling of something growing—something that must be given time to grow.

We were learning a lot about each other, beginning to understand and reach out a little. All very tentative and delicate, so that we were careful with each other and a little wary. Though on my part, not always. I loved his new gentleness. I needed a man to be gentle with me.

At Windtop action was finally being taken on the burned-out section of the house. Geneva had given her permission at last. But there would be no bulldozers, she ordered. She couldn't stand that. Let Pete start to work on it manually, if he wanted to. Perhaps something could be accomplished before cold weather set in.

Pete went to work with shovel and wheelbarrow, and this caused a surprising development. Luther discovered what he was doing, and volunteered to work along with him. Perhaps Luther, more than anyone else, wanted to wipe out all evidence of the night when Mary had set the fire that had left him scarred both physically and psychologically.

When I went walking I would see them both working energetically in the ruins, though never talking to each other. I still felt uneasy with Luther, and now with Pete Evans too, and I gave that area of the house a wide berth. Liz was right—Pete had turned into something of a wild man.

I kept putting from my mind the fact that he had been working around the garage when Norris's car had been there. The police had already gone into all that, and there was no real evidence that anyone had tampered with the brakes of the car. And no one could have expected me to be in that car with Norris when he left, so whatever had happened hadn't been directed at me. Small comfort. Norris had known more than he wanted to tell me, and he'd been determined to get me away from Windtop, even if he had to kidnap me. Now I ought to leave on my own. But how could I before I knew the final answers? I owed it to those who had died. And to myself. Songs would never flow freely for me again until I was free of so many terrible questions.

In the week or so before the weather changed, I began to feel that I was somehow being hunted inside the house. It was more than a sense of someone watching. It was as though I had become to the others a question mark that needed to be answered. I had uneasy encounters now and then with all of them—even with Luther, who liked me no better than before. I hoped no one realized that I too was watching, becoming in my own quiet way a hunter.

19

On the Saturday morning when the snow came I awoke to a gray day with a tune drifting through my head. "Dark Morning," I might call it. A song about that feeling of snow in the air before everything changes.

I put on a jacket and stood on my balcony looking out toward the silvery waters of the harbor, and down into the garden where nothing moved. There was a stillness in the air, a smell of snow, and that almost charged sense of waiting. Of culmination?

Weather reports promised a storm, and when I went downstairs the house was bustling. Luther and Pete had brought in extra wood for the fireplaces, and both Alan and Tim were checking for loose shutters.

I went for a walk while the ground was still bare, and I felt the first cold flake on my cheek when it drifted down. Even after three years in New York, snow seemed exciting to a Californian like me, and my spirits lifted. New York snow changed so quickly to gray slush. For a little while it hid the city's ugliness, with shop windows shining through. Then the streets turned to muck, and snowplows left piles that were all too soon a dirty gray. Out here in the country the landscape would be pristine and beautiful.

Birdy was already complaining about snow arriving too early. It could at least wait until Christmas, she grumbled. The driveway would turn icy, and we'd need to be plowed out. Everything would become difficult living on top of a hill. For her, snow was an offense that she wanted to postpone as long as possible.

Now when it came, the wind came with it, and a white curtain blew in thick and fast. Swiftly all the trees were coated with a frosting that thickened almost as one watched, growing heavy along each branch, and mounding over the shrubbery. By noontime the storm was a small blizzard, blowing hard, whining about the house, setting windows to rattling, whispering against glass with thickening flakes. So beautiful, so entrancing! Outside, drifts piled high, and it took only a few hours to bury the world.

Geneva wandered about, looking out the windows, perhaps savoring the snow, or perhaps restless and distracted. I could tell only that a tension grew in her too. At noon Birdy served us steaming hot bean soup, and even Geneva ate with the rest of us in the warmth of the kitchen. Windtop at its best could be filled with drafts, and only a few rooms were comfortable. Mine were among them, and after lunch I retreated to spend a lazy afternoon reading, and sometimes jotting down bits for a "Dark Morning."

Now and then I went to look out through the balcony door to a blowing, snowy world.

Then, as suddenly as it had started, there came a change. In the late afternoon the day grew lighter as the wind died and the snow stopped falling. An edging of sun streaked low in the sky. I put on woollen slacks, high boots, and a warm jacket, and went downstairs. In the closet near the door I found a red muffler with a matching cap and mittens. I wound the muffler around my neck, pulled on the knitted cap and mittens, and went outside through knee-high drifts to roll snowballs that I hurled at the lady with the urn.

For the first time in a long while I felt exhilarated, keyed to a state of high excitement. As though the snowstorm had brought me an unexpected gift. Perhaps it had—the gift of being a child again for a little while.

Though the temperature was rising, the sky glowed with a lavender light that tinged the clouds and seemed to threaten more storm. Windtop's roofs wore blankets of white that had already begun to slide, and sometimes a mass would fall over the edge of a gutter with a soft "whoosh." Tree shadows looked blacker than ever across the snow, and every twig that was freed of its burden quivered against the eerie lavender, its tracery sharply beautiful. Now and then a branch came crashing down under the snow weight—a startling sound in the quiet world of blanketing snow—only to land silently when it reached the ground.

Lamps came on inside the house, and glowed yellow through the big beech tree. Here and there cinnamon-colored leaves blew about on top of snow that took a purplish cast in the strange light.

I could hear Tim out in front shoveling a path to the door, and I'd seen Luther at work with the snow blower. Where Pete was, I didn't know. More and more lately, he seemed to avoid everyone in the house, even though he was staying under its roof in his high attic room—warmed now with a space heater that Geneva had sent up to him.

I was about to offer my help in snow clearing when Alan came out the door from the music room. He'd put on a thermal jacket, corduroy pants, and lumberjack boots. His dark hair was quickly frosted with snow as a branch shed its load on him.

"You make a wonderful splash of color in all the white," he said as he came toward me. "Everyone should wear red in the winter. How do you like Windtop after a snowstorm, Hollis?"

"I love it!" I cried, stirred by an excitement, an anticipation that had nothing to do with the storm.

He smiled as he took my red-mittened hand, and we stamped through drifts together.

We followed the leg of the "T" that formed the house, lifting our boots high, sinking into drifts, sometimes losing our balance, so that we tumbled in the snow, laughing together, getting up to brush patches of snow from each other. I sensed excitement in him too and my own heightened.

For a few moments before it set, the sun came out gloriously, and rainbow colors sparkled from a million crystals on every tree branch and bush. A diamond-studded white quilt covered all of Windtop, and at the edge of the roof where icicles grew, their daggers caught the light and dazzled the eye with a lovely shining.

I stood looking up at the nearest tower of the house, admiring its cap of snow, when Alan put gloved fingers beneath my chin and turned my face toward him.

"Beautiful," he said softly. "Beautiful and honest and giving. Hollis, will you marry me?"

His words came without warning. I could see my own breath clouding the cold air, and it was something to watch when I couldn't meet his eyes. Why must excitement and exhilaration die all in an instant? What was the matter with me? Why didn't I just say "Yes!" and go straight into his arms? Why hesitate and be uncertain when this was what a part of me clamored for?

He read my uncertainty and put his hands on my shoulders. "I know. That was too abrupt. I didn't intend to do it that way. But it seems as though I've been watching you from a distance long enough. This could work out well for us, Hollis. We could even move in here. Geneva would welcome us, and someday Windtop would be ours. You'd fit into it so splendidly. I know now how much I need you. No—don't worry, I won't press you. You've been through too much. But when I saw you that day after the accident, I knew I mustn't wait too long. How many chances can a man have?"

I put my cheek against his shoulder and felt comforted, with no need to speak. He held me for a moment and then took my hand again and drew me toward the kitchen entrance to the house. As we went, I looked back at the capped tower, and saw Pete Evans standing at one of its windows, staring down at us.

The knowledge that Pete had seen Alan's tenderness with me wasn't reassuring. Instinctively I knew that Pete wouldn't approve, and while I wouldn't let that bother me, I wished he hadn't seen.

Soon after the light faded, it began to rain. A freezing rain that pocked the snow and laid sheets of ice across the walks. Geneva's spirits seemed to droop, and she decided to have supper alone in her room downstairs. I wondered if she too had seen me in Alan's arms, and would perhaps be less welcoming toward me than he thought.

Since help couldn't reach Windtop in the storm, Birdy was on her own, and for once she didn't spurn my offer to help in the kitchen. Alan disappeared into the room he'd taken for himself near Geneva, and I wondered miserably if I'd hurt him by holding back. That was the last thing I'd intended. He didn't appear, however, for dinner, though Birdy went to summon him.

Pete came downstairs from his attic quarters, looking different. He had decided to shave off his beard at last, and without it he seemed a stranger with whom I felt less comfortable than ever. He and Tim and I sat at the kitchen table for our meal, shunning the big dining room, and we ate mostly in silence.

Tim grumbled because the snow hadn't come on a school day, while Pete seemed lost in thoughts of his own, paying us little attention.

When we'd finished our salads and cheese omelets, and eaten some crisp fall apples, Tim went off to Windtop's library to get his school-work out of the way, and Pete disappeared on some quest of his own.

He and Birdy had been whispering together, though I didn't know what about.

I helped Birdy with the dishes, and afterward, finding myself restless again, I went into the music room and turned on a blaze of lights—as though to get ready for a concert. From her portrait on the wall Geneva Ames watched me without curiosity, too remote in years for me to turn to her for counsel. The piano drew me. Music would help quiet me, and that was what I needed. First, however, I went once more to a long glass door and opened it upon cold rain.

Across the garden light standards revealed a world that was still white, though surface snow had pocked and was melting fast. The ground hadn't frozen yet for the winter, and none of the beauty I'd seen this afternoon would last. When snow came again it would never be quite the same as this magical first fall at Windtop.

Was this house to be my home? I wasn't sure I could ever grow fond of it, though I liked Geneva, who had behaved with great kindness and concern for me during the aftermath of Norris's death. Yet a little while ago, when Alan had drawn me into his arms, my sense of excitement had faded—as though its source lay somewhere else, whether I liked it or not. I was young and I'd been sad for too long. Just to be out in the snow and feel free for a little while had brought my spirits up—not love for Alan. Wouldn't I know if I loved him? Wouldn't I be sure? I'd known from the first with Ricky. Or was that sort of love the kind that came only once in a lifetime? Perhaps I mustn't expect it with Alan. I was drawn to him, certainly—but how was I to know for sure if this was right?

I closed the door upon the sounds of rain and went to the piano. I didn't know what I would play. When I'm making up songs, I sometimes feel as though my fingers think for themselves, and know what key to choose, what notes to play. But now the music that came unbidden from the keys was nothing new.

One after another, I played Ricky Sands's songs. Some were from the time before I knew him, and others were songs I'd written for him. Some of the choruses I repeated, and sometimes I hummed the tune softly as I played, or whispered the words. And as I played it was as though all that was old and wounding and painful flowed away through my fingertips. These songs didn't bring Ricky close to me as they had in the past. Rather, they seemed nostalgic, belonging to something long gone, and having little to do with today. Strangely, it was as though I played away my own pain, so that it could be accepted and borne; so that I could move on to the rest of my life and not always hold back in doubt and confusion.

I finished with "Sweet Rain" and it brought a lump to my throat. This was my song more than it was Ricky's, and it was a song of hope, of courage. Human courage that stood against the forces of destruction and looked to a brighter future.

Yet I was not entirely free. There was something more to be done before I could move into Alan's arms and into his life. I must know the truth about Ricky's death. There was no freedom for me until I knew. That was what held me back. In spite of all the hurt I'd suffered, I had loved Ricky Sands deeply, and I owed him the truth.

Pete Evans—Peter Barron—knew what that truth was. I grew more and more certain of this—and certain that he could tell me what I must know. If he held back because the truth might wound me still more, then I must make him understand that it would only free me. That I *must* know.

I had no fear of Pete. He made me uncomfortable at times, but I was not afraid of him. I must see him alone, and see him right now.

I went up to my room and put on a sweater against the attic chill. Then I climbed the stairs to the dark space beneath the roof—a space that spread away on either side along the top of the "T" between the two towers. I hadn't thought to bring a flashlight, and I couldn't find switches in the dark, but the clouds must have broken overhead, because faint moonlight showed at windows set into the roof. I fumbled my way among old trunks and discarded furniture toward the closed door of Pete's tower—the same room where a young Mary Ames had once had her studio.

The attic seemed to echo at every sound, and I tried to move without bumping into things because the echoes disturbed me. I detoured around objects I could hardly make out, expecting that at any moment Pete would hear me and fling open his door. But it was still closed when I reached the steps that wound up to it. I climbed them and rapped on the panel. Again the attic picked up the sound and hurled it back at me harshly, but no one answered from inside the room.

I called Pete's name, and when there was no answer I tried the door and found it open. No light burned inside, but as I stepped up into the tower room I found a switch by the door and turned on an overhead light. The heat was off, and it was even colder up here than in the attic below. I buttoned my sweater to my throat and blew on my fingers, seeing my breath mist on the cold air. For a moment I stood looking around, wondering about Pete.

Evidence of his presence was here. The cot bed was made, and once more the pillow bore the indentation of a head, as it had borne Tim's. A man's clothes hung on the rack, and there was a record player, a radio, books, some writing things laid out on a table. The old paint boxes and brushes that I'd seen here before were gone, though Mary's face still looked down from the wall, bubbling with laughter in Luther's portrait. A sad picture, now that I knew what had become of her. Ricky had known the answer to her death—I was sure of that now. Pete knew as well—and about Ricky too. As soon as I could find him, I would make him tell me.

On the table a big scrapbook lay open and I went to look at it idly. It contained newspaper clippings, snapshots, and a few photographs of the young Mary Ames. I remembered that Geneva had been looking for a scrapbook in the opposite tower room, and I wondered if this was the one she'd had Birdy search for. Had Pete brought it here?

As I turned the pages, I discovered that the back section was devoted, not to Mary, but to Coral Caine. Clippings of her reviews were here, and her last professional photographs.

These were all glossies, and I stared at the first one, shocked. Undoubtedly it had been a photo of Coral Caine in the early days when she was doing well on television. In fact, her signature was scrawled across one corner. The pose of the head was jaunty, the blond hair, which wasn't her true color, had been combed attractively, her neckline flattered the lovely column of her throat—all were intended for the camera. The only thing wrong was that the photo had no face.

Someone must have used a chemical solution that had carefully erased Coral's features. Where the face had been there was only a grayed and smudgy blank. I turned the remaining pages quickly, to discover that every photo of Coral Caine had been defaced in the same way. Literally defaced. The earlier pictures of Mary Ames hadn't been touched at all.

Such destruction seemed unbalanced—demented. If Pete had done this, I didn't want him to find me here. Until now I hadn't been afraid. But this treatment of Coral's pictures seemed pathological. A sort of vicarious "murder." As if to destroy her image again and again was to destroy her. No wonder Birdy hadn't wanted Geneva to find the scrapbook. Though why it had been brought to this tower I couldn't even guess. The important thing now was for me to get away as quickly as I could.

I hurried to the steps that led down to the big room below, and as I moved I heard a sound out in the darkness of the main attic. As though someone had bumped into one of the stored objects that crowded the area. If someone was there, I'd already been seen, silhouetted against the light behind me.

"Pete?" I called. "Pete, are you there?"

No one answered, but out in crowded space, which was too dense to allow moonlight to penetrate, something moved again.

Once more I called his name. "Pete?"

There was still no answer, and I felt a stirring of panic. This was what it was like to be stalked. I stepped back into the tower room and closed the door. There was no key, no bolt, so whoever was there could reach me when he pleased. But there must be a way out, and I looked about for any path of escape. There were plenty of windows, but no sound, no call for help that I could make would be heard on the first floor of the house. So shouting out a window was useless.

The time when I'd caught Tim here he had gone out a window overlooking the roof, and he'd run across the slates to escape through the opposite tower. I went to the same window and looked out. Pale moonlight gilded the roof, shining on patches of snow and ice. A light burned in the opposite tower, but the distance was too far for me to call for help, whoever was there. The slates could never be crossed now.

Someone had reached the tower steps and was coming up. I flung the window open, wondering if I could crawl out and hide there just below the sill. Cold wind rushed in, chilling me, and I felt wet drops on my face. Racing clouds closed overhead, and the moonlight dimmed. All the vast stretch of roof looked black where snow had melted, and it would be treacherous with rain falling on ice. To go out there would be to fall to the flagstones far below.

I wanted to live.

20

Across the room the door opened slowly. I clung to the windowsill and watched. When Alan walked into the room I nearly collapsed with relief. I'd been so sure it was Pete out there stalking me, not answering to his name. Now I could close the window and shut out the cold rain.

"You frightened me!" I cried. "Why didn't you tell me you were there when I was calling Pete?"

"It couldn't have been Pete," he said easily. "He's downstairs doing some chore or other for Geneva."

Alan glanced around the room and saw the scrapbook lying open on the table, its mutilated photographs in plain view. He walked over and stood looking down at them.

"How did this get here?" he asked without surprise.

He had known. The earlier pictures of Mary Ames hadn't been touched. Only those of Coral Caine had been disfigured. And now I knew why.

Alan's voice was low, compelling, as he continued. "I'd have taken her back—even after all that happened. I gave her another chance—and she refused it."

His words seemed wondering—like those of a man who was unaccustomed to rejection and still couldn't accept it. I listened in growing horror as the calm, assured voice went on.

"She deserved what happened, Hollis. It was the only choice she could make." He glanced up from the book and saw my expression. "Don't look so shocked. I never touched her. It was just that she frightened so easily, once I began to carry out my plan. She had to understand that she could make only one of two choices. She could come back to me, to Windtop—which, of course, was the sensible choice. As far as her career went, she was through. And Ricky had married you."

I must have made a choking sound, for he looked at me again, his eyes kind, and a little reproachful.

"Hollis, I want you to understand. She knew that she was destroying herself with liquor and drugs. Though I could have helped her to recover. With me she could have had another chance. She could have been Mary Ames again. But she chose to go the other way. It *was* her choice."

"You drove her to it," I said.

"Drove? Not really. I just kept following her at unexpected times, turning up, phoning her, pointing out the desperate truth of her situation. I tried to help her—until her final rejection. I don't accept rejection, Hollis. I've always been a winner, and I always will be. I know how to manage my life, how to do what needs doing. When I understood the choice she'd made, I sent her those roses of a special color—the coral color that Ricky used to send her so sentimentally."

He smiled at my stunned look. "Of course the roses were the last straw for her. When she saw them she thought Ricky was coming back. Until she read the card. I didn't need to sign it. I just wrote, 'These aren't from him.' Of course I was never sure what would prove the last straw with her, but the roses did it. I found it curious that the police never found the card. Though it wouldn't have meant anything, since the words were typed."

"Pete took the card," I said dully.

That surprised him. "Something will have to be done about Pete. He came here to watch me, didn't he?"

"I don't know anything about that."

"I think you do. Of course Ricky was easier than Coral. He was ready to be driven out of his wretched mind. How could you care about what he'd turned into, Hollis? There was nothing left of his career—as I kept telling him. Oh, yes, I saw him on and off in New York. I pointed out that he was to blame for Coral's suicide, and he knew if he hadn't rejected her she'd still be alive. He really deserved what happened to him, just as she did."

"The roses?" I said. "There were roses in Ricky's room." My mouth was so dry that it was hard to speak.

"An inspiration! The stupid fool tried to run away and hide from me —he was that desperate. But of course I followed him to his sleazy little hotel. And I sent up the coral roses. Again—the finishing touch! It worked the second time too. Of course he'd brought drugs with him, and he knew well enough what to do. He knew that I'd never let him go, and his life was over. If he couldn't sing, he had no life. So he paid for all he'd done to Coral. Yet I never laid a finger on either of them, Hollis. I'm not a violent man."

His blind self-esteem was appalling. He had an unshakably good opinion of himself—and he was completely mad. A calm, calculating, reasonable madman, in whom all moral principles had been twisted askew! And whose dangerous logic was his own.

"Of course there was Wahl." He sounded almost apologetic. "I'm sorry about that. But what other choice did I have? He'd begun to find out too much, and he was comparing notes with Pete. He'd already upset Geneva, and he probably told you a great deal too much. So he had to go. It was tricky to get at his car during the little while when Pete went into the house, but I managed. Of course I had no idea that Wahl would take you with him when he drove down the hill. I never intended you to be injured, Hollis. And I don't intend it now."

I hadn't moved from the window, and I wondered about opening it again.

He went on and I heard the calm persuasion in his voice—as though everything he said was perfectly reasonable. "Geneva will leave everything to me, and you can be part of that, Hollis. I won't have to skimp and save or ask anyone for money. We'll have children here at Windtop. A son who will continue my work at Sea Spray. I can accomplish what I want most, what I care about."

"I think you care more about plants than you do about people!" I cried.

"Plants are clean and they live according to natural laws—unless they're interfered with by men. Only humans can be filthy and despicable."

"I'm sorry for you," I said.

I saw by his face that I'd touched him at the quick. No one should dare to be sorry for Alan Gordon. This too would be a form of rejection.

"So you've decided against me," he said calmly. "That's very foolish of you, Hollis. But I like you well enough to make you a gamble."

I didn't know what he intended, and I cast a quick look out over the roof—my only path of escape. I could never cross it and live. Nevertheless, I threw open the window again.

He nodded as though I'd pleased him. "That's right—you're going out there now. You're terribly despondent, aren't you? Everyone knows how strangely you've been acting. The loss of your husband by suicide, the death of your manager and friend—your own despair, is driving you to this one end. So now you'll go out on that icy roof and you will throw yourself off. There isn't any other way, Hollis."

"I would never commit suicide!" I cried. "I want to live! I'll always want to live. You can't talk *me* into this!"

"That's because you haven't considered the alternatives. To stay here in this room with me could be a lot worse. Plants suffer too, you know. But I would never hurt them. When it comes to human suffering, I'm not convinced that it matters as much, or that our suffering counts for anything. But there can be slow, ugly pain. And no matter how loudly you scream, Hollis, no one will hear you up here."

I was even more afraid of the open window, and I made a last attempt to dash across the room and reach the door. If I could get down into the attic I could hide. But he caught and held me, and I felt his strength again. He was capable of anything he promised. When I struggled in his arms, fighting him, he slapped me across the face.

"Sorry," he said. "That was crude. I can do much better." He picked up my hand almost lovingly and examined my fingers.

I snatched my hand away and he shook his head in reproach. "I said I was willing to gamble. The roof offers you a choice. If you can get across in spite of the ice and snow, maybe you can reach the opposite tower and climb in a window."

There was no way I could make it in the dark across that glazed roof, but I ran back to the window. There was no reasonable way to deal with madness either. The "logic" was so horribly different.

He started after me. "If you like, I'll help you out the window."

If I waited he might push me out and send me crashing down the roof. Now I really had no other choice.

I climbed over the sill, and put one foot onto the slanting roof. At least I was wearing slacks and rough-soled shoes, but the icy slates offered no purchase. I tried another spot a little higher, expecting at any moment to feel his hands on my back. This patch of roof was wet, but not frozen, and my foot stayed where I put it. Just as Alan reached out his hand, I swung my other leg over the sill, and found myself standing in drizzling rain on a tiny patch of wet slate.

I dropped to a crouch at once, and huddled myself against the steep rise, out of Alan's reach, but unable to move in any direction. When I felt about me I could find only snow and ice. Then, though light rain was still coming down, a rift in the clouds let the moon shine through, so that a faint glow was cast over the roof. A horned moon, with two points sharp in the sky, and somehow eerie.

Trees below still carried soft, melting snow, and I was all too aware of the precipitous pitch of the roof into darkness that would end at the bricks of the terrace.

"Go ahead, Hollis," Alan called behind me. "Go on across the roof. You can't stay there."

"You know I can't cross it!" I shouted. "I can't cross it and live!"

"Oh, come on! You've got more courage than that."

I hadn't given up. Not yet. I was still looking for a way. Edging out on my hands and knees so that I could see across the long "T" bar of the roof, I braced myself against the steep slant. Rain streaked my face and I wiped it away with one hand. There were four chimneys in a row out there, with the far tower rising behind the last one, its windows dark. No one would hear me, but I had to try.

"Pete!" I shouted. "Help me! Pete! Tim! Birdy—anyone!"

No one heard my shouting with all the windows closed downstairs. Moonlight showed me another patch of roof that didn't glisten slickly with ice, and I crawled across on all fours. If I slipped I would go flat on my face and slide feetfirst toward the edge. Only the gutters might stop me, and probably they wouldn't hold the jar of my weight.

A little farther down I could see another small square of slates that were free of ice. But as I tried to move toward them I began to slide. A bank of snow intervened and I lay in the heap of melting snow until a chunk of it broke away beneath me and dropped over the edge of the roof.

Once more I shouted. But all I could hear was Alan laughing softly in the window behind me. I cast about for another clear patch that would hold me and let me crawl a foot or so closer to the nearest chimney. The rain was letting up, but pale moonlight showed me nothing but slick ice. Drizzle had melted the surface, but underneath still lay a dangerous glaze.

Until now the pitch of the roof had sheltered me to some extent, but a sudden wind rushed over the ridge and tore at me—as though it would pluck me from the slates by its own force and hurl me toward the ground. It came in gusts, and I had to wait until there was a lull before I could move again.

"It's so easy, Hollis." That was Alan's voice again, with its dreadful appeal. "You're miserable and frightened, aren't you? You haven't been happy since you came here. You're tortured and wretched, and there's nothing left to live for. Can't you feel the freezing cold getting into your bones? It will get colder as the temperature drops in the night, and pretty soon you'll be so numb you can't move at all. Are your toes freezing, Hollis? And your fingers? Don't think about them. Think about peace. About letting go. There was no pain for Coral or Ricky. And there won't be for you, either—this way. You won't feel anything at all when you hit."

I was just as miserable and cold and frightened as he claimed, but I wouldn't be seduced by his voice. This was what he'd done to the others. I mustn't listen.

Someone shouted at me from the ground, and I looked down to see Tim standing on the front driveway, his head tipped back, so that his face shone white in the moonlight.

"Don't do it, Hollis! Please don't do it!"

I took a deep breath and tried to speak to him through numbed lips. "I'm not going to jump. I have to get across the roof. Alan—"

His brother called down to him. "Maybe you can talk her out of it, Tim. She won't listen to me."

Tim shouted again. "You stay right there. I'm coming up to help you."

"No, Tim, no!" I screamed after him, but he was already on his way inside. And I knew Alan would stop him.

I sat huddled with my knees drawn to my chin, shivering with a chill I couldn't control. The slates beneath me were icy cold. I don't know how long I sat there, unable to move, waiting for whatever would happen in the tower behind me. Then, suddenly, I was aware of a yellow glow from the farther tower, and I heard the sound of a window opening. I could hardly lift my head because my neck was so stiff, but when I looked, Pete was there in the opening. A tiny flare of hope came to life in me.

"Come toward me, Hollis," he called. "You're not going to fall.

Crawl sideways—just to the nearest chimney. That will give you something to hold on to. Move—*now!*"

On my hands and knees I could feel for the iced places. The first chimney wasn't that far off. I shoved a patch of snow with one cold hand and it slid away, leaving a bare place that hadn't frozen over.

Somehow I crawled crabwise to the chimney and held on to its bricks desperately. But the next chimney seemed a mile away, and the roof between glittered with ice.

Behind me I could hear sounds—Alan struggling with his brother. Then a moment of deep quiet, before Alan himself climbed out on the roof. Again he began to urge me.

"It's getting colder, Hollis. The rain has stopped and the temperature's already dropping. You can freeze out there holding on to that chimney. That's not a pleasant way to go. It hurts a lot at first. It's up to you to end the pain. Just stay there and I'll help you."

I knew what such "help" would mean.

Pete crawled out the other window, and I found my voice to shout to him. "No, Pete—don't try it!"

"Then come to me, Hollis. On your knees again. Crawl!"

I had to try. I had to reach him somehow. Pete was sanity and safety —as he had been all along, if only I'd known.

My knees slipped from under me, and I slid flat on my face, my hands clutching at nothing. A spot that was drying in the wind stopped my descent, but now I was too near the edge of the roof, and too far from the next chimney.

Alan had come a little closer. "Put out your hand, Hollis. Just take mine. There's peace down there. Sleep. No more torment."

"Don't listen to him, Hollis!" Pete shouted.

I crawled again—and made it to the second chimney. My hands were raw and parts of me that weren't aching felt numb. I could barely hold on to the bricks, and I knew I'd never make it the rest of the way. Not over the roof past two more chimneys before I could reach Pete's tower. No matter what happened, I couldn't move another inch. I couldn't even look around to see what Alan was doing. If he reached me . . .

"I can't!" I croaked to Pete. "I can't make it. Just go back. My hands won't hold on any longer." I was going to pieces as my own dangerous panic took over.

Pete had reached the first chimney on the other side and was leaning against it. "Listen to me, Hollis. Just listen."

I tried to quiet myself in order to hear him, even as my fingers slipped on the bricks. He had begun to whistle, and a strange sort of wonder came over me. The tune was gentle, beautiful, soothing. The sound of it calmed and strengthened me as words began to flow through my mind.

Let the rain fall sweetly . . .

That was *my* song. *I* had given that song to the world. It was a song about life—the life I still had to live. I got to my knees and crawled again. Now I could hear Alan coming behind me.

Pete had reached the next chimney, and was holding out his hand. Alan, still closer, reached for me. I crawled wildly, sliding, slipping, working my way back up the roof again.

Let the sweet rain fall . . .

The words sang through my mind. I wasn't going to die tonight. I would reach Pete and I would be safe.

Alan's shout stopped me as I crawled again on my hands and knees, but I didn't dare to look around. There was a shout of triumph as I heard him go slamming down the roof. Seconds of silence that seemed endless followed before the terrible crash on the terrace far below.

In his warped way Alan had won—*he* had rejected defeat.

I reached out for Pete's hand, touched his fingers, and pulled myself along. I held on to the belt of his jacket as we both crept toward the lighted tower window. Together we reached it and climbed through—to hold each other tightly, shivering but safe.

When we went downstairs into the warmth of the house, Birdy and Geneva were standing in the great hallway staring out the open front door to where Alan lay still upon the bricks.

21

I have rented one of the old sea captain's houses on the hill above Cold Spring Harbor, and I'm living there for now. When Geneva closed Windtop after Alan's death and flew to California, taking Birdy with her, Tim moved back to live with Liz Cameron, who needed him as he needed her.

Before Geneva left she gave me her greatest treasure—the Bechstein. "I can't do it justice anymore," she told me. "And I won't be coming back. So make your own beautiful songs on it, Hollis. The piano needs a new life."

It crowds my living room now, but I know it will always be the heart of any house I live in. It doesn't intimidate me anymore, and I'm working on new songs. I've even made some fresh contacts in New York on my own.

The details of what happened that terrible night at Windtop all came clear in the next day or two after Alan's death. Geneva had been restless that night. She'd been upset ever since Norris had tried to talk to her about Alan, though she'd refused to listen. After Norris died, she began to feel haunted, but where she'd have once let the Valkyries ride, she wanted no more of that dramatic self-indulgence. Instead, that last evening she'd opened a window in her sitting room and stood breathing cold, rainy air and listening to the night.

That was when she heard someone calling Pete's name, though she couldn't be sure of where the sound came from. She went into the library, where Tim was doing his homework, and sent him outside to look around. He saw me and rushed back in. When he passed Birdy in the hall, he told her to find Pete and tell him I was out on the roof. Then he dashed upstairs to the nearest tower, meaning to climb out the window that would be close to where I crouched. Of course he never expected that Alan would try to stop him. There was a scuffle, and Alan knocked Tim out easily enough.

Pete had gone at once to the opposite tower, and had begun the tricky task of coaxing me across the roof. When he brought me downstairs, Birdy took charge. She drew a hot bath for me, and afterward wrapped me in one of Geneva's warmest wool robes. She brought me hot milk, laced with rum, as I toasted before the fire in my azalea sitting room.

By the time Tim recovered and stumbled downstairs, Geneva was talking to the police—and not telling everything. I didn't have to talk to them that night—which was a good thing. I felt broken up inside, somehow damaged, as though I might never mend again. It was Pete Evans who began to mend me.

He persuaded Birdy to let him come to sit with me before the fire, though he wasn't drinking hot milk, but something stronger. I lay back with my eyes closed and listened to his quiet voice and the spell of calm and reason it wove around me. Not like Alan's dreadful "persuasion."

First he talked a little about Ricky. "Now you can be free of that worry you've had. I mean that Ricky might have had a deliberate hand in Coral's death."

"I know." That burden, at least, had slipped away. What Alan had done was something else—something I would push away with horror for a long time to come.

Pete went on. "After Coral died, Ricky talked to me a few times, and I suspected that Alan was tormenting him. I took the card from the roses to show Ricky—and he *knew*. He knew that Alan must have helped to drive Coral over the edge. He also blamed himself in part, and he became afraid of Alan. Though Ricky would never tell me all of it."

"You really did come here to watch him, didn't you? But why didn't you tell me?"

"I had no real proof, and if you knew too much you'd have been in danger from Alan yourself. Your manner toward him would have changed, and he'd have suspected. I had to know more first. And I thought I could watch out for you, protect you. A few times I sat out in the garden, watching your room."

"You have protected me," I said. "Did you know about that awful scrapbook?"

"Yes. Birdy was getting edgy about Alan. She hated the way he'd treated Tim, so when she found the scrapbook she guessed who must have wiped out those faces of Coral Caine. She gave me the book, and I took it upstairs until I could decide what to do. I waited too long. But now it's over, Hollis, and we all have to let it go."

I knew that was so, but it would take a while longer before I could heal.

We were quiet, watching the flames, thinking our own thoughts. I could still hear Alan's last shout ringing in my ears.

Pete reached out to touch my hand lightly. "You couldn't know," he said, "but I've loved you for a long time. Loved you and been afraid of you—and for you. I may have damaged one young woman, and I didn't want to repeat that with you. First I knew you through your songs, and I watched you with Ricky, though always from a distance. That time I talked to you in Greenwich Village, after you'd visited Coral Caine, I sensed how vulnerable you were, and I knew how Ricky was behaving. But there was nothing I could do for you then. Though perhaps I could help Coral. So I went back to her apartment—and you know the rest."

I remembered Pete's kindness that day—it had been a bracing kindness that had brought me back to life. Yet what he was telling me now seemed unreal. I wanted to accept what he was saying, but there was a numbness in me that I couldn't fight.

"Don't worry," Pete said. "I'm not asking anything. But I'll be around. You know that, don't you?"

This was a reassuring thought. I did know. And I also knew that I would want him there.

He's teaching again now at a local school, as he should be, and I've seen how the kids love him. Tim has come to trust him too, looking up to him, as he never could to Alan. Tim and I have become good friends since that terrible night.

Liz is recovering too. She's too strong a woman to be permanently damaged by what happened. Now I could better understand the frantic state of mind she'd been trying to hide. She had done what Alan asked, even to making those appalling phone calls he wanted her to make to the Wahls. Except for that last call, when Norris had taped her. She had done that on her own, because she'd begun to fear for my safety at

Windtop and wanted me away. She had already guessed that her brother had come to Windtop to watch Alan, and later understood that he'd come on my account too. She didn't want anything to happen to me.

Pete seemed more a "Peter" to me now. He looked different without his beard, and I liked his sensitive, rather angular features. I trusted him, and I began to love him in a new way that was more satisfying than the dangerous excitement that Alan had sometimes stirred in me. This was a feeling that would grow, given time. Perhaps that was what love really was—a growing—something I'd never had with Ricky.

Once we paid a visit to Windtop, Peter and Tim and I, and we talked to Luther. What the future of the house will be, we don't know yet, but Luther is staying on for now to keep an eye on things. At Christmastime he brought me some sprigs of holly as a peace offering.

I believe I have more to say in my songs these days, because I really have gone deep into myself and tried to understand, as Pete Evans once told me to do. The songs are flowing richly, and some top talent is interested in two or three.

I sit now on the front porch of my rented house overlooking what was once called Bedlam Street, and I feel a real affection for this little town that I'm just beginning to know.

In a few moments Peter will be here. We have plans to talk about. My father will fly out from San Francisco soon, and this time I don't think he'll mind my interest in a musician. An ex-musician.

It will soon be May in Cold Spring Harbor, and I'm looking forward to all the new beginnings. A song is stirring in my head, and perhaps I can get a snatch of it down before Peter comes. I have an idea for the theme. Something like this:

> Wait a little while, just wait.
> Everything that's wrong will change;
> It always has, it always will . . .
> It's never really late.

That's not right yet. But I'll find it.
I go inside and open Geneva's piano.